Flower o' the Lily

by

Baroness Orczy

Double9
BOOKS

Flower o' the Lily
by Baroness Orczy

ISBN: 978-93-57484-38-1

Published by

DOUBLE 9 BOOKS

2/13-B, Ansari Road
Daryaganj, New Delhi – 110002
info@double9books.com
www.double9books.com
Tel. 011-40042856

This book is under public domain

ABOUT THE AUTHOR

Baroness Emmuska Orczy was born in Tarnaors, Hungary in 1865. She was a notable artist, playwright and author. Her father Baron Felix Orczy was a composer and mother Countess Emma Orczy. Due to a peasant revolt her family fled to Brussels then Paris and lastly to London. With her sister Emma studied in convent schools in Brussels and Paris. She learned music and paintings but gained success in paintings at the West London School of Art and at Heartherley. In collaboration with her husband Montague Barstow, Baroness Hungarian fairy tales and began writing romance and fiction. She was appreciated for the translation of Old Hungarian Fairy Tales. Her first novel, The Emperor's Candlesticks faced rejection for being too short. But her second novel 'The Scarlet Pimpernel' proved a boon for him, she earned name and fame. As a prominent author she wrote dozens of romantic novels, plays and detective stories. Her memorable works-The Man in Grey, The Laughing Cavalier, Skin O' My Tooth, Eldorado- a sequel to the Scarlet Pimpernel, The Old Man in the Corner, The Divine Folly, The Old Scare Crow, Lady Molly of Scotland Yard etc. She was died in London in 1947.

CONTENTS

CHAPTER I.
HOW MESSIRE GILLES DE CROHIN WENT FOR
AN EXCURSION INTO THE LAND OF DREAMS....................9

CHAPTER II.
HOW A NOBLE PRINCE PRACTISED
THE GENTLE ART OF PROCRASTINATION............................21

CHAPTER III.
HOW A CLEVER WOMAN OUTWITTED
AN OBSTINATE MAN 32

CHAPTER IV.
HOW MONSIEUR KEPT HIS WORD..49

CHAPTER V.
WHAT MARGUERITE OF NAVARRE DID
WHEN SHE HEARD THE NEWS...58

CHAPTER VI.
WHAT MONSEIGNEUR D'INCHY AND
MESSIRE GILLES DE CROHIN MUTUALLY
THOUGHT OF ONE ANOTHER 76

CHAPTER VII.
WHY MADAME JACQUELINE WAS SO LATE
IN GETTING TO BED 88

CHAPTER VIII.

WHAT BECAME OF THE LILIES 106

CHAPTER IX.

HOW MESSIRE GILLES WAS REMINDED

OF A DREAM..113

CHAPTER X.

HOW THE QUARREL BEGAN 127

CHAPTER XI.

AND HOW IT ENDED 150

CHAPTER XII.

HOW TWO LETTERS CAME TO BE WRITTEN........175

CHAPTER XIII.

HOW MADAME JACQUELINE WAS

GRAVELY PUZZLED 183

CHAPTER XIV.

WHICH TREATS OF THE DISCOMFITURE

OF M. DE LANDAS...195

CHAPTER XV.

HOW M. DE LANDAS PRACTISED THE

GENTLE ART OF TREACHERY 211

CHAPTER XVI.

WHAT NEWS MAÎTRE JEHAN BROUGHT

BACK WITH HIM...221

CHAPTER XVII.

HOW MESSIRE DE LANDAS' TREACHERY

BORE FRUIT...231

CHAPTER XVIII.

    HOW A SECOND AWAKENING MAY
BE MORE BITTER THAN THE FIRST............................243

CHAPTER XIX.

    WHAT JACQUELINE WAS FORCED TO HEAR.................253

CHAPTER XX.

    HOW MORE THAN ONE PLOT WAS HATCHED 262

CHAPTER XXI.

    HOW SOME OF THESE SUCCEEDED 273

CHAPTER XXII.

    WHILE OTHERS FAILED 282

CHAPTER XXIII.

    WHILE TRAITORS ARE AT WORK...............................301

CHAPTER XXIV.

    THE DEFENCE OF CAMBRAY....................................310

CHAPTER XXV.

    HOW CAMBRAY STARVED AND ENDURED.........................326

CHAPTER XXVI.

    WHAT VALUE A VALOIS PRINCE SET
UPON HIS WORD...345

CHAPTER XXVII.

    AND THIS IS THE END OF MY STORY............................354

CHAPTER I.
HOW MESSIRE GILLES DE CROHIN WENT FOR AN EXCURSION INTO THE LAND OF DREAMS

I

When Gilles de Crohin, Sire de Froidmont, received that sabre-cut upon his wrist—a cut, by the way, which had been dealt with such efficacy that it very nearly severed his left hand from his arm—he swore, so I understand, both lustily and comprehensively. I have not a faithful record of what he did say, but from what I know of Messire, I can indeed affirm that his language on the occasion was as potent as it was direct and to the point.

As for the weapon which had dealt that same forceful stroke, its triumph was short-lived. Within the next few seconds its unconscious career upon this earth was brought to a sudden and ignominious close: it was broken into three separate pieces by a blow more vigorous than even Messire Gilles himself had ever been known to deal. The hilt went flying sky-high above the heads of the nearest combatants; part of the blade was ground into the mud under the heel of Messire's stout leather boot, whilst the point itself—together with a few more inches of cold steel—was buried in the breast of that abominable spadassin who had thought to lay so stalwart an enemy low.

And, mind you, this would have been exceedingly satisfactory— the life of a rascally Spaniard in exchange for a half-severed wrist— had not some other rogue of the same ilk, who happened to be close by, succeeded at that very instant in delivering a vigorous thrust into the body of Maître Jehan le Bègue, the faithful friend and companion of the Sire de Froidmont. Whereupon Gilles, maddened with rage, slashed and charged upon the enemy with such lustihood that for an instant the valiant French troops, which indeed were sore pressed, rallied about him, and the issue of the conflict hung once more in the balance. But alas! only for a few moments. The Spaniards, more numerous and undoubtedly more highly skilled in the science of arms, soon regained the advantage, and within a few hours after that, they were driving the Netherlander and the French helter-skelter before them, having gained a signal and decisive victory.

This all occurred at Gembloux in Brabant, three and more years before the events which I am about to put on record in this veracious chronicle, and at the time when the Sire de Froidmont and his faithful henchman, Jehan—surnamed le Bègue because he stuttered and spluttered like a clucking hen—happened to be fighting in the Netherlands at the head of a troop of French Protestants who had rushed to support the brave followers of Orange against the powerful armies of Alexander Farnese, Duke of Parma; and I use the word 'happened' advisedly, because in these days the knights and gentlemen of France—aye, and the marshals and princes of blood, far finer noblemen and lords than was the poor Sire de Froidmont— were wont to fight now on one side, now on the other—now on the Catholic side, hand-in-hand with the Spaniards; now on the Huguenot, according if they 'happened' to be in good friendship with the Queen Mother or with the King's favourite, or with the Protestant Henry of Navarre.

On this occasion, and despite his broken wrist, Messire Gilles de Crohin was the very last to lay down his sword before the victorious Spaniard; nor is the expression 'lay down his sword' altogether the right one to use, for the Sire de Froidmont never did lay down his sword either to the Spaniards or to any other enemy, either then or on any other occasion. But it seems that, in addition to that half-severed wrist, he had several and sundry wounds about his body, and all the while that the victorious Spanish army pursued the Netherlanders even as far as the territory of the King of France, Messire Gilles lay as one dead, bleeding, half-frozen, and only sufficiently conscious to curse his own fate and the disappearance of Maître Jehan le Bègue, the most faithful servant and most expert henchman, man ever had. The trouble, indeed, was that Master Jehan was nowhere within sight.

II

Now it happened that that memorable night of February, 1578, which followed the grim fight in the valley below Gembloux, was a very dark one. Toward eight or nine o'clock of the evening, Messire Gilles woke from his state of unconsciousness by feeling rough and unfriendly hands wandering about his body. Had I not already told you that his language was apt to be more forceful than reverent, I would tell you now that he utilized his first return to actuality in sitting up suddenly and pouring forth such a volley of expletives against the miscreants who were even then trying to divest him of his boots, that, seized with superstitious fear, these human vultures fled, scattered and scared, to rally again at some distance from the spot, in order to resume their nefarious trade with less forcible interruption.

Messire Gilles listened to their scurrying footsteps for awhile; then with much difficulty, for he was sorely hurt and bruised, he struggled to his feet.

The darkness lay upon the plain and wrapped in its grim pall all the suffering, all the horror which the fiends of hatred and of fanaticism had brought in the wake of this bloody combat. Silence absolute reigned in the valley, save for an occasional sigh, a moan, a cry of pain or a curse, which rose from the sodden ground up to the sombre firmament above, as if in protest to the God of battles against so much misery and so much unnecessary pain.

Gilles—accustomed as he was to all these sounds—shook himself like a shaggy dog. Though he was comparatively a young man still, these sounds had rung in his ears ever since, as a young lad, he had learned how to fight beside his father's stirrup leathers, and seen his father fall, wounded and bruised, in much the same plight as he— Gilles himself—was at this hour. Nor had the night any terrors for him. The groans of dying men no longer stirred his senses, and only moved his heart to transient pity. What did worry Messire Gilles de Crohin, however, was the disappearance of Maître Jehan.

'So long as those hellish body-snatchers do not get hold of the poor fool!' he sighed dolefully.

Just then his ear, trained of old to catch the slightest sound which might bring a ray of hope at moments such as this, perceived above the groanings and the sighs the distant tinkle of a bell.

'Now, Gilles, my friend,' he murmured vaguely to himself, 'collect your scattered senses and find out exactly where you are.'

Dizziness seized him again, and he came down on one knee.

'Jehan, you dog!' he exclaimed instinctively, 'where the devil are you?'

To which summons Maître Jehan was evidently unable to give reply, and Messire Gilles, very sore and very much out of humour, once more contrived to struggle to his feet. The tinkling of that bell seemed more insistent now; his re-awakened consciousness worked a little more actively.

'We fought just below Gembloux,' he reflected. 'The tinkling which I hear is the monastery bell on the heights above. Now, if it will go on tinkling till I have struck the right direction and see a light in the monastery windows, I doubt not but that those worthy monks will let me lie in the kennel of one of their dogs until I can find my way to a more congenial spot.'

From which cynical reflection it can be gathered that Messire Gilles had not a vast amount of faith in the hospitality of those good Benedictines of Gembloux; which doubt on his part is scarce to be wondered at, seeing that he had been fighting on the side of the heretics.

'If only that ass Jehan were here!' he added, with a final despondent sigh.

It was no earthly use for a wounded, half-fainting man to go searching for another in the darkness on this field littered with dead and dying. Gilles, whom a vague instinct drove to the thought, had soon to give up all idea of it as hopeless. The same acute sense of hearing which had brought to his semi-consciousness the sound of the tinkling bell, also caused him to perceive through the murky blackness the presence of the human vultures taking their pickings off the dead.

Gilles shuddered with the horror of it. He felt somehow that poor old Jehan must be dead. He had seen him fall by his side in the thick of the fight. He himself was only half-alive now. The thought that he might once more fall under the talons of the body-snatchers filled him with unspeakable loathing. He gave himself a final shake in order to combat the numbness which had crept into his limbs in the wake of the cold, the faintness and the pain. Then, guided through the darkness by the welcome tintinnabulation of the monastery bell, he started to make his way across the valley.

III

Why should I speak of that weary, wretched tramp of a sorely-wounded man, in the dead of night, on sharply-rising ground, and along a track strewn with dead and dying, with broken bits of steel and torn accoutrements, on sodden ground rendered slippery with blood? Messire Gilles himself never spoke of it to any one, so why should I put it on record? It took him five hours to cover less than half a league, and he, of a truth, could not have told you how he did it even in that time. He was not really fully conscious, which was no doubt one of God's many mercies, for he did not feel the pain and the fatigue, and when he stumbled and fell, as he very often did, he picked himself up again with just that blind, insentient action which the instinct of self-preservation will at times give to man.

Whenever he recalled this terrible episode in his chequered career, it took the form in his brain of a whirl of confused memories. The tinkling of the bell ceased after a while, and the moans which rose from the field of battle were soon left behind. Anon only a group of tiny lights guided him. They came from the windows of the monastery on the heights above, still so far—so very far away. Beyond those lights and the stillness—nothing; neither pain, nor cold, nor fatigue, only a gradual sinking of sense, of physical and mental entity into a dark unknown, bottomless abyss. Then a sudden, awful stumble, more terrible than any that had gone before, a sharp agonizing blow on the head—a fall—a fall into the yawning abyss—then nothing more.

IV

Everything that happened after this belongs to the world of dreams. So, at any rate, did Messire Gilles aver. The sensation of waking up, of opening his eyes, of feeling sweet-smelling straw beneath his aching body, was, of course, a dream. The sense of well-being, of warm yet deliciously cooling water, and of clean linen upon his wounds was a dream; the murmur of voices around him was a dream.

Perhaps Messire Gilles would have thought that they were realities, because all these sensations, remember, were not altogether unknown to him. How many times he had lain wounded and insensible during his stormy life-career, he could not himself have told you. He had oft been tended by kindly Samaritans—lay or clerical; he had oft lain on fresh, clean straw and felt that sense of well-being which comes of complete rest after dire fatigue. But what he had never experienced in his life before, and what convinced him subsequently that the whole episode had only been the creation of his fevered fancy, was that wonderful vision of a white-robed saint or angel—good Messire Gilles could not have told you which, for he was not versed in such matters—which flitted ever and anon before his weary eyes. It was the sound of a voice, whispering and gentle, which was like the murmur of butterflies' wings among a wilderness of roses; it was the perfume of spring flowers with the dew fresh upon them which came to his nostrils; it was a touch like unto the velvety petals of a lily which now and again rested upon his brow, and above all it was a pair of deep blue eyes, which ever and anon met his aching ones with a glance full of gentleness and of pity.

Now, although Messire Gilles was quite willing to admit that some angels might have blue eyes, yet he had never heard it said that they had a tiny brown mole on the left cheek-bone—a mole which, small as it was, appeared like a veritable trap for a kiss, and added a quaint air of roguishness to the angelic blue eyes.

But then Gilles de Crohin, being a heretic and something of a vagabond, was not intimately acquainted with the outward appearance of angels. Moreover, that wee, tantalizing mole was far removed from the reach of his lips.

'Think you he'll recover, Messire?'

Just at that moment Gilles de Crohin could have sworn that he was conscious and awake; but that whisper, which suddenly reached his hazy perception, could not have been aught but a part of his dream. He would have liked to pinch or kick himself to see if he were in truth awake, but he was too weak and too helpless to do that; so he lay quite still, fearful lest, if he moved, the vision of the white-robed angel who had just made such tender inquiry after him, would vanish again into the gloom. Thus he heard a reply, gruff and not over tender, which, of a truth, had nothing dreamlike about it.

'Oh, he'll recover soon enough, gracious lady. These rascals have tough hides, like ploughing oxen.'

Messire Gilles de Crohin, Sire de Froidmont, tried to move, for he was impelled to get up forthwith in order to chastise the malapert who had dared to call him a rascal; but it seemed as if his limbs were weighted with lead—for which fact he promptly thanked his stars, since if he had moved, those heavenly blue eyes would, mayhap, not scan his face again so anxiously.

'Think you he fought on the side of our enemies?' the dream-voice queried again; and this time there was an awed, almost trembling tone in its exquisite music.

'Aye,' answered the graft one, 'of that I have no doubt. Neither psalter nor Holy Bible have I found about his person, and the gracious lady should not have wasted her pity upon a spawn of the devil.'

'He looked so forlorn and so helpless,' said the angel-voice with gentle reproach. 'Could I let him lie there, untended in a ditch?'

'How did he get there?' retorted the real—the human—voice. 'That is what I would wish to know. The fighting took place over half a league away, and if he got his wounds on the battlefield, I, for one, do not see how he could have walked to the postern gate and deposited himself there, just in time to be in your way when you deigned to pass.'

'God guided him, Messire,' said the angel softly, 'so that you might do one of those acts of goodness and of charity for which He will surely reward you.'

Some one—a man, surely—seemed to mumble and to grumble a good deal after that, until the human voice once more emerged clearly out of the confused hubbub.

'Anyhow, gracious lady,' it said, 'you had best let yourself be escorted back to your apartment now. Messire is already fuming and fretting after you; nor is it seemly that you should remain here any longer. The fellow will do quite well, and I'll warrant be none the worse for it. He's been through this sort of thing before, my word on it. His wounds will heal...'

'Even that horrid one across his wrist?' queried the white-robed saint again. (Gilles by now was quite sure that it was a saint, for the tender touch upon his burning hand acted like a charm which soothed and healed.)

'Even that one, gracious lady,' replied the swine who had dared to speak of the Sire de Froidmont as a 'rascal' and a 'fellow.' 'Though I own 'tis a sore cut. The rascal will be marked for life, I'll warrant. I've never seen such a strange wound before. The exact shape of a cross it is—like the mark on an ass's back.... But it'll heal, gracious lady ... it'll heal ... I entreat you to leave him to me.'

Anger again rose hotly to Messire Gilles' fevered brow, whereupon everything became more and more confused. The darkness closed in around him; he could no longer see things or hear them; he was once more sinking into the dark and bottomless abyss. He opened his eyes, only to see a white-robed vision far, far above him, fading slowly but certainly into nothingness. The last thing which he remembered was just that pair of blue eyes—the most luminous eyes he had ever gazed into; eyes which looked both demure and tantalizing—oh, so maddeningly tantalizing with that adorable little mole, which was just asking for a kiss!

And the rest was silence.

V

When Gilles de Crohin, Sire de Froidmont, once more recovered consciousness, it was broad daylight. The slanting rays of a genial, wintry sun had struck him full in the face, and incidentally had been infusing some warmth into his numbed body. He opened his eyes and tried to visualize his position. It took him some time. He still felt very giddy and very sick, and when he tried to move he ached in every limb. But he was not cold, and his temples did not throb with fever. As he groped about with his right hand, he encountered firstly the folds of a thick woollen cloak which had been carefully wrapped around him, and then, at a foot or so away, a pitcher and a hunk of something which to the touch appeared very like bread.

Messire Gilles paused after these preliminary investigations, closed his eyes and thought things out. He had been dreaming, of that there was no doubt, but he would be hanged, drawn and quartered if he knew whence had come the pleasing reality of a cloak, a pitcher and a hunk of bread.

It was some time after that, and when the sun was already high in the heavens, that he managed to sit up, feeling the pangs of hunger and of thirst intensified by the vicinity of that delectable bread. The pitcher contained fresh, creamy milk, which Messire Gilles drank eagerly. Somehow the coolness of it, its sweetness and its fragrance made his dream appear more vivid to him. The bread was white and tasted uncommonly good. After he had eaten and drunk he was able to look about him.

As far as he could recollect anything, he was lying very near the spot where he had fallen the day before—or the day before that, or a week, or a month ago—Messire Gilles was not at all clear on the point. But here he was, at any rate, and there were all the landmarks which he had noted at the time, when first his troop was attacked by the Spaniards. There was the clump of leafless shrubs, trampled now into the mud by thousands of scurrying feet; there was the group of broken trees, stretching gaunt arms up to the skies, and beyond them the little white house with the roof all broken in—a miserable derelict in the midst of the desolation.

He, Gilles, had been propped up against a broken tree-trunk which lay prone upon the ground. Underneath him there was a thick horse-blanket, and over him the aforementioned warm cloak. His cut wrist had been skilfully bandaged, the wounds about his body had been dressed and covered with soft linen, and, hidden away under the trunk, behind where he was lying, there was another loaf of bread, another pitcher containing water, the limbs of a roasted capon and a pat of delicious-looking cream cheese.

The Benedictine monastery which, from the distant heights had dominated the field of battle, was on Gilles' right. All around him the valley appeared silent and deserted save by the dead who still lay forgotten and abandoned even by the human vultures who had picked them clean. There were no more dying on the field of Gembloux now. Here and there a clump of rough shrubs, a broken tree with skeleton arms stretched out toward the distance, as if in mute reproach for so much misery and such wanton devastation; here and there the crumbling ruins of a wayside habitation, roofless and forlorn, from which there still rose to the wintry firmament above, a thin column of smoke. From somewhere far away came the rippling murmur of the stream and through it the dismal sound of a dog howling in this wilderness, whilst overhead a flight of rooks sent their weird croaking through the humid air.

All other sounds were stilled—the clash of arms, the call of despair or of victory, the snorting of horses, the cries of rage and of triumph had all been merged in the mist-laden horizon far away. Was it indeed yesterday, or a cycle of years ago that Gilles de Crohin had lain just here, not far from this same fallen tree-trunk, a prey to the ghoulish body-snatchers who, by their very act of hideous vandalism, had brought him back to his senses?

VI

Later on in the forenoon when, having eaten some of the capon and the cream cheese, he was able to struggle to his feet, Gilles started out to look for his friend.

Though his thoughts and impressions were still in a state of confusion, the possible plight of Maître Jehan weighed heavily on Messire's soul.

He remembered where Jehan had fallen right down in the valley, not far from the edge of the stream and close to the spot where he, Gilles, had received that terrible blow upon his wrist, and had then lashed out so furiously into the Spaniard in his wrath at seeing his faithful henchman fall.

And there indeed he found him—stark naked and half-frozen. The human vultures had robbed him even of his shirt. The search had been long and painful, for in addition to his own weary limbs, Messire Gilles had dragged the horse-blanket and the warm cloak about with him. He knew, alas! in what plight he would find Master Jehan—if indeed he were fortunate enough to find him at all; and he had also carried the pitcher half-filled with water and had thrust bread and capon into his breeches' pocket. Now that he had succeeded in his quest, he laid the blanket and the cloak over the inanimate body of his friend, moistened poor Jehan's cracked lips with the water, then he laid down beside him and fell into another swoon.

Sometime during that long and bitter day he had the satisfaction of hearing Master Jehan both groan and curse. He was able to feed him with bread and to ply him with water; and when the night came the two of them rolled themselves up in the one blanket and kept one another warm and comforted as best they could.

It is not my purpose to speak of the vicissitudes, of the ups and downs which befell Messire Gilles de Crohin and his faithful Jehan during the next few days and weeks, whilst they struggled from a state of moribundity into one of life and vigour once again, tended and aided now by one Samaritan, now by another; helped, too, by a piece of gold which Messire Gilles most unaccountably found in the inner pocket of his doublet. He swore that he had no idea he had ever left one there.

All that I desire to remind you of is that, as soon as he could again struggle to his feet, he went on another quest—one that to him was only second in importance to the search for his friend. It was a quest connected with the Benedictine monastery up yonder on a spur of the Ardennes. Messire Gilles now was quite conscious enough to remember that the monastery had been his objective when, sorely wounded and aching in every limb, he had started on a weary tramp which had culminated in an exquisite dream. To the monastery, therefore, he meant to go, for he wished to ascertain if somewhere near by there was a postern gate, beside which angels with blue eyes and perfumed hands were wont to pass, and to minister to the sick and to the weary. Messire Gilles, you perceive, trusted a great deal to intuition first and then to observation. He was quite certain in his own mind that if there was a postern gate he would come across it; and he was equally certain that in the rough grass or the scrub close by he would recognize traces of a sorely-wounded man falling headlong against a very hard wall, and the footsteps of the kindly Samaritan who, at the aforesaid angel's bidding, had carried him to shelter.

As for the angel, it was obvious of course, that such celestial beings did not walk and would not therefore leave imprints upon the sordid earth; still, even so, Messire Gilles clung to the vain hope that he would see tiny footprints somewhere, such as fairies make when they dance in a ring, and that from the very ground there would arise the perfume of spring flowers when the dew is fresh upon them in the morn.

VII

I may as well put it on record here and now that Gilles de Crohin, Sire de Froidmont, after having tramped along half a league or more, came upon the purlieus of the Benedictine monastery of Gembloux, which is famed far and wide, and that after much exploration he did discover a postern gate which was let into a high stone wall. But neither in front of that gate, nor anywhere near it, were there any traces of Samaritans, of angels or of a wounded man. The ground round about that gate had at some time or another been strewn with sand and raked over very smoothly and evenly, after which the humid air and the rain had had their way with it.

Messire Gilles uttered a comprehensive oath. Then he turned on his heel and went his way.

CHAPTER II.
HOW A NOBLE PRINCE PRACTISED THE GENTLE ART OF PROCRASTINATION

I

Now, all that which I have related occurred during the month of February in the year 1578—three years and more ago.

After which I come to my story.

We will leave the subject of Messire Gilles' dream, an it please you; we will even leave that gallant if somewhat out-at-elbows gentleman in the tap-room of the only hostelry of which the little town of La Fère could boast, where he must needs wait for the good pleasure of no less a personage than François Hercule, Duke of Alençon and of Anjou—usually styled 'Monsieur'—who was own brother to His Very Christian Majesty, King Henry III of France, and whom Gilles de Crohin, Sire de Froidmont, was serving for the nonce.

M. le Duc d'Alençon and d'Anjou was closeted upstairs with the Queen of Navarre, that faithful and adoring sister who had already committed many follies for his sake, and who was ready to commit as many more. What she saw to adore and worship in this degenerate and indolent scion of the princely house of Valois, in this foppish profligate devoid alike of morals and of valour, no historian has ever been able to fathom. That he had some hidden qualities that were as noble as they have remained unknown to tradition, we must assume from the very fact that Marguerite, Queen of Navarre, one of the most brilliant women of that or any epoch and the wife of one of the most dazzling and fascinating men of his day, lavished the resources of her intellect and of her sisterly love upon that graceless coxcomb.

Picture her now—that beautiful, clever woman—full of energy, of vitality and of burning ambition, pacing the narrow room in the humble hostelry of a second-rate city, up and down like some caged and exquisite wild animal, the while that same fondly-adored brother sat there silent and surly, his long legs, encased in breeches of delicate green satin, stretched out before him, his not unattractive face, framed in by an over-elaborate ruffle, bent in moody contemplation of his velvet shoes, the while his perfumed and slender hands fidgeted uneasily with the folds of his mantle or with the slashings of his doublet.

On the table before him lay a letter, all crumpled and partly torn, which Marguerite had just thrown down in an access of angry impatience.

'By all the saints, François,' she said tartly, 'you would provoke an angel into exasperation. In Heaven's name, tell me what you mean to do.'

Monsieur did not reply immediately. He stretched out his legs still further before him; he shook his mantle into place; he smoothed down the creases of his satin breeches; then he contemplated his highly polished nails. Marguerite of Navarre, with flaming cheeks and blazing eyes, stood by, looking down on him with ever-growing irritability not unmixed with contempt.

'François!' she exclaimed once more, evidently at the end of her patience.

'Gently, my dear Margot; gently!' said *Monsieur*, with the peevishness of a spoilt child. 'Holy Virgin, how you do fume! Believe me, choler is bad for the stomach and worse for the complexion. And, after all, where is the hurry? One must have time to think.'

'Think! Think!' she retorted. ''Tis two days since M. d'Inchy's letter came and he sends anon for his answer.'

'Which means,' he argued complacently, 'that there is no cause to come to a decision for at least half an hour.'

An angry exclamation broke from Marguerite's full lips.

'My dear Margot,' said the Duke fretfully, 'marriage is a very serious thing, and — —'

He paused, frowning, for his sister had burst into ironical laughter. 'I am well aware,' he resumed dryly, 'that you, my dear, look upon it as a cause for levity, and that poor Navarre, your husband — —'

'I pray you, dear brother,' she broke in coldly, 'do not let the pot call the kettle black. 'Tis neither in good taste nor yet opportune. M. d'Inchy will send for his answer anon. You must make up your mind now, whether you mean to accept his proposal or not.'

Again *Monsieur* remained silent for awhile. Procrastination was as the breath of his body to him. Even now he drew the letter—every word of which he probably knew already by heart—towards him and fell to re-reading it for the twentieth time.

II

Marguerite of Navarre, biting her lips and almost crying with vexation, went up to the deep window embrasure and, throwing open the casement, she rested her elbow on the sill and leaned her cheek against her hand.

The open courtyard of the hostelry was at her feet, and beyond it the market-place of the sleepy little town with its quaint, narrow houses and tall crow's foot gables and curious signs, rudely painted, swinging on iron brackets in the breeze. It was early afternoon of a mild day in February, and in the courtyard of the hostelry there was the usual bustle attendant upon the presence of a high and mighty personage and of his numerous suite.

Men-at-arms passed to and fro; burghers from the tiny city, in dark cloth clothes and sombre caps, came to pay their respects; peasants from the country-side brought produce for sale; serving-men in drab linen and maids in gaily-coloured kerchiefs flitted in and out of the hostelry and across the yard with trays of refreshments for the retinue of M. le Duc d'Anjou and of Madame la Reyne de Navarre, own brother and sister of the King of France. Indeed, it was not often that so great a prince and so exalted a lady had graced La Fère with their presence, and the hostelry had been hard put to it to do honour to two such noble guests. Mine host and his wife and buxom daughters were already wellnigh sick with worry, for though Madame la Reyne de Navarre and M. le Duc, her brother, were very exacting and their gentlemen both hungry and thirsty, not one among these, from *Monsieur* downwards, cared to pay for what he had. And while the little town seethed with soldiery and with loud-voiced gentlemen, the unfortunate burghers who housed them and the poor merchants and peasants who had to feed them, almost sighed for the Spanish garrisons who, at any rate, were always well-paid and paying.

Down below in the courtyard there was constant jingling of spurs and rattle of sabres, loud language and ribald laughter; but when the casement flew open and the Queen of Navarre's face appeared at the window, the latter, at any rate, was at once suppressed. In the shade and across a narrow wooden bench on which they sat astride, a couple of gentlemen-at-arms were throwing dice, surrounded by a mixed and gaping crowd—soldiers, servants, maids and peasants— who exchanged pleasantries while watching the game.

Marguerite looked down on them for a moment or two, and an impatient frown appeared between her brows. She did not like the look of her brother's 'gentlemen,' for they were of a truth very much out-at-elbows, free of speech and curt of manner. The fact that they were never paid and often left in the lurch, if not actually sold to their enemies by *Monsieur*, accounted, no doubt, for all the laxity, and Marguerite swore to herself even then, that if ever her favourite brother reached the ambitious goal for which she was scheming on his behalf, one of his first acts of sovereignty should be to dismiss such down-at-heel, out-at-elbows swashbucklers as were, for instance, Messire Gilles de Crohin and many others. After which vow Marguerite de Navarre once more turned to her brother, trying to assume self-control and calmness which she was far from feeling. He appeared still absorbed in the contemplation of the letter, and as he looked up lazily and encountered her blazing eyes, he yawned ostentatiously.

'François!' she burst out angrily.

'Well, my dear?' he retorted.

'M. le Baron d'Inchy,' she continued more quietly, 'hath taken possession of Cambray and the Cambrésis and driven the pro-Spanish Archbishop into exile. He offers to deliver up the Cambrésis and to open the gates of Cambray to you immediately, whilst M. le Comte de Lalain will hand you over, equally readily, the provinces of Hainault, of Flanders and of Artois.'

'I know all that,' he muttered.

'You might be Duke of Hainault and Artois,' she went on with passionate enthusiasm. 'You might found a new kingdom of the Netherlands, with yourself as its first sovereign lord—and you hesitate!!! Holy Joseph! Holy Legions of Angels!' she added, with a bitter sigh of pent-up exasperation. 'What have I done that I should be plagued with such a nincompoop for a brother?'

François d'Alençon and d'Anjou laughed and shrugged his shoulders.

'The provinces are worth considering,' he said coolly. 'Cambray is attractive, and I would not object to the Duchies of Artois and Hainault, or even to a Kingdom of the Netherlands. But...!'

'Well?' she broke in testily. 'What is the "but"?'

He sighed and made a sour grimace. 'There is a bitter pill to swallow with all that sugar,' he replied. 'You appear to be forgetting that, my very impetuous sister!'

It was Marguerite's turn to shrug her pretty shoulders.

'Bah!' she said contemptuously. 'A wife! You call that a bitter pill! Jacqueline de — —what is her name?'

Monsieur referred to the letter.

'Jacqueline de Broyart,' he said dryly.

'Well! Jacqueline de Broyart,' she continued, more composedly, 'is said to be attractive. M. d'Inchy says so.'

'A merchant must praise the goods which he offers for sale,' remarked Monsieur.

'And even if she be ill-favoured,' retorted Marguerite dryly, 'she brings the richest duchies in the Netherlands and the influence of her name and family as her marriage portion. Surely a kingdom is worth a wife.'

'Sometimes.'

'In this case, François,' urged Marguerite impatiently. Then, with one of those sudden changes of mood which were one of her main charms, she added with a kind of gentle and solemn earnestness: 'You in your turn appear to forget, my exasperating brother, that 'tis I who have worked for you, just as I always have done heretofore, I who made friends for you with these loutish, ill-mannered Flemings, and who prepared the way which has led to such a brilliant goal. Whilst you wasted your substance in riotous living in our beloved Paris, I was half-killing myself with ennui in this abominable Flemish climate, I was drinking the poisonous waters of Spa so as to remain in touch with the governors of all these disaffected provinces and insidiously turning their minds towards looking for a prince of the house of France to be their deliverer and their ruler. Now my labours are bearing fruit. Don John of Austria is more hated throughout the Netherlands than he was before my coming hither, the provinces are more wearied of the Spanish yoke—they are more ready to accept a foreign ruler, even though he be a Catholic to boot. You have now but to stretch a hand, and all the golden harvest prepared by me will fall into it without another effort on your part save that of a prompt decision. So let me tell you, once and for all, Monsieur my brother, that if you refuse that golden harvest now, if you do not accept the Baron d'Inchy's offer, never as long as I live will I raise another finger to help you or to advance your welfare. And this I hereby do swear most solemnly and pray to the Virgin to register my vow!'

The Duke, unaccustomed to his charming sister's earnestness, had listened to her without departing from his sullen mood. When she had finished her tirade he shrugged his shoulders and yawned.

'How you do talk, my dear Margot!' he said coolly. 'To hear you one would imagine that I was an incorrigible rogue, an immoral profligate and a do-nothing.'

'Well, what else are you?' she retorted.

'A much maligned, overworked prince.'

She laughed, and despite her choler a look of genuine affection crept into her eyes as she met the reproachful glance of the brother whom she loved so dearly, and whose faults she was always ready to condone.

'By the Mass!' quoth he. 'You talk of having worked and slaved for me—and so you have, I'll own—but, far from leading a dissipated life in Paris the while, I toiled and slaved, intrigued and conspired, too—aye, and risked my life a hundred times so that I might fall in with your schemes.'

'Oh!' she broke in with a good-natured laugh. 'Let us be just, Monsieur my brother. You allowed others to toil and slave and intrigue and conspire, and to risk their life in your cause——'

''Tis you are unjust, Margot,' he retorted hotly. 'Why, think you then, that I was arrested by order of my brother the King, and thrown into the dungeon of Vincennes——?'

'You would not have been arrested, my dear,' said Marguerite dryly, 'if you had not chosen to be arrested.'

'The King, our brother, does not approve of your schemes, my Margot.'

'He is the dog in the manger,' she replied. 'Though Flanders and Hainault and the Netherlands are not for him, he does not wish to see you a more powerful prince than he.'

'So, you see — —'

'But you knew,' she broke in quickly, 'you knew four and twenty hours before the order of your arrest was issued that the King had already decided on signing it. You had ample time for leaving Paris and joining me at Spa. Six precious months would not have been wasted — —'

'Well! I escaped out of Vincennes as soon as I could.'

'Yes!' she retorted, once more fuming and raging, and once more pacing up and down the room like a fretful animal in a cage. 'Procrastination! Time wasted! Shelving of important decisions!...'

He pointed leisurely to the letter.

'There's no time lost,' he said.

'Time wasted is always lost,' she argued. 'The tone of M. le Baron d'Inchy is more peremptory this time than it was six months ago. There is a "take it or leave it" air about this letter. The provinces are waxing impatient. The Prince of Orange is rapidly becoming the idol of the Netherlands. What you reject he will no doubt accept. He is a man — a man of action, not a laggard — —'

'But I am not rejecting anything!' exclaimed *Monsieur* irritably.

'Then, for God's sake, François — —!'

Marguerite de Navarre paused, standing for a few seconds quite still, her whole attitude one of rigid expectancy. The next moment she had run back to the window. But now she leaned far out of the casement, heedless if the men below saw the Queen of Navarre and smiled over her eagerness. Her keen ears had caught the sound of an approaching troop of men; the clatter of horses' hoofs upon the hard road was already drawing perceptibly nearer.

'Messire Gilles!' she called out impatiently to one of the dice-throwers, who was continuing his game unperturbed.

In a moment the man was on his feet. He looked up and saw the Queen's pretty face framed in by the casement-window; and a pretty woman was the only thing on God's earth which commanded Gilles de Crohin's entire respect. Immediately he stood at attention, silhouetted against the sunlit market-place beyond—a tall, martial figure, with face weather-beaten and forehead scarred, the record of a hundred fights depicted in every line of the sinewy limbs, the powerful shoulders, the look of self-assurance in the deep-set eyes and the strong, square jaw.

III

There was nothing very handsome about Messire Gilles de Crohin. That portrait of him by Rembrandt—a mere sketch—done some years later, suggests a ruggedness of exterior which might have been even repulsive at times, when passion or choler distorted the irregular features. Only the eyes, grey and profound, and the full lips, ever ready to smile, may have been attractive. In a vague way he resembled the royal master whom he was serving now. The features were not unlike those of François, Duc d'Alençon et d'Anjou, but cast in a rougher, more powerful mould and fashioned of stouter clay. The resemblance is perhaps more striking in the picture than it could have been in the original, for the Duke's skin was almost as smooth as a woman's, his hair and sparse, pointed beard were always exquisitely brushed and oiled; whereas Gilles' skin was that of a man who has spent more nights in the open than in a downy bed, and his moustache—he did not wear the fashionable beard—was wont to bristle, each hair standing aloof from its neighbour, whenever Messire Gilles bridled with amusement or with rage.

Then, again, Gilles looked older than the Duke, even though he was, I think, the younger of the two by several years; but we may take it that neither his cradle nor his youth had been watched over with such tender care as those of the scion of the house of France, and though dissipation and a surfeit of pleasure had drawn many lines on the placid face of the one man, hard fighting and hard living had left deeper imprints still on that of the other. Still, the resemblance was there, and though Gilles' limbs indicated elasticity and power, whereas those of the Prince of Valois were more slender and loosely knit, the two men were much of a height and build, sufficiently so, at any rate, to cause several chroniclers—notably the Queen of Navarre herself—to aver that Gilles de Crohin's personality ofttimes shielded that of *Monsieur*, Duke of Anjou and of Alençon, and that Messire Gilles was ofttimes requisitioned to impersonate the master whom he served and resembled, especially when any danger at the hand of an outraged husband or father, or of a hired assassin lurked for the profligate prince behind a hedge or in the angle of a dark street. Nor was that resemblance to be altogether wondered at, seeing that the de Froidmonts claimed direct descent from the house of Valois and still quartered the Flower o' the Lily on ground azure upon their escutcheon, with the proud device: 'Roy ne suys, ne Duc, ne Prince, ne Comte; je suys Sire de Froide Monte.'[1] They had indeed played at one time an important part in the destinies of the princely house, until fickle Fortune took so resolutely to turning her back upon the last descendants of the noble race.

[1] 'Am neither King, nor Duke, nor Prince, nor Count;
am Sire de Froide Monte.'

Marguerite of Navarre was too thoroughly a woman not to appreciate the appearance of one who was so thoroughly a man. Gilles de Crohin may have been out-at-elbows, but even the rough leather jerkin which he wore and the faded kerseymere of his doublet could not altogether mar a curious air of breeding and of power which was not in accord with penury and a position of oft humiliating dependence. So, despite her impatience, she gazed on Gilles for a moment or two with quick satisfaction ere she said:

"'Tis Monseigneur d'Inchy's messenger we hear, is it not, Messire?'

'I doubt not, your Majesty,' replied Gilles.

'Then I pray you,' she added, 'conduct him to my brother's presence directly he arrives.'

And even whilst the sound of approaching horsemen drew nearer and nearer still, and anon a great clatter upon the rough paving stones of the courtyard announced their arrival, Marguerite turned back into the room. She ran to her brother's chair and knelt down beside him. She put fond arms round his shoulders and forced him to look into her tear-filled eyes.

'François,' she pleaded, with the tenderness of a doting mother. '*Mon petit* François! For my sake, if not for yours! You don't know how I have toiled and worked so that this should come to pass. I want you to be great and mighty and influential. I hate your being in the humiliating position of a younger brother beside Henri, who is so arrogant and dictatorial with us all. François, dear, I have worked for you because I love you. Let me have my reward!'

Monsieur sighed like the spoilt child he really was, and made his habitual sour grimace.

'You are too good to me, Margot,' he said somewhat churlishly. 'I would you had left the matter alone. Our brother Henri cannot live for ever, and his good wife has apparently no intention of presenting him with a son.'

'Our brother Henri,' she insisted, 'can live on until you are too old to enjoy the reversion of the throne of France, and Louise de Lorraine is still young—who knows? The Duchies of Artois and Hainault and the Sovereignty of the Netherlands to-day are worth more than the vague perspective of the throne of France mayhap ten or a dozen years hence— —'

'And my marriage with Elizabeth of England?' he protested.

'Elizabeth of England will never marry you, François,' she replied earnestly. 'She is too fanatical a Protestant ever to look with favour on a Catholic prince. She will keep you dangling round her skirts and fool you to the top of her bent, but Milor of Leycester will see to it that you do not wed the Queen of England.'

'If I marry this Flemish wench I shall be burning my boats— —'

'What matter?' she retorted hotly, 'if you enter so glorious a harbour?'

There was nothing in the world that suited *Monsieur's* temperament better than lengthy discussions over a decision, which could thereby be conveniently put off. Even now he would have talked and argued and worn his sister's patience down to breaking point if suddenly the corridor outside had not resounded with martial footsteps and the jingling of swords and spurs.

'François!' pleaded Marguerite for the last time.

And the Duke, still irresolute, still longing to procrastinate, gave a final sigh of sullen resignation.

'Very well!' he said. 'Since you wish it— —'

'I do,' she replied solemnly. 'I do wish it most earnestly, most sincerely. You *will* accept, François?'

'Yes.'

'You promise?'

Again he hesitated. Then, as the footsteps halted outside the door and Marguerite almost squeezed the breath out of his body with the pressure of her young strong arms, he said reluctantly: 'I promise!' Then, immediately—for fear he should be held strictly to his word—he added quickly: 'On one condition.'

'What is that?' she asked.

'That I am not asked to plight my troth to the wench till after I have seen her; for I herewith do swear most solemnly that I would repudiate her at the eleventh hour—aye, at the very foot of the altar steps, if any engagement is entered into in my name to which I have not willingly subscribed.'

This time he spoke so solemnly and with such unwonted decision that Marguerite thought it best to give way. At the back of her over-quick mind she knew that by hook or by crook she would presently devise a plan which would reconcile his wishes to her own.

'Very well,' she said after an almost imperceptible moment of hesitation. 'It shall be as you say.'

And despite the half-hearted promise given by the arch-procrastinator, there was a look of triumph and of joy on Queen Marguerite's piquant features now. She rose to her feet and hastily dried her tears.

There was a rap at the door. Marguerite seated herself on a cushioned chair opposite her brother and called out serenely: 'Enter!'

CHAPTER III.
HOW A CLEVER WOMAN OUTWITTED
AN OBSTINATE MAN

I

The door was thrown open and Messire Gilles de Crohin, Sire de Froidmont, stood at attention upon the threshold.

'Monseigneur le Baron d'Inchy's messenger, is it not, Messire?' asked Marguerite of Navarre quickly, even before Gilles had time to make the formal announcement.

'Messire de Montigny has arrived, your Majesty,' he replied. 'He bears credentials from Monseigneur the governor of Cambray.'

'Messire de Montigny?' she said, with a frown of puzzlement. 'In person?'

'Yes, your Majesty.'

'Has he come with a retinue, then?' broke in *Monsieur* with his wonted peevishness. 'There is no room in the city. Already I have scarce room for my men.'

'Messire de Montigny is alone, Monseigneur,' replied Gilles de Crohin, 'save for an equerry. He proposes to return to Cambray this night.'

Monsieur uttered a fretful exclamation, but already Marguerite had interposed.

'We cannot,' she said curtly, 'keep Messire de Montigny on the doorstep, my dear brother. And you must remember that I have your promise.'

'Holy Virgin!' was *Monsieur's* only comment on this timeful reminder. 'Was ever man so plagued before by a woman who was not even his mistress, Gilles!' he added peremptorily.

'François!' admonished his sister sternly.

'*Mon Dieu*, my dear!' he retorted. 'May I not speak to Gilles now? Gilles, who is my best friend— —'

'Messire de Montigny is in the corridor,' she broke in firmly.

'I know! I know! Curse him! I only wished to order Gilles—my best friend, Gilles—not to leave me in the lurch; not to abandon me all alone between an impetuous sister and a mulish Fleming.'

'François!' she exclaimed. 'What folly!'

'Gilles must remain in the room,' he declared, 'during the interview.'

'Impossible!' she affirmed hotly. 'Messire de Montigny might not like it.'

'Then I'll not see him— —'

Marguerite de Navarre was on the verge of tears. Vexation, impatience, choler, were wellnigh choking her.

'Very well!' she said at last, with a sigh of infinite weariness. 'I pray you, Messire,' she added, turning to Gilles, 'introduce Monseigneur le Baron d'Inchy's messenger and remain in the room, as *Monsieur* bids you, during the interview.'

II

Messire de Montigny was a short, stout, determined-looking gentleman who, very obviously, despite his outward show of deference to a scion of the house of France, had received his instructions as to the manner in which he was to deal with that procrastinating and indolent prince. He had clearly come here resolved to be firm and not to yield an inch in his demands, nor to allow any further delay in the negotiations wherewith he had been entrusted.

But with François, Duc d'Alençon et d'Anjou, a promise given was not of necessity a promise kept. No one knew that better than the sister who adored him, and whose quasi-maternal love for him was not wholly free from contempt. Therefore, all the while that Messire de Montigny was paying his devoirs to *Monsieur* and to herself, all the while that the preliminary flummery, the bowings and the scrapings, the grandiloquent phrases and meaningless compliments went on between the two men, Marguerite of Navarre was watching her brother, noting with a sinking of the heart every sign of peevish fretfulness upon that weak and good-looking face, and of that eternal desire to put decisions off, which she knew in this case would mean the ruin of all her ambitious plans for him. At times, her luminous dark eyes would exchange a glance of understanding or of appeal with Gilles de Crohin who, silent and apparently disinterested, stood in a corner of the room quietly watching the comedy which was being enacted before him. Marguerite de Navarre, whose sense of the ridiculous was one of her keenest attributes, could well appreciate how a man of Gilles' caustic humour would be amused at this double-edged duel of temperaments. She could see how, at *Monsieur's* perpetual parryings, Gilles' moustache would bristle and his deep-set eyes twinkle with merriment; and though she frowned on him for this impertinence, she could not altogether blame him for it. There certainly was an element of farce in the proceedings.

'I have come for Monseigneur's answer,' Messire de Montigny had declared with uncompromising energy. 'My brother de Lalain and M. d'Inchy cannot, and will not, wait!'

'You Flemings are always in such a devil of a hurry!' Monsieur had said, with an attempt at jocularity.

'We have endured tyranny for close upon a century, Monseigneur,' retorted de Montigny curtly. 'We have been long-suffering; we can endure no longer.'

'But, Holy Virgin, Messire!' exclaimed the Duke fretfully, 'ye cannot expect a man to risk his entire future in the turn of a hand.'

'Monsieur le Baron d'Inchy had the honour to send a letter to Monseigneur two months ago,' rejoined the other. 'The Provinces have fought the whole might of Spain and of Don Juan of Austria on their own initiative and on their own resources, for the recovery of their ancient civil and religious liberties. But they have fought unaided quite long enough. We must have help and we must have a leader. The Prince of Orange has his following in Holland. We in the Cambrésis, in Hainault and Artois and Flanders want a sovereign of our own—a sovereign who has power and the might of a great kingdom and of powerful alliances behind him. 'Our choice has fallen on *Monsieur*, Duc d'Alençon and d'Anjou, own brother to the

King of France. Will he deign to accept the sovereignty of the United Provinces of the Netherlands and give them the happiness and the freedom which they seek?'

With a certain rough dignity Messire de Montigny put one knee to the ground and swept the floor with his plumed hat ere he pressed his hand against his heart in token of loyalty and obeisance. Marguerite de Navarre's beautiful face became irradiated with a great joy. Her fine nostrils quivered with excitement and she threw a look of triumph on Messire Gilles, who had, in his appearance just then, the solemnity of a Puck—and one of encouragement on the beloved brother. But *Monsieur* looked as sullen and as gloomy as he had done before. If there was a thing on this earth which he hated more than any other, it was a plain question which required a plain answer. He was furious with Messire de Montigny for having asked a plain question, furious with his sister for looking triumphant, and furious with Gilles for seeming so amused.

So he took refuge in moody silence, and Messire de Montigny, with a flush of anger on his round face, quickly rose to his feet. Even to one less keenly observant than was the clever Queen of Navarre, it would have been obvious that all these obsequious marks of deference, these genuflexions and soft words were highly unpalatable to the envoy of Monseigneur le Baron d'Inchy, governor of the Cambrésis. They were proud folk, these Flemings—nobles, burgesses and workers alike—and it had only been after very mature deliberation and driven by stern necessity that they had decided to call in a stranger to aid them in their distress. The tyranny of the Spaniards had weighed heavily upon them. One by one they saw their ancient privileges wrested from them, whilst their liberty to worship in accordance with the dictates of their conscience was filched from them under unspeakable horrors and tyrannies. They had fought on doggedly, often hopelessly, loth to call in outside aid for fear of exchanging one oppressor for another, and a while ago they had a goodly number of victories to their credit. Orange had freed many provinces, and several cities had driven the Spanish garrisons from out their gates. M. le Baron d'Inchy had seized Cambray and the Cambrésis and driven the Catholic Archbishop into exile. Flemish governors were established in Hainault, Brabant, in Artois and in Flanders; the Dutch were the masters in Holland, Zeeland and Frise—a splendid achievement! For, remember that these burghers and their untrained bands were pitted against the finest military organization of the epoch.

But lately, the Spaniards, alarmed at these reverses, had sent fresh troops into the Netherlands, and Alexander Farnese, Duke of Parma, their most distinguished soldier, had obtained signal victories over the war-wearied Dutch and Flemish troops. Since Orange had suffered a signal defeat at Gembloux three years ago several cities had fallen back once more under the Spanish yoke. It was time to call in foreign aid. On the one hand, Elizabeth of England had given assurances of money and of troops; on the other, Marguerite of Navarre had made vague promises in the name of the Duc d'Alençon. A Catholic prince was a bitter pill to swallow for these staunch Protestants, but when d'Inchy offered *Monsieur* the sovereignty of the Netherlands, with immediate possession of the Cambrésis, of Hainault, Artois and Flanders, he had first of all insisted—respectfully but firmly—on certain guarantees: the guarantee which to *Monsieur's* fastidious taste was like a bitter pill in the sugary offer—a Flemish wife and a Protestant to boot—one who would hold the new sovereign lord true to his promise to uphold and protect the reformed faith.

III

"I hate being forced into a marriage!" *Monsieur* repeated for the third time, as he cast lowering looks upon the bowed head of M. de Montigny.

'There is no question of force, Monseigneur,' rejoined the latter firmly. 'M. d'Inchy, speaking in the name of our provinces, had the honour to propose a bargain, which Monseigneur will accept or reject as he thinks fit.'

'But this Jacqueline—er—Jacqueline——?' queried Monsieur disdainfully.

'Jacqueline de Broyart, Dame de Morchipont, Duchesse et Princesse de Ramose, d'Espienne et de Wargny,' broke in Messire de Montigny with stern pride, "is as beautiful and pure as she is rich and noble. She is worthy to be the consort of a King.'

'But I have never seen the lady!' argued *Monsieur* irritably.

'Jacqueline de Broyart,' retorted de Montigny curtly, 'cannot be trotted out for Monseigneur's inspection like a filly who is put up for sale!'

'Who talks of trotting her out?' said *Monsieur*. '*Mon Dieu*, man! Can I not even see my future wife? In matters of beauty tastes differ, and——'

'You will admit, Messire,' here interposed Marguerite quickly, seeing that at *Monsieur's* tone of thinly-veiled contempt frowns of anger, dark as thunder-clouds, were gathering on Messire de Montigny's brow. 'You will admit that it is only just that my brother should see the lady ere he finally decides.'

'Jacqueline, Madame la Reyne,' riposted de Montigny gruffly, 'is wooed by every rich and puissant seigneur in four kingdoms. Princes of the blood in Germany and Austria and Spain, noble lords of England and of France are at her feet. She is a mere child—scarce nineteen years of age—but she has a woman's heart and a woman's pride. She is my cousin's child; d'Inchy and my brother are her guardians. They would not allow an affront to be put upon her.'

'An affront, Messire?' queried Marguerite coldly. 'Who spoke of an affront to the Duc d'Alençon's future wife?'

'If Monseigneur sees the child,' argued de Montigny stiffly, 'and then turns against her, she is quite old enough to look upon that fact as an affront.'

'The devil take you for a stiff-necked Fleming, Messire!' quoth the Duke angrily.

'Then Monseigneur refuses?' was de Montigny's calm retort, even though his rough voice was shaking with suppressed choler.

'No, no, Messire!' once more broke in Marguerite hastily. 'Did Monseigneur say that he refused?'

'Monseigneur seems disinclined to accept,' rejoined de Montigny. 'And so much hesitation is a slur cast upon the honour of a noble Flemish lady who is my kinswoman.'

'Believe me, Messire,' said Marguerite gently and with unerring tact, determined to conciliate at all costs, 'that we of the house of Valois hold all honour in high esteem. Meseems that you and my brother do but misunderstand one another. Will you allow a woman's wit to bridge over the difficulty?'

'If you please, Madame,' replied de Montigny stiffly.

IV

Marguerite de Navarre gave a short sigh of satisfaction. One look of warning only did she cast on her brother, and with an almost imperceptible movement of finger to lip she enjoined him to remain silent and to leave the matter in her hands. François d'Anjou shrugged his shoulders and smothered a yawn. The whole matter was eminently distasteful to him, and gladly would he have thrown up the promised throne and be rid of all these serious questions which bored him to tears.

De Montigny stood erect and stern; his attitude remained deferential, but also unyielding. He was deeply offended in the person of the child who in his sight stood for all that was most noble and most desirable in the Netherlands. The indifference with which the offer of such a brilliant alliance had been received by this Prince of France had angered the stiff-necked Fleming beyond measure. But Marguerite, feeling the difficulties around her, was now on her mettle. None knew better than she how to make a man unbend—even if he be a bitter enemy, which de Montigny certainly was not.

'Messire,' she said with that gentle dignity which became her so well, 'I pray you be not angered with my brother. He has had much to worry him of late. Indeed, indeed,' she continued earnestly, 'his heart is entirely given over to your magnificent country and he is proud and honoured to have been chosen by you as your future Sovereign Lord.'

But to this conciliating harangue de Montigny made no reply, and Marguerite resumed, after a slight pause.

'Perhaps you do not know, Messire, that the King of France, our brother, hath not such goodwill towards his kindred as they would wish, and that, fearing that *Monsieur* would be overproud of your offer and would nurture further ambitious plans, he did order *Monsieur's* arrest, thereby causing us much delay.'

'Yes, your Majesty,' replied de Montigny curtly, 'I knew all that. But the offer hath been made to Monseigneur now—and I still await his answer.'

'His answer is yes, Messire!' said Marguerite firmly.

'A grudging "yes," forsooth,' quoth de Montigny with an impatient shrug of the shoulders.

'An eager "yes," an you'll believe me,' retorted Marguerite. 'All that he asks is to see the noble Dame Jacqueline de Broyart and to pay her his devoirs ere he is formally affianced to her.'

'Hang it all!' quoth *Monsieur* resolutely. 'You cannot expect a man to wed a woman whom he has never seen!'

'A man in Monseigneur's position,' retorted de Montigny gruffly, 'must do many things which humbler folk can afford to leave undone, and I have explained my objections to that plan; so that if Madame la Reyne hath none other to offer——'

'Nay! but I entreat you to listen to me, Messire,' urged Marguerite with exemplary patience. 'And you, François,' she added, turning to her brother, who at de Montigny's last words had muttered an angry oath under his breath, 'I beg that you will let me unfold my plan ere you combat it. Messire,' she continued earnestly, once more addressing the Flemish lord, 'let me assure you again that I both understand and appreciate your objection and, on my soul I never dreamed of suggesting that so noble and great a lady as Madame Jacqueline de Broyart should, as you justly remark, be trotted out for the inspection of Monseigneur, like a filly which is put up for sale.'

'Well, then——?' retorted de Montigny.

'Tell me, Messire,' she interposed irrelevantly, 'how old exactly is Madame Jacqueline?'

'Not yet twenty,' he replied. 'But I do not see——'

'You will in a moment,' quoth she with a smile. 'Twenty, you said?'

'Not quite.'

'And beautiful, of course?'

'Ask the men of Hainault and of Flanders,' was his proud reply. 'They will tell you how beautiful she is.'

'Twenty—not quite—and beautiful,' said Marguerite of Navarre slowly. 'And of a romantic turn of mind, shall we say, as young girls so often are?'

'Oh, as to that,' replied de Montigny with a puzzled frown, 'I dare swear that she hath a romantic turn of mind. She certainly would not allow herself to be offered up for sale like a bundle of goods. Therefore——'

'Easy, easy, Messire!' urged the Queen gently. 'I entreat you to reply to my questions without choler. Are we not both striving to find a way out of an impasse which might wreck the very welfare of your country and Monseigneur d'Inchy's most cherished scheme?'

De Montigny sighed impatiently. 'You are right, Madame la Reyne,' he said grudgingly. 'I pray you continue. I'll not lose my temper again. My word on it.'

'You were about to assure me, Messire,' resumed Marguerite gently, 'that Madame Jacqueline is as romantic as she is beautiful.'

'Jacqueline has been spoilt and adulated,' replied de Montigny, determined to speak calmly. 'Poets have dedicated their verses to her. Musicians have sung her praises——'

'And love-sick swains have died of love for her, or sighed impassioned tirades beneath her casement-window,' concluded Marguerite, with a smile which was so winning that, despite himself, after a moment or two, it found a pale reflex in de Montigny's stern face.

'Who should know better than the Queen of Navarre,' he retorted, with a crude effort at gallantry, 'the power which beauty wields over all men?'

'Very well, then, Messire,' quoth she gaily. 'Listen to my plan, for I swear 'tis a good one, since it will marry your pride to my brother's hesitation. I propose that *Monsieur* le Duc d'Anjou shall first approach Madame Jacqueline under an assumed name. She hath never seen him—he is totally unknown in these parts; his incognito could therefore be easily kept up.'

'I don't quite understand,' muttered de Montigny with a frown.

'You will in a moment,' she rejoined. 'I propose, then, that *Monsieur* shall enact a part—the part of an unknown and noble prince who hath become secretly enamoured of Madame Jacqueline. I would suggest that he should appear before her closely masked and begin his part by sighing dolefully beneath her casement-window. Thus, at the outset, Madame Jacqueline, being what she is—romantic and not yet twenty—will feel an interest in this unknown swain. Her curiosity will be aroused, and she will not be loth to grant him the interview for which he will have sighed and begged in all humility.'

'But that is sheer folly, Madame!' broke in de Montigny, who had been at great pains to check his growing truculence.

'Folly?' she queried blandly. 'Why?'

'Because—because——' he argued gruffly.

'You promised on your honour, Messire,' she admonished gaily, 'that you would not again lose your temper.'

'But the folly of it!'

'Again I ask you—why folly?'

'Jacqueline is not a foolish child. She is not like to be taken in by so transparent a comedy.'

'It will not be transparent, Messire. Under my guidance the comedy will be exceedingly well acted. Madame Jacqueline will never know that her love-sick swain is the Duke of Anjou.'

'Then 'tis greater folly still!'

'Ah, that I swear it is not!' retorted Marguerite de Navarre hotly. 'Your Jacqueline is not twenty—she is proud and beautiful and romantic. Well! give her some romance and she'll thank you for it presently on her knees.'

'But——' protested de Montigny.

'Is not the whole thing simplicity in itself?' she broke in eagerly. 'The fame of Madame Jacqueline's beauty hath spread far and wide; what more rational than that a noble prince—too insignificant or too poor to enter the lists for her hand—should choose a romantic method to approach her? After all, what are we all striving for? That *Monsieur* shall see the lovely Jacqueline without her knowing that he proposes to woo her. If, in addition to that, we cause the two young people to fall in love with one another, we shall have done well; whilst, on the other hand, if, after having seen her, *Monsieur* retires from the candidature, the susceptibilities of the Flemish nation and of Madame Jacqueline will have been safeguarded.'

'How?'

'The unknown prince can vanish as mysteriously as he came. The story can reach Madame Jacqueline's ear that he was found killed by some other jealous swain outside her garden-gate.'

'Folly, Madame! Folly, I say!' protested de Montigny, perhaps a shade less forcibly than he had done before.

'Nay, then, 'tis a blessed folly, Messire, which oft outweighs counsels of wisdom.'

'But— —'

'Ah! but me no more buts, Messire! Ye cannot bring forth one objection which I cannot easily combat. Think on it! A romantic girl, whose life will be brightened by this pretty adventure!'

'Perchance— —'

'Perchance what?'

'She fall in love with the unknown swain.'

'So much the better, when she discovers he is her future lord.'

Then, as de Montigny really appeared to be struggling between consent and refusal, and doubt, anger, contempt, irresolution were alternately depicted in his rugged face, she continued persuasively:

'Think, Messire, how you safeguard your niece's feelings, her just pride, her maidenly reserve. *Monsieur* le Duc d'Anjou will either himself fall madly in love with Madame Jacqueline—in which case you will have added the leaven of passion to the stodgy dough of matrimony—or else he'll withdraw from the candidature, unknown, unsuspected; and the child will only have one pleasant dream the more to add to her illusions.'

Montigny was yielding. Who could, indeed, resist for long the insinuating tongue of Marguerite of Navarre, the eager glitter of her eyes, the strength of her will and of her personality. The sober-minded, stiff-necked and somewhat slow-witted Fleming felt himself literally swept off his feet in this whirlpool of adventure and of intrigue, and his language was not sufficiently glib to meet objection with objection, to parry or to thrust in this unequal duel of wits. Perhaps—had he not desired so passionately the alliance which he had been sent to conclude, had he been less firmly convinced that a union with France would prove the salvation of his people and of the country which he worshipped—he might have opposed an obstinate and gruff refusal to Marguerite's subtle scheme. But as it was, his resistance was soon disarmed; she even managed to conquer the irritation which *Monsieur's* very personality had aroused in his mind.

'We have not yet heard,' he said at last, 'what Monseigneur le duc d'Anjou hath to say on the matter.'

'Oh!' *Monsieur* hastened to say with mock sincerity, 'all that I have to say is that throughout my life I have from time to time and on many a momentous occasion, registered on oath that I would never be affianced to a woman whom I had not previously learned to love.'

'You will own, Messire,' broke in Marguerite gently, 'that this is a laudable sentiment.'

Nor did she think it desirable to let Messire de Montigny know that her unreliable brother had vowed but half an hour ago that if a wife were thrust upon him now he would, an he did not like her, repudiate her even at the foot of the altar. Shifty and irresponsible in most things, she knew him well enough to understand that in matters which affected himself and his desires, he would prove dangerous, obstinate and cruel.

'On my soul!' added *Monsieur* with well-assumed earnestness, 'I do assure you, Messire, that I knew nothing of my sister's project.'

'There was no time to put it before you, François,' rejoined Marguerite. 'It arose in my brain even while you parleyed together with Messire de Montigny and seemed unable to come to an understanding.'

'Then what says Monseigneur now?' reiterated the Flemish lord curtly.

'Well!' drawled *Monsieur* in his usual indecisive way, 'I say—I say that— —'

'François!' admonished Marguerite sharply.

He felt himself driven into a corner, from which procrastination would no longer free him. In a manner the proposed adventure suited his temperament, and in any case it would help to put off the final and irrevocable decision. Therefore he was willing to fall in with it.

Sentimental dalliance was an art which he knew to his finger-tips, and there was much in his sister's project which pleased his lazy, pulpy nature. To sigh beneath a woman's window, to woo a woman's love with honeyed words beneath a silken mask, to plan secret meetings and steal to lovers' trysts at dead of night, had always been an absorbing occupation for this degenerate prince. Now he felt de Montigny's stern gaze fixed upon him and his sister's admonitions rang in his ears. He knew that he had worn her love and patience almost to a breaking thread. He threw a final appealing look on Gilles de Crohin, but the latter's glance of amusement appeared as an encouragement. Well, Gilles would know! Gilles would appreciate! He, too, loved masks and casement-windows and fair women, tearful with love. Gilles also loved fighting, so he could do that, if any of it barred the way to *Monsieur's* comfort and peace.

'François!' came once more, appealing yet severe, from Marguerite of Navarre.

'What says Monseigneur?' reiterated de Montigny for the third time.

'I say that you have left me no choice, Messire,' quoth François due d'Anjou at last. 'It shall be as my sister desires.'

V

What was said after this is not much to the point. Enough that de Montigny yielded—very reluctantly, very slowly, be it admitted—but still, he did yield, and Marguerite, Queen of Navarre, was triumphant because she had got her way and because she would be allowed now to weave one of those subtle and sentimental plots which was as the breath of life to her inventive brain. She was also triumphant because she felt that nothing now stood in the way of the ambitious plans which she had framed for her favourite brother. She was triumphant because she felt the romance which she had concocted for his benefit would end in substantial gain for him—a richly-dowered wife and a sovereignty as rich as a crown. Then, at last, when she had won Messire de Montigny over absolutely and completely with her ready wit and her glib tongue, she extended a gracious hand to the somewhat shamefaced Fleming. 'Ah, Messire!' she said. 'You little realize how much you have done for your country this day!'

'I certainly have sacrificed my sanity and my better judgment,' he said gruffly. But he did bend the knee, and kissed the delicately-perfumed hand.

'And Madame Jacqueline will be at Cambray?' she asked.

'She is at Cambray now,' he replied.

'Then *Monsieur* had best repair thither right away. You yourself will be there, Messire?'

'Not I, alas, Madame!' he replied. 'After I have seen my brother and d'Inchy and obtained their consent to this wild-cat scheme, I join the army of the Prince of Orange at Utrecht.'

'But you'll see that my brother has a safe conduct and is sure of a welcome from Monseigneur d'Inchy?'

'Oh! d'Inchy will consent and so will my brother. They will make Monseigneur quite welcome,' rejoined de Montigny with a sigh. 'All of us would do much, Madame, in order to bring about this alliance, on which we have set our hearts.'

He was as wax now in the hands of this fascinating intriguer. In his heart of hearts he knew that sober reflection would come anon; he knew that it would take much persuasion ere his brother, and the other sober-minded Flemings who ruled the destinies of a great nation and of a rich heiress, would finally consent to these wild and romantic plans which had found their origin in an imaginative woman's brain; he knew that, mayhap, when he returned to Cambray, he would have to argue in his turn as the Queen of Navarre had argued with him. But in the meanwhile, now that he had given in, he was man enough and gentleman enough to fulfil his share of the bargain loyally and completely.

'That's brave!' exclaimed Marguerite. 'And I entreat you, lose no time. *Monsieur* could start for Cambray this night.'

'Would Monseigneur go alone?' queried de Montigny.

'No, no,' broke in the Duke fretfully. 'I could not go unattended. Think on it, Messire! A prince of the house of France!'

'Monseigneur would not, I presume, enter Cambray incognito with a retinue of men-at-arms,' retorted the other with a grim smile.

'No! not a retinue,' he rejoined unperturbed. 'I'll have Gilles with me and a serving-man; that is all.'

'Gilles?'

'Gilles de Crohin, Sire de Froidmont,' interposed Marguerite, as with a graceful gesture of the hand she indicated Gilles, who still stood silent and impassive in the corner of the room. 'This gallant gentleman is devoted to Monsieur's service and accompanies him wherever he goes.'

De Montigny's sharp, scrutinizing glance swept approvingly over Gilles de Crohin's martial figure.

'Very well then, so be it,' he said. 'I will give a safe conduct to Monseigneur under any name he will choose to assume, and one to Messire Gilles de Crohin, Sire de Froidmont, who will travel as his equerry. Is that what Madame la Reyne desires?'

'It is! It is!' cried Marguerite joyfully. 'Ah!' she added as she directed a reproachful glance on her brother, 'dilatoriness is not a part of your method, Messire de Montigny!'

'*Mon Dieu*, my good Margot!' quoth *Monsieur* tartly. 'You do not give Messire sufficient time to breathe.'

'Who wants to breathe,' she retorted gaily, 'when the destinies of kingdoms are at stake? The safe conducts, Messire! The safe conducts, I entreat! Why not sign them here and now?'

She jumped up from her chair, eager, young, full of vitality. In a moment, with her own dainty hands, she had placed ink-horn, sand, a quill, a sheet of paper upon the table.

'The safe conduct, Messire!' she reiterated excitedly. 'I vow that I'll don male attire and start for Cambray with my brother this night!'

And she would have done it, too, had not prudence dictated otherwise. Her fine, clever face, however, was well known in this part of Belgium. She had been at Cambray but a few weeks ago, moving heaven and earth and stirring up those heavy Flemings to activity on behalf of her brother. But she would have loved to be of that adventurous party. The conception of it had been born in her brain; it was her thing, her creation, her child, and she fretted at the thought that her brother's indolence, his shiftlessness and indecision might even yet jeopardize these glorious projects which she had formed.

'Sainte Vierge and chorus of angels, grant me patience!' she murmured as she watched, frowning and fretful, the deliberate movements of M. de Montigny. The Duc d'Anjou chortled quietly to himself. He loved to see his impetuous sister fuming over the dilatoriness of another, and now he gave a low cackle of delight when the Fleming first drew a chair slowly to the table, then sat down and settled himself to write. He next took up the quill pen, examined it, tested it on his thumb-nail, turned the sheet of paper over and over. Obviously he was not very much used to rapid caligraphy, and Marguerite's temper was oozing out of her very finger-tips as she watched that quill pen travelling with ponderous slowness along the paper.

'In what name shall I make out the safe-conduct?' he asked presently.

'Oh, ye gods!' exclaimed Marguerite impatiently. 'Any name, Messire—or leave the name in blank— —'

'I cannot do that,' rejoined de Montigny deliberately. 'M. d'Inchy, who is governor of the city and of the province, would not wish it. And since Monseigneur desires to enter Cambray incognito— —'

'Any name will do,' she retorted.

'Still, I must have one— —'

'Then, in God's name, make out the safe-conduct in the name of Monseigneur le Prince de Froidmont, travelling with his equerry Messire Gilles de Crohin and with his serving-man. Will that satisfy Monseigneur le Baron d'Inchy?'

De Montigny thought the matter over for a moment or two ere he replied, wholly unperturbed, 'I think so.'

And thus did the document stand. A permit to enter the City of Cambray was granted to Monseigneur le Prince de Froidmont, to his equerry Messire Gilles de Crohin and to his serving-man, by Edmond, Sire de Montigny, acting on behalf of Roger, Baron d'Inchy, governor of the province of Cambrésis, and safe conduct was assured them on their way thither.[1]

[1] This document which Messire de Montigny made out and signed on that memorable occasion is still preserved

among the archives of the City of Cambray. At any rate, it was still extant in the spring of 1914, when the writer of this veracious chronicle was granted a sight of it. Since then the hordes of the modern Huns have swept over the fair lands of Belgium and France. They may have destroyed these archives as they did so much of what had historical and romantic interest.

'Well! you have your wish, my dear sister,' was the Duc d'Anjou's sole comment as he saw the look of impatience on Marguerite's fair face give place to one of triumph and of joy.

CHAPTER IV.
HOW MONSIEUR KEPT HIS WORD

I

When M. de Montigny—after much ponderous leavetaking—finally took his departure, accompanied by Messire Gilles de Crohin, it is positively averred that Marguerite, Queen of Navarre, forgot for a moment her position and her dignity and danced around the narrow room like a child who has had its way after much fighting and arguing. It is even said that she dragged her dearly-loved François up from his chair and that, seizing both his hands, she forced him to join her in a whirl which literally swept him off his feet, raised a cloud of dust from the old wooden floor, and finally sent him sprawling and dizzy, and thoroughly out of temper, up against the table, from whence he poured a volley of abuse upon his devoted sister.

But I have oft marvelled if this story be true, for, of a truth, there was no one there to witness these events, and Queen Margot herself never put them on record. But there was Messire Gilles, and where he was at the moment I, for one, cannot say. He did accompany Messire de Montigny as far as the courtyard, and saw that noble Fleming ride off with an obviously heavy heart, after what had only been a partially successful errand. We are not going to suppose that Messire Gilles paused on his way back to the apartments of his princely master in order to listen at the keyhole. He was more like to have kicked open the door with scant ceremony and seen the young Queen of Navarre dancing a rigadoon in the middle of the floor with her reluctant brother. Certain it is, that anon he did stand there under the lintel, coughing and spluttering as the dust caught in his throat, and coughing so loudly, be it said, that the noise which he made drowned some of *Monsieur's* most sanguinary expletives. The next moment he had once more entered the room and closed the door behind him;

and Marguerite paused in her mad dance in order to clap her hands gleefully together.

'Ah, Messire Gilles!' she exclaimed excitedly. 'Is it not wonderful? Is it not great? All arranged, and both Monsieur and that tiresome Fleming satisfied! Is it not a triumph, I say?'

'A triumph, indeed, your Majesty!' replied Gilles with a grim smile. ''Tis only our chief actor, methinks, who doth not look overjoyed.'

'I know,' rejoined Marguerite, with a sigh. 'But, then, Monsieur never really looks pleased. So I entreat you, Messire, remain with him now and make all arrangements for the journey to-morrow. Nay! 'twere far better you started this very night, slept and rested at St. Quentin and arrived at Cambray the day after to-morrow. I leave you with Messire Gilles, François,' she added, turning to Monsieur who, ill-humoured and still growling like a frowsy dog, was putting his rumpled toilet in order. 'Let him make all arrangements for your journey. He is always of good counsel.'

'Good counsel!' muttered *Monsieur*. 'Good counsel! I am sick to death of good counsels. Had I been left to myself— —'

'Nothing would have happened, *c'est entendu*,' she riposted gaily. 'Nay! you'll not damp my ardour again, François; and you cannot deny that I have satisfied M. de Montigny whilst keeping my solemn promise to you. So I leave you now with Messire Gilles. The way is prepared. And, remember,' she added earnestly, 'that you are pledged to me as I was to you. I have fulfilled my share of the bargain. If you fail me now, I will never look upon your face again!'

II

As soon as Marguerite de Navarre had gone from the room, Gilles de Crohin drew a folded missive from inside his doublet and handed it to Monsieur.

'Just came by messenger from Paris,' he said curtly.

Monsieur snatched eagerly at the missive. It had been carefully folded into a tiny compass, tied with a shell-pink ribbon and sealed with mauve-coloured wax. *Monsieur* broke the seal and read the letter. A flush—which might have been one of pleasure, of excitement or of anger, or of all three combined—spread over his face. He read the letter again, and a dark frown appeared between his brows. Then he looked up into the face of the one faithful friend whom his many treacheries had not driven from his side.

'Gilles,' he said dolefully, 'I cannot go to Cambray.'

'I thought as much, Monseigneur,' replied Gilles dryly. 'That letter is from Madame de Marquette.'

'It is, my good Gilles,' sighed *Monsieur*. 'It is!' Then as Gilles said nothing, he added fretfully: 'She had promised to let me know as soon as Monsieur le Comte, her husband, would be absent from Paris.'

'Ah!' was Gilles' simple comment. 'And is M. le Comte de Marquette absent from Paris at this moment?'

'Cooling his heels in the dungeons of Vincennes, my good Gilles,' replied *Monsieur* lightly.

'Ah!' uttered Gilles once more; this time without any comment.

'Yes. I let His Majesty, my brother, know indirectly of certain doings of Monsieur de Marquette. I have no doubt, therefore, that that estimable worthy is incarcerated at Vincennes by now.'

'Under a false charge of conspiracy?'

'False? No!' retorted *Monsieur*. 'Doth he not conspire to keep his charming wife a virtual prisoner in his own palace?'

'Therefore he is to be kept a real prisoner under a denunciation from *Monsieur* le Duc d'Alençon and d'Anjou,' riposted Gilles dryly.

'Oh! not a denunciation, my good Gilles!' said *Monsieur*, wholly unperturbed. 'I only gave His Majesty a hint that M. de Marquette was not quite so faithful a subject as one would desire.'

'And the hint has landed M. de Marquette in Vincennes rightly enough.'

'Apparently,' concluded *Monsieur* placidly, as he held the delicately-scented missive of Madame de Marquette to his nose. 'So you see, my good Gilles,' he continued after a slight pause, 'how inconvenient it will be for me to go a-wooing a ponderous Flemish wench just now. Madame de Marquette is so dainty, so exquisite, so— so—what shall I say? ... What would you do, now, Gilles?' he added, with a sudden change of tone, 'if you were in my shoes?'

'Oh, I, Monseigneur,' quoth Gilles, with a careless shrug of the shoulders. 'Not being a prince of the blood I would probably stick to my promise and go and woo the Flemish wench at Cambray.'

'I believe you would, you dog!' retorted *Monsieur* with a yawn. 'And then hurry back to Paris, eh, in order to console Madame de Marquette?'

'Possibly, Monseigneur,' concluded Gilles simply.

'Well, then, the only difference 'twixt you and me, my dear Gilles—that is, 'twixt your moral sentiments and mine—is that I'll hie me first to console Madame de Marquette, and having done that, I'll—I'll——'

'Gravely offend the most devoted of sisters, Queen Marguerite of Navarre,' broke in Gilles quickly.

'Yes,' admitted *Monsieur*. 'I imagine that dear Margot will be in one of her most fretting humours when she finds that I am half-way to Paris instead of to Cambray. She hath vowed that if I fail her now in her schemes she'll never look on my face again. And she won't—for at least six months,' he added peevishly. 'Trust her for that! Margot is nothing if not obstinate! And my chance of getting a rich wife and some rich provinces of these accursed Netherlands will have vanished for ever. Ah, Gilles! my good Gilles!' he concluded, with naïve induction. 'You see what comes of it, if a man allows himself to be overruled by women!'

'Well!' retorted the other with a careless laugh. 'Meseems that Monseigneur hath not much cause to quarrel with his fate this time. King of the Netherlands!' he exclaimed, and gave a long, low whistle of appreciation. ''Tis no small matter——'

'Bah!' rejoined *Monsieur* with a shrug of the shoulders. 'To be a king among these dull-witted, slow-going Flemings is not altogether an enviable existence. Would you care for it, Gilles?'

'Oh, I, Monseigneur?' riposted Gilles gaily. 'I have so few kingly attributes.'

'Better to be Duc d'Alençon in Paris, eh, than King in Antwerp or in Ghent? Brrr!' added *Monsieur*, with a mock shudder. 'Think of the Flemish women, my good man!'

'I have thought of them, Monseigneur,' replied Gilles dryly, 'once or twice since we came into Flanders.'

'Well! and what did you think of them?'

'That God has fashioned uglier ones.'

'Where?'

'In many places—even in Paris.'

'Not often, Gilles.'

'I'll grant that, Monseigneur, an you command.'

'Now this Jacqueline, for instance——'

'Madame Jacqueline, Monseigneur?'

'Yes!' And Monseigneur sighed. 'I have got to marry her, Gilles, if I wish for the sovereignty of the Netherlands.'

'Messire de Montigny hath been at pains to tell us, Monseigneur, that Madame Jacqueline is very beautiful—very beautiful, an it please you.'

'It would please me if she were beautiful. But have you ever seen a beautiful Fleming, Gilles?'

Gilles de Crohin was silent.

'Have you, Gilles?' insisted the Duke.

'Yes, Monseigneur,' replied Gilles curtly. 'Once.'

'The devil you did! Where?'

'In the land of dreams, Monseigneur.'

'Then it could not have been Madame Jacqueline. She is reality, alas! Ponderous reality, I fear! I have got to woo her, Gilles.'

'Yes, Monseigneur.'

'Under a mask and an assumed name.'

'No better way hath yet been found for wooing a wench.'

'I shall have to sing and sigh beneath a casement, and by the light of the moon risk breaking my neck in trying to climb up to a window.'

''Twill not be the first time Monseigneur hath done any of these things, and with a less worthy object to boot.'

'But this time, Gilles, I might be so much better employed in consoling Madame de Marquette for the absence of her lord.'

'Whereas, now, Monseigneur will have to send word back by the messenger—who, by the way, still waits below—that the denunciation against M. de Marquette was an error, and that you desire his immediate release.'

'Gilles!' retorted *Monsieur* coolly, 'have you become an idiot?'

'I didn't think so, Monseigneur.'

'Very well, then, do not talk as one. M. de Marquette cannot be better occupied than in cooling his heels at Vincennes. I am going to Paris, Gilles, in order to explain this to a charming grass-widow.'

'Yes, Monseigneur. When?'

'To-night.'

'Monseigneur goes to Paris to-night?'

'Yes. I have said so.'

'And Monseigneur means it?'

'*Mon Dieu*! Of course I mean it! You don't suppose that I am going to allow that exquisite Madame de Marquette to pine away in solitude, do you?'

'But Madame Jacqueline, Monseigneur?' protested Gilles de Crohin. 'The crown of the Netherlands— —'

'Madame Jacqueline may go to the devil, Gilles, and the crown of the Netherlands after her— —'

'But, Madame la Reyne— —!'

'Ah! that is another matter. My dear sister can go to the devil if she likes, but I cannot send her thither. You must remain here and explain matters to her, Gilles.'

'I, Monseigneur?' exclaimed Gilles, very much crestfallen at this prospect.

'Yes. Not to-night, of course. To-morrow morning. I shall be a long way off by then—too far for her to run after me and bring me back like a whipped schoolboy; which, I doubt not, she were quite capable of doing! Once I get to Paris, I'll take care that she does not find me, and she'll have to pacify these tiresome Flemings as best she can.'

Gilles de Crohin looked down for a moment or two on the sprawling figure of the master whom he served—the long, loose limbs stretched out lazily, the narrow shoulders decked in exquisite satin, the perfumed beard, the delicate hands, the full, sensual lips and weak chin and jaw which characterized this last descendant of the Valois. But not a line of his own strong, rugged face betrayed just what he thought, and after a while he resumed in his dry, quiet way:

'I doubt, Monseigneur, that the tiresome Flemings will allow themselves to be pacified—nor will Madame la Reyne de Navarre, I'm thinking,' he muttered under his bristling moustache.

'She must, and they must, my good Gilles,' riposted *Monsieur* airily; and, with a wide gesture of his beringed hand, he appeared to wave aside all the obstacles which threatened the even course of his path of pleasure. '*Mordieu*, man! If you are going to raise difficulties——' he said.

'The difficulties are there, Monseigneur. I am not raising them.'

'Well, then, you will have to smoothe them down for me, that's all! What do I pay you for?' he added roughly.

'I was not aware that Monseigneur was paying me for anything,' replied Gilles good-humouredly; 'or had paid me anything these three years past.'

'Then why do you serve me, I wonder?'

'I have oft wondered, too!' rejoined Gilles calmly.

'My brother Henri would pay you better; so would my brother-in-law of Navarre.'

'That's just it, Monseigneur. Since there is not much fighting to do just now, other princes would pay me for doing dirty work for them, no doubt. But, being constituted as I am, if I have to do dirty work for any one I would sooner not be paid for doing it. This may sound curious morality, but so it is.'

The Duke laughed.

'Morality? From you, my good Gilles?'

'It does sound incongruous, does it not, Monseigneur?' said Gilles placidly. 'A soldier of fortune, like myself, cannot of a truth afford to have any morality. Mine consists in forgetting the many sins which I have committed and leaving others to commit theirs in peace.'

'Admirable in sentiment, my friend,' concluded *Monsieur*, with a cynical laugh. 'You will, therefore, leave me in peace to join Madame de Marquette, if I wish?'

'How can I prevent it, Monseigneur?'

'You cannot. But you can serve me by conciliating my sister during my absence.'

'I will serve Monseigneur to the best of my ability.'

'Very well, then. I start for Paris this night.'

'So Monseigneur hath already deigned to say.'

'I will let my sister understand that you and I are starting for Cambray. She will be overjoyed. You will ride with me as far as Noyon, and then under cover of the darkness you will return hither.'

'Yes, Monseigneur?'

'To-morrow, during the forenoon—not too early, remember—you will seek audience of Her Majesty and explain to her that unavoidable business caused me to change my mind at the eleventh hour; that I have gone—whither you know not—but that I shall return within a few weeks, or a few months, as soon as I have tired of my present business, and that in the meanwhile I adjure her, as she loves me, to keep those stodgy Flemings in a good humour. You understand?'

'I understand, Monseigneur.'

'Of course, Madame Marguerite will fume and fret——'

'Of course.'

'She will also probably throw books, or a slipper, or a cushion at your head——'

'Or the fire-irons, Monseigneur'

'But you won't mind that——'

'On the contrary, I shall enjoy it.'

'The more my sister frets the quicker will her choler be over.'

'The quicker, too, will the furniture of the hostel be smashed to pieces.'

'And when she hath calmed down, you and she can sit together quietly and make plans for the conciliation of my future loyal Flemish subjects.'

'I shall greatly look forward to so peaceful a *tête-à-tête*.'

'Then, that's settled!' concluded *Monsieur* airily, as he finally rose from his chair, yawned and stretched. '*Palsambleu!* what a day of it I have had! Own to it, my good Gilles, I have well deserved a holiday and the company of Madame de Marquette after all this business and the scoldings and objurgations of my impetuous sister!'

'I doubt not, Monseigneur,' responded Gilles dryly, 'that Fate will, as usual, be kind and give you the full measure of your deserts.'

'Amen to that, my friend. Now, see to it that we get to horse within the hour. I'll to my dear Margot and receive her embraces and her praises for my readiness. And, remember,' he added warningly, just as Gilles, turning on his heel, was striding towards the door, 'that you will have to impress it upon Her Majesty most emphatically in your interview to-morrow that it will be no use her trying to find out where I am. Madame de Marquette and I will be beyond her reach. Between you and me, my good Gilles, I know of a cosy nest where — —'

But Gilles de Crohin was apparently no longer in a mood to listen patiently to his Royal master's rigmarole.

'What about the safe conduct?' he broke in curtly. And he pointed to the papers which Messire de Montigny had been at such pains to complete.

'Oh! put it away, my good Gilles,' replied *Monsieur* carelessly. 'Put it away! It will be very handy a month hence, or two months, or three, when I am ready to go and woo that very solid Flemish maid.'

Without another word, Gilles de Crohin picked up the safe-conduct, folded it carefully and slipped it into the inner pocket of his doublet. Then, after a somewhat perfunctory obeisance, he strode out of the room.

Monsieur listened in complacent silence to the firm footsteps as they gradually died away down the corridor. Then he shrugged his shoulders and whistled softly to himself.

'A good fellow, that Gilles,' he murmured. 'I wonder what my dear sister will do to him to-morrow when she hears— —?'

CHAPTER V.
WHAT MARGUERITE OF NAVARRE
DID WHEN SHE HEARD THE NEWS

I

When Messire Gilles de Crohin sought audience of Her Majesty the Queen of Navarre on the following day at noon, she had just finished dressing. She had been up betimes, been for a ride in the cool of the early morning; she had broken her fast with a hearty appetite, for she was young and full of health and vitality. All night she had had happy dreams. The brother whom she loved, just as a mother loves her most fractious and most unmanageable child, had at last been brought to act decisively for himself; the goal of her ambitions for him was in sight; in a very few months she — Marguerite — would have the satisfaction of seeing him Sovereign Lord — King, perhaps — of one of the finest countries in Europe, as powerful and more than was brother Henri, King of France.

She woke up happy, gay as a lark, contented in mind and merry of humour. After her ride and her breakfast she had a rest, then she put on a pretty gown, for she was a beautiful woman and knew the value of clothes. Her intention now was to remain in La Fère while her dear brother was in Cambray and to watch over his interests until after he had been formally betrothed to Jacqueline de Broyart. After that, she would proceed to Nerac to rejoin her husband.

Having dressed and dismissed her waiting-women, Marguerite de Navarre sat down beside the open casement-window in order to indulge in pleasant daydreams. Five minutes later, one of her serving-men entered in order to announce to Her Majesty that Messire Gilles de Crohin, Seigneur de Froidmont, respectfully begged for an immediate audience.

There are moments in life when to all the senses it appears as if a blow of sledge-hammer power and weight has suddenly fallen upon the brain, numbing every thought, every capability and every sentient action. Just such a moment was this one for Marguerite of Navarre. That simple announcement—that Messire Gilles de Crohin desired an audience—was the sledge-hammer blow which seemed to crush in the one instant her entire volition and energy and to leave her unthinking, spell-bound, a mere breathing, human machine, alive only by the power of the eyes, which remained fixed upon the doorway wherein presently she would see Messire Gilles.

It was quite unconsciously that she had intimated to the serving-man that she would receive Messire de Crohin. After that, she sat on and gazed upon the doorway and listened as the familiar footfall resounded along the corridor. Something had happened, or Gilles would not be here. He would be on his way to Cambray with *Monsieur*. Strangely enough, it never occurred to Marguerite of Navarre that some simple, easily-explained if untoward accident had brought Messire back to La Fère. She knew that something terrible had happened, even before she saw Gilles standing at attention upon the threshold.

But while the serving-man was still within earshot, she found the courage to say quite quietly and almost naturally:

'Enter, Messire, I pray you, and close the door behind you. You are right welcome.'

Then, as soon as the door was closed, she added rapidly and in a curious choked and hoarse voice:

'My brother?' And as Gilles made no immediate reply, she continued: 'He hath met with an accident? He is dead?'

'No! No!' protested Gilles quickly.

'Then, what is it?' she queried. 'Speak, man, or I die of terror!'

'Monseigneur le Duc d'Anjou did not go to Cambray last night, your Majesty,' said Gilles quietly.

Marguerite frowned. She did not understand. The news now appeared trivial after what she had feared.

'Not gone to Cambray?' she said slowly. 'But I saw him go—with you, Messire.'

'We started together, your Majesty, and rode together as far as Noyon. Then Monseigneur went on his way and I returned hither.'

'Monseigneur went on his way? What do you mean? And why did you go to Noyon, which is not on the way to Cambray?'

Gilles de Crohin sighed with impatience. But for his respect for the exalted lady, he would have thought her strangely dull-witted to-day.

'Monseigneur did not go to Cambray,' he reiterated slowly, like one who is trying to infuse a lesson into the mind of a doltish child. 'He hath gone to Paris, on his way to some spot unknown to any one—certainly unknown to me. He will be absent weeks—perhaps months. He desired your Majesty to try and conciliate Monseigneur le Baron d'Inchy and the other Flemish lords as best you can.'

Marguerite of Navarre listened to Gilles until the end. Slowly, very slowly, the perception of what had happened penetrated into her brain. Her eyes were fixed upon him, glowing with an intense inward fire. Gradually her breath came and went with ever-increasing rapidity. Her left hand, which rested on the arm of her chair, gripped the carving with a more and more convulsive clutch. Then suddenly, without a cry or warning, her right hand fastened on a heavy, unloaded pistol which lay, carelessly flung aside, upon the table close to her, and she flung it at Gilles de Crohin's head.

He dodged, and the massive weapon struck the door behind him and fell with a clatter to the floor.

'I could kill you,' said Marguerite de Navarre huskily, 'for bringing me this news!'

'If killing me would bring Monseigneur back,' riposted Gilles quietly, 'your Majesty would be more than welcome to do it.'

This sobered her, and she pulled herself together, blushing to the roots of her hair when she realized that her hand had already seized upon the small Italian dagger which, in accordance with the prevailing fashion, she wore fastened to her girdle. These were but semi-civilized times, and the days were not very far distant when the messenger of evil tidings was slain for his pains. But now, when Marguerite de Navarre encountered Gilles de Crohin's quiet, good-humoured gaze, she dropped the little dagger and laughed almost shamefacedly.

'I ought not to have let him out of my sight,' she said simply.

'It would have been wiser, your Majesty,' rejoined Gilles with a sigh.

'Madame de Marquette sent for him, I suppose.' Then, as Gilles made no reply to that, she added with sudden fierce contempt: 'And you helped him to commit this treachery?'

'Would you have me betray the man who trusts me?' he retorted.

'He ordered you to play the farce of starting for Cambray?'

'Yes.'

'To throw dust in my eyes?'

'Yes.'

'To accompany him as far as Noyon?'

'Yes.'

'Then to return hither under cover of darkness?'

'Yes.'

'And to greet me on the morrow with the *fait accompli*?'

'Yes.'

'Holy Virgin!' she exclaimed. 'That men should be so base!'

Tears of mortification, of humiliation, of wild, passionate anger, had risen to her eyes. Heavy sobs choked the words in her throat. For once in her life Marguerite of Navarre felt weak and undone and was not ashamed of her weakness. She had piloted the chariot of her brother's destiny with such marvellous success up to the dizzy heights of her own restless ambition only to see it fall crashing to the ground through his own treachery.

'Oh, Messire Gilles!' she cried with bitter reproach; 'if only you had served me as well as you have served my brother!'

'I would give my life in your Majesty's service now,' he rejoined simply, 'if anything that I could do could retrieve Monseigneur's folly.'

'If anything that you could do could retrieve Monseigneur's folly?' murmured Marguerite slowly, laboriously, like a child repeating a lesson. 'Alas! nothing can be done now to retrieve that, Messire.'

II

Outside, a soft-toned bell struck the midday hour. The little market-place beyond the courtyard lay bathed in wintry sunlight. Men and women were moving to and fro, stopping to chat with one another or exchanging a hasty greeting; men-at-arms jingled their spurs upon the uneven pavements; burghers in dark cloth surtouts flitted solemnly across the place. Marguerite watched with dreamy, unconscious eyes the pulsating life of the somnolent little city. With her, even life appeared at a standstill. With this hideous treachery on the part of her beloved François, with this unexpected shattering of all her hopes in sight of goal, she felt as if she herself no longer existed, as if some other entity had chased her soul away—her loving, ambitious, romantic soul—and taken possession of her body.

Gilles stood by, silent—looking down on her with infinite compassion. He, the poor, homeless, penniless soldier of fortune, found it in his heart to pity this young and adulated queen. He would have liked to help her if he could. But the situation was now a hopeless impasse. The curtain had rung up upon a brilliant drama of glory and of satisfied ambition; but the principal actor was not there to play his part, and the drama *must* fail for want of him.

'Shall I go now, your Majesty?' asked Gilles at last.

But she made no reply. She sat on in the high-backed chair, looking out upon the world beyond. There were happy people out there, contented people. People who had humble aspirations, but who saw them fulfilled. Better far to long for mere subsistence, to have few and simple desires and see them satisfied, than to let one's ambition soar to impossible heights which must for ever remain unattainable. And Gilles remained standing some distance away from the Queen, watching a whole world of varied emotions flitting rapidly over her mobile face. First came anger and despair, hot resentment and bitter contempt. The eyes looked steely and glittered with a fierce, inward wrath, whilst not one line of tenderness softened the curve of the closely set mouth. At this stage of her grim meditations it was obvious to the keen watcher that Marguerite de Navarre felt that she would never quite forgive the dearly loved brother this culminating act of treachery.

Then something of the hardness of the look went, and gave place to one of utter hopelessness which, to Gilles who knew her buoyant disposition, appeared quite heartrending. It were absolutely useless now, that look seemed to say, to try and redeem so much folly, such black and despicable cowardice. And there was the shameful humiliation too, to endure, the necessary abasement before those stiff-necked Flemish lords, those proud purists, rigid in their code of honour. There was the bitter acknowledgment to come that a prince of the House of France could so vilely break his word.

But presently, even as the tears of wrath and humiliation still glistened in Marguerite de Navarre's beautiful eyes, there crept gradually into her face a strange look of puzzlement. It came slowly, very slowly, just as if Fate, having struck her blow, was beginning to relent and to whisper words of hope. Frowns came and went between the pencilled brows, and inaudible whispers seemed to come through the slightly parted lips. Then, still quite gradually, a glow of excitement spread over the face, the eyes shone less sombre, a ray of light, like unto a faint smile, played round the corners of the lips.

Then Marguerite de Navarre turned her pretty head and fixed her eyes upon Gilles. And he who stood by, listening and watching, heard distinctly that her lips murmured the two little words: 'Why not?'

A quarter of an hour had gone by. Both the actors in this palpitating little interlude had lost count of time—Gilles gazing pityingly, almost remorsefully, on the Queen, and she, thinking, thinking, wrestling with Fate, unwilling even now to give in.

And all the while she was looking on Gilles with a puzzled frown, whilst her lips kept on murmuring, as if unconsciously: 'Why not?'

III

'Messire de Crohin,' said Marguerite of Navarre at last. 'You said just now that you would give your life in my service if anything that you could do at this hour would retrieve Monsieur's folly. Did you mean all that you said, Messire?'

Gilles smiled. 'I am not a Royal prince, Madame,' he said simply. 'I cannot afford the luxury of playing with my word. 'Tis all I have.'

She sighed and looked on him with those appealing yet compelling eyes of hers, which had such marvellous power to bend poor, feeble man to her will.

'Oh! but do repeat what you said, Messire,' she said naïvely. 'If you only knew how I long for an assurance of fidelity from one who is really a man!'

'I do repeat then, your Majesty, what I said before,' rejoined Gilles solemnly; 'that I would give my life in your service if aught that I can do will retrieve Monseigneur's folly.'

She seemed to drink in his simple words as if they were nectar to her soul—her soul, which was thirsting for loyalty, for service, for strength and truth. Then she said quietly:

'I'll put you to the test, Messire.'

'If your Majesty pleases,' he replied.

'I pray you,' she then resumed, speaking very quietly and with slow but firm emphasis, 'to listen in silence and to the very end to what I am going to say. However surprised or—or—unwilling you may feel, do not raise any objections till after I have told you of the scheme which I have just evolved in my mind, and which I firmly believe will yet retrieve our family honour and secure for my brother the throne of the Netherlands. God knows,' she added with a bitter sigh, 'that he hath not deserved that you or I should still be working for him! But when a prince of the House of Valois breaks his word, the shame of it bears upon us all.'

She paused, and in accordance with her desire Gilles remained silent, listening.

'Messire Gilles,' resumed Marguerite after awhile. 'There is, so I am told, Valois blood in your veins. That blood hath given you a glibness of tongue, at times wholly out of keeping with your adventurous temperament. It has also given you—so gossip avers—that persuasive eloquence which tickles pleasantly the ear of women. In temperament and in bearing Nature hath favoured you more generously than she did my brother. This perhaps is the only possible hitch in the plan which I have devised.'

Gilles frowned. It was his turn now to be exceedingly puzzled.

'It has been arranged, Messire—and to this the Flemish lord gave his consent—that *Monsieur* Duc d'Anjou et d'Alençon shall woo his future wife under a mask—under a mask,' she reiterated slowly. 'Ah!' she exclaimed, seeing that Gilles had suddenly given an involuntary gasp. 'I see that already you understand! There is something that you can do, Messire, to retrieve *Monsieur's* folly. You can act the rôle which I had assigned to him. You can don a mask and woo Madame Jacqueline from beneath her casement window. How oft in the past years have you impersonated your princely master in a less avowable cause? How many blows and sabre-cuts have you received on his behalf whilst he pursued some less worthy adventure? Nay! you cannot deny that. I know so much of what my dear brother would conceal from me. It can be done, Messire Gilles,' she added eagerly. 'It can be done, if you will loyally and faithfully serve me to this end.'

She paused, breathless and excited, and with glowing eyes fixed upon Gilles de Crohin as if to probe his very soul and to extract from him not only a consent, of which she was already assured, but the same enthusiasm for her scheme which she felt herself.

'Messire Gilles!' she exclaimed. 'It can be done! And now, in Heaven's name, I pray you, speak! I can endure your silence no longer!'

Gilles smiled at her quaint inconsequence. Then he passed his toil-worn hand through his rumpled hair. His look of utter bewilderment was so ludicrous that, despite her anxiety, Marguerite could not help but laugh.

'Oh, Messire Gilles!' she cried. 'If you only knew how comical you look!'

'Comical, Madame?' retorted Gilles with a growl. 'So would you look comical if you were suddenly confronted with so wild a proposition!'

'Wild, Messire?' riposted the Queen. ''Tis the Flemish lords who would be wild if my inventive brain had not conceived the proposition.'

'But, Madame— —' protested Gilles feebly.

'But, Messire,' retorted the Queen, mimicking the unfortunate man. 'Tell me,' she added more soberly, 'have you or have you not impersonated *Monsieur* before now?'

'Well!' murmured Gilles, 'I confess that I...'

'There was the affair with Monsieur de Ravache, for instance,' she continued firmly. 'The sword-thrust which that invincible duellist received in a certain affair of honour last June was openly attributed to *Monsieur*; but those who were in the know have averred that it was Messire Gilles de Crohin, and not the Duc d'Anjou, who fought Monsieur de Ravache that night.'

Gilles shrugged his shoulders and Marguerite went on glibly:

'And in the fracas in a low booth outside Arras, when an irate father and three bellicose brothers vowed vengeance against the princely lover of an over-trusting wench, was it indeed *Monsieur* Duc d'Anjou who, beneath a mask and cloak, kept half a dozen sturdy swordsmen at bay for close on half an hour? Or was it not rather Messire Gilles de Crohin who fought single-handed thus valiantly, even while *Monsieur*, disguised and furtive, found safety in flight?'

'Your Majesty, I protest,' broke in Gilles firmly, 'that rumour is nearly always a lying jade— —'

'Bah!' quoth Marguerite lightly. 'I'll challenge you to deny either of these tales on your oath. And there is the story of the jeweller's daughter, and that of Madame de Franqueville. The latter, I believe, is still under the impression that M. le Duc d'Anjou is the most ardent lover and the most chivalrous foe in France and that he wears about his person all the evidences of a hard and adventurous life. But why argue, Messire?' she continued impatiently. 'Even if you had never in your life impersonated the shifty prince whom you serve, I would ask you to do it now for his sake as well as for mine own.'

'But, in the name of all the saints in the calendar!' exclaimed Gilles with an air of laughable-helplessness, 'how is it all going to be done? I shall be seen ... recognized ... the fraud exposed within the first few hours ... and our second state will be distinctly worse than our first.'

'Exposed?' rejoined the Queen coolly. 'Who by? *Monsieur* hath never been in Cambray. Who should be acquainted with his appearance? And, moreover, there will be the mask to ward off any untoward or chance recognition.'

'But hath your Majesty thought of Messire de Montigny?' retorted Gilles dryly. 'He hath just spent half an hour in Monseigneur's presence and is not blind, I imagine. A mere mask would not deceive him.'

'Ah! I thought that you would mention Messire de Montigny,' riposted Marguerite triumphantly. 'Have you forgotten that he said he would only just have time to see his brother and M. d'Inchy in Cambray, as he was on his way to join the army of the Prince of Orange at Utrecht?'

'He may return at any time.'

'He may,' said Marguerite calmly. 'I did not say,' she added with a significant little smile, 'that there would be no risks, no dangers, connected with the undertaking. If you fear to affront them, Messire ... why, there's nothing more to be said.'

Marguerite de Navarre was far too clever not to know that in uttering the word 'danger' she would be playing her trump card. 'Gilles' objections were suddenly dissolved like smoke in thin air. He laughed and said good-humouredly:

'That was a clever move, Madame! I hated the affair until you spoke of danger.'

'And now?' she queried, smiling.

'Now? Now?' he said. 'I merely repeat: how is it going to be done?'

'In exactly the same manner in which the affair, say, with Madame de Franqueville was conducted,' she replied.

'But there we had an object to attain, Madame—a none too avowable one, I own, but still an object. But here ... suppose I sigh beneath Madame Jacqueline's window effectually? Suppose she falls in love with her unknown swain? Suppose she grants him an interview?.... We should still be where we now are! 'Tis Monseigneur who will have to marry Madame Jacqueline de Broyart—not I.'

'Do not trouble your head about that, good Messire,' retorted Marguerite dryly. 'We only want to gain time. You do your wooing; I'll see that *Monsieur* is there to wed.'

'But——'

'Oh! I know him well enough,' she continued with an impatient sigh. 'His present caprice—I suppose it is Madame de Marquette— will not last a week. At the end of a sennight or less he will come back fawning to me, satiated, bored and repentant, ready to do anything— even to marry Madame Jacqueline blindfolded—in order to regain my good graces. All that we want,' pleaded Marguerite with a sudden softening of her voice and of her whole attitude, 'is to gain time—a few days' time, Messire—while I go hunting for my faithless brother. I cannot go and tell Monseigneur de Lalain and M. le Baron d'Inchy that *Monsieur* Duc d'Anjou of the princely House of Valois hath fled from his obligations. Those obligations must be fulfilled at all costs, Messire ... at all costs, you understand? Nominally, Monsieur must be in Cambray within three days, and you must keep Madame Jacqueline amused and happy until I send you word that *Monsieur* is on his way—ready to take your place.'

'But——' murmured Gilles again, in a final attempt at protest.

She, however, would not allow him to get in a word edgewise now.

'When Monseigneur arrives,' she went on with eager volubility, 'you, Messire, will give up your dual rôle, become once again the one and only Sire de Froidmont. When *Monsieur* appears unmasked before his promised bride, we must see to it that plenty of padding do supplement his somewhat narrow shoulders and sunken chest, for Madame Jacqueline and her entourage will have been accustomed by then to your broad stature, Messire; but no one will have seen the face of the masked swain. Oh, Messire Gilles! Messire Gilles!' she exclaimed, clasping her hands together with a gesture of passionate entreaty. 'With a little thought, a little care and a little luck, it can all be done so easily if you will but consent! Say yes, Messire! and the prayers of a harassed Queen and a doting sister will bring blessings down upon your loyal head!'

IV

The tears were in Marguerite de Navarre's eyes as she extended an appealing hand to Gilles de Crohin. He, poor wretch, had not much choice. His loyalty had been requisitioned in such terms that he could not refuse. And, remember, that Gilles de Crohin, the soldier of fortune, was nothing if not adventurous. Deep down in his heart something was already stirring which tickled his imagination and fired his ardent blood. Like a war-horse scenting battle, he scented excitement, danger, hair-breadth escapes, sword-thrusts given and received—all of which was to him the very essence of life. And there was something exceedingly pleasant, too, in the gratitude of this beautiful and accomplished woman—a Queen indeed, in the highest acceptance of the word.

Messire Gilles' life had been very dull and dreary of late. He had set out once—very long ago and when he was a mere lad—to carve out his own fortune in the world. Penniless, and bearing a noble name which the penury of two generations had somewhat tarnished, he dreamed, when he was still in his teens, that Fate reserved something very glorious and very wonderful for him. A decade and more had gone by since then, and Messire Gilles had found that the cornucopia of Fate held more thistles than roses for him. The wars now were so inglorious; the days of chivalry had gone, never to return. The princes in high places, whom adventurers such as he were destined to serve, had nothing to offer for devoted allegiance save a miserable pittance often withheld.

As a matter of fact, Messire Gilles de Crohin had of late been heartily sick of life. The spirit of adventure that glowed within him was gradually becoming somnolent. He felt that even his blood would become sluggish in time if he dragged on this uneventful existence in the wake of an indolent and dissolute prince.

Then, in the midst of all this dreary dullness, came this ray of sunshine—an adventure such as he, Gilles, had not dreamed of since his boyhood—an adventure proposed to him by the fairest lips in Europe—which would bring all the excitement with it for which he yearned so passionately. No wonder that every objection seemed to him all at once to be futile, every obstacle mere child's play.

And Marguerite, keen and clever, saw at once that he was wavering, just as de Montigny had done yesterday. Long before either of these two men realized themselves that they were yielding, she *knew* that she had gained her point.

'You gave me your word, Messire,' she said gently.

'And I'll not go back on it, Madame,' he replied.

'Yet you hesitate!'

'Your pardon, Madame,' he rejoined with a smile. 'I was only bewildered.'

'Then you consent?' she exclaimed joyfully.

He shrugged his shoulders with his habitual easy-going good-humour.

'Madame gives me no choice,' he said. 'I cannot go back on my word.'

He bent the knee and kissed the gracious hand which was extended to him. Marguerite's eyes were still bathed in tears.

'If anything that I can do,' reiterated Gilles de Crohin solemnly, 'will retrieve Monseigneur's folly I'll do it.'

'Ah!' she riposted gently. 'But 'tis your solemn oath I want, Messire Gilles.'

'My word of honour, Madame,' he retorted bluntly, 'hath always been found sufficient.'

'Nay! your oath!' she insisted, pleading once more. 'A solemn, binding oath! One,' she added naïvely, 'which, if broken, would land you in hell.' Then, as a sudden scowl gathered on Gilles' brow, she continued in a tone of sadness and self-pity: 'Do not be angered, Messire. I know you for a loyal gentleman and have no doubt that, to you, your word is as good as your oath. But I have been so oft deceived, so oft befooled, that a man's word of honour hath lost its value in mine eyes. Can you blame me, remembering what I am suffering now?'

Gilles' sense of humour saved the situation. His word of honour had of a truth never been doubted, but in face of this sorely outraged woman, he could not take offence.

'What oath shall I take,' he queried, with a good-humoured smile, 'that will satisfy the Queen of Navarre?'

'On your immortal soul, Messire,' she said solemnly; 'on your hopes of salvation; on all that you hold most precious and most dear, swear to me that you will serve me in this matter as I shall direct you, and until I myself do release you from this bond.'

He drew his cross-hilted sword and held it fixed before his eyes. Then he placed his right hand upon the hilt and said with solemn earnestness: 'I swear.'

Marguerite gave a quick sigh of content. She watched Gilles with evident satisfaction as he rose to his feet, sheathed his sword and then stood before her in all his picturesque ruggedness, a perfect presentment of a man, strong, reliable—oh! above all, reliable!!!

'Now, Madame,' said 'Gilles finally, 'will you deign to tell me just
what I am to do?'

V

For an hour and more after that, these two—veritable conspirators
now—sat together, the Queen of Navarre talking and explaining
eagerly and Gilles listening; for of a truth he was still rather
bewildered at the proposition and at the part which he would have
to play in it. Not that the rôle itself was unfamiliar to him. He had
played it often enough, as Marguerite had very shrewdly said, and in
far less avowable causes; but never for any length of time. It had been
a matter of fighting a duel or meeting an inconvenient interlocutor; a
matter of stepping into his Royal master's shoes for half an hour or so,
and as oft as not under cover of a dim light. But now he would have to
sustain the part for days—weeks, perhaps—never forgetting, always
on the alert, always fearful lest a word, a gesture, an inflexion of the
voice, should betray him. And he had sworn so solemnly on what
he held most sacred and most dear that he would see the business
through! Ye gods! but it was a hard proposition for a simple-minded
soldier of fortune to tackle!

Marguerite of Navarre, however, was for laughing away every
difficulty which stood in her path.

'It has got to be done, Messire!' she said more than once, and with
ever-increasing earnestness. 'For the honour of France and of her
Royal House.'

She began by giving Gilles more money than he had ever seen
before, taking purse after purse of gold from her private coffer and
watching him as, puzzled and confused, he stowed these away in the
inner pockets of his doublet and breeches.

'I haven't earned all this yet,' he muttered ruefully.

'You will want it,' she rejoined. 'You are a prince, remember, and
though you will be travelling incognito, you must live like a prince.'

But the question of clothes was the most difficult one to settle.
Gilles de Crohin possessed none save those in which he stood up at
this moment: a well-worn doublet of faded kerseymere, a stout jerkin
and cloth trunks. His hose showed a multiplicity of darns, and his

boots, though stout and solid, were not exactly suited to a lady's drawing-room.

'Time is too short to fashion new ones,' said Marguerite thoughtfully; 'even if this little town did boast of silken materials and Court tailors; which it certainly does not!'

'It certainly doth appear in the light of an insurmountable difficulty,' rejoined Gilles with a hopeful sigh.

'No difficulty is insurmountable, Messire, when the honour of France is at stake,' she retorted with a frown.

'But— —'

'What hath *Monsieur* done with his wardrobe?' asked Marguerite. 'He always travels with trunk-loads of frippery.'

'Monseigneur left all his clothes here and most of his jewellery. I am to convey them to his house in Paris when an opportunity occurs.'

'Very well,' she rejoined firmly; 'we must find what you want among them.'

'But— —' he broke in once more, disconcerted at the suggestion.

'But what?'

'The trunks are locked.'

'I'll break them open,' she rejoined simply. 'Have no fear, Messire; I am taking all the responsibility of this affair upon my shoulders.'

'But I cannot strut about in another man's clothes!' protested Gilles dolefully.

'Why not?'

'Because ... because ... *parbleu!* because they would not fit me!'

Marguerite smiled. Then she threw another admiring glance on Gilles' massive figure.

'My brother is very nearly as tall as you are, Messire, she said,' even though not quite so broad. I have two very skilful seamstresses who will adjust *Monsieur's* doublets across your splendid shoulders. With his love of slashings and puffings, such alterations are very easily done.'

'But the boots— —' protested Gilles again.

'You have the small foot, Messire,' she replied dryly, 'which you inherit from your Valois ancestor.'

'The Lord help me, your Majesty!' he exclaimed piteously. 'You have thought of everything, and I am a puppet in your august hands.'

'Therefore I entreat you not to argue any further,' she retorted gaily, 'or I shall think that you are repenting of your bargain—and of your oath.'

Which suggestion caused Gilles to cease from further protests, even though he did express a hope that Her Majesty's seamstresses would not make gossip all about the town that he—the Sire de Froidmont—was going to walk about in another man's clothes.

'My women never gossip,' said Marguerite dryly, after which she abruptly changed the subject. 'And now tell me,' she said. 'A man like you must have a friend, a comrade or a servant—some one, in fact, who would be faithful and trustworthy. You will want a companion on your journey. Messire, have you such a friend?'

'Aye! that I have,' replied Gilles fervently, his whole face beaming with joy at thought of having his faithful Jehan with him in this mad expedition.

'One who would serve you faithfully?' she continued.

'To the death, your Majesty.'

'And cleverly?' she insisted. 'You will both have to keep your wits about you.'

Gilles smiled. 'Maître Jehan,' he said, 'hath no wits to speak of, Madame; but he hath a heart of gold and muscles of steel. Nature hath forced him to hold his tongue, for he stutters like a clucking hen. He is invaluable for circumventing an inopportune visitor or misunderstanding an imperative command. We have fought side by side these past ten years and have nearly bled to death or been frozen to death together before now. Jehan will do for me what I would do for you, Madame.'

'You are lucky, Messire,' rejoined Marguerite simply, 'to have such a friend. And I,' she added, with an engaging smile,' to have such an one, too. Maître Jehan shall journey to Cambray with you as your serving-man. With his prowess and your own invincible courage and strength, the very thought of failure appears treasonable. Ah, Messire Gilles!' she continued eagerly, 'I beg of you to cast all doubts aside! Have no fear, I entreat you—no fear of failure or of gossip! And, above all, trust me! Trust me, Messire, that whatever happens,

I will not leave you in the lurch. Only trust me! Trust me! You shall not suffer through serving me! On the faith of Marguerite of Navarre!'

She gave him her hand again, and through tears of emotion gave him a glance of appreciation and of confidence. Gilles had no more resistance left in him; and as he looked into those lovely eyes which had already played such havoc with men's wills and with men's hearts, he sighed with resignation and with only a transient thought for the morrow. None knew better than the Sire de Froidmont the exact value of promises made by princes or by women. To-day Marguerite of Navarre's clever mind and warm heart were filled with enthusiasm for this new scheme of hers; a week hence, mayhap, she would have thought of something else, and Gilles—as like as not—would indeed be left to bear the brunt of failure.

But these were just the vicissitudes which were wont to attend the career of a soldier of fortune these days. A dazzling prize or a gibbet might await the adventurer at the end of his goal. For the nonce, Gilles had sworn to serve this gracious lady and to redeem the unpardonable folly of a faithless prince, and with a careless shrug of the shoulders he left the future in Dame Fortune's hands.

'I will give you an autograph letter,' resumed Marguerite more quietly after awhile, 'for M. le Baron d'Inchy, governor of Cambray, and one for Maître Julien at the hostelry of "Les Trois Rois." These will serve as your credentials in addition to the safe-conducts which Messire de Montigny delivered to *Monsieur*. You have those, I hope.'

'Yes, Madame,' replied Gilles. 'Monseigneur left them with me. If your Majesty deigns to remember, they were e'en made out in my name.'   –

'In the name of Messire Gilles de Crohin, the equerry and of Monseigneur le prince de Froidmont!' she exclaimed gleefully. 'Indeed, I mind it well! You will not even have to change your name, Messire; and the title shall be yours, an' you desire it, when my brother is King of the Netherlands.'

Gilles shrugged his shoulders. 'Oh! a title, Madame...!' he said lightly.

'I know! I know!' she riposted, with the volubility of intense excitement. 'I know your proud device: "Roy ne suys, ne Prince, ne Duc, ne Comte. Je suys Sire de Froide Monte." Ah, Messire Gilles! you were fated to belie that device! Prince de Froidmont—'tis no mean title.'

'I prefer that of Friend of the Queen of Navarre,' he said simply.

'You are that indeed, Messire, and more,' she rejoined solemnly. 'Ah! if my brother were only like you, what glorious destiny would have been his!'

'Our destinies are of our own making, Madame,' he retorted.

'You have started to carve them out for yourself now, Messire Gilles, on the tablets of my memory.'

'Then may God and the Fates favour me!'

'The Fates?' she cried gaily. 'Why, you and I have conquered the Fates, Messire. Will you deny that they are our handmaidens now?'

CHAPTER VI.
WHAT MONSEIGNEUR D'INCHY AND MESSIRE GILLES DE CROHIN MUTUALLY THOUGHT OF ONE ANOTHER

I

And three days later, an' it please you, Messire Gilles presented himself, his safe-conduct and his faithful Jehan at the Porte de Cantimpré.

The safe-conduct being made out in the name of Monseigneur le Prince de Froidmont, his equerry, Messire Gilles de Crohin, and his serving-man, the absence of one of the three personages was casually commented on by the Captain of the Guard.

'My equerry hath fallen sick on the way,' explained Gilles airily. 'He lies at a village inn close by and will come as soon as may be.'

It was at once arranged that whenever the equerry did present himself at the gate, Monseigneur le Prince de Froidmont was immediately to be apprised of his arrival so that he might at once stand guarantee for the man's identity. Needless to say that no such equerry existed, nor does the Captain of the Guard appear to have worried his head over so small a matter. But, anyway, Gilles now was inside Cambray, the scene of his coming adventure, and I can assure you that on this first occasion—it was late evening then and a cold, drizzling rain was blurring every outline of the picturesque city— Gilles did not stride about the streets with that careless jauntiness which characterized his usual demeanour.

After some searchings and many wanderings through the most unfrequented portions of the city, Messire did finally espy the Rue aux Juifs, at one end of which there dangled on a ricketty iron bracket a half-obliterated sign that still bore the legend 'Les Trois Rois' in black paint on a crimson ground and three dabs of pink paint, surmounted by dabs of yellowish paint, which might still pass muster as kingly faces surmounted by their crowns. Now, if you remember, the Rue aux Juifs in Cambray is a narrow street which runs behind the Place aux Bois, and links the latter with the Porte Notre Dame. Owing to the elaborate corbelling of the old houses on either side, it appeared far narrower in the year 1581 than it does to-day,[1] and the hostelry so pretentiously styled 'Les Trois Rois' was of the humblest description.

[1] In the spring of 1914.

Gilles was satisfied to find it so. He liked its seclusion and had never been *difficile* in the matter of his creature comforts. Secrecy and mutual confidence were the greatest desiderata for the moment in the pursuit of his adventure, and he knew enough about the exquisite Queen of Navarre that if any male creature who dwelt within 'Les Trois Rois' had come within the magic circle of her fascination, that man would go through fire and water, torture and hell itself, in order to serve her.

So he knocked boldly at the ricketty front door of the humble hostelry. A young man, thin and pale, wearing a long doublet of dark woollen stuff and a black cap above his scanty yellow hair, opened the door and bade him welcome. He had a lanthorn in his hand and held it high above his head, surveying the stranger with that pathetic air, half-fear, half-entreaty, wherewith the very poor are wont to regard those who might bring about a small measure of change in their misery.

Gilles at once presented the letter which Madame la Reyne de Navarre had given him for his prospective host. The young man glanced at the latter, recognized the signature, and at once his almost cadaverous-looking face became transfigured. His hollow eyes took on a glow of joy, his cheeks assumed a warm hue, his long, bony hands clutched the welcome missive as an idolater might clutch the relic which he worshipped.

There was no doubt that Messire Gilles would be made welcome — and right welcome — in the humble hostelry. Not only would discretion be assured him, but also unswerving devotion, of which indeed he might presently stand in sore need.

'My mother,' stammered the youth, after he had recovered from his primary emotion, 'is bedridden now, alas! but I will do my best to serve you, Messire, and your henchman, to the best of my ability. I will tend you and wait on you, and whatever this humble abode hath to offer is entirely at your disposal. My liege lady commands,' he added, drawing up his spare frame with the air of a devotee in the presence of his hero. 'I will obey her in all things!'

We will not say that Gilles was exactly gratified to hear that the hostess of 'Les Trois Rois' was bedridden and would be unable to attend on him, but it is certain that he was not grieved. With this young enthusiast alone to attend on him and to share the secret of his adventure, he was as secure from untimely discovery as it was possible under the circumstances to be.

II

At eleven o'clock the next morning, Gilles sent word round to Monseigneur the governor of the Cambrésis that he would wait on him within the hour. Together with this message he sent the sealed letter wherein the Queen of Navarre commended her dear brother François, Duc d'Anjou, to the good graces of Monseigneur the governor.

At the hour when the messenger arrived, M. le Comte de Lalain, who was governor of Flanders and one of d'Inchy's closest associates, was closeted with the latter in one of the stately rooms of the Archiepiscopal Palace where M. d'Inchy had taken up his abode after he had dispossessed the Archbishop and taken possession of the city. D'Inchy, obviously nervy and anxious, quickly dismissed the messenger; then he turned to de Lalain and, throwing the Queen's letter across the table to him, he said briefly: 'Well, he has come!'

De Lalain in his turn read the letter through. Then he sighed.

'Yes,' he said. 'He, at any rate, seems determined to carry the adventure through.'

'I hope to God that we have done right,' rejoined d'Inchy. 'The whole thing, now that it is upon us, appears to me more foolish than ever it did before.'

'And there is no drawing back now, unfortunately.'

'The whole affair is in God's hands,' quoth d'Inchy sententiously.

'In the hands of an irresponsible and dissolute prince,' said the other moodily. 'I blame de Montigny for having consented so readily.'

'Then you must blame yourself too, my friend,' retorted d'Inchy dryly. 'You, too, consented, and so did I....'

'I know that well enough! Like yourself, de Montigny and I acted for the best, though I for one could even now with zest strike that Valois Prince in the face for this insult upon our ward.'

But d'Inchy apparently was all for a conciliating attitude and a cheerful view of the situation.

'Do not,' he said lightly, 'let us use grandiloquent words, my dear de Lalain. There is no insult in a man's desire to see the woman whom he is asked to wed. For the time being Jacqueline will hold herself aloof. She will appear little in public, and then only wearing a mask. After a few days, if affairs seem to be shaping to our satisfaction, we can always allow a certain degree of intimacy. Jacqueline is so beautiful that we really run no risk of refusal. And,' he added with a quick sign of finality, 'in any case we had no choice.'

'Alas, no!' rejoined de Lalain ruefully. 'For of a truth I cannot bring myself to believe in Orange as the saviour of the Netherlands. He thinks that he can rally the burghers and the mass of the people to his standard. But I doubt it. And if he fails in his present campaign we shall all fall into a veritable abyss of humiliation and dependence on those abominable Spaniards—far worse than ever before.'

'And all our friends think the same, as you well know, my good de Lalain,' continued d'Inchy firmly. 'An alliance with a prince of the House of France is safer than a submission to the leadership of Orange. We want the help of France; we want her well-trained armies, her capable generals, the weight of her wealth and influence to drive the Spaniards out of our provinces. Elizabeth of England promises much but holds little. She is on the side of Orange. I am on the side of France.'

'So am I, my good d'Inchy,' rejoined de Lalain; 'else I had never consented to the Queen of Navarre's madcap scheme.'

'Nor I,' concluded d'Inchy with the solemn earnestness of political fanaticism. 'So why all these misgivings, my good friend?'

'Was it fair to the girl?' murmured the other almost involuntarily. 'Monsieur is as fickle as he is unprincipled. Had we the right to toy with a woman's heart—a young girl's—our kinswoman——?'

'You wrong Jacqueline by such doubts, my friend. She is not a child nor yet an irresponsible girl. She knows that her person and her fortune are powerful assets in the future of her country. She is a patriot, and will never allow sentiment to overrule her duty.'

Perhaps de Lalain would have liked to continue the argument. Obviously his conscience was smiting him a little now that the curtain had actually rung up on the first act of the foolish adventure. The ill-fame of the Valois prince had preceded him long ago. De Lalain knew—and so did d'Inchy, so did de Montigny—that *Monsieur* was both profligate and faithless. He, like the others, had entered into a bargain with one whom they could never trust. Was it fair? Was it just? Would God's blessing descend upon the proposed Kingdom of the Netherlands if its foundations rested on so infamous a base? And yet de Lalain, though conscious of that vague feeling of remorse, had no thought of turning back. Even now, as a tall, masked figure appeared under the lintel of the door in the wake of the usher, and then stepped boldly into the room, he made a great effort to control his resentment. Though his hand ached to drag the mask away from the man's face, to try and read him eye to eye, his reason re-asserted itself, re-adjusted his thoughts and his sentiments. 'This,' it whispered insistently, 'this man who has come to Cambray masked and disguised, is a prince of the House of France. If he approve of the beautiful Flemish heiress and consents to take her for wife, the future of the Netherlands is assured, even though he were twenty times as base as he is depicted.'

And reason gained the victory. D'Inchy already had gone a few steps forward in order to greet his exalted visitor. De Lalain composed himself too, even paid an involuntary tribute of admiration to that tall and martial-looking figure which enshrined, so rumour had it, a soul that was both weak and false.

III

And Messire Gilles de Crohin, the penniless soldier of fortune, the mountebank set to play an unworthy part, was greeted by these two proud Flemish nobles with all the respect due to a prince of the

House of France. And indeed there was nothing mean or humble about his appearance even though he had come to Cambray with only one man to serve him, and that man a rough and uncouth soldier with a ludicrous stutter which would at once have provoked the gibes of Monseigneur, the governor's servants, but for the fact that Maître Jehan's fists appeared as hard and harder than their heads, and that his temper was so hot that he had already put the first scoffers to flight by the mere rolling of his eyes. He was standing at this precise moment immediately behind his master, and as soon as the usher had withdrawn and the door been closed, he slipped quite unostentatiously into the nearest corner and remained there, with his eyes fixed on Messire like a faithful watch-dog, silent and keen.

The two Flemish lords had also waited until the usher had disappeared; then only did they make obeisance, with all the ceremonious empressement which the presence of a Royal personage demanded.

Let us admit at once that Gilles looked magnificent in Monsieur le Duc d'Anjou's splendid clothes—doublet and trunks of fine satin, slashed and puffed after the latest fashion; hose of Italian silk and short mantle of Genoa velvet, exquisitely embroidered in dull silver and gold, the whole of that sombre bottle-green hue specially affected by *Monsieur* and a miracle of the dyer's subtle art. He had ruffles at neck and wrist of delicate Mechlin lace, wore a mask with a frill of black lace pendant from it, which effectually hid the whole of his face, and at his side a rapier which obviously hailed from Toledo. Altogether a splendid prince! And it was difficult indeed to credit the rumours which averred that he had undermined his constitution by high living and drinking and a life of profligacy and excess.

He received the greetings of the Flemish lords with just the necessary measure of gracious condescension, and through the slits of his mask he was studying with keen anxiety what might be hidden behind those stolid and stern faces and the frowning glances wherewith two pairs of eyes were steadfastly regarding him.

D'Inchy waited in dutiful respect till *Monsieur*, Duc d'Anjou, was pleased to be seated; then he said:

'Monseigneur understood, I hope, how it was that we did not present our respects to you in person. Such a ceremony would have set the tongues of our town gossips wagging more furiously than before.'

Already, it seemed that the presence of the stranger inside Cambray had created some comment. In these days, when the Spanish armies swarmed all over the province, when plots and counter-plots were being constantly hatched in favour of one political side or another, strangers were none too welcome inside the city. There was the constant fear of spies or of traitors, of emissaries from Spain or France or England, of treason brewed or brewing, which might end in greater miseries yet for any unfortunate province which was striving for its own independence and the overthrow of Spanish tyranny. Gilles, listening with half an ear to Monseigneur d'Inchy's elaborate compliments, was inwardly marvelling whether spies had not already come upon his track and would upset the Queen of Navarre's plans even before they had come to maturity. He had a curious and exceedingly uncomfortable sensation of unreality, as if these two stern-looking Flemings were not actual personages but puppets moved by an unseen hand for the peopling of his dreams. He answered the elaborate flummeries of the governor with a vague: 'I thank you, Messire.' Then he added a little more coherently: 'I understood everything, believe me, and must again thank you for acceding to my wishes and to those of my sister, the Queen of Navarre.'

'Our one desire, Monseigneur,' continued d'Inchy stiffly, and still speaking very deferentially, 'our one desire is to see the sovereignty of the Netherlands secure in your keeping.'

Gilles roused himself. It was no use and ill policy to boot to allow that feeling of unreality to dominate his mood so utterly. If he let himself drift upon these waves of somnolence he might, with one unguarded word, betray the grave interests which had been committed to his care.

'That is understood, Messire,' he said dryly. 'Messire de Montigny put the whole matter before me and before my sister of Navarre. We both fell in readily with your schemes. As for me, you know my feelings in the matter. I only asked for delay and consideration ere I pledged myself irrevocably to so grave an affair.'

'And we, equally readily, Monseigneur,' asserted de Lalain, 'do place ourselves entirely at your service.'

After which preliminary exchange of compliments, the Flemings were ready to discuss the matter in all its bearings. All the arguments which had been adduced by de Montigny when the proposed marriage was being discussed before the Queen of Navarre, were once more dished up for the benefit of *Monsieur*. Gilles played his part with as much ease as his want of experience would allow; but he was a soldier and not a courtier, ill-versed too in the art of guarded speeches. He fumed and fretted over all these pourparlers quite as much and more than *Monsieur* would have done, and once or twice he caught sight through the slits of his mask of certain glances of puzzled wonderment which passed between the two men at a more than usually rough retort which had escaped his lips.

Half an hour drew its weary length along while the discussion proceeded, and it was at the very end of that time that M. le Baron d'Inchy said quite casually:

'Of course, you, Monseigneur, will understand that since you choose to do your wooing under a mask, our ward, Madame Jacqueline de Broyart, Dame de Morchipont, Duchesse et Princesse de Ramèse, will not appear in public either, save also with a mask covering her face.'

Now Madame la Reyne de Navarre had not thought of this eventuality, and indeed if it had truly been *Monsieur* Duc d'Anjou who had received this ultimatum, he would undoubtedly have then and there turned on his heel and left these mulish Flemings to settle their own affairs as they wished. But Gilles had sworn to see the business through. Left to himself in this difficulty, he was for the moment puzzled, but never tempted to give up the game. The two Flemish lords appeared so determined, and with it all so pleased, with their counter-stroke, that any kind of argument would only have ended either in humiliating acquiescence or in the breaking off of the negotiations then and there. The latter being of course unthinkable, Gilles thought it best to take this part of the adventure as lightly as he had taken the rest.

''Tis hard for a man to woo a maid whose face he is not allowed to see,' he said, by way of protest.

'Oh, Monseigneur is pleased to jest!' was d'Inchy's calm rejoinder. 'It was agreed that you should come to Cambray and see the noble lady who holds in her dainty hand the sovereignty of the Netherlands for her future lord; but, as Messire de Montigny had the honour to tell you, Madame Jacqueline de Broyart is not going to be trotted out for any man's inspection—be he King or Emperor, or Prince—like a filly that is put up for sale.'

'But man——' retorted Gilles, nettled by the Flemish lord's coolness.

'I crave Monseigneur's pardon,' broke in d'Inchy with perfect outward deference; 'but we must remember that Monseigneur also is here for inspection. If Madame Jacqueline refuses the alliance, neither I nor my co-guardian would dream of forcing her choice.'

'That is understood, Messire,' rejoined Gilles coldly. 'And I have set myself the task of wooing the lady with ardour, so as to win her affection as well as her hand.'

'Oh, Monseigneur....' protested the Fleming with a deprecating smile. 'That is hardly the position, is it? You have reserved unto yourself the right to withdraw. Well, we arrogate that same right for our ward.'

'A just arrogation, Messire,' riposted Gilles. 'But why the mask?' he added blandly.

'If Monseigneur will woo Madame definitely and openly,' replied d'Inchy firmly, 'she will not wear a mask either. But then there can be no question of withdrawal if she consents.'

Now, to woo Madame Jacqueline definitely and openly was just the one thing Gilles could not do. So there was the difficulty and there the cunning and subtlety of these Flemish lords, who had very cleverly succeeded in getting *Monsieur* into a corner and in safeguarding at the same time the pride and dignity of the greatest heiress in Flanders. Gilles would have given all the worlds which he did not possess for the power to consult with Madame la Reyne de Navarre over this new move on the part of the Flemings. But, alas! she was far away now, flying across France after her faithless brother, hoping soon to catch him by the tails of his satin doublet and to drag him back to the feet of the rich heiress whom that unfortunate Gilles was deputed to woo and win for him. And Gilles was left to decide for himself, which he did with a 'Very well, Messire, it shall be as you wish!' and as gracious a nod and bow to these two obstinate men as he could bring himself to perform; for, of a truth, he would gladly have given each a broken head.

Thus the actual discussion of the affair was ended. After that, there were only a few minor details to talk over.

'You two gentlemen,' Gilles said after a slight pause, during which he had been wondering whether it were a princely thing to do to rise and take his leave. 'You two gentlemen are alone in the secret of this enterprise?'

'For the moment, yes,' replied d'Inchy guardedly. 'But others will have to know ... some might even guess. I shall have to explain the matter to my private secretary, and one or two members of my Privy Council have certain rights which we could not disregard.'

'And what about Messire de Montigny?' queried Gilles warily.

'He hath gone to Utrecht to join the Prince of Orange.'

'When doth he return?'

'Not before the summer.'

A short, quick sigh of relief escaped Gilles' lips. At the back of his mind there had always lurked the ever-present fear of one who wilfully deceives his fellow-men—the fear of being found out. In this, Montigny was the greatest, nay! the only danger. With him out of the way, the chances of discovery became remote.

'To every one else, then, Messire,' he continued more firmly, 'I shall pass as the Prince de Froidmont.'

'To every one else, Monseigneur,' replied d'Inchy.

'To Madame Jacqueline de Broyart?'

'Certainly, Monseigneur.'

'She hath no suspicions?'

'None.'

'Doth she know that it is your desire she should become the wife of the Duc d'Anjou ... that she should become my wife, I mean?'

'No, Monseigneur; she does not.'

'Then I have a clear field before me!' he exclaimed gaily.

'A clear field, Monseigneur,' broke in de Lalain firmly, 'for two weeks.'

'Two weeks?' retorted Gilles with a quick frown. 'Why only two weeks?'

'Because,' said the other with solemn earnestness, 'because the Duke of Parma's armies are already swarming over our province. If they should invest Cambray we could not hold out alone. Monseigneur must be ready by then to support us with influence, with men and with money. If you turned your back on us and on the proposed alliance with a Flemish heiress, we should have to look once more to Orange as our future Lord.'

'I understand,' rejoined Gilles dryly. ''Tis an "either—or" that you place before me.'

Then, as d'Inchy remained respectfully silent, M. de Lalain broke in abruptly:

'Think you, Monseigneur, that the people of the Netherlands, after all that they have suffered in intolerance and religious persecution, would accept a Catholic sovereign unless his wife, at least, were of *their* nation and of their faith?'

A sharp retort hovered on Gilles' lips; already a curt 'Pardi, Messire——' had escaped him, when suddenly he paused, listening. A loud ripple of laughter, merry, sunny, girlish, rang out clearly from beyond the monumental doors, rising in its joyous cadence above the oppressive silence and solemnity of this gloomy Palace and the grave colloquy of Monsieur d'Inchy and his colleagues. Only for a moment, and the laughter died away again, making the silence and solemnity seem more gloomy than before. It seemed to Gilles as if it all were part of that same dream, that it was really intangible and non-existent, just like these sober seigneurs, like himself, like the whole situation which had landed him—Gilles de Crohin—into the midst of this mad adventure.

He threw back his head and laughed in hearty echo. The whole humour of the situation suddenly struck him with the full force of its irresistible appeal. Life had been so dull, so drab, so uneventful of late! Here was romance and excitement and gaiety; a beautiful maid— Gilles had become suddenly convinced that she was beautiful—some blows; some knocks; a master to serve; a beautiful, sorrowing Queen to console; spurs to be won and a fortune to be made!

'And, by Heaven, Messire!' he exclaimed lightly, 'The God of Love shall favour me. Your ward is exquisite and I am very susceptible.

What are two weeks? 'Tis but two seconds a man requires for losing his heart to a beautiful wench. And if the fickle god fails me,' he added with a careless shrug of the shoulders, 'well, where's the harm? After this—this romantic episode, shall we say?—Madame Jacqueline will either be Duchesse d'Anjou et d'Alençon, a happy and worshipped bride, or the Prince de Froidmont will disappear from her ken as unobtrusively as he came. And you, Messeigneurs,' he concluded lightly, 'will have to offer the sovereignty of the Netherlands to one who is worthier than I.'

Neither d'Inchy nor de Lalain appeared to have anything to say after that. They were both looking moody—even forbidding—for the moment, though they bowed their heads in humble respect before this prince whose light-heartedness jarred upon their gravity.

And here the matter ended for the nonce. Gilles took leave of his stiff-necked hosts and returned to 'Les Trois Rois,' having declared most solemnly that he must have time to prepare himself for so strange a wooing. A masked wench; think on it! It changed the whole aspect of the situation! A respite of four days was, however, all that was respectfully but firmly granted to him for this preparation, and Messire Gilles spent the next few hours in trying to devise some means whereby he could outwit the Flemish lords and catch sight of Madame Jacqueline ere he formally set out to woo her. Of a truth, the dull-witted and stodgy Flemings whom *Monsieur* affected to despise, had not much to learn in the matter of finesse and diplomacy from the wily Valois! This counter-stroke on their part was a real slap-in-the-face to the arrogant prince who was condescending to an alliance, of which every other reigning house in Europe would have been proud.

CHAPTER VII.
WHY MADAME JACQUELINE WAS
SO LATE IN GETTING TO BED

I

Old Nicolle, restless and cross, was fidgeting about the room, fingering with fussy inconsequence the beautiful clothes which her mistress had taken off half an hour ago preparatory to going to bed — clothes of great value and of vast beauty, which had cost more money to acquire than good Nicolle had ever handled in all her life. There was the beautiful gown which Madame had worn this evening at supper, fashioned of black satin and all slashed with white and embroidered with pearls. There was the underdress of rich crimson silk, worked with gold and silver braid; there were the stockings of crimson silk, the high-pattened shoes of velvet, the delicately wrought fan, the gloves of fine chamois skin, the wide collarette edged with priceless lace. There was also the hideous monstrosity called the farthingale — huge hoops constructed of whalebone and of iron which, with the no less abominable corset of wood and steel, was intended to beautify and to refine the outline of the female figure and only succeeded in making it look ludicrous and ungainly. There were, in fact, the numberless and costly accessories which go to the completion of a wealthy lady's toilet.

Madame had divested herself of them all and had allowed Nicolle to wrap a woollen petticoat round her slender hips and to throw a shawl over her shoulders. Then, with her fair hair hanging in heavy masses down her back, she had curled herself up in the high-backed chair beside the open window — the open window, an it please you! and the evening, though mild, still one of early March! Old Nicolle had mumbled and grumbled. It was ten o' the clock and long past bedtime. For awhile she had idled away the hour by fingering the exquisite satin of the gown which lay in all its rich glory upon the carved dowry chest. Nicolle loved all these things. She loved to see her young mistress decked out in all the finery which could possibly be heaped up on a girlish and slender body. She never thought the silks and satins heavy when Jacqueline wore them; she never thought the farthingale unsightly when Jacqueline's dainty bust and shoulders emerged above it like the handle of a huge bell.

But gradually her patience wore out. She was sleepy, was poor old Nicolle! And Madame still sat squatting in the tall chair by the open window, doing nothing apparently save to gaze over the courtyard wall to the distance beyond, where the graceful steeple of St. Géry stood outlined like delicate lace-work against the evening sky.

"Tis time Madame got to bed,' reiterated the old woman for the twentieth time. 'The cathedral tower hath chimed the quarter now. Whoever heard of young people not being abed at this hour! And Madame sitting there,' she added, muttering to herself, 'not clothed enough to look decent!'

Jacqueline de Broyart looked round to old Nicolle with amusement dancing in her merry blue eyes.

'Not decent?' she exclaimed with a laugh. 'Why, my dear Colle, nobody sees me but you!'

'People passing across the courtyard might catch sight of Madame,' said Nicolle crossly.

'People?' retorted Jacqueline gaily. 'What people?'

'Monseigneur had company to-night.'

'They all went away an hour ago.'

'Then there are the varlets and maids— —'

'E'en so,' rejoined Jacqueline lightly, 'my attire, meseems, is not lacking in modesty. I am muffled up to my nose in a shawl and— — Oh!' she added with a quick sigh of impatience, 'I am so comfortable in this soft woollen petticoat. I feel like a human being in it and not like a cathedral bell. How I wish my guardian would not insist on my wearing all these modish clothes from Paris! I was so much more comfortable when I could don what I most fancied.'

'Monseigneur le Baron d'Inchy,' said Nicolle sententiously, 'knows what is due to your rank, Madame, and to your wealth.'

'Oh! a murrain upon my rank and upon my wealth!' cried the young girl hotly. 'My dear mother rendered me a great disservice when she bare me to this world. She should have deputed some simple, comfortable soul for the work, who could have let me roam freely about the town when I liked, run about the streets barefooted, with a short woollen kirtle tied round my waist and my hair flying loose about my shoulders. I could have been so happy as a humble burgher's daughter or a peasant wench. I do so loathe all the stiffness and the ceremony and the starched ruffles and high-heeled shoes. What I want is to be free—free!—Oh!——'

And Jacqueline de Broyart stretched out her arms and sighed again, half-longingly, half-impatiently.

'You want to be free, Madame,' muttered old Nicolle through her toothless gums, 'so that you might go and meet that masked gallant who has been haunting the street with his music of late. You never used to sigh like this after freedom and ugly gowns before he appeared upon the scene.'

'Don't scold, old Colle!' pleaded the girl softly. And now her arms were stretched towards the old waiting-woman.

Nicolle resisted the blandishment. She was really cross just now. She turned her back resolutely upon the lovely pleader, avoiding to look into those luminous blue eyes, which had so oft been compared by amorous swains to the wild hyacinths that grow in the woods above Marcoing.

'Come and kiss me, Colle,' whispered the young charmer, 'I feel so lonely somehow to-night. I feel as if—as if——'

And the young voice broke in a quaint little gasp which was almost like a sob.

In a moment Nicolle—both forgiving and repentant—was kneeling beside the high-backed chair, and with loving, wrinkled hands holding a delicate lace handkerchief, she wiped the tears which had gathered on Jacqueline's long, dark lashes.

'My precious lamb, my dove, my little cabbage!' she murmured lovingly. 'What ails thee? Why dost thou cry? Surely, my pigeon, thou hast no cause to be tearful. All the world is at thy feet; every one loves thee, and M. de Landas—surely the finest gentleman that ever walked the earth!—simply worships the ground thy little foot treads on.

And—and'—added the old woman pitiably—'thy old Colle would allow herself to be cut into a thousand pieces if it would please thee.'

Whereupon Jacqueline broke into a sudden, gay and rippling laugh, even though the tears still glistened on her lashes.

'I shouldn't at all enjoy,' she said lightly, 'seeing my dear old Colle cut into a thousand pieces.'

'Then what is it, my beloved?'

Jacqueline made no reply. For a few seconds she remained quite silent, her eyes fixed into nothingness above old Colle's head. One would almost have thought that she was listening to something which the old woman could not hear, for the expression on her face was curiously tense, with eyes glowing and lips parted, while the poise of her girlish figure was almost rigidly still. The flame of the wax candles in the tall sconces flickered gently in the draught, for the casement-window was wide open and a soft breeze blew in from the west.

'Come, my cabbage,' pleaded Nicolle as she struggled painfully to her feet. 'Come and let thy old Colle put thee to bed. Thou must be tired after that long supper party and listening to so much talking and music. And to-morrow yet another banquet awaits thee. Monseigneur hath already desired thy presence— —'

'I don't want to go to another banquet to-morrow, Colle,' sighed the young girl dolefully. 'And I am sick of company and of scrapings and bowings and kissing of hands—stupid flummery wherewith men regale me because I am rich and because they think that I am a brainless nincompoop. I would far rather have supper quietly in my room every night—quite alone— —'

But old Colle evidently thought that she knew better than that. 'Heu! heu!' she muttered with a shrug of the shoulders, accompanied by a knowing wink. 'What chance wouldst thou have then of seeing M. de Landas?'

'I hardly can speak with M. de Landas during those interminable banquets,' rejoined Jacqueline with a sigh. 'My guardian or else M. de Lalain always seem in the way now whenever he tries to come nigh me.'

'I'll warrant though that M. de Landas knows how to circumvent Monseigneur,' riposted the old woman slyly. Like so many of her sex who have had little or no romance in a dull and monotonous life, there was nothing that old Colle enjoyed more than to help forward a love intrigue or a love adventure. M. de Landas she had, as it were, taken under her special protection. He was very handsome and liberal with money, and in his love-making he had all the ardour of his Southern blood, all of which attributes vastly appealed to old Colle. The fact that Monseigneur le Baron d'Inchy did not altogether favour the young man's suit—especially of late—lent additional zest to Nicolle's championship of his claims.

'Even so,' said Jacqueline with sudden irrelevance, 'there are moments when one likes to be alone. There is so much to think about—to dream of——'

'I know, I know,' murmured the old woman crossly. 'Thy desire is to sit here half the evening now by the open window, and catch a deathly ague while listening to that impudent minstrel who dares to serenade so great a lady.'

She went on muttering and grumbling and fidgeting about the room, unmindful of the fact that at her words Jacqueline had suddenly jumped to her feet; eyes blazing, small fists clenched, cheeks crimson, she suddenly faced the garrulous old woman.

'Nicolle, be silent!' she commanded. 'At once! Dost hear?'

'Silent? Silent?' grumbled the woman. 'I have been silent quite long enough, and if Monseigneur were to hear of these doings 'tis old Nicolle who would get the blame. As for M. de Landas, I do verily believe that he would run his sword right through the body of the rogue for his impudence! I know.... I know,' she added, with a tone of spite in her gruff voice. 'But let me tell thee that if that rascally singer dares tō raise his voice again to-night——'

She paused, a little frightened at the fierce wrath which literally blazed out of her mistress's eyes.

'Well?' said Jacqueline peremptorily, but in a very husky voice. 'Why dost thou not finish? What will happen if the minstrel, whose singing hath given me exquisite joy these three nights past, were to raise his heavenly voice again?'

'Pierre will make it unpleasant for him, that's all!' replied the old woman curtly.

'Pierre?'

'Yes; Pierre! M. de Landas' serving-man. I told him to be on the look-out, outside the postern gate, and—well!—Pierre has a strong fist and a heavy staff, and...'

In a moment Jacqueline was by Nicolle's side. She seized the old woman by the wrist so that poor Colle cried out with pain, and it was as the very living image of a goddess of wrath that the young girl now confronted her terrified serving-maid.

'Thou hast dared to do that, Nicolle?' she demanded in a choked and quivering voice. 'Thou wicked, interfering old hag! I hate thee!' she went on remorselessly, not heeding the looks of terror and of abject repentance wherewith Colle received this floodgate of vituperation. 'I hate thee, dost hear? And if Pierre doth but dare to lay hands on that exquisite singer I'll ask M. de Landas to have him flogged—yes, flogged! And I'll never wish to see thy face again—thou wicked, wicked Colle!'

Mastered by her own emotion and her passionate resentment, Jacqueline sank back into a chair, her voice broken with sobs, and tears of genuine rage streaming down her cheeks. Nicolle, quite bewildered, had stood perfectly still, paralysed in fact, whilst this storm of wrathful indignation burst over her devoted head. In spite of her terror and of her remorse, there had lingered round her wrinkled lips a line or two of mulish obstinacy. The matter of the unknown singer, who had not only ventured to serenade the great and noble Dame Jacqueline, Duchesse et Princesse de Ramèse and of several other places, just as if she were some common burgher's wench with a none too spotless reputation, had not ended with a song or two: no! the malapert had actually been impudent enough last night to scale the courtyard wall and to stand for over half an hour just below Madame's window (how he knew which was Madame's window Satan, his accomplice, alone could tell!) singing away to the accompaniment of a twangy lute, which she—Nicolle—for one, could never abide.

Fortunately, on that occasion Madame Jacqueline had been both modest and discreet. She had kept well within the room and even retired into the alcove, well out of sight of that abominable rascal; but she would not allow Colle to close the window and had been very angry indeed when the old woman with a few gruff and peremptory words had presently sent the malapert away.

That was yesterday. And now this outburst of rage! It was unbelievable! Madame Jacqueline of a truth was hot-tempered and passionate—how could she help being otherwise, seeing that she had been indulged and adulated ever since, poor mite of three, she had lost both father and mother and had been under the guardianship of Monseigneur d'Inchy and of half a dozen other gentlemen. Never, however, had Colle seen her quite like this, and for such a worthless cause! Colle could scarce credit her eyes and ears. And alas! there was no mistaking the flood of heartrending weeping which followed. Jacqueline sat huddled up in her chair, her face buried in her hands, sobbing and weeping as if her heart would break.

II

All the obstinacy in the worthy old soul melted away in an instant, giving place to heartrending remorse. She fell on her knees, she took the small feet of her adored mistress in her hands and kissed them and wept over them and cried and lamented tearfully.

'Lord God, what have I done?' she called out from the depths of her misery. 'My dove, my cabbage! Look at me—look at thy old Colle! Dost not know that I would far sooner bite my tongue out than say one word that would offend thee? My lamb, wilt not look at Colle?—I vow—I swear that I'll die here on the spot at thy feet, if thou'lt not smile on me!'

Gradually as the old woman wept and pleaded, Jacqueline became more calm. The sobs no longer shook her shoulders, but she still kept her face hidden in her hands. A few minutes went by. Colle had buried her old head in the young girl's lap, and after a while Jacqueline, regally condescending to forgive, allowed her hand to fall on the bowed head of the repentant sinner.

'I'll only forgive thee, Colle,' she said with solemn earnestness, 'if Pierre doth not lay a finger upon that heavenly singer—but, if he does——'

Colle struggled to her feet as quickly as her stiff joints would allow.

'I'll go and find the varlet myself,' she said fiercely, ready to betray with cowardly baseness the confederate of awhile ago, now that she had propitiated the mistress whom she adored. 'M. de Landas hath not yet left the Palace, and if Pierre dares but raise his hand against that mal—hem!—against the noble singer whom thou dost honour with thine attention, well! he'll have to reckon with old Colle; that is all!'

With Jacqueline de Broyart—who in herself appeared the very embodiment of spring, so full of youth, of grace and of vitality was she—sunshine and storm came in rapid succession over her moods, just as they do over the skies when the year is young. Already her eyes, bathed in tears of rage awhile ago, were glistening with pleasure, and her lips, which had pouted and stormed, were parted in a smile.

'Go, Colle!' she said eagerly. 'Go at once, ere it be too late and that fool Pierre——'

The words died upon her lips. The next instant she had jumped down from her chair and run to the window. From some distance down the street there had come, suddenly wafted upon the wings of the wind, the sound of a voice singing the well-known verses of Messire de Ronsard:

'Mignonne, allons voir si la rose
   Qui ce matin avait desclose
Sa robe de pourpre au soleil
   A point perdu cette vesprée
Les plis de sa robe pourprée
   Et son teint au vostre pareil.'[1]

[1] 'Mignonne, come see if the rose
   That this morning did unclose
Her purple robe to the sun
   Hath not ere this evening lost
Of those purple petals most
   And the tint with your tint one.'

(Translation by Mr. Percy Allen. *Songs of Old France*.)

Jacqueline knelt upon the window-seat, but she could see nothing, so she turned back piteously to murmur to old Colle: 'Oh! if I could only see him!'

The old woman, after the experience of the past few minutes, was ready to do anything, however abject, to further her mistress' desire.

'Put on thy mask, my pigeon,' she said, 'and then lean well out of the window; but not too far, for fear M. de Landas should happen to be passing in the courtyard and should see thee with thy hair down. No, no!' added the old hypocrite obsequiously, 'there is no harm in listening to so sweet a singer. I'll get thy purse, too, and thou canst throw him a coin or two. No doubt the poor fellow is down-at-heels and only sings to earn his supper.'

And humble, fussy, still snivelling, Nicolle shuffled across the room, found the satin mask and brought it to her mistress. Jacqueline fixed it over her face; then she leaned as far out of the window as she dared to do without fear of falling out. And, if M. de Landas saw her, why! he would be so gladdened at the sight that he would have no ear for a mere street musician, whilst she—Jacqueline—was just now in so soft a mood that if M. de Landas happened to scale the wall to her casement-window—as he had more than once threatened to do—she would return his kisses in a way that she had never done before.

For she was deeply in love with M. de Landas, had been for years. She had plighted her troth to him when she was a mere child, and she loved him—oh yes! she loved him very, very much, only...

III

There was the width of the courtyard and the tall wall between Jacqueline and the street where stood the singer whom she so longed to see. She had caught sight of him yesterday when, to Nicolle's horror, he had boldly scaled the wall and then had lingered for nigh on half an hour beneath her window, singing one merry song after another, till her young heart had been filled with a new joy, the cause of which she herself could not quite comprehend.

She had watched him unseen, fearful lest some of the serving-men should see him and drive him away. Fortunately Chance had been all in favour of her new romance. M. de Landas was on duty at the Forts that night; her guardian was still closeted with some other grave seigneurs, and the serving-men were no doubt too busy to trouble about a harmless minstrel. As for the wenches about the place, they had stood about in the doorways, listening with delight at the impassioned songs and gaping in admiration at the splendid bearing of the unknown cavalier.

Thus the singer had stood in the courtyard for some considerable time, his martial figure silhouetted against the clear, moonlit sky, his voice rising and falling in perfect cadence to the accompaniment of a soft-toned lute, whilst Jacqueline, hidden within the shadow of the window-embrasure, listened spellbound, her whole youth, her ardent, loving soul exultant at this romance which was taking birth at her feet.

And now he had come back, and the very night seemed to bid him welcome. It was still quite early in March, yet the air was soft as spring. All day the birds had been twittering under the eaves, and on the west wind had come wafted gently the scent of budding almond blossom and of the life-giving sap in the branches of the trees.

The stately city with its towers and steeples and cupolas lay bathed in the light of the honey-coloured moon. Far away on the right, the elegant church of Saint Géry up on the Mont-des-Boeufs seemed like a bar of silver which attached old Cambray to the star-studded firmament above, and around it were grouped the tall steeples of St. Martin, St. Waast and St. Aubert, with the fine hexagon of Martin et Martine which crowned the Town Hall; whilst, dominating this forest of perfect and rich architecture, was the mass of the cathedral close by, with its tall pointed steeple, its flying buttresses, its numberless delicate pinnacles picked out as by a fairy hand against the background of deep azure.

But Jacqueline de Broyart had for the nonce no eyes for all that beauty. What cared she if the wintry moon outlined all these lovely heights with delicate lines of silver? What cared she if the shadows of stately edifices appeared full of a golden glow by contrast with the cold blue of the lights? Her eyes were fixed, not on the tower of St. Géry nor on the steeple of Notre Dame: they rested upon that high and cruel wall which hid the unknown singer from her sight.

'Mignonne!' he sang out gaily. 'Allons voir la rose——'

'Oh!' sighed Jacqueline with passionate longing. 'If I only could——!'

And her fancy went soaring into a world of romance—a world far away from the sordid strifes, the political intrigues, the quarrels of to-day; a world wherein men were all handsome and brave and women were all free to grant them their hand to kiss, to listen to their songs, to reward their prowess, to receive their homage unfettered by convention—a world, in fact, such as Messire de Froissart had chronicled and of which Messire Villon had sung so exquisitely.

Then suddenly Jacqueline's dreams were rudely interrupted, as was also the song of the unseen minstrel. Loud voices were raised and there was a clash which made Jacqueline's very heart turn cold in her bosom.

'Colle!' she cried excitedly.

But Colle had shuffled out of the room some little while ago, in search of Pierre, no doubt, whom evidently she had failed to find. And out there behind that cruel wall the rough hands of that abominable varlet were being laid on the precious person of the unsuspecting minstrel. Jacqueline felt literally paralysed both with terror and with wrath. Colle had spoken of Pierre's stout arm and still stouter stick, but there was also the possibility of M. de Landas himself being about, and then—oh, then! ... Ye heavens above! anything might happen! ... Oh! the wicked, wicked old woman and that execrable Pierre! ... and ... and of course M. de Landas' jealousy was sometimes terrifying!

'God in Heaven!' sighed Jacqueline. 'I entreat Thee to protect him!'

The noise of the scuffle in the street became louder and louder. There were cries of rage as well as of pain. Blows were evidently raining freely—on whom? My God, on whom? Then, from further up the street, came the sound of running footsteps as well as the stern voice of the night watchmen hurrying to the scene. Jacqueline would have bartered some years of her life to see what was going on the other side of the wall. Only a minute or two had gone by: to the young girl it had seemed like hours of suspense. And now these people all rushing along, no doubt in order to give a hand to Pierre—to fall on the unarmed minstrel—to lay hands upon him—to belabour him with sticks—to wound or hurt him—to— —

Jacqueline uttered a loud cry of horror. It was the echo of one of terror, of pain and of rage which came from the other side of the wall. The next moment a dark mass appeared over the top of the wall, silhouetted against the moonlit sky. To Jacqueline's straining eyes it seemed like the body of a man which, for the space of a brief second, seemed to hover in mid air and then fell with a dull thud upon the paving-stones of the courtyard below.

Jacqueline closed her eyes. She felt sick and faint. To her ears now came the sound of loud groans and vigorous curses. And then—oh, then!—loud laughter and the last bar of the interrupted song—a sound indeed which caused her at once to open her eyes again; whereupon she, too, could have laughed and sung for joy. The inert mass still lay in a heap at the foot of the wall; Jacqueline could vaguely discern its outline in the gloom, whilst up on the top of the wall, astride, hatless, lute in hand, sat the masked minstrel with his head turned gazing toward her window.

She clapped her hands with glee, and he, with a loud cry of 'Mignonne!' swung himself down from the wall and ran across the courtyard until he came to a halt just beneath her window, and even in the dim light of this wintry moon Jacqueline thought that she could see his eyes glowing through the holes in the mask.

It was all so joyous, so gay, so romantic; so different—ah! so very, very different—to the dreary monotony of Jacqueline's daily existence! This masked and unknown minstrel! His daring, his prowess, aye! his very impudence, which laughed at high walls and defied an army of varlets! There was Pierre moaning and groaning, disarmed and helpless, having been tossed over the wall just as if he were a bale of cumbersome goods! Serve him right well, too, for having dared to measure his valour against that of so proud a cavalier! Pierre was not hurt—oh, Jacqueline was quite sure that he was not hurt! Nothing, nothing whatever, was going to be wrong on this lovely, glorious evening! No! Pierre would soon be healed of his wounds; but it was ludicrous to see him stretched out just there, where he thought he could lay the noble singer low!

'Mignonne, allons voir si la rose,' sang the mysterious minstrel; and Jacqueline's young heart, which was filled with the joy of romance, the exquisite rapture of ideals, suddenly ached with a passionate longing for—for what? She did not know. She had had so many things in life: riches, beauty, adulation, aye! and the love of a man whom she loved in return. But now it seemed to her as if, in spite of all that, in spite of M. de Landas and his love, she had really lacked something all the time—something that was both undefinable and mystic and yet was intensely and vividly real, something that would fill her life, that would satisfy her soul and gladden her heart, in a way that M. de Landas' love, his passionate kisses, had never succeeded in doing hitherto.

And somehow all this longing, all this thirst for a still-unknown happiness, seemed personified in the singer with the tall, broad stature and the mellow voice; it was embodied in the honey-coloured moon, in the glints of silver and gold upon the steeples of Cambray, in the scent of the spring and the murmurs of the breeze. Jacqueline pressed her hands against her heart. She was so happy that she could have cried.

Beside her on the window-sill stood a tall vase fashioned of Dutch clay. It was filled with tall-stemmed Madonna lilies, which had been produced at great cost in the hot-houses belonging to her own estate in Hainault. Their powerful scent had filled the room with its fragrance. Without thought or hesitation, Jacqueline suddenly pulled the sheaf out of the vase and gathered the flowers in her arms. The tender, juicy stems were wet and she took her embroidered handkerchief out of her pocket and wrapped it round them; then she flung the whole sheaf of lilies out of the window and watched to see them fall, bruised and sweet-smelling, at the minstrel's feet.

Then, half-ashamed, laughing a little hysterically, but thoroughly happy and excited, she drew quickly back into the room and hastily closed the casement.

IV

When, ten minutes or so later, Nicolle came back, shame-faced, remorseful and not a little frightened, she was surprised and delighted to find her young mistress sitting quite composedly in a high-backed chair in the centre of the room, the window closed, and the lady herself quite eager to go to bed.

'Thou hast been gone a long time, Colle,' said the young girl carelessly. 'Where hast thou been?'

Old Colle sighed with relief. The Lord be praised! Madame had evidently seen and heard nothing of that vulgar scuffle which had ended in such disaster for poor Pierre, and in such a triumph for the impudent rascal who had since disappeared just as quickly as he came.

'I just went round to see that those wenches were all abed and that their lights were safely out,' replied the old woman with brazen hypocrisy.

'And didst speak to Pierre on the way?' queried Jacqueline, who had assumed the quaintest possible air of simple ingenuousness.

'Aye!' replied the old woman dryly. 'I spoke to Pierre.'

'What did he say?'

'Nothing of importance. We talked of to-morrow's banquet.'

'To-morrow's banquet?'

'Do not feign surprise, my pigeon,' rejoined old Colle, who was decidedly out of humour. 'I even asked thee to-night, before taking off thy gown, if thou wouldst wear that one or another on the morrow.'

'I remember,' replied Jacqueline with a yawn, 'I said that I did not care what I wore, as I hated banquets, and company and bowings and——'

'But Monseigneur said that the banquet to-morrow would be for a special occasion.'

'When did he say that?'

'A moment or two ago—to Pierre.'

'And what will the special occasion be to-morrow?'

Nicolle looked mysterious.

'Maybe,' she said, 'that it is not altogether unconnected with Monseigneur de Landas.'

'Why with him?' asked Jacqueline eagerly.

'Oh! I am only putting two and two together, my cabbage,' replied old Colle with a sly wink. 'There is talk of distinguished guests in Cambray, of betrothals, and ... and ...

'Betrothals?'

'Why, yes. Thou art nearly twenty, my pigeon, and Monseigneur, thy guardian, will have to make up his mind that thou wilt marry sooner or later. I always thought that he did favour Monseigneur de Landas, until——'

'Until what?' queried Jacqueline impatiently.

'There are so many rumours in the air,' replied Colle sententiously. 'Some talk of the Duc d'Anjou, who is own brother to the King of France.'

Jacqueline made a little moue of disdain.

'Oh! *Monsieur!*' she said carelessly.

'A very great and noble prince, my pigeon.'

'I am tired of great and noble princes.'

'But Monseigneur, the Duc d'Anjou...'

'Is one of the many, I suppose, who want my fortune, my family connexions, the Sovereignty of the Netherlands. Bah!' she added with an impatient sigh. 'They sicken me!'

'A great lady, my cabbage,' said Nicolle solemnly, 'cannot follow the dictates of her heart like a common wench.'

'Why!' exclaimed Jacqueline. 'Methought thou wast all for M. de Landas!'

'So I am, my pigeon, so I am!' rejoined the old woman. 'He is a very distinguished gentleman, who loves thee ardently. But if there's one who is own brother to the King of France....' And old Colle gave an unctuous sigh when she spoke the exalted name.

'Bah!' retorted Jacqueline with a careless shrug of the shoulders. 'There are others too! And no one can force me into a marriage whilst my heart is pledged to M. de Landas.'

'No, no! Thank God for that!' assented Colle piously. 'As for the others ... well! their name is legion ... some of them will be at the banquet to-morrow.... There is the Marquis de Hancourt, a fine-looking youth, and that horrid German prince whom I cannot abide! The English lord hath gone away, so they say, broken-hearted at thy refusal; but there's the Spanish duke, whose name I cannot remember, and Don José, own son to the Emperor.... As for that stranger — —' she added with a contemptuous shrug of the shoulders.

'The stranger?' queried Jacqueline lazily. 'What stranger?

'Well, I don't know much about him. But Pierre, feeling crestfallen, did admit that Monseigneur chided him severely for having shown a want of respect to a gentleman who ought to have known better than to pretend to be a street musician.'

But Jacqueline appeared all of a sudden to have lost interest in the conversation. 'Ah!' she said with well-assumed indifference, 'then the street musician of awhile ago was a gentleman in disguise?'

'Aye! so Pierre said—the fool!' quoth old Colle unblushingly. 'Monseigneur was very angry with him when he heard of the altercation with the singer, threatened to speak of the matter to M. de Landas and have Pierre flogged or dismissed for his interference. Then he hinted that the stranger, far from being a street musician, was a foreign seigneur of high degree, even if of scanty fortune.'

'Oh!' commented Jacqueline carelessly.

'And he e'en ordered Pierre to go and apologize most humbly to the stranger, who it seems is lodging in a very poor hostelry known as "Les Trois Rois," just close to the Porte Notre Dame.'

Jacqueline ostentatiously smothered a yawn.

'I think I'll go to bed now, Colle,' she said.

But Colle's tongue, once loosened, could not so easily be checked.

'Town gossip,' she went on with great volubility, 'has been busy with that stranger for the past two days. 'Tis said that he is styled Monseigneur le Prince de Froidmont; though what a prince should be doing in a shabby hostel in that squalid quarter of the city I, for one, do not know—nor why he should be going about masked and cloaked through the city in the guise of a vagabond.'

'Perhaps the vagabond is no prince after all,' suggested Jacqueline.

'That's what I say,' asserted Colle triumphantly. 'And that's what Pierre thought until Monseigneur told him that if he did not go at once and offer his humble apologies he surely would get a flogging, seeing that the Prince de Froidmont would actually be a guest at the banquet to-morrow, and would of a certainty complain to M. de Landas.'

'A guest at the banquet!' exclaimed Jacqueline involuntarily.'

'Aye!' assented Colle. 'Didst ever hear the like! But he must be a distinguished seigneur for all that, or Monseigneur would not bid him come.'

'No, I suppose not,' said Jacqueline with perfect indifference. 'The Prince de Froidmont?' she added with a little yawn. 'Is that his name?'

'So the town gossips say,' replied Colle, who was busy just then in wrapping the bed-gown round her young mistress's shoulders.

'And he comes to the banquet to-morrow?'

'So Monseigneur said to Pierre.'

Jacqueline said nothing more for the moment, appeared to have lost all interest in the masked musician and in Pierre's misdeeds. She stretched out her arms lazily while vigorous old Colle picked her up as if she were a baby and carried her—as she was wont to do every night—to her bed.

She laid her down upon the soft feather mattress and spread the fine coverlets over her. The alcove wherein stood the monumental bedstead was in semi-darkness, for the light from the wax candles in the sconces about the room failed to penetrate into the recess. But that semi-darkness was restful, and for awhile Jacqueline lay back against the pillows, with eyes closed, in a state of that complete well-being which is one of the monopolies of youth. Nicolle, thinking that Madame would be dropping off to sleep, made a movement to go; but Jacqueline's small white hand had hold of the old woman's bony fingers, and old Colle, abjectly happy at feeling the pressure, remained quite still, waiting and watching, gazing with doglike devotion on the lovely face—lovely in repose as it was when the light of gaiety and roguishness danced in the blue eyes.

After a few minutes of this silent beatitude, Jacqueline opened her eyes and said in a dreamy voice, half-asleep:

'Tell me, Colle, which is my prettiest gown?'

And Nicolle—herself more than half-way to the land of Nod—roused herself in order to reply: 'The white one with the pearls, my pigeon.'

She was sufficiently awake to feel quite happy at the thought that Madame was suddenly taking an interest in her clothes, and continued eagerly: 'It hath an underdress of that lovely new green colour which hath become the mode of late, and all embroidered with silver. Nothing more beautiful hath ever been fashioned by tailors' art, and in it Madame looks just like an exquisite white lily, with the delicate green stem below.'

'Well then, Colle,' rejoined Jacqueline dreamily, 'to-morrow evening I will wear my white satin gown with the pearls and the underdress of green and silver, and Mathurine must study a new way of doing my hair with the pointed coif which they say is so modish now in France. I will wear my stockings of crimson silk and my velvet shoes, and round my neck I'll wear the ropes of pearls which my dear mother did bequeath to me; in my ears I'll have the emerald earrings, and I'll wear the emerald ring upon my finger. I wish I had not that ugly mole upon my left cheek-bone, for then I could have had one of those tiny patches of black taffeta which are said to be so becoming to the complexion....'

She paused, and added with quaint wistfulness: 'Think you, Colle, that I shall look handsome?'

'As lovely as a picture, my dear one,' said Nicolle with enthusiasm. 'As exquisite as a lily; fit only to be the bride of a King.'

Jacqueline gave a quick sigh of satisfaction, after which she allowed Colle to give her a kiss and to bid her a final 'good night.'

And even as she fell gradually into the delicious and dreamless sleep of youth, her lips murmured softly: 'I wonder!'

CHAPTER VIII.
WHAT BECAME OF THE LILIES

I

Gilles had spent four days at the hostelry of 'Les Trois Rois,' and here he would have liked to remain indefinitely and to continue the sentimental romance so happily begun beneath the casement-windows of the Archiepiscopal Palace. With the light-heartedness peculiar to most soldiers of fortune, he had during those four days succeeded in putting his rôle out of his mind. Though he had not yet caught sight of Madame's face at her window, he quite thought that he would do so in time, and already he had received more than one indication that his singing was not unwelcome. The casement had been deliberately thrown open when he had scaled the courtyard wall, and had resumed his song immediately beneath the window which he had ascertained belonged to Madame's private apartment. He had felt, even though he did not actually see, that some one was listening to him from up there, for once he had perceived a shadow upon the casement curtain, and once a hand, small and delicate, had rested upon the window-sill. Gilles would have continued this wooing—aye! perhaps have brought it to a happy conclusion, he thought—without being forced to assume another personality than his own: a thing which became more and more abhorrent to Messire Gilles' temper, now that the time for starting the masquerade in earnest was drawing nigh.

'We could make ourselves very happy here, honest Jehan,' he had said to the faithful companion of his many adventures. 'Waited on by that silent and zealous youth, who of a truth looks like the very ghost of silence and discretion. With judicious economy, the money which a gracious Queen hath placed in our hands would last us a year. It seems a pity to fritter it all away in a few weeks by playing a rôle which is detestable and unworthy.'

'B-b-b-but——' stammered old Jehan.

'You are quite right,' broke in Gilles gravely. 'Your argument is very sound. The money, my friend, was given unto us in order to play a certain rôle, and that rôle we must now play whether we like it or not, on pain of being branded as vagabonds and thieves.'

'V-v-v-very——' stammered poor Jehan.

'As you say,' remarked Gilles dryly, 'I have always found you of good counsel, my friend. Very likely—that is what you would say, is it not?—very likely, unless we played our parts as Madame la Reyne de Navarre did direct, Monseigneur le Baron d'Inchy would discover the fraud and have us both hanged for our pains. And if the hangman did happen to miss us, Madame Marguerite would certainly see to it that a gibbet was ready for us somewhere in France. So for this once, I think, mine honest Jehan, we must take it that honesty will be the best policy.'

'O-o-o-only th-th-th-that——'

'Quite so!' assented Gilles, 'only that in this case we cannot contrive to remain honest without being dishonest, which is a proposition that doth gravely disturb my mind.'

'Th-th-th-the o-o-o-only——'

'Hold your tongue, friend Jehan,' broke in Gilles impatiently. 'Verily, you talk a great deal too much!'

II

And now, at the very close of the fourth day, Messire Gilles made noisy irruption into the tiny room which he occupied in the hostelry of 'Les Trois Rois.' Maître Jehan—after the stormy episode outside the postern gate wherein he had taken part—was in the room, waiting for his master.

Gilles was in the rarest of good humour. As soon as he had closed the door behind him, he threw his plumed toque and the lute upon the table and, sitting down on the narrow paillasse which was his bed, he fell to contemplating a bunch of white lilies which he had in his hand. The stems of these lilies were carefully wrapped in an embroidered handkerchief, but they hung their bruised, if still fragrant, heads in a very doleful manner.

Gilles laughed softly to himself. Then he held the flowers out at arm's length and called out gaily to Jehan:

'Congratulate me, honest Jehan!' he said. 'The first act of our adventurous comedy is over. The curtain has rung down on a veritable triumph! I have received a token! ... I have captured the first bastion in the citadel of the fair one's heart! Give me a week, and I hold the entire fortress for and on behalf of *Monsieur* Duc d'Anjou, our august master!'

'Th-th-th-then you h-h-h-have— —'

'No, I have not seen her, my good man. All that fine fight outside the walls, the complete discomfiture of our assailants, my perilous position inside the courtyard, from whence a reinforcement of varlets might easily have put me to flight, did not win for me even a glimpse of the lady. But her window was wide open this time, and I could see her shadow flitting past the casement. Then suddenly these lilies were flung at me. They were crushed and bruised against the pavement as they fell; but they are a token, friend Jehan, and you cannot deny it! Madame Jacqueline's heart is already touched by the song of the unknown troubadour, and he hath but to present himself before her to be graciously received.'

'B-b-b-b-but— —' said Jehan with grave solemnity.

'That's just it!' broke in Gilles with a laugh. 'You have a way, my friend, of hitting the right nail on the head. As you say, the four days' respite which have been granted to us have now expired, and we have not yet seen the future Duchesse d'Anjou face to face.'

'N-n-n-not yet! Th-th-th-that— —'

'That is the trouble, I grant you. There is that infernal masquerade; and of a truth, I am more convinced than ever that the reason why those noble mynheers are so determined that Madame shall not show her face ere I have irrevocably committed myself—I—that is, the Duc d'Anjou—that is— — Oh, my God!' he exclaimed. 'What a tangle!! Well, as I was saying.... By the way, what was I saying just now?'

'Th-th-th-that— —'

'Of course! You incorrigible chatterbox! I would have explained my meaning before now if you had not talked nineteen to the dozen all the time! I mean that I have completely changed my mind, and that I have become convinced that Madame Jacqueline is as ugly as sin, else those wily Dutchmen would not be so anxious to cover up her face.'

'Th-th-th-therefore— —' asserted Jehan stoutly.

'Therefore, my good man, good fortune is in our debt. She did not favour me with a sight of the lady ere I meet her in my official capacity. But Madame Jacqueline hath given me a token: she is prepared to love me, and I am still in the dark as to whether she squints or is pitted with pock-marks. A terrible position for any man to be in!' he sighed dolefully, 'even though he is out a-courting for a friend.'

'B-b-b-but— —'

'You mean well, my friend,' quoth Gilles, who fell to contemplating the bunch of faded lilies with a rueful expression of face. 'You mean well, but you talk too much, and thus I am thrown on mine own resources for counsel in an emergency. As for arguments! Why, you would argue the devil's horns from off his head! Still,' he added, as he finally flung the lilies away from him with a careless gesture of indifference, 'still, in spite of what you say, I must stick to my bargain. Those mulish mynheers will not grant us any further delay, and to-morrow I am pledged to appear at the governor's banquet—yes, even I!—*Monsieur* Duc d'Anjou et d'Alençon, own brother to the King of France, and you as my faithful servitor.'

'N-n-n-not a m-m-minute t-t-too soon,' Maître Jehan managed to blurt out quickly whilst Gilles had paused for breath.

'Ah! there you are wrong, my friend,' retorted Gilles. 'For my taste, the dénouement is coming along at far too rapid a pace. To-morrow, already our troubles will begin—peace will know us no more. I for one will never rightly know who I am; nor will I know who it is who will know who I am not. Oh, my Lord!' he added in mock despair, as he rested his elbows on his knees and buried his head in his hands. 'My head will split ere I have done! Tell me, Jehan, who I shall be to-morrow.'

'T-t-t-to-morrow,' stammered Jehan with painful earnestness, 'you—you—you— —you will b-b-b-b-be— —'

'Own brother to His Majesty the King of France,' said Gilles, 'and as great blackguard as ever disgraced a Royal house. To Monseigneur the governor, and maybe also to some of his friends, I shall be a Royal prince. To others, and notably to Madame Jacqueline de Broyart, I shall be the Prince de Froidmont—an insignificant and penniless seigneur who only dares approach the far-famed heiress under cover of a mask, having fallen desperately in love with her. Ah, Jehan! Jehan!' he added with mock solemnity, 'thou art of a truth a lucky devil! Thou canst keep thine own name, thine own rank, even thine own ludicrous stutter: whereas I,—what shall I be? A mime! A buffoon! And what's more, a fraudulent varlet, pledged to deceive an innocent wench into the belief that her future lord is both sentimental and amorous and can sing the love ditties writ by Messire de Ronsard with passable tunefulness.... Ye gods, Jehan, hast ever heard *Monsieur* Duc d'Anjou—the real one, I mean—sing?'

'N-n-n-no!' objected Jehan in pious horror, for he did not like to hear so exalted a personage derided.

'Then hast ever heard the barn-door rooster calling to his favourite hen?'

'S-s-s-s-sometimes!'

'Well!' quoth Gilles lightly, 'so have I. And I prefer the barn-door rooster! And now to bed, friend Jehan,' he added as he jumped to his feet. 'To-morrow is the great day! Didst take my letter to the governor's palace?'

'I d-d-d-did.'

'And didst see Monseigneur the governor himself?'

Jehan nodded affirmatively.

'Gave him my letter?'

Another nod from Jehan.

'Did he look pleased?'

A shrug of the shoulders this time.

'Said he would be honoured to see Monseigneur le Duc d'Alençon et d'Anjou at the banquet to-morrow?'

Once again a nod.

'Then to bed, chatterbox!' concluded Gilles gaily, 'for to-morrow I begin my career as a low, deceitful hound, fit only for the gibbet, which I dare swear is already prepared for me!'

III

Jehan helped his master to undress. He pulled off the heavy boots and laid aside the cloth jerkin, the kerseymere trunks and worsted hose. Then, when Messire Gilles lay stretched out upon the hard paillasse, honest Jehan bade him a quiet good night and went off carrying the guttering candle. For one candle had to do duty for two customers, or even at times for three, at the hostel of 'Les Trois Rois.' These were not days of luxurious caravanserai: eight square feet of floor space, a tiny leaded window, a straw paillasse, perhaps a table and a rickety chair, made up the sum total of a furnished bedroom, if destined for a person of quality. Men like Maître Jehan had to be content with the bare boards and a horse-blanket outside their master's door, or behind a wooden partition set up inside the latter's room.

Jehan went off, then, with the candle, and Gilles de Crohin remained in almost total darkness, for the light of the moon failed to penetrate through the narrow aperture which went by the name of window. For a long time Messire Gilles lay motionless, staring into the gloom. Vague pictures seemed to flit before his gaze: the unknown girl whom he was pledged to woo appeared and disappeared before him, now walking across his line of vision with stately dignity, now dancing a wild rigadoon like some unruly country wench; but always, and with irritating persistence, wearing a mask which he longed to drag away from her face. Then he saw pictures of fair Marguerite of Navarre, imperious yet appealing, and of his own cross-hilted sword, upon the sacred emblem of which he had pledged himself to an ugly deception; Monsieur Duc d'Anjou, indolent and vapid, dressed in that ludicrous green satin suit, came and mocked him through the darkness.

Gilles de Crohin, wearied with all these phantasmagoria, began tossing restlessly upon his hard bed, and as he did so he flung his arm out over the coverlet and his hand came in rough contact with the floor. And there, close to his touch, was something soft and velvety, the drooping, fading lilies which an unknown lady of high degree had flung out to him and which he had so carelessly tossed aside. His hand closed tightly upon the flowers, crushing the last spark of life out of the fragrant blossoms, and even as he did so—quite unconsciously and mechanically—an unpleasant pang of remorse shot right through his heart. Was this unconscious act of his a presage of the cruel rôle which he had set out to play? Would the young soul of an innocent girl droop and wither beneath his careless touch?

Very gently now Gilles, turning on his side, gathered the flowers together and drew them towards him. Something of their fragrance still lingered in the bruised petals. Gilles got out of bed. His eyes had become accustomed to the darkness, or perhaps something of the radiance of the moonlit night had penetrated into the narrow room. Gilles could see his way about, and he remembered that in the further corner there had stood a pitcher filled with fresh water. With infinite precaution he unwound the handkerchief from around the stems and then dropped the flowers one by one into the pitcher. After awhile he picked up the handkerchief. It was nothing now but a damp and sodden little ball, but it smelt sweetly of lilies and of lavender. Gilles marvelled if the lady's initials and coronet were embroidered in the-corner. He felt with his fingers in order to make sure; but he was too inexperienced in such matters to arrive at any definite conclusion, so with a sudden impulse which he would not have cared to analyse, he searched the darkness for his doublet, and having found it he thrust the damp little rag into its breast-pocket.

Then, with a laugh at his own folly and a light shrug of the shoulders, he went back to bed. This time he fell at once into a dreamless sleep.

CHAPTER IX.
HOW MESSIRE GILLES WAS
REMINDED OF A DREAM

I

In Maître C. Calviac's treatise on the manners and tone of good society, which he published in the year 1560[1] for the guidance of those who desired to frequent the company of the Great, we are told that 'when we enter the presence of exalted personages, we must walk on the tips of our toes, incline our body and make a profound obeisance.' And further, Maître Calviac goes on to explain the many different modes of saluting, which we might adopt for the occasion: 'Firstly,' he says, 'we can uncover our right hand, with it lower our hat by stretching the arm down along our right thigh and leaving our left hand free. Secondly, we can regard humbly and reverentially the exalted one whom we desire to salute. Thirdly, we can lower our gaze and advance our right foot whilst drawing the left one slightly back. We can also take off the glove from our right hand, incline our body, and after nearly touching the ground with our hand, carry our fingers to our lips, as if in the act of imprinting a kiss upon their tips.'

[1] La Civile Honnêteté, par C. Calviac. Paris 1560. in-12.

Finally, our accomplished monitor tells us that the embrace is yet another form of salute which cannot, however, be practised save between persons of equal rank or those who are bound to one another by ties of kinship or of especial friendship. In that case, the most civil manner of thus saluting is for each to place the right hand on the top of the other's shoulder and the left hand just below, and then present the left cheek one to the other, without touching or actually kissing the same.

We may take it that Monseigneur le Baron d'Inchy, governor of the province of Cambrésis, being an exalted personage himself and closely connected by family ties with Madame Jacqueline de Broyart—whose guardian and protector he was—did adopt the latter mode of salutation when, at eight o'clock precisely of the following evening, he presented himself before his young ward for the purpose of conducting her to the State dining-room, where a banquet in honour of several distinguished guests was already spread. We may take it, I say, that Monseigneur the governor did take off his right-hand glove, advance his right foot and walk on the tips of his toes; that he did place one hand on Madame Jacqueline's shoulder, whilst she did the same to him, and that they each presented the left cheek to one another in accordance with the laws of propriety laid down by Maître Calviac.

Monseigneur was accompanied by a young man whose manners and demeanour were even more punctilious and ceremonious than those of his companion. The airs and graces wherewith he advanced in order to greet Madame Jacqueline would have done honour to a Grand Master at the Court of the Spanish King. And, indeed, many did aver that M. le Marquis de Landas had Spanish blood in his veins, and that, though he was a Netherlander by birth, and a Protestant by practise, he was a Spaniard and a Papist by tradition—which fact did not tend to make him popular in the Cambrésis, where the armies of Alexander Farnesse, Duke of Parma, were already over-running the villages, rumour being rife that they were about to threaten Cambray.

'Twas well said of M. le Marquis de Landas that none knew better than he how to turn a compliment. Perhaps that same strain of Spanish blood in him had given him glibness of tongue and the languorous look in the eyes which had rendered many a favoured lady proud. He was known to be of exalted lineage but not endowed with fortune, connected too with some of the noblest families both in Flanders and in Spain, and had lately come to the Cambrésis as aide-de-camp to his kinsman, the baron d'Inchy, who had promptly given him command of the garrison of Cambray.

So much for facts that were known. But there were rumours and conjectures, not altogether false, it seems, that M. de Landas was a suitor for Madame Jacqueline's hand—one of the many, of course; for her hand was sought far and wide. She would bring a rich dowry as her marriage portion to any man who was lucky enough to win her, and also the influence of her Flemish kinsmen, who had already boldly asserted that the Sovereignty of the Netherlands would go with the hand of Madame Jacqueline de Broyart.

Many favoured the French alliance; others preferred the Netherlander with the strain of quasi-royal Spanish blood in him. The Marquis de Landas would prove a useful link between the Spaniards and the Netherlanders, would know how to smoothe many difficulties, calm the obstinate temperament of the Dutch and gloss over the tyranny of their masters. He had suave manners and a persuasive tongue, useful in politics. The ladies of Cambray at once adored him: his olive skin, his dark hair which clustered in heavy waves above the well-cut oval of his face, his large brown, velvety eyes, were all destined to please the fair sex. He wore a silky moustache and the small, pointed beard on his chin, and his cheeks were of a blue-black colour all down where the barber shaved him every day. Whene'er he gazed on a young and pretty woman his eyes would assume an amorous expression and his lips were curved and of a bright cherry-red, like those of a girl.

II

Between Jacqueline and her young kinsman there had sprung just that kind of love which is made up of passion on the one side and innocent devotion on the other. At first it had flourished almost unopposed—ignored, probably, as being of no importance. Monseigneur d'Inchy's plans for his ward had been both immature and vague, for, until a year or so ago Jacqueline had a brother living— Jan, a couple of years older than herself, who was the owner of the rich Netherlands duchies and on the point of taking unto himself a wife. But, with the death of that brother, Jacqueline at once became a personage of vast importance. She had remained the sole possessor of the princely heritage and thereby a pawn in the political game in which the Sovereignty of the Netherlands was the priceless guerdon.

Monseigneur d'Inchy's plans began to mature: ineligible and obscure suitors were quickly given the cold shoulder and an imaginary barrier was drawn around Madame Jacqueline into the inner circle of which only scions of kingly or great princely houses were allowed to enter. Jacqueline's dowry rendered her a fit mate even for a King.

Even M. de Landas, more highly connected than most, backed too by his Royal Spanish kindred, found that his position as an approved suitor had suddenly become gravely imperilled. Monseigneur d'Inchy no longer looked on him as an altogether desirable mate for the richest heiress in the Netherlands, now that one of the sons of the Emperor, a reigning German duke, and the brother of the King of France, were among those who had entered the lists for her favours.

But, as is nearly always the case in such matters, the boy and girl affection ripened, with this growing opposition, into something more ardent and more passionate. M. de Landas, who hitherto had dallied with his pretty cousin just to the extent that suited his wayward fancy, suddenly realized that he was very deeply enamoured of her; jealousy did the rest, transforming transient sentiment into impetuous and exacting fervour.

As for Jacqueline, though she was no longer a mere child, she was totally inexperienced and unversed in the knowledge of human hearts—not excepting her own. She loved de Landas dearly, had loved him ever since he first began to speak of love to her. It is so difficult for a girl, as yet untouched by searing passion, to distinguish between sentimental affection and the love which fills a life. Landas whispered amorous, tender, flattering words in her ear, had fine, flashing eyes which, with their glance of bold admiration, were wont to bring the warm blood to her cheeks. He had a way with him, in fact, which quickly swept her off her feet in the whirlpool of his infatuation, long before she had learned that there were other streams whereon she could have launched her barque of life, with a greater certainty of happiness.

Her heart was touched by his ardour, even though her senses were not fully awakened yet; but she yielded to his caresses with a girlish surrender of self, not realizing that the thrill of pleasure which she felt was as ephemeral as it was shallow. She admired him for his elegant manners, which he had acquired at the Spanish Court, for they stood out in brilliant contrast to the more uncouth Flemish ways; whilst his admiration for her was so unbounded that, despite herself, the young girl felt enraptured by his glowing looks.

To-night she knew that she was beautiful, and that consciousness lent her a quaint air of dignity and self-possession. An unwonted excitement which she could not account for caused her eyes to shine like stars through the slits of her mask. De Landas could only gaze in rapt wonderment at the vision of radiant youth and loveliness which stood before him in the person of Jacqueline de Broyart.

'You are more adorable to-night than ever, my beloved,' he contrived to whisper to her behind Monseigneur d'Inchy's back. 'And I am thankful that Monseigneur's orders have decreed that so much beauty shall remain hidden from unworthy eyes.'

Monseigneur, it seems, just caught these last few words, but mistook their exact meaning. 'All the ladies, my dear de Landas,' he said somewhat tartly, 'who belong to our circle will appear masked at all future public functions until I myself do rescind this order.'

'I was not complaining, Messire,' retorted de Landas dryly. 'On the contrary, I, as a devoted friend, have reason to rejoice at the order, seeing that several strangers will be at your banquet this night, and it were certainly not seemly for ladies of exalted rank to appear unmasked before them.'

He paused awhile, noting with pleasure that his bold glance had brought a glow to Jacqueline's delicate throat and chin. Then he murmured softly:

''Tis only when the strangers have departed that we, who have the privilege of intimacy, can call on the ladies to unmask.'

'Even you, my dear de Landas,' broke in d'Inchy curtly, 'must be content to wait until I decide to grant you special favours. Shall we go below, Madame?' he added, turning to Jacqueline. 'The banquet is spread for nine o'clock.'

Jacqueline, who had scarce uttered a word since the gentlemen entered the room, appeared almost as if she were waking from a trance. Her eyes had a vague, expectant look in them which delighted de Landas, for his vanity at once interpreted that look as one caused by his presence and his own fascination. But now that she encountered her guardian's cold, quizzical glance, the young girl pulled herself together, laughed lightly and said with a careless shrug of her pretty shoulders:

'Nay, then, Monseigneur; 'twill not be my fault if we are late, for I've been dressed this past half-hour, and oh!' she added with a mock sigh of weariness, 'Ye gods! How bored I have been, seeing that I detest all these modish Parisian clothes almost as much as I do a mask, and have chafed bitterly at having to don them.'

'You would not have been bored, Madame,' riposted de Landas with elaborate gallantry, 'had you but glanced once or twice into your mirror, for then you would have been regaled with a sight which, despite the cruel mask, will set every man's heart beating with joy to-night!'

She received his formal compliment more carelessly than was her wont, and he, quick to note every shade of indifference or warmth in her demeanour, frowned with vexation, felt a curious, gnawing pang of jealousy assail him. Jacqueline was so young, so adulated, so very, very beautiful! This was not the first time of late that he had asked himself whether he could hope to enchain her lasting affection, as he had done her girlish fancy ... and had found no satisfactory answer to the bitterly searching question. But she, equally quick to note his moods, quite a little in awe of his outbursts of jealousy, which she had learned to dread, threw him a glance which soon turned his moodiness into wild exultation. After which, Jacqueline turned to Nicolle, who was standing by, gazing on her young mistress in rapt adoration.

'Give me my fan and gloves, dear Colle,' she said.

And when Colle had given her these things, she put on her gloves and, holding her fan in one hand and the edge of her satin skirt with the other, she made a low curtsey before her guardian, looking shy and demure in every line of her young figure, even though the mask hid the expression of her face.

'Does my appearance,' she asked, 'meet with Monseigneur's approval?'

The answer was so obvious that M. d'Inchy—who was somewhat nervy and irritable this evening—said nothing but a sharp, 'Come, Jacqueline!' Whereupon she placed her hand upon his left arm, and without glancing again in her lover's direction, she walked sedately across the room.

III

The dining hall on the floor below was brilliantly lighted for the occasion. At one end of it three tables had been laid for eighty-two guests; they were spread with fine linen and laden with silver dishes and cut glass.

In the centre of the room the company was already assembled: gentlemen and ladies whom Monseigneur, governor of Cambray and the Cambrésis, desired to honour and to entertain. They had entered the room in accordance with their rank, those of humble degree first— one or two of the more important burghers of the town and their wives, members of the municipal council and mayors of the various guilds. The gentlemen of quality followed next, for it was necessary, in accordance with usage, that persons of lower rank should be present, in order to receive those who stood above them in station.

It would be a laborious task to enumerate all the personages of exalted rank who filed into the stately hall, one after another, in a veritably brilliant and endless procession. The Magistrate—elected by the Governor—was there as a matter of course, so was the Provost of the City, and one or two of the Sheriffs. Naturally, the absence of the Archbishop and of the higher clergy detracted somewhat from the magnificence of the pageant, but Monseigneur d'Inchy had taken possession of the city, the province and the Palace, and the Archbishop was now an exile in his own diocese. On the other hand, the Peers and Seigneurs of the Province were well represented: we know that Monseigneur de Prémont was there, as well as Monseigneur d'Audencourt and Monseigneur d'Esne and many other wealthy and distinguished gentlemen and their ladies.

Most of the ladies wore masks, as did many of the men. This mode had lately become very general in Paris, and the larger provincial towns, who desired to be in the fashion, were never slow in adopting those which hailed from the French capital. The custom had its origin in the inordinate vanity of the time—vanity amounting to a vice—and which hath never been equalled in any other epoch of history. Women and men too were so vain of their complexions and spent so much upon its care, used so many cosmetics, pastes and other beautifiers, that, having accomplished a veritable work of art upon their faces, they were loth to expose it to the inclemencies of the weather or the fumes of tallow candles and steaming food. Hence the masks at first, especially out of doors and during meals. Afterwards, they became an attribute of good society. Ladies of rank and fashion wore them when strangers were present or when at a ball they did not desire to dance. To remove a mask at the end of a meal or before a dance was a sign of familiarity or of gracious condescension: to wear one became a sign of exalted rank, of high connexions and of aloofness from the commoner herd of mankind. Whereupon those of humbler degree promptly followed suit.

IV

When M. le Baron d'Inchy entered the dining hall, having Madame Jacqueline de Broyart on his arm and followed by M. le Marquis de Landas, the whole company was assembled in order to greet the host.

Jacqueline's entry was hailed with an audible murmur of admiration and a noisy frou-frou of silks and satins, as the men bowed to the ground and the ladies' skirts swept the matting of the floor. The murmur of admiration increased in boldness as the young girl went round the company in order to welcome her friends.

And, indeed, Jacqueline de Broyart fully deserved that admiration. As you know, Messire Rembrandt painted her a year or so later in the very dress in which she appeared this night—a dress all of shimmering white satin and pearls, save for the peep of delicate green and silver afforded by the under-dress, and the dark crimson of her velvet shoes and silk stockings. The steel corset encased her young figure like a breastplate, coming to a deep point well below the natural waist, whilst round her hips the huge monstrosity of the farthingale hid effectually all the natural grace of her movements. In Rembrandt's picture we see the dainty face, round and fresh as a flower, with the nose slightly tip-tilted, the short upper lip and full, curved mouth; we also see the eyes, large and blue, beneath the straight brow—eyes which had nothing of the usually vapid expression of those that are blue—eyes which, even in the picture, seem to dance with merriment and with joy, and to which the tiny brown mole, artfully placed by nature upon the left cheek-bone, lent an additional air of roguishness and of youth.

To-night, her girlish figure was distorted by hoops of steel, but even these abominations of fashion could not mar the charm of her personality. Her figure looked like an unwieldy bell, but above the corset her shoulders and her young breasts shone like ivory set in a frame of delicate lace; her blue eyes sparkled with unwonted excitement, and beneath the flickering light of innumerable wax candles her hair had gleams of coppery gold.

But, above all, there was in Jacqueline de Broyart the subtle and evanescent charm of extreme youth and that delicious quality of innocence and of dependence which makes such an irresistible appeal to the impressionable hearts of men. Just now, she was feeling peculiarly happy and exhilarated, and, childlike, being happy herself she was prodigal of smiles: the small element of romance which had so unaccountably entered into her life with the advent of the mysterious singer had somehow made the whole world seem gay and bright in a way which de Landas' passionate and exacting love had never succeeded in doing. It had dissipated the pall of boredom and ceremonious monotony which was as foreign to Jacqueline's buoyant nature as was the corselet to her lissom figure. The light of mischief and frolic danced in her eyes, even though at times, for a moment or two, de Landas, who observed her with the keenness and persistence of a jealous lover, would detect in her manner a certain softness and languor which made her appear more alluring, more tantalizing perhaps, then she had ever been.

As she entered the room, she gave a quick and comprehensive glance on the assembled company.

'Tell me, Monseigneur,' she whispered in her guardian's ear, 'has the stranger arrived?'

'The stranger?' retorted d'Inchy. 'What stranger?'

'Pardi! Monsieur le Prince de Froidmont,' she said. 'Who else?'

'Oh!' replied d'Inchy with well-assumed indifference, 'the Prince de Froidmont has certainly arrived before now. He is not a person of great consequence. Why should you be interested in him, my dear Jacqueline?'

To this Jacqueline made no answer, looked down her nose very demurely, so that only her blue-veined lids could be seen through the slits of her mask. She drew up her slim figure to its full height, looked tall and graceful, too, despite that hideous farthingale. Friends crowded round her and round Monseigneur the governor, and she was kept busy acknowledging many greetings and much fulsome flattery. M. le Marquis de Landas never swerved from her side. He, too, wore a mask, but his was a short one which left the mouth and chin free, and all the while that other men—young ones especially—almost fought for a look or a smile from the beautiful heiress, his slender hand was perpetually stroking and tugging at his moustache—a sure sign that his nerves were somewhat on edge.

V

Monseigneur d'Inchy left his ward for a moment or two in the midst of all her friends and admirers and drew Monseigneur de Lalain into a secluded portion of the room.

'Well!' he began curtly, as soon as he felt assured that there were no eavesdroppers nigh. 'He is here.'

'Yes!' said de Lalain, also sinking his voice to a whisper. 'He came early, as one who is of no account, and at once mixed with the throng.'

'You were here when he arrived?'

'No. But I came soon after.'

'Was there much curiosity about him?'

'Naturally,' replied de Lalain. 'Our good bourgeois of Cambray do not often have the chance of gossiping over so mysterious a personality.'

'But did they receive him well?'

De Lalain shrugged his shoulders and, by way of reply, pointed to the further end of the room, where a tall figure, richly though very sombrely dressed and wearing a mask of black satin, stood out in splendid isolation from the rest of the crowd.

Gilles, from where he stood, caught de Lalain's gesture and d'Inchy's scrutinizing look. He replied to both by a scarce perceptible obeisance. His keen eyes under the shield of the mask had already swept with a searching glance over the entire company. Strangely enough, though the success of his present adventure was bound up in a woman, it was the men's faces that he scanned most eagerly at first. A goodly number of them wore masks like himself, but when he drew himself up for a moment to his full height with a movement that was almost a challenge, he felt quite sure in his own mind that he would at once detect—by that subtle instinct of self-preservation which is the attribute of every gambler—if danger of recognition lurked anywhere about.

He himself had never been to Cambray, it is true, and he was a knight of such humble degree that it was not very likely that, among this assembly of Flemish notabilities, some one should just happen to know him intimately enough to denounce him as the adventurer that he really was. Still, the danger did exist—enough of it, at any rate, to add zest to the present situation. Light-hearted and careless as always, Gilles shrugged his broad shoulders and turned his attention to the ladies.

Here, though there also was suspicion, there was undoubtedly keen interest. Over the top of Monseigneur d'Inchy's head Gilles could see at the end of the room the group of ladies, gay in their brilliantly-coloured satin dresses and their flashing jewels, like a swarm of butterflies, and standing as closely together as their unwieldy hoops would allow. He felt that at least a score pairs of eyes were fixed upon him through the narrow slits of satin masks, and that murmured comments upon him and his appearance, conjectures as to his identity and his rank, flew from many a pair of lovely lips.

Right in the very centre of that group was a woman all dressed in white, with just a narrow peep of pale green showing down her skirt, which gave to her person the appearance of a white lily on its stem. Something immature about the shoulders and the smooth, round neck—something shy yet dignified about the poise of the head, suggested youth not yet fully conscious of its beauty and its power, while the richness of her attire and of her jewels proclaimed both wealth and high position. Murmurs and remarks among the gentlemen around him soon made it clear to Gilles that this was the lady whom he had been sent to woo. Agreeably thrilled by the delicate curves of her throat and breast, he thought that he might spend some very pleasant hours in sentimental dalliance with so fair a maid.

'We must have that mask from off your face, madonna,' he said to himself; 'and not later than this night! In affairs of the heart, even by proxy, one does not like to venture in the dark.'

So intent was he on his own meditations that he failed to note the approach of a young cavalier, dressed in rich garments of sober black, who suddenly addressed him in a slightly ironical tone, which however appeared intended to be friendly.

'You seem to be a stranger here, Messire,' the young cavalier said lightly. 'Can I be of any service?'

He spoke French very fluently but with a slight guttural accent, which betrayed Spanish blood and which for some unexplainable reason grated unpleasantly on Gilles de Crohin's ear.

'Oh, Messire!' replied the latter quietly, 'I pray you do not waste your time on me. I am a stranger, it is true; but as such, the brilliant picture before me is full of interest.'

'You are visiting Cambray for the first time?' asked the other, still with an obvious effort at amiability.

'For the first time—yes, Messire.'

'In search of fortune?'

'As we all are, methinks.'

'Cambray is scarce the place to find it.'

'Is that your experience of it, Messire?'

De Landas frowned and a sharp retort obviously hovered on his lips. He appeared morose and captious about something; probably the fact that Jacqueline had evinced an extraordinary interest in the masked stranger had acted as an irritant on his nerves.

But already Gilles appeared to have completely forgotten his presence, had only listened with half an ear to the Spaniard's laboured amenities. For the nonce he was vaguely conscious that through the slits of her mask, the lily-like maid kept her eyes fixed very intently upon him.

'Monseigneur the governor,' de Landas was saying just then, 'desires your presence, Messire. He wishes you to pay your respects to the noble Dame Jacqueline de Broyart.'

The name acted like magic on Gilles' temper. He pulled himself together and with a cool 'At your service, Messire!' he followed de Landas across the room.

VI

The presentation had been made. It was very formal and very distant; it even seemed to Gilles as if Jacqueline had somewhat ostentatiously turned away from him as soon as he had gone through the ceremonious bowings and kissing of hand which convention demanded. For a moment or two after that, M. d'Inchy kept him in close converse, whilst de Landas, evidently reassured by Jacqueline's indifference toward the stranger, appeared much more amiable and serene. But the young Spaniard's mind was apparently still disturbed. He studied the other man with an intentness which, in those days of fiery and quarrelsome tempers, might almost have been construed into an insult. He appeared to chafe under the man's cool confidence in himself and M. d'Inchy's obvious deference towards one who outwardly was of no account.

Gilles took no further notice of him; but, as he would have told you himself, he felt an atmosphere of hostility around him, which appeared to find its origin in de Landas' attitude. D'Inchy, aided by de Lalain, did his best to dissipate that atmosphere, but evidently he, too, felt oppressed and nervy. Unversed in the art of duplicity, he was making almost ludicrous efforts to appear at his ease and to hide his profound respect for a prince of the House of France under a cloak of casual friendliness—an elephantine effort which did not deceive de Landas.

Gilles alone appeared unconscious of embarrassment. His mind was not properly enchained either to M. d'Inchy's difficulties or to the young Spaniard's growing enmity. His thoughts were for ever breaking bounds, turning at every moment to the girlish figure in the unwieldy hoops and the white satin gown, whose merry laugh was like the twittering of robins in the early days of spring. Even at this moment his attention had been arrested by a little episode which occurred at the end of the room, where she was standing. A little, sudden cry of pain rang out from beneath one of the satin masks. Some one had evidently been hurt—a prick from a pin, perhaps, or a toe trodden on. Anyhow, there was the cry, and Messire Gilles would have thought nothing more of it only that the next moment a girlish voice reached his ear—a voice quite tearful and trembling with compassion.

'Think you it will heal?' the voice said tenderly.

And then it appeared to Gilles as if something in his brain had suddenly been aroused, as if memory—a vague, dreamy memory— had become quickened and like some intangible sprite had taken a huge leap backwards into some dim and remote past which the brain itself was still unable to reach or to seize upon. It was not a recollection, nor yet a definite thought; but for one moment Gilles remained absolutely still and was conscious of a curious, swift beating of his heart, and a still more strange, choking sensation in his throat.

The whole episode had occurred within the brief compass of half a dozen heart-beats, and Gilles, when he looked once more on Monseigneur d'Inchy, still saw that same look of perplexity upon the Fleming's face, whilst from the group of ladies in the distant part of the room there came only the same confused murmur of voices of awhile ago.

So Gilles sighed, thinking that his excited fancy had been playing him an elusive trick.

And the next moment the loud clanging of a bronze bell proclaimed to the assembled guests that the banquet was ready to be served.

CHAPTER X.
HOW THE QUARREL BEGAN

I

Monsieur le Baron D'Inchy took his seat at the head of the principal table; beside him sat his ward, Madame Jacqueline de Broyart, who had M. le Comte de Lalain on her left. Gilles sat some little way down one of the side tables. Outwardly, he was a person of no importance—a stranger, travelling incognito and enjoying for the time being the hospitality of Monseigneur the governor. Maître Jehan, watchful and silent, stood behind his master's chair. The tables had been lavishly and sumptuously laden with good things: a perpetual stream of butlers, pages and varlets had walked in and out of the hall, bringing in dish after dish and placing them upon the boards.

The company sat down amidst much laughter and facetious conversation, and, we take it, every intention of enjoying their host's good cheer. And, of a truth, it was a brilliant assembly, a veritable kaleidoscope of colours, an almost dazzling sparkle of jewels. The dark doublets worn by the men acted as foils to the vivid satins worn by the ladies. The host and his principal guests had high-backed chairs to sit on, but every one else sat on low stools, set very far apart so as to give plenty of room for the display of the ladies' dresses and their monstrous farthingales. Indeed, the men almost disappeared between the billows of satin-covered hoops and the huge lace collars, the points of which would tickle their nose or scratch their ear or even get into their eye.

While the serving-men and wenches went the round of the tables with serviettes over their shoulders and silver ewers and basins in their hands, offering to the guests tepid water perfumed with orange flower, with myrtle, lavender and rosemary, for washing their hands, Gilles de Crohin was watching Jacqueline de Broyart. From where he sat, he could see her dainty head above a forest of silver dish-covers. She had not removed her mask; none of the ladies would do that till, mayhap, after the banquet was over, when conviviality and good cheer would breed closer intimacy. To Gilles' senses, rendered supersensitive by his strangely adventurous position, it seemed as if that piece of black satin, through which he could only perceive from time to time the flash of glowing eyes, rendered Jacqueline's personality both mysterious and desirable. He was conscious of an acute tingling of all his nerves; his own mask felt as if it were weighted with lead; the fumes of rich soups and sauces, mingled with those of wine and heady Flemish ale, appeared to be addling his brain. He felt as if he were in a dream—a dream such as he had never experienced before save once, when, sick, footsore and grievously wounded, he had gone on a brief excursion to Paradise.

Gilles did not know, could not explain it satisfactorily to himself, why the remembrance of a far-off, half-forgotten dream-voice came, with sweet persistency, between him and reality, a voice tender and compassionate, even whilst a pair of eyes, blue as the firmament on an April morning, seemed to be gazing on him through the slits in the mask.

II

It would have been difficult for any stranger who happened to have landed in Cambray, unacquainted with the political circumstances of its province, to have realized, at sight of Monsieur le gouverneur's table, that the Spanish armies were even then ravaging the Cambrésis, and that provisions in the city were becoming scarce owing to the difficulties which market-gardeners and farmers had of bringing in their produce. Gilles, who had been in the service of a Royal prince of France and who had oft risen from the latter's table with his stomach only half filled, was left to marvel at the prodigality and the sumptuousness of the repast. Indeed, one of the most interesting documents preserved until recently in the archives of the city of Cambray, is the account of this banquet which M. le Baron d'Inchy, governor of the Cambrésis, gave ostensibly in honour of the notabilities of the province, but which, I doubt not, was really in honour of *Monsieur* Duc d'Anjou et d'Alençon, brother of the King of France, who we know was present on the occasion, under a well-preserved incognito.

And the menu! Ye gods who preside over the arts of gastronomy, what a menu! Eighty-two persons sat down to it, and of a truth their appetite and their digestion must have been of the staunchest, else they could never have grappled successfully with half the contents of the dishes which were set before them. Three separate services, an' it please you! and each service consisting of at least forty different dishes all placed upon the three tables at once, with the covers on; then, at a given signal, the covers removed, and the guests ready to help themselves as they felt inclined, using their knives for the purpose, or else those curiously shaped pronged tools which Monseigneur d'Inchy had lately imported out of England, so the town gossips said.

Ye gods, the menu! For the first service there were no fewer than eight centre dishes, on each an *oille*—that most esteemed feat of gastronomic art, in which several succulent meats, ducks, partridges, pigeons, quails, capons, all had their part and swam in a rich sauce flavoured with sundry aromatic substances, pepper and muscat, thyme, ginger, basil and many sweet herbs. Oh, the *oille*, properly cooked, was in itself a feast! But, grouped around these noble dishes were tureens of partridges, stewed with cabbage; tureens of fillets of duckling; several pigeon pies and capons in galantine; fillets of beef with cucumbers and fricandeaus of lard; and such like insignificant side dishes as quails in casserole and chickens baked under hot cinders—excellent I believe!

After the platters and dishes had become empty, the first service was removed, clean cloths spread upon the tables—for by this time the first ones had become well spattered with grease—and perfumed water once more handed round for the washing of hands. Knives were washed too, as well as the forks—the few of them that were used. Then came the second service. Breasts of veal this time, larded and braised, formed the centre dishes and the minor adjuncts were fowls garnished with spring chickens and hard-boiled eggs, capons, leverets, and pheasants garnished with quails: there were sixteen different kinds of salads and an equal number of different sauces.

Again the service was removed and clean cloths laid for the third service. A kind of dessert—little things to pick at, for those who had not been satisfied. Such little things as boars' heads—twelve of them—

which must have looked magnificent towering along the centre of the table; omelettes à la Noailles—the recipe of which, given in a cookery book which was printed in the beginning of the sixteenth century, does suggest something very succulent—dishes of baked custards, fritters of peaches, stewed truffles, artichokes and green peas, and even lobsters, sweetbreads and tongues!

Such abundance is almost unbelievable, and where all the delicacies came from I, for one, do not pretend to say. They were there, so much we know, and eighty-two ladies and gentlemen must have consumed them all. No wonder that, after the first few moments of formal ceremonies—of bowings and scrapings and polite speeches— tongues quickly became loosened and moods became hilarious; wine too and heady Flemish ales were copiously drunk—not a little of both was spilled over the fine linen cloths and the rich dresses of the ladies. But these little accidents were not much thought of these days; fastidiousness at meals had not yet come to be regarded as a sign of good breeding, and a high-born gentleman was not thought any the worse of for vulgar and riotous gorging.

A very little while ago, M. d'Inchy himself—a man of vast wealth and great importance—would have been quite content to help himself with his fingers out of his well-filled platters and to see his guests around his board doing the same. But ever since the alliance with France had been discussed by his Council, he had desired to bring French manners and customs, French fashions in dress, French modes of deportment, into this remote Belgian province. Indeed, he was even now warmly congratulating himself that he had quite recently imported from England for his own use some of those pronged tools which served to convey food to the mouth in a manner which still appeared strange to some of his guests. The civic dignitaries of Cambray and more than one of the Flemish nobles assembled here this night looked with grave puzzlement, even with disapproval, at those awkward tools which had so ostentatiously, they thought, been placed beside their platter: French innovations, some of them murmured contemptuously, of which they certainly did not approve; whereupon they scrambled unabashed with their fingers in the dishes for their favourite morsels.

III

Jacqueline, silent at first, began after awhile to chatter merrily. Monsieur de Landas, who sat opposite to her, having lately come from Paris, she begged earnestly for all the latest gossip from the Court. Madame la Reyne de Navarre? What was she like? Jacqueline had heard such marvels of her grace and of her intellect. And the Duc d'Anjou? Was he as handsome as women averred? And was he — was he really such a rogue as irate husbands and brothers would have every one believe? Then she wanted to know about the fashions. Were hoops really growing in size or had a revulsion of feeling set in against them, and what was the latest mode for dressing the hair? Was it true that the new green dye specially invented by *Monsieur* Duc d'Anjou was so unhealthy to the wearer that many mysterious deaths had already followed its introduction?

And all the while that she talked she affected to eat heartily; but Gilles, who was watching her, saw that she scarce touched a morsel, only played with her fork, the use of which was evidently still unfamiliar to her. From time to time she seemed to pause in her chatter in order to gaze across the table in the direction where he sat silent and absorbed, somewhat isolated, as if shunned by the rest of the company; and whenever she did so it seemed to him as if her eyes called to him through the slits of that mysterious mask. After awhile, that call seemed so insistent that Gilles had the greatest difficulty in the world to force himself to sit still. He wanted to jump up and to go and sit near her, force her to remove that forbidding mask and let him see just what kind of a face was concealed behind it.

By now, you see, his imagination had once more veered right round and he had quite made up his mind that she was fair to look upon. The length of the table which separated him from her obsessed his mood, till he felt a perfect fever of desire and impotence coursing through his veins. And with this tingling of the nerves came a sense of jealousy. He could not see the man with whom Jacqueline was conversing so animatedly, had only given passing attention to Monsieur de Landas when the latter had spoken with him. But gossip had already reached his indifferent ear that M. le Marquis de Landas had — at any rate at one time — been an approved suitor for the hand of the rich heiress, whereupon Messire Gilles became satisfied within himself that that unpleasant feeling of dislike, which he was feeling toward the other man, was solely on account of *Monsieur* Duc d'Anjou, his master, over whose interests vis-à-vis that same heiress, he—Gilles—was set here to watch.

Still Jacqueline chattered away, and quite ten minutes had gone by since she had cast a glance in Gilles' direction. So he felt curious as well as angered and leaned forward in order to get a better view of Monsieur de Landas. He let his eyes travel along the line of faces which he saw for the most part only in profile: men and women, some old, some young, some grave and sober, others frivolous, rowdy, not a little vulgar, thought the fastidious Sire de Froidmont, who had Valois blood in his veins and had seen a good deal of the super-civilization of Paris. All of them appeared intent on devouring huge slabs of meat, and licking their fingers for the last drops of sauce. All, that is, except one—the man with whom Jacqueline was conversing so gaily; a young man, with masses of wavy black hair, a blue chin and an oval face, which he kept resolutely turned toward Madame Jacqueline.

'The favoured lover,' mused Gilles. 'The possibly dangerous enemy of *Monsieur* Duc d'Anjou, and spoiler of Madame la Reyne's best laid schemes.'

The young man ate very little, but he drank copiously. When he was not looking at Jacqueline he appeared to be staring moodily before him and bit furiously at his nails.

'Attention, friend Gilles!' Messire said to himself. 'There's the rock against which you may well bruise your head presently if you are not careful. Madame Jacqueline may, for aught I know, have a fancy for that amorous, olive-complexioned swain, who, as soon as I begin to take the centre of the stage—as take it I must—will become, a fierce and cunning enemy. I shall have to see to it that Madame's fancy for him turns to indifference. After that, beware, friend Gilles! Satan hath no finer henchman than a rejected lover.'

IV

As the banquet drew to its close there was little gravity or decorum left around the festive board. Even the oldest and the gravest had yielded to the delights of untrammelled gorging. The food was excellent, the wines beyond praise; every one knew every one else; they were all friends, companions together, allied by political or business interests — in many cases by blood. The veneer of civilization as shown by sober manners had not yet come to be thought more necessary than good cheer and conviviality.

The heat in the room had become oppressive. The smoke from innumerable wax candles made a blue haze overhead, a veil of mist which hid the high, vaulted ceiling and caused the lights to flicker dimly. The men had cast aside their mantles and loosened their sword-belts; the ladies used their plumed fans vigorously. There was little left on the table even of the elaborate dishes pertaining to the third service: platters and silver épergnes were for the most part empty; only now and again some one would lean over and desultorily pick at a piece of lobster or a truffle — an excuse, mayhap, for washing down the highly-spiced food with another bumper of wine.

Conversation, loud jests — some of them both ribald and coarse — flew over and across the tables, loud calls were made to friends who sat far away. The time had come for casting off the last shred of ceremonial decorum which stood in the way of unbridled hilarity. The ladies, at the instance of their respective cavaliers, had cast aside their masks one by one, and their comely faces appeared, crimson and steaming even beneath the thick layers of cosmetics.

Jacqueline was one of the few who remained quite calm and cool. She plied her fan with lazy grace and kept on her mask — despite the earnest, whispered entreaties of M. de Landas and of a group of young gallants who had gathered round her.

Gilles had already made up his mind to go. He felt stifled under his mask and the heat of the room, the heady fumes of wine and food rendered him stupid and dizzy. There appeared to be no chance of his being able to approach Jacqueline again, short of provoking a quarrel with her Spanish watch-dog, which Gilles would have thought impolitic to do. On the whole, he thought that it would be best to retire for the nonce from the scene. His day had not been altogether unsuccessful: it was the fifth since his arrival in Cambray, and surely Madame la Reyne de Navarre would by now be on the track of her truant brother. Gilles' probation could not last many days longer, and in the meanwhile he had definitely made up his mind that *Monsieur's* future bride was adorable, and that she already evinced a more than passing interest in the masked stranger who had serenaded her so boldly from beneath her casement-window.

Not a bad beginning, thought Messire, as he gave a wink to Jehan to follow him and rose from his seat. The moment which he chose appeared a favourable one: the etiquette of the supper table was considerably relaxed; those of Monseigneur's guests who wished to do so had taken to moving about from place to place, according as they desired to speak with friends; whilst some who wished to hold private converse together, or who were on the point of leaving, actually walked out of the room.

This was Gilles' opportunity. Just then Monseigneur d'Inchy rose also. Monsieur le Prince d'Eremberghe and his lady were about to take their leave. They were personages of vast importance and the host desired to do them special honour. Accompanied by de Lalain, he escorted his departing guests to the door, and thence, having the Princess on his arm, he went out into the antechamber, followed by de Lalain and the Prince. He had not noticed Gilles, and the latter stood for a moment or two in the centre of the room, alone with Jehan, and momentarily undecided. He surveyed the group at the head of the table with a critical frown: the young gallants—there were six of them—were crowding round Madame, some leaning across the table, others pressing close to her chair. She may have been amused at the platitudes wherewith they were regaling her; she may have enjoyed their conversation and M. de Landas' ardent glances—she may have done all that, I say, and thought no more of the man standing there alone in the middle of the room than if he had been one of her lacqueys. But, as chance would have it—or was it indeed Gilles' compelling look which drew her own?—certain it is that she turned her head in his direction and that he *felt* that she was regarding him quizzically, searchingly, through the eye-slits of her mask.

Quickly he gave a few whispered instructions to his faithful Jehan; then he calmly strode across the room.

Monseigneur the governor was still absent: his seat beside Madame Jacqueline was empty. Gilles walked up the length of the table—no one heeded him—and before any one—least of all M. de Landas—was aware of his intention, sat down quite coolly on M. d'Inchy's vacant chair, immediately next to Jacqueline.

V

If you can imagine a cannon ball exploding in the very centre of that festive board, you will have some dim idea of the effect produced upon M. d'Inchy's guests by this manoeuvre. Every head was at once turned in that direction, for M. de Landas and his friends had uttered an exclamation that was almost ludicrous in its bewildered wrath.

The ladies round the supper tables could not do more than utter shrill little screams of disapproval, and many of the men were, alas! too deep in their cups to do aught save mutter bibulous imprecations against the malapert. A few rose and ran to give the weight of their moral and social support to de Landas, who had already jumped to his feet and appeared ready to make of this incident a quarrel—and that quarrel, his own. Of a truth, it was de Landas who had been most grievously insulted. The vacant chair beside Madame Jacqueline could only be taken by an intimate friend such as he. Already his hand was on his sword-hilt; his eyes, somewhat dimmed by the effect of copious libations, were rolling with unbridled fury; beneath his mask a hot flush had risen to his forehead, whilst below the curly masses of his dark hair his ears appeared white and shiny like wax. Unfortunately, he, like several other gentlemen present here this night, had drunk a vast quantity of Burgundy and Rhenish wine, not to mention several bumpers of excellent Flemish ale, and when choler came to mingle with the fumes of so much heady liquor, M. de Landas on rising, turned very giddy and had to steady himself for a moment or two against the table.

Just at that moment a veritable pandemonium reigned in the stately banqueting hall.

'The insolence!' said some of the ladies to the accompaniment of piercing little shrieks.

'A stranger!'

'A prince from Nowhere at all!'

'Bah! A Prince!'

'A mere fortune hunter!'

'Probably a Spanish spy!'

'Only a Spaniard would have such insolence!'

'Such impudence passes belief!'

The men—those who could speak coherently—sent encouraging calls to de Landas:

'Seize him by the collar, M. le Marquis!'

'Throw him out!'

'Have him kicked out by the varlets!'

Enough noise, in fact, to break the drum of a sensitive ear. But Gilles appeared superbly unconscious of the storm which was brewing round him. He had his back to M. de Landas, leaned an elbow on the table and faced Madame Jacqueline as coolly as if he had been invited by every one here to pay her his respects.

Jacqueline, demure and silent, was smiling beneath her mask. To look at her, you would have sworn that she was stone-deaf and heard nothing of the tumult around her.

It soon raged furiously. M. de Landas had quickly recovered himself. His towering rage helped to dissipate the fumes of wine and ale which had somewhat addled his brain, and backed by all his friends he made preparation to throw the malapert to the tender mercies of M. d'Inchy's varlets, and as a preface to the more forcible proceeding, he turned in order to smite the impudent stranger in the face—turned, and found himself confronted by a short, square-shouldered man, with a round head and fists held clenched on a level with a singularly broad chest.

The man stood between Gilles and M. de Landas; he had the table on his right and the monumental mantelpiece on his left, and behind him was the tall carved oak back of the chair on which Gilles was sitting—all equally strong barriers to the young Marquis' bellicose intentions.

'Out of the way, lout!' shouted de Landas furiously, and would have seized Maître Jehan by the collar but for the fact that it was a very difficult thing indeed to seize Maître Jehan by any portion of his squat person unless he chose to allow so unceremonious a proceeding, and just now he was standing guard between a number of enraged gentlemen and the back of his master's chair—a trying position, forsooth, for any man of Maître Jehan's prowess, for ... well! he would not have dared to lay hands on such a great gentleman as was M. le Marquis; but, against that, M. le Marquis had no chance of laying hands on Maître Jehan either.

VI

And all the while, Gilles sat so near to Jacqueline that his knees touched the hoops of her skirt. Instinctively she drew her own chair back with that same little demure air which was apparent in every one of her movements, even though her face was concealed by the mask.

'An' you move an inch further, fair one,' he said boldly, 'I vow that I shall be ready to commit a crime.'

'You are committing one now, Messire,' retorted Jacqueline. 'A crime against decorum, by sitting in my guardian's place.'

'Then I'll no longer sit—I'll kneel at your feet,' he riposted, and made a movement as if to push away his chair.

'Heaven forbid!' she exclaimed lightly. 'M. de Landas would kill you!'

'I am not so easily killed,' he rejoined. 'And M. de Landas is, for the moment, engaged with my man.'

'Who is getting sorely pressed, Messire!' cried Jacqueline with sudden, eager excitement. 'Will you not go to his aid?'

She had caught sight of Jehan, standing with his back to his master's chair, fists levelled, shoulders squared, defying not only M. de Landas but a crowd of other gentlemen, who had rushed forward to support their friend.

'Not before you have promised to unmask, fair one,' Gilles said calmly.

'I?' she exclaimed, now really staggered by his cool impudence. 'You are dreaming, Messire!'

'I think I am, Madame,' he replied; 'therefore I must have your promise ere I wake.'

'You are presumptuous!'

'Just now you said that I was dreaming. A man who dreams is a man asleep—and a man asleep is too helpless to be presumptuous.'

'That is sophistry, Messire,' she retorted. 'And while you parley thus idly, your man is in serious danger through the wrath of these gentlemen.'

'My good Jehan's danger is not so pressing as mine. He hath my orders to hold these gentlemen at arm's length until I give the word, whilst Monseigneur d'Inchy may be back any moment before I wake up from my dream.'

'Oh!' she urged now with well-feigned alarm. 'But your poor man cannot stand long before these gentlemen, and you, Messire, will surely not allow him to receive all those knocks which are intended for you!'

'I have received many a score which were intended for him,' retorted Gilles with a laugh. 'Jehan and I have long ceased to reckon up accounts. Your promise, fair one,' he pleaded; 'ere Monseigneur return to place a spoke in my wheel!'

She felt now as if she were trapped, no longer combated his desire, but merely appeared anxious to gain time until her guardian came to release her from the strange, compelling power of this man, who was arrogating unto himself rights which could only be claimed by a friend or lover.

'Oh, mon Dieu!' she exclaimed agitatedly, half rising from her chair in her eagerness to catch sight of Jehan. 'He cannot long parry the attack——'

'Your promise, fair one,' he insisted quietly, 'to let me see your sweet face to-night! I swore it to myself just now, when you threw me a glance across the room, that I would look into your eyes untrammelled. Your promise!—or I vow that I'll do something desperate!'

'Heavens above!' she exclaimed, keeping her attention deliberately fixed on Maître Jehan. 'If he should strike one of these gentlemen— he—a mere servant!...'

'If he does,' riposted Gilles lightly, 'I will take up his quarrel, with this token tied to my sword-hilt.' And from the inner pocket of his doublet he drew a tiny, perfumed rag, held it in his hand and waved it with an ostentatious flourish for her to see.

She gave a quick, involuntary little cry of alarm: 'My handkerchief!'

'Undoubtedly, fair one!' he said coolly. 'It hath your initials and crown embroidered in the corner! Think you Messire de Landas' choler will cool at sight of it?'

Her forehead, her tiny ears, her neck and chin, everything that he could see of her dainty face, had become suffused with a warm blush.

'Messire!' she said firmly, 'I command you to give me back that handkerchief, which you stole unawares.'

'It was flung at me with a sheaf of lilies, which, alas! have withered. 'Tis my right hand which shall wither ere I part from the handkerchief.'

'My handkerchief!' she reiterated impatiently.

'Only with my life! But it shall lie for ever hidden against my heart if you will promise...'

'Messire, you are committing a base and unworthy act!'

'I know it,' he said with a smile. 'But I must have that promise.'

'Promise of what?' she asked breathlessly, driven into a corner by his obstinacy.

'To let me look straight into your eyes to-night,' he said, 'unfettered by that hideous mask.'

He leaned forward so that his face now was quite close to hers, and he could feel her quick breath against his cheek.

'No, no!' she said with a little gasp. 'My guardian—and—and M. de Landas——'

'Very well!' he said dryly, and began quietly winding the little rag around his sword-hilt.

'Messire!' she said in a peremptory tone, through which a note of appeal, if not of genuine alarm this time, could be distinctly perceived.

'Promise!' he reiterated relentlessly.

Just then she caught sight of de Landas, who, flushed with choler, was thrusting somewhat wildly at Maître Jehan. She thought that his eyes were constantly wandering in her direction and that he was vainly trying to get near her, past his sturdy opponent, who was guarding the approach to his master's chair with all the fierceness of a Cerberus. Somehow, at sight of de Landas thus fighting with almost savage violence, she lost her head for the moment. Of a truth, the matter of the handkerchief might lead to a very bitter quarrel between her lover and this stranger. A very bitter quarrel—and worse! De Landas was wont to lose all self-control when jealous rage had hold of him, was as quick with his dagger as with his rapier! And here was this tantalizing troubadour calmly preparing to flaunt upon his sword-hilt the handkerchief which bore her name and coronet. He looked up and caught the sparkle of her eyes.

'Promise!' he insisted quite coolly.

And she—very reluctantly—murmured: 'Very well; I promise!'

'To-night!' he insisted.

'No!—no!' she protested. 'Not to-night!'

'To-night!' he reiterated firmly, smiled at her too beneath his mask as if in triumph—Oh, the insolence of him!—and continued to toy with the compromising bit of white rag.

If only Monseigneur would return! There was nothing for it but to acquiesce. De Landas even then looked the very image of wild and unreasoning fury. Jacqueline shuddered and murmured a quick: 'Very well! To-night! I promise!'

Gilles gave an equally quick sigh of satisfaction.

'When?' he asked.

But before she could reply, there came a loud curse from Jehan. He had been seized round the legs by two varlets, even while he was engaged in warding off the blows which were aimed at his head by half a dozen gallants. It was when he came down with a dull thud upon his knees and felt that he could no longer stand between his master and these evil-intentioned gentlemen that he gave forth a prolonged and uproarious stutter:

'The d-d-d-d-d——'

Gilles jumped to his feet. In less than three completed seconds he was round by the side of Jehan, had kicked the two varlets out of the way and interposed his massive person between his faithful henchman and the seething group of bellicose gallants.

'Silence, chatterbox!' he said coolly to Jehan. 'These seigneurs are not here to listen to your perorations. Anything that must be said can be referred to me.'

He had one hand on the elegant hilt of his Spanish rapier; the other rested on the shoulder of Maître Jehan, who had struggled very quickly to his feet. His mocking glance, veiled by the black satin mask, swept coolly over de Landas and his friends.

'Insolent!' exclaimed one of the men.

'Unmask the spy!' cried out another.

'Leave the rogue to me!' quoth de Landas, who was getting beside himself with rage.

Already half a dozen swords were drawn. Every one who had been drunk before became sobered in the instant; those who had remained sober felt suddenly drunk with choler. Some of the ladies thought it best to scream or to feign a swoon, others made a rush for the door. No one dared to come nigh, for de Landas was a man who was not good to trifle with when his ire was aroused. But those who were not taking part in the quarrel were certainly not eyeing the stranger with any degree of benevolence, and Jacqueline felt more than she actually heard the adverse comments made upon this Prince de Froidmont—so he was styled, it appeared—who had come no one knew whence and who seemed to arrogate unto himself privileges which only pertained to favoured friends.

Thus a wide circle was formed at one end of the room, leaving at the other, in splendid isolation, the group which was made up of half a dozen young gallants standing in threatening attitudes in front of the masked stranger, who now had his henchman on one side of him and on the other the monumental mantelpiece, in which the fire had been allowed to die down.

'Out of the way, malapert!' cried de Landas savagely to Gilles, as he advanced towards him with sword clutched and eyes that glowed with a fierce flame of unbridled wrath. His desire was to reach Jacqueline, who stood a little way behind Gilles, near the table, watching in an attitude of tense excitement the progress of this quarrel, and with an eye on the door through which she hoped every moment to see her guardian reappear.

But, quick as lightning, Gilles had barred the way. He appeared highly amused and perfectly at his ease, laughed boldly in M. de Landas' heated face; but would not let him pass.

It was easy to perceive that he was enjoying this quarrel, loved to see the glint of those swords which threatened him even while they promised to vary the monotony of this sentimental adventure. He had not drawn his own. In France, fighting in the presence of ladies was thought highly unseemly. These Flemings were different, very uncouth, not a little brutal and abominably hot-headed. Well! the quarrel once begun would of a surety not end here and now, even though M. d'Inchy were to return and peremptorily order it to stop. There was something in M. de Landas' sullen and defiant attitude which delighted Gilles: and when half a dozen irate gentlemen shouted hoarsely, 'Out of the way!' he laughed and said:

'Impossible, Messeigneurs! 'Tis for you to retire. Our gracious hostess will grant me the favour of unmasking. An' I am much mistaken, she will not do the same for you.'

'Madame Jacqueline,' retorted de Landas hotly, 'will not unmask before the first jackanapes who dares to approach her unbidden.'

'Ah! but I am not unbidden,' riposted Gilles gaily. 'Have I not told you that Madame will deign to unmask ere I bid her good-night?'

'Insolent coxcomb!' shouted the other excitedly.

'A spy!' cried one of the others.

'Tear off his mask, de Landas! Let us see the colour of his skin!'

'An impudent rogue!' added a third.

'M. le Marquis de Landas,' here interposed Jacqueline peremptorily, 'you forget that M. le Prince de Froidmont is our guest.'

'Oh!' retorted de Landas with a sneer, 'if he is under the protection of the ladies...'

'Under no protection save that of my sword, Messire!' broke in Gilles carelessly. 'And that will be entirely at your service as soon as I have taken leave of our fair hostess.'

'Nay! that you shall not do!' riposted de Landas. 'Your impudent assertion of awhile ago has put you outside the pale. You shall not take your leave! 'Tis we who'll throw you out; unless you relieve us of your company now—at once!'

'Well said, de Landas!' came in an approving chorus from the irate group of de Landas' friends.

'We'll throw him out!' cried some of them. 'Leave him to us.'

'A spy!' came from others.

'Now, Messire—whoever you may be,' concluded de Landas with ironic emphasis, 'will you go willingly or shall my friends and I— —'

'For shame, Messire!' broke in Jacqueline loudly and firmly. 'You are six against one— —'

'So much the better!' riposted de Landas with a harsh laugh. 'At him, friends!'

'Madame,' said Gilles, turning to Jacqueline with perfect calm, 'your promise will remain for ever unredeemed if these gentlemen succeed in throwing me out of the room; for this, I vow, they cannot do while I am alive.'

'Jacqueline,' interposed de Landas impulsively, 'I forbid you to unmask before this man.'

He had guessed her purpose, for already her hand was raised towards her mask; and so enraged was he that she should thus yield to this stranger whom already he had come to hate, that he forgot himself, lost all self-control, and said just the one word which decided Jacqueline. At the word 'forbid,' she drew herself up to her full height and faced her lover with calm and hauteur.

'There is nothing,' she said coolly, 'that any one here has the right to command or forbid.' Then she turned to Gilles: 'I'll bid you good-night now, Messire, and can but offer to you—a stranger—my humble apologies in mine and my guardian's name for the uncouth behaviour of my countrymen.'

'Jacqueline!' exclaimed de Landas with a hoarse cry of rage.

But even before this final protest had reached her ear, she had extended one hand to Gilles and with the other slowly detached the mask from her face. He had stooped very low in order to kiss her finger-tips; when he straightened out his tall figure once more he was face to face with her.

He never spoke a word or made a sign. He did not look into her eyes at first, though these were as blue as the skies in Southern France; he did not gaze at the delicate mouth with the deep corners and the roguish smile, or at the chiselled, slightly tip-tilted nose with the sensitive nostrils that were quivering with excitement. No! all that Messire Gilles gazed on at the moment was a tiny brown mole which nestled tantalizingly on the velvety cheek, just below the left eye. And for that moment he forgot where he was, forgot the storm of enmity which was raging around him, the unworthy rôle which he had set out to play for the deception of a confiding girl. He lost count of time and of space and found himself once more lying on cool, sweet-smelling straw, with a broken wrist and an aching head, and with a vision as of an angel in white bending over his fevered brow and murmuring in tones of exquisite compassion, 'Think you it will heal?'

And as he gazed on that little mole, that veritable kissing-trap which had tantalized him long ago, his lips murmured vaguely:

'My dream!'

VII

Of course the little interlude had all occurred within a very few seconds: the kiss upon the soft, warm hand, the look upon that roguish face, the swift and sudden rush of memory—it had all happened whilst poor M. de Landas was recovering from the shock of Jacqueline's cold rebuke. Her stern taunt had come down on him like a hammer-blow upon the head; he felt dazed for a moment; speechless, too, with a white rage which was too great at first for words. But that kind of speechless fierceness seldom lasts more than a few seconds. Even as Gilles de Crohin was quietly collecting his scattered senses and Jacqueline, vaguely puzzled, was readjusting her mask in order to be able to gaze on him unobserved, marvelling why he should have murmured 'My dream!' and looked so strangely at her, de Landas had recovered some measure of self-control. The anger which he felt against the stranger was no longer impetuous and ebullient; it had become cold and calculating, doubly dangerous and more certain to abide.

He put up his sword, motioned to his friends to do likewise—which they did, murmuring protestations. They were itching to get at the stranger who had triumphed so signally over them all. But de Landas was waiting with apparent calm whilst Gilles took leave of Jacqueline. This Gilles did with all the ceremony which etiquette demanded. He still felt dazed with the strange discovery which he had just made, the knowledge that the dream which he had only cherished as a vague memory was a living, breathing, exquisite reality. Ye gods! how exquisite she was!

But he had no excuse for lingering—had, on the other hand, a wild desire to be alone, in order to think, to remember and to dream. So, having bowed his last farewell, he turned to go, and found de Landas barring his way.

'You will pay for this outrage, Messire,' said the latter in a quick whisper through his set teeth.

'Whenever you please,' replied Gilles imperturbably.

'To-night— —'

'Surely not while ladies are present,' broke in Gilles quietly.

''Tis in Madame's presence,' retorted de Landas roughly, 'whom you have insulted, that I and my friends— —'

'Messire!' protested Jacqueline firmly.

'Ah! a valorous half-dozen then?' rejoined Gilles lightly. 'I see that you—and your friends, Messire—have no intention of taking any risks.'

'Our intention is to tear that mask off your impudent face and make you lick the dust at Madame Jacqueline's feet.'

'And mine,' riposted Gilles gaily, 'is to collect a trophy of half a dozen masks—yours, Messire, and those of your friends—on the point of my sword and to place these with my homage at Madame Jacqueline's feet.'

'Insolent!'

'I therefore am completely at your service, gentlemen,' concluded Gilles, with an ironical bow directed at his opponents. 'Whenever, wherever you please.'

'Here and now!' broke in de Landas, whose self-control—never of long duration—had already given way. 'At him, friends! And, by Satan, we'll teach this malapert a lesson!'

It was in vain that Jacqueline tried to interpose; in vain that the ladies about the room screamed and swooned, that the men even began loudly to protest. Neither de Landas nor his friends were in a state to hear either commands or protests. All decorum, chivalry, breeding, was thrown to the winds. Hatred had descended like an ugly night-hawk upon these young gallants, and with her frowzy, sable wings had enveloped their brain and hearts till they were deaf to the most elementary dictates of honour. With de Landas, a wild, insensate jealousy had fanned that hatred to a glowing brazier of unreason and of madness. He saw—or thought he saw—that Jacqueline displayed unwonted interest in this stranger, that her eyes followed his movements with anxiety not unmixed with admiration. And de Landas became conscious of a red veil before his eyes and of a furious desire to humiliate that man first and to kill him after.

'At him, friends!' he called again hoarsely. 'We'll teach him a lesson!'

It was most fortunately at this very moment, and when the tumult was at its height, that Monseigneur d'Inchy re-entered the room. Just for a second or two he did not pay much heed to the noise. In these days, when political and religious controversies oft raged with bitter acrimony, it was not very unusual that a hot quarrel marred the close of a convivial gathering. D'Inchy at first did not do more than glance round the room, to see if his interference was really necessary. Then, to his horror, he realized what was happening, saw *Monsieur* Duc d'Anjou, own brother to the King of France and future Sovereign Lord of the Netherlands, standing in the midst of a group of young hotheads, who were actually threatening Monseigneur the governor's exalted guest!

And de Landas, that impetuous quarrelsome young coxcomb, was talking of giving *Monsieur* a lesson! It was unbelievable! Appalling! D'Inchy was a middle-aged man, but it was with a degree of vigour which many young men might have envied that he pushed his way through the jabbering and gesticulating throng of men and women, right across the room to the top of the table, where he arrived just in time to avert what would indeed have been a terrible calamity.

'By Heaven, M. de Landas,' he interposed stoutly, ''tis I will teach you and these gentlemen a lesson which you are not like to forget!'

And, regardless of de Landas' and his friends' glowering looks, he pushed his way to Gilles' side and stood facing that angry little crowd who, suddenly abashed, drew back a step or two, muttering wrathful expletives. Monseigneur, of course, was their host and an old man; but why should he interfere and spoil what promised to be really fine sport?

'M. le Prince de Froidmont is my guest,' M. d'Inchy went on calmly. 'Who quarrels with him, insults me and my house.'

A real sigh of relief came from Madame Jacqueline. Already, at sight of her guardian, she had felt reassured, and now he had voiced just what she had wished to say all along. She felt grateful to him for this and for his dignified attitude, and with a pretty, clinging gesture, sidled up to him and took hold of his arm.

What could the young gallants do? They were helpless for the moment, even though still raging with choler. De Landas tried to look as if nothing of importance had happened, even though from beneath his mask he shot a last glance of hatred and menace at his unperturbed enemy. The others quickly followed suit and for the moment the incident was at an end. Fortunately it was not likely to have unpleasant consequences, for already Gilles had interposed with his habitual good-humour.

'Your pardon, Monseigneur,' he said. 'These—these gentlemen and I had no intention of insulting one another. We were only having a little argument, and as your hospitality hath been over-lavish, we became somewhat heated; that is all!'

'Somewhat heated!' riposted d'Inchy gruffly. 'With mine own ears I heard M. le Marquis Landas here...'

'Yes, that's just it!' broke in Gilles imperturbably. 'M. de Landas and I were indulging in a friendly argument, which your presence, Monseigneur, at once rendered futile.'

M. d'Inchy sighed with relief. Gilles' coolness was contagious; even de Landas ceased to growl and the others to mutter. Thank Heaven! the quarrel was fizzling out like an unfanned flame, and in any case Monsieur was taking the situation with perfect good-humour. D'Inchy, bent, as always, on conciliation, smiled with impartial blandness on every one, whilst Jacqueline, silent and demure now as if nothing had happened, was once more looking straight down her nose. D'Inchy took hold of her hand, which still rested upon his arm, and patted it gently with an indulgent, fatherly caress.

'Then all is for the best, Messeigneurs,' he said, 'and with your leave my ward will now take her leave of you. I fear me that your friendly argument has somewhat fatigued her. By the way,' he added lightly, 'you have not yet told me what that argument was about.'

'Oh!' rejoined Gilles with a quiet smile, 'we only argued as to whose should be the privilege of placing a trophy at the feet of our fair hostess.'

'A trophy? What trophy?'

'Oh, something quite insignificant. A—a mask—or half a dozen——'

'Just like so many 'prentices a-quarrelling,' said d'Inchy with gruff good-humour. 'A mask or half a dozen, forsooth! You'd far better all be going to bed now. Madame cares nothing for your masks or your trophies. She is too tired for any such nonsense. Eh, Jacqueline?'

'Not too tired, Monseigneur,' replied Jacqueline demurely, 'to forgo the pleasure of bidding you good-night ere you go to rest.'

'There, you see, gentlemen,' rejoined d'Inchy gaily, 'that age has certain privileges which youth seeks for in vain. Whilst you go moodily, unsatisfied, to bed, the fairest of the fair will be sitting with her old guardian in his living-room, prattling away on the events of this night, quizzing you all, I'll warrant; laughing at your quarrels and your trophies. Is that not so, my dear? ... One mask or half a dozen! ... Are they not like children, these gallants, with their senseless quarrels? But there, while women are beautiful, men will quarrel for their favours—what?'

And he looked down with fatherly pride on the golden head which was kept so resolutely bent.

'C'est entendu, Monseigneur,' replied Jacqueline softly. 'I'll come to your living-room as usual and bid you good-night after all our guests have departed.'

Far be it from me even to hint that, as she said this, Jacqueline threw more than a cursory glance on Gilles or on M. de Landas, for nothing could have looked more demure, more dignified and aloof than she did at this moment, when, having spoken, she bowed with stiff grace to the group of gentlemen before her. And even Maître Calviac would have felt that he was a mere bungler in the matter of bowings and scrapings if he could have seen these gallants responding to Madame's salute; the right leg outstretched, the left foot kept back, the hand almost touching the floor with a wide sweep of the arm, then brought back to the lips as for an imaginary kiss.

The next moment Jacqueline had turned and presently could be seen, still with that same stiff grace, receiving the adieux of her guardian's guests. She held her small head very erect and with one hand plied her fan with lazy nonchalance, whilst the other was perpetually being extended to those whose privilege it was to kiss it.

As for the group of young gallants—well! they had the immediate future to look forward to. True, that for the nonce they were forbidden to continue the quarrel for fear of incurring their host's displeasure; but it was only a matter of putting off the happy hour when one could be even with that insolent stranger. De Landas turned with a significant gesture and a knowing wink to his friends. After that, the small group dispersed and ostentatiously mingled with the rest of the departing crowd.

D'Inchy, before he left Gilles' side, managed to murmur fulsome apologies.

'I do assure Monseigneur,' he whispered earnestly in Gilles' ear, 'that these young jackanapes will not be tempted to repeat their impudence, and that I...'

'And that you, Messire,' broke in Gilles a little impatiently, 'are entirely innocent of any intention of offending me. That is, of course, understood. Believe me,' he added gaily, 'that the little incident was more than welcome as far as I am concerned. Your lavish hospitality had made us all drowsy. M. de Landas' aggressive temper brought life and animation into the entertainment. I, for one, am grateful to him for the episode.'

Five minutes later he too had taken leave of his host. Jacqueline he did not see again. She was entirely surrounded by friends. Nevertheless, he left the banqueting hall in a state of exhilaration, and as he passed through the doors between the rows of Monseigneur's obsequious serving-men, they all remarked that Monsieur le Prince de Froidmont was humming a lively tune, the words of which appeared to be:

> 'Les plis de sa robe pourprée
> Et son teint au vostre pareil!'

CHAPTER XI.
AND HOW IT ENDED

I

When Gilles de Crohin found himself alone with Maître Jehan in the corridor which led straight to the main entrance hall, he paused for a moment, irresolute, wondering what he had best do. That there had been murder in the eyes of that gallant Marquis de Landas no one could doubt for a moment, and there lay a long stretch of dark streets and narrow lanes between the Archiepiscopal Palace and the safe shelter of 'Les Trois Rois.'

But you cannot imagine Messire Gilles de Crohin quaking even for a moment at the thought.

'Careful we must be,' he said in a whisper to his faithful *alter ego;* 'for my choleric friend will not, I imagine, be above lying in wait for us within the shelter of a convenient doorway, and I should ill serve the cause of the Queen of Navarre by getting spiked between the shoulders at such an early stage of the proceedings. But between that and showing that gallant Spaniard a clean pair of heels and foregoing the pleasure of threading his mask on my blade, there is a world of difference; eh, my good Jehan?'

'Above all things,' he added to himself, under his breath, so that even Jehan could not hear, 'I must find out whether a certain provoking glance, which flashed from out a pair of the most adorable blue eyes I have ever seen, were intended for me or not.'

And his thoughts flew riotously back to Jacqueline—Jacqueline, his dream, his tantalizing, exquisite dream—Jacqueline of the blue eyes and the captivating mole—Jacqueline of the roguish smile and the demure glance.

'I wonder, now!' he murmured softly. Had she perchance meant to give him a hint? Had she thrown him a warning glance? Gilles just then could have sworn that she had done both when she spoke of Monseigneur's living-room, where she would sit prattling after the last of the guests had departed.

'Did she mean me to take refuge there against de Landas' murderous intentions?' he asked himself. But the supposition did not appear likely. Gilles was no coxcomb and had not had many dealings with women during the course of his chequered career; but he had an innate respect for them, and would not credit Jacqueline—proud, demure, stately Jacqueline—with the intention of offering a gratuitous rendezvous to an unknown gallant. Rather was her glance intended for de Landas—the assignation was for him: 'perhaps,' thought Messire Gilles with a vague stirring of hope in his heart, 'perhaps with a view to keeping that fiery lover of hers out of harm's way, till I myself was safely abed.'

Be that as it may, the most elementary dictates of prudence demanded that he should go back to his hostelry before his enemies had time to concoct any definite plans for his undoing. So, calling to Jehan to follow him, he found his way quickly out of the Palace.

It was raining heavily just then; the streets were dark and, after a while, quite deserted. Gilles and Jehan, keeping a sharp look-out around them, walked rapidly and kept to the middle of the streets. Fortunately for them both, they had had plenty of leisure in the last four days to wander through the intricate by-ways of the Flemish city. They knew the lay of the land pretty well by now, and at this moment when the thought of a possible *guet-apens* was foremost in their minds, they were able to outwit any potential assassin who might be lurking on the direct route by going to the hostelry along devious ways usually unfrequented by strangers.

Thus it took them nearly half an hour to reach 'Les Trois Rois,' and Jehan, for one, was heartily congratulating himself that those murderous gentlemen had been comfortably thrown off the scent and were mayhap cooling their tempers somewhere in the cold and the wet, when, just as they entered the porch of the hostelry, a shadowy figure detached itself from out the gloom.

Gilles was already prepared with a quick, 'Qui va là?' but the figure proved inoffensive-looking enough: a woman, wrapped in a mantle and hood from head to foot. She had a small roll of paper in her hand, and this she held out timidly to Gilles.

'Monseigneur le Prince de Froidmont?' she inquired under her breath.

'Myself,' replied Gilles curtly. 'What is it?'

He took the paper and unrolled it. By the light of a small lanthorn which hung just inside the porch he saw that it was a letter—just a few lines—written in a small, pointed hand, and signed with the letter 'J.'

'Jacqueline!' he murmured, bewildered—so dazed that it took him some time before he was able to read. At last he deciphered the brief message.

> 'I do entreat you, Mesire,' it ran, 'to return to
> the palace within the hour. Nay! I do not entreat, I
> command! Go to the postern Gate: you will find it
> unlatched. Then cross the Courtyard till you come
> to a door on the left of the main Perron—this will be
> unlocked. You will find yourself in one of the chief
> Corridors which give on the grand Staircase. Remain
> there concealed, and await further Orders.'

A strange enough missive, of a truth, and one, no doubt, which would have made an older and more prudent man pause ere he embarked on so dubious an adventure. But Gilles de Crohin was neither old nor prudent, and he was already up to his neck in a sea of adventure which had begun to submerge his reason. Even before he had folded up the paper again and slipped it into the inner pocket of his doublet, he had made up his mind that no power on earth, no wisdom or warning, would deter him from keeping the tryst. Did I think to remind you that he was no coxcomb? Well! he certainly was absolutely free from personal vanity, and it was not his self-conceit which was stimulated by the mysterious message; rather was it his passion for adventure, his love for the unforeseen, the unexpected, the exhilarating. The paper which he hid so tenderly inside his doublet had a delicious crisp sound about it, which seemed to promise something stimulating and exciting to come.

'Run up, Jehan,' he called to his man. 'I follow you. Let me get out of these damnable slashed and puffed rags—these velvet shoes and futile furbelows. Up, man! I follow in a trice! We have not done with adventure yet to-night.'

Then he turned, with a piece of silver in his hand ready to reward the bearer of such joyful tidings. But the messenger had disappeared into the night as quietly, as mysteriously as she had come

II

Less than half an hour later, Gilles de Crohin once more found himself within the precincts of the Archiepiscopal Palace. He had been so quick in changing his clothes and so quick in covering the distance which separated him from the trysting place, that he had no occasion to use the postern gate or the small door which had been indicated to him. The great entrance portals were still wide open when he arrived; some of the corridors still thronged with people — guests of Monseigneur and their servants on the point of departure — whilst others appeared entirely deserted. At one point, Gilles caught sight of M. de Landas taking elaborate leave of a group of ladies. He had his usual circle of friends around him, who — a moment or two later — followed him out of the Palace.

Gilles, with Jehan close behind him, kept well within the shadows, away from the throng. He had exchanged his elaborate and rich costume for a suit that was both plain and sombre; he had washed the perfume out of his hair and the cosmetics from off his hands. He felt unfettered in his movements now and in rare good humour. The only thing which he had borrowed from his former accoutrement was the magnificent Toledo rapier, which, after a moment's hesitation, he had buckled into his own sword-belt. It had been a parting gift from Madame la Reyne de Navarre and was a miracle of the steel-worker's art; supple as velvet, it would bend point to hilt like a gleaming arc and when it caught a ray of light upon its perfect edge, it flashed a thousand coloured rays like a streak of vivid lightning in a storm-laden sky.

Jehan, on the other hand, was not altogether at his ease. Having less cause to feel exhilarated, he had a greater mistrust of the mysterious missive, had vainly tried to argue prudence where his master would only hearken to folly. But he had never succeeded in getting beyond a laboured: 'I th-th-th-think — —' Upon which, he was peremptorily ordered to hold his tongue, even while Messire went merrily singing to face this questionable adventure.

At one point Gilles stopped in order to speak to a serving-man, asked him to tell him where was Monseigneur's private apartments, and when the man appeared to hesitate—for indeed he did not like to give this information to a stranger—Messire had seemingly lost his temper, and the man, trembling in his shoes, had stammered out the necessary directions. Monseigneur's private apartments and those of the household were in the right wing of the Palace. This was reached by mounting the grand staircase, then continuing along the main corridor which connected the different portions of the vast building, until the wing containing the living-rooms was reached. No one, the man went on to explain, slept in this portion of the Palace, which held only the reception rooms and one of the chapels; but there were always night-watchmen about the place to see that no malefactors were about.

Whilst the man spoke, Jehan felt as if his eyes were searching him through and through. The worthy soul was liking this adventure less and less every moment.

Indeed, very soon after this all the corridors became deserted. Singly, in pairs, or in groups, all Monseigneur's guests and their servants had taken their departure. For awhile the varlets and wenches belonging to the household were busy clearing up the disorder and the débris attendant on so large a gathering and on so copious a supper, and one could hear them jabbering and laughing in the distant dining hall or in the offices down below. Then that noise, too, became stilled, and one felt that this portion of the vast Palace was indeed completely uninhabited.

Up at the Town Hall, the belfry of Martin et Martine had just chimed the midnight hour. Messire Gilles and his faithful Jehan found themselves in the vast hall at the foot of the grand staircase, and the main entrance with its monumental gates was then immediately behind them. A strange stillness reigned all around: the great Palace seemed here like a city of the dead.

Jehan vainly tried to protest once more. For what was Messire waiting, he wondered. Surely it was unwise and worse to linger here now, when every one had gone and all servants were abed. Presently, of course, the night-watchmen would be making their rounds. Jehan had a swift and exceedingly unpleasant foreboding that he and his master would be ignominiously turned out! and then God alone knew in what rows and quarrels they would be involved, or how hopelessly they would jeopardize their own position; not to speak of the Queen of Navarre's cherished scheme. Poor Jehan would have given five years of his life and half his savings for five minutes' glib speech with his master.

III

Even at this very moment, Jehan's vague terrors took on a definite form. Footsteps and voices raised in merry converse were heard, resounding from the distance, and the next instant two serving-men carrying torches came leisurely down the corridor in the direction of the hall. Immediately behind them walked Monseigneur the Governor, who had Madame Jacqueline on his arm. Jehan felt as if his heart had stopped its beating; his knees shook under him, whilst tiny drops of perspiration rose at the roots of his hair.

Ye gods! if they were discovered now! They would be under grave suspicion of evil intent ... burglary ... assassination.... There had been talk at the banquet of 'spy' and 'Spaniard.' Jehan's scanty hair stood up on end with horror.

Fortunately, Messire was equally aware of danger, gave a quick glance round, and perceived a door close beside him on the right. This part of the hall was, equally luckily, in shadow. There was also just sufficient time to reach the door, to open it, and to step incontinently behind it, closing it again noiselessly. Phew! it had been a narrow escape!

The footsteps and the voices came rapidly nearer; a minute or two later they passed within a foot of the door behind which Gilles and Jehan were crouching, hardly daring to breathe. The glint of the torches could be distinctly seen through a narrow chink between two panels, as well as the shimmer of Madame's white satin gown. There were but a few inches of wood and a foot of floor-space between Messire and shameful discovery, and Maître Jehan fell to wondering what particular form of torture would be applicable to a man who was found lurking at dead of night in the dark, and with obviously evil designs on the life or property of the governor of a Flemish province.

Thank Heaven and all the protecting angels, however, the footsteps passed by, and presently were heard ascending the main staircase, and whilst Maître Jehan was feeling as if his whole body would melt in a sea of cold perspiration, Madame Jacqueline's rippling laughter came only as an echo from a considerable and comparatively safe distance.

After awhile Gilles ventured to open the door very cautiously. A faint murmur of people stirring came from very far away; the shuffling footsteps of the torch-bearers died away in the distant corridors.

And once more all was still.

IV

Gilles gave vent to his feelings by a long-drawn-out 'Phew!' of obvious relief; but the next moment he said, quite coolly:

'Pardi, my good Jehan! but we did not want to be caught hiding in this place like a couple of malefactors, did we?' and made straightway to re-open the door. Jehan seized him by the arm and clung to him with all his might.

'Why shouldn't we st-st-st-stay here?' he urged almost glibly.

Gilles shrugged his shoulders. 'Why not, indeed?' he retorted. 'Something has got to happen presently,' he added carelessly. 'Somebody has got to come. If it is not Madame Jacqueline—and, honestly, my good Jehan, I have small hopes of that—If it is not Madame, then——'

He paused and frowned. For the first time a sharp suspicion had crossed his mind. Had he proved himself to be a vanity-ridden coxcomb after all? Should not the most elementary prudence have dictated....? Bah! whatever prudence had dictated, Gilles would not have listened. He was out for adventure! Whether gallant or dangerous he did not care! Once more he shrugged his broad shoulders and unconsciously his slender hand gripped the hilt of his splendid Spanish sword.

He threw a quick glance around him. Through the open door, the huge metal lamps which illumined the hall beyond threw a wide shaft of golden light into the room where he and Jehan had found such welcome refuge. It appeared to be something of a boudoir or library, for the shaft of light revealed rows of books, which lined the walls all round. There was a window at the far end of the room, and that was closely curtained, and there was no other door save the one through which the two men had entered. The fire in the large open hearth had been allowed to die down. A massive desk stood not far from the window, and there were a few chairs about and a small, iron-bound coffer. Papers littered the desk and a finely wrought candelabra hung from the ceiling.

'The room,' said Gilles lightly, 'looks as if it had been closed for the night. There is no reason why we should not await here the future course of events.' He drew one of the chairs into a comfortable position and sat down, then added: 'I do not know, of course, how long we may have to cool our heels in this place, until the writer of the mysterious epistle chooses to explain his or her commands. I am beginning to think, as you do, my friend, that the missive should have been signed with an "L" rather than with a "J". What say you?'

'Aye! Aye!' muttered Jehan.

'Well, 'tis no matter! I'd as soon meet mine ebullient friend of the languorous eyes to-night as to-morrow, and inside this deserted Palace as out there in the rain. And a little sword-play would be very stimulating after the sentimental dalliance of the last few days.'

'H'm!' murmured Jehan equivocally.

'In the meanwhile, there is no reason why we should not have a rest. I confess to feeling rather sleepy. Just take a last look at the corridor,' concluded Gilles, as he stretched his long limbs out before him. 'And if you are satisfied that all is well, come and join me in an excursion to the land of Nod.'

Jehan went to the door as he was told and peered cautiously to right and left of him. Seeing nothing suspicious, he went as far as the great hall to listen if all was clear and still. It was whilst he was gone that something arrested Gilles' attention. Furtive footsteps this time—a number of them—moving stealthily along the corridor. With a quick gesture, he adjusted the mask over his face—instinct led him to do that first and foremost; then he jumped to his feet and went to the door, but had no time to step across the threshold, for the next instant a compact group of moving figures emerged straight in front of him out of the gloom, intercepting him and barring the way.

'À moi, Jehan!' he called aloud.

But it was too late. From the hall beyond there came the sound of a vigorous scuffle. Jehan, caught unawares, was putting up a good fight seemingly against heavy odds; but he could no longer reach his master—whilst some half-dozen gentlemen, all wearing masks, were pushing their way into the room.

'We've run our fox to earth at last, Messeigneurs,' came with a mocking laugh from out this dense and aggressive-looking group. 'And without cooling our heels in the wet—what? I told you that this would be the better plan. His own egregious vanity hath led him straight into our trap and 'tis mighty fine sport that we'll have with this abominable spy, without fear of interruption.'

It was the voice of M. de Landas, unmistakable owing to the slight guttural pronunciation of the French language peculiar to his Spanish blood. Before Gilles could forestall him, he and his friends were all around him: six of them, fine young gallants—those who had supported de Landas in the quarrel after the banquet.

Gilles surveyed them all with a rapid glance, measured his own position, which of a truth was not an advantageous one. The light from the lamps in the hall fell, through the open doorway, full upon him, whilst his aggressors appeared only like a dense mass in the heart of the shadow. They were evidently intent on forcing him back into the room; their movements appeared like part of a concerted plan of action, to get him into a corner where they could more comfortably hold him at their mercy.

Gilles realized his position, the danger in which he stood and his best chance of defence, with the unerring rapidity of a born soldier.

'It must have taken a huge effort of intelligence, Messire,' he said ironically, 'to concoct this pretty plan. What was there in an open challenge to frighten so many stalwart gallants?'

He gave ground, retreated into the room while he spoke. De Landas and his friends pressed in closely after him.

'I have yet to learn,' retorted the young Spaniard with a sneer, 'that you are worthy of crossing swords with one of us. You may draw, an' you have a mind; but you cannot escape the lesson which I and my friends have vowed to administer to you, and which, forsooth, you have so richly deserved.'

"'Tis no use,' he added with an intaking of the breath like an angry snake, "'Tis no use calling for help. The night-watchmen are in my pay: my own men have settled with your servant, and no sound short of an earthquake could reach the distant wing of the Palace where Monseigneur and his household are abed.'

He drew his sword, and his friends immediately did likewise. Still they advanced, the solid phalanx of them, and so cunningly that Gilles was kept in the shaft of light whilst they remained under cover of the shadow.

'A murder!' said Gilles quietly.

'A lesson, first and foremost,' was de Landas' curt reply. 'After that, we shall see.'

'What shall we see, Messire?' riposted Gilles with a mocking laugh. 'A Spanish cavalier stooping to assassination — —?'

'Who spoke of assassination?' queried one of the gallants.

'Why else are you here?' retorted Gilles, 'the six of you, whilst half a dozen or more of your varlets are overpowering my man outside, after ye have bribed or threatened the watchmen into silence? Methinks it looks uncommonly like projected murder.'

'Whatever it is,' broke in de Landas savagely, 'it will be a lesson which you are not like to forget.'

'The lesson of how to lay an ignoble trap for an unsuspecting foe? A lesson, indeed, in which the teacher is well-versed in infamy. The assignation; the forged signature! The watchmen bribed, a dozen of you to attack two men, and, as you say, the wings of the Palace where our host and his servants lie abed, well out of earshot. My compliments, M. de Landas! I have met much knavery in my time, but none, I think, quite so cleverly devised. France, it seems, hath still a great deal to learn from Spain, and — —'

He had not yet drawn in response to the other's challenge, but stepped back and back until he was almost up against the desk at the far end of the room. Then, suddenly, with a movement so swift that his antagonists were taken completely unawares, he skipped behind the desk and with a push of his strong arms threw it down straight at his assailants, forcing them in their turn to give ground or the massive piece of furniture would have fallen on the top of them. As it was, it came to the ground with a crash, the noise as it fell being to a certain extent subdued by the thickness of the matting which covered the floor.

When de Landas and his friends recovered from the suddenness of this unexpected shock, positions for them were unpleasantly reversed. They were now in full light, a good target for an experienced swordsman, whilst Messire le Prince de Froidmont lurked somewhere in the shadow. Fortunately he was comfortably outnumbered, and his henchman quite helpless by now; to disarm him and give him the long promised chastisement was only a question of time.

'And I have sworn,' cried de Landas spitefully, 'to deposit at Madame Jacqueline's feet the mask which still hides his impudent face.'

Gilles, however, was determined to sell his life or his discomfiture dearly. He had not been slow in consolidating his new position. Losing not one second of precious time, he drew the overthrown desk close to him, picked up a couple of chairs that were close by, then reached out for two or three more, piled these up over and around the desk, and by the time de Landas and his crowd had recovered their bearings and returned to the attack, he was magnificently ensconced behind a barricade of heaped-up furniture, and, having drawn his sword, was ready for defence.

'Now, Messeigneurs,' he said with those same mocking tones which had already exasperated de Landas beyond endurance, 'see to it that you escape well-merited chastisement; for, on my oath, I swear that 'tis I who will deposit half a dozen masks at Madame Jacqueline's feet ere I give you a chance of carrying out that nice little murder plot which was destined to cover six stalwart seigneurs with glory.'

De Landas gave a harsh laugh.

'Your ruse will not protect you,' he said, 'though I confess 'twas well manoeuvred. À moi, friends! 'Twill not be the first time that you have aided me in extirpating noisome vermin from its hidden burrow. You, La Broye, and du Prêt, hold the right; Herlaer and Maarege the left; de Borel, you and I wherever we are needed, and en avant. At him, friends! No barricade on earth nor protecting darkness shall save him from the punishment which he hath so richly deserved. At him, and unmask the rogue, so that I can at last smite the impudent spy in the face!'

De Borel, young, impetuous, a fiery nincompoop, easily led by the nose by his more brilliant friend, was not slow in following the lead given him. He and Herlaer made a swift rush for the improvised barricade whilst de Landas attacked in the centre and the others, with equal vigour, both on right and left. They thrust their swords somewhat wildly through the interstices provided by the legs of the chairs which towered above the overturned desk, lunged blindly into the darkness, for they could not see their opponent. For a few minutes all was confusion—the din of clashing steel, the hoarse cries of the assailants, and Gilles' ironical taunts as he parried all these aimless thrusts with the coolness of a consummate swordsman—all merged into a chaotic uproar. The next moment, however, Herlaer went down, and then de Borel, each with a deep gash in the leg, which had ripped up the flesh from the ankle to midway up the calf.

The front of the desk happened to be kidney-shaped, and it was through the aperture formed by that front as it lay on its beam end that Gilles' sword had suddenly darted out once and then again, like some vicious snake, with maddening rapidity and stealth, inflicting the sharp flesh wounds which had so disconcerted his assailants. They, entirely taken unawares, irritated by this attack from a wholly unforeseen quarter, not only fell back with some precipitancy, but also with a marked cooling off of their primary ardour. They had come straight from a festive gathering, were wearing silk hose and low shoes of velvet, and at this moment were wishing that their ankles had been protected by substantial leather boots. Somewhat sulkily they set to to staunch their wounds with their lace-edged handkerchiefs. De Landas watched them with a scowl, giving the while a short respite to his opponent—the latter, of a truth, well ensconced behind his barricades, was more difficult to get at than had at first been supposed.

There ensued a hasty council of war. Herlaer, limping, was despatched for reinforcements. The varlets who had effectually dealt with Jehan might as well come and lend a hand to dress their masters' wounds. Jehan, indeed, lay prone upon the flagstones of the hall, having apparently succumbed to a blow on the head, of which one of those same varlets was even now boasting with inordinate vainglory to his companions, when they were all incontinently called away to attend upon the young seigneurs.

De Landas in the meanwhile had returned to the assault. Leaving Herlaer and de Borel in the hands of their henchmen, he called the others lustily to him.

'À moi, du Prêt, Maarege, La Broye!' he cried. 'Beware of the fox's underground burrow, and en avant!'

He had espied the small coffer, seized it by one of its handles and dragged it across the floor. Aided by Maarege, they succeeded in placing it in position so as to block the aperture below the barricade. Now there was no longer any danger from that quarter; the enemy was getting foiled at every turn. And with renewed valour they once more rushed to the assault.

Gilles now was on his feet, ensconced in the angle of the wall, so as to allow his sword arm full play; and indeed, in his skilful hands the magnificent Toledo blade seemed like a living, breathing thing—a tongue of steel which darted in and out of the improvised barricade, forward, to right, to left, parry, en garde, thrust, lunge—out of the darkness, now and then only catching a glint of light upon its smooth surface, when it would flash and gleam like a streak of vivid lightning, to subside again, retire, disappear into the gloom, only to dart out again more menacing, more invincible than before.

And every time that this tongue of living flame shot out of the darkness it left its searing trail behind. Maarege was bleeding from the shoulder, du Prêt from the thigh; La Broye had a gash across the forehead, and de Landas' forearm was torn from the wrist to the elbow. On the other hand, de Landas' sword was also stained with blood. He gave a cry of triumph.

'À moi, de Borel! Herlaer!' he called to the other two. 'At the barricades, while we keep the rogue busy. He cannot hold out much longer!'

And, indeed, the combat was far too unequal to last. One man against six, and his only ally was the darkness. That too was failing him, for his assailants' eyes were becoming accustomed to the gloom. They were able to descry him more easily than before, and there was not a mean swordsman amongst them, either. Even now, under cover of a vigorous onslaught made by de Landas and his three seconds, de Borel and Herlaer—their wounds temporarily dressed—rushed for the barricade and dragged first one chair and then the other away, and finally succeeded in throwing the two others right into Gilles' legs, thus hampering the freedom of his movements. True, that during this rapidly executed manoeuvre, de Borel received a gash across the cheek and Herlaer a thrust in the arm; but the solitary fighter's position had been rendered decidedly more precarious.

'Throw up your hands, you fool!' exclaimed de Landas with grudging admiration at his opponent's swordsmanship. 'Unmask, and go your way, and we will call quits over this affair!'

Gilles' only reply to the taunt was an ironical laugh. The chairs encumbered his legs, but his sword arm was free, and he had once been counted the finest swordsman in France. Attack and parry again, thrust and en garde—six blades menaced him, and he, ensconced in the dark angle, kept the six of them at bay! Now du Prêt's sword, with a vigorous blow, was knocked clean out of his hand; anon Maarege's blade was broken in two close to the hilt.

Confusion now reigned supreme. Fight and excitement had whipped up the blood of all these young gallants till a perfect fury of hatred for the invincible opponent drew a blood-red, veil-like mist before their eyes. The frantic desire to kill was upon them; their wounds no longer ached, their arms felt no weariness; the breath came with a hissing sound through their quivering nostrils. Now Maarege and La Broye succeeded in further demolishing the barricade, dragging away the table, overthrowing the chairs, making the way clear to right and left of these for a concerted attack upon the foe. Gilles, quick as a bird that scents an attack, skipped over the obstacle, darted to the right, where the curtained window was, and shadows still hung dark, almost impenetrable.

Already he was en garde again, close to the window this time— seemed still fresh and full of vigour though bleeding from more than one wound. He loved this fight, as a hungry man loves the first morsel of food which a kindly hand places before him; loved it for its excitement—one of the keenest he had ever sustained. De Landas' fury stimulated him, maddened jealousy was so obviously its mainspring; and Gilles felt as if he were fighting for the possession of Jacqueline. His fine Toledo blade filled him with joy—at this very moment it pierced de Borel's thigh as easily as it would have done a pat of butter.

'There's for one of you!' exclaimed Gilles in triumphant exhilaration.

De Borel was now out of action, and La Broye was weakening perceptibly; but du Fret had recovered his sword and Maarege was brandishing the broken stump of his rapier, whilst de Landas, drunk with jealousy and with rage, returned to the assault again and again, heedless of his wounds. The room was a mass of wreckage. Overturned furniture, broken débris, scraps of silken doublets and velvet mantles, shoulder knots, tassels and bits of priceless lace, littered the floor; the matting in places showed dark crimson stains and had become slippery under the ceaseless tramp of feet. With his barricade all tumbled about him, Gilles was more open to attack, for there were still four of them at least against him, and they pressed him closely enough just now.

'At him, friends!' de Landas contrived to shout, in a voice rendered husky with exhaustion. 'At him! The rogue is weakening rapidly! One more effort, and we have him!'

'Nay, by God! Ye have not!' exclaimed Gilles lustily, and parried with dazzling skill an almost simultaneous attack from de Landas and Herlaer on one side and Maarege and du Prêt on the other. They fell on him with redoubled energy, wellnigh frenzied by the seeming invincibility of their foe, their own impotence. They had thought to make sure of victory, had come in their numbers to administer humiliation and correction, and now were half crazy with impending defeat. And so vigorous became their attack, so determined were they to bring that hated foe to his knees, that it seemed for the moment as if he must succumb, as if only some sort of magic could save him.

But for a man of Gilles' temperament there could be no such thing as defeat. Defeat for him meant humiliation, which he could not tolerate, and the failure of Madame la Reyne's cherished plan. He was not only defending his life now, but her schemes and her happiness. His perfect blade accomplished miracles of defence; again and again his enemies returned to the charge. But that blade lived; it breathed; it palpitated with every thrust and every parry, swifter than lightning's flash. Now it was du Prêt's turn to stagger under a slashing cut on the shoulder, whilst La Broye was almost swooning with loss of blood.

'For two! And for three!' cried Gilles with a laugh. 'Three more of you, and I have done!'

With a cry of rage de Landas turned to the serving-men who, appalled by the fury of this combat, were cowering together in a far corner of the room, hardly daring to breathe.

'Here, Jan!' he shouted hoarsely. 'Peter! Nikolas! All of you! Seize that man! Fall on him! Seize him! At him! At him, I say!'

For just the fraction of a second the men shrank away still further into the angle of the room, terrified at the uncontrolled rage which had prompted the monstrous and cowardly command. They hesitated but only for one instant, and during that instant there was breathing time for all. But the next, egged on by de Landas' threatening commands, they gathered themselves together and came forward at a rush.

Gilles at once saw this new, this unexpected source of danger. The utter cowardice of this fresh attack lent him strength and power to act. With one of those swift, masterful gestures of his which were as unexpected as they were unerring, he threw aside his sword and seizing one of the heavy chairs which lay prone close by, he raised it above his head and brandishing it like a gigantic swivel he stood there, towering, menacing, breathing hatred too now against the dastardly foe who could thus outrage every canon of chivalry and of valour.

He struck out with the heavy chair, to right, to left. The varlets paused, really terrified. De Landas egged them on, prodded them with his sword. He had wandered so far now on the broad road of infamy, he was ready to go on to its ignominious end.

'Fall on him, Jan! Nikolas! All of you, you abominable knaves!' he cried huskily. 'Fall on him; or by Satan, I'll have you all hanged to-morrow!'

He beat them with the flat of his sword, kicked them and struck at them with his fist, till they were forced to advance. The heavy chair came down with a crash on the head of one man, the shoulder of another. There were loud curses and louder groans; but numbers were telling in the end. One more assault, one more rush, and they were on him. Then Gilles, as if by instinct, felt the folds of the heavy window curtain behind him.

To gain one second's time, he threw the chair straight at the compact mass of men, disconcerting the attack; then with both hands he seized the curtain, gave it a mighty wrench which brought it down in a heaped up medley of voluminous folds and broken cornice, and threw the whole mass of tangled drapery on his onrushing foes. De Landas, who was in the forefront of the aggressors, was the first to lose his footing. Already weak with loss of blood, he stumbled and fell, dragging one or two of the varlets with him. The edge of the cornice struck du Prêt on the head and completed the swoon which had already been threatening him, whilst Maarege, dazed, uncomprehending, stared about him in a state of semi-imbecility.

The other knaves, paralysed by some kind of superstitious fear, gazed on him open-mouthed while Gilles, still moved only by the blind instinct of self-preservation, extricated himself from his newly-improvised stronghold.

His first instinctive act was to stoop in order to pick up his sword again. A momentary lull—strange and weird in its absolute stillness had succeeded the wild confusion of awhile ago. Gilles staggered as he straightened out his tall figure once more, was at last conscious that even his splendid endurance had been nigh to breaking point. There was a mist before his eyes, through which he could vaguely perceive a cowering group of lacqueys quite close to him, huddled up together almost at his feet in the gloom; others, whose vague forms could be discerned under the fallen tapestry: further on, de Borel, lying helpless beside Herlaer; Maarege still clutching his broken sword; La Broye in a swoon, lying across the upturned desk, and de Landas, half-sitting, half-reclining, on an overthrown chair, obviously struggling against dizziness, his hand outstretched, with convulsed fingers that still threatened and pointed at the hated foe.

For the moment Gilles could not move. The mask on his face scorched his brow and cheeks as if it had been made of hot iron, and yet, though he longed to tear it off, his arm, from sheer exhaustion, refused him service. He longed to get out of that door, to find Jehan; but his limbs felt as if they were weighted with lead: his very brain was in a state of torpor.

V

Just then, through that semi-conscious state, he heard swift footsteps approaching down the main staircase, then across the hall.

The serving-men, almost blind with terror, heard them too, crouched yet closer together in the gloom. They dragged themselves along the floor, nearer to Gilles, as if for protection. Experience had taught the poor wretches that, whatever else happened, they would be made to suffer for all that had occurred. True, they deserved all that they would get, for they too had played an ignoble part; but whatever else happened there would be floggings or worse for them. Their employers were too weak now to protect them even if they would. M. le Marquis, enraged at defeat, would perhaps be the first to give his men away. So they gathered round Gilles now — round the man whom they had helped almost to murder. They clung to him in their sheer, unreasoning cowardice — the instinct to get behind something that was still stalwart and strong. They crawled away into the shadow, out of sight of Monseigneur's serving-men if these should come, of the night-watchmen or of the Palace guard if they appeared upon the scene.

Thus Gilles, when he tried to move towards the door, could not do so because of that cringing mass of humanity that clung, terror-stricken, round his legs. He was too utterly weary to kick them all aside, so he remained quite still, listening to those approaching footsteps. One of these he could have sworn to — heavy, and with a slight dragging of the feet — which could only have belonged to Jehan. He tried to call to his faithful henchman, but his throat was so dry he could not utter a sound.

The footsteps were quite close now, and through the open doorway he could see that a new and flickering light threw every nook of the corridor into bold relief. A torch-bearer was coming along; other lighter footsteps followed, and anon it seemed as if a woman's satin skirts swept the marble floor with its melodious frou-frou.

Gilles now was in a trance-like state on the borders of unconsciousness, a state wherein the body's utter exhaustion seems to render the mental perceptions abnormally acute. He could only stand and gaze at the open doorway; but he knew that in a very few seconds she would appear. He knew that it was she who was coming: she and Jehan. Old Jehan had found her and brought her along, and now that he — Gilles — was weary and sick she would minister to him and tend him as she had done that night, long ago, in what still seemed to him so like a dream.

The next moment the second half of the folding door was flung open and a torch, held aloft by a serving-man, threw a flood of light into the room. Immediately afterwards, under the lintel of the door, Jacqueline appeared, just as Gilles had expected her to do, like a vision of the angel of peace, in her shimmering white satin gown, with the pearls round her neck and her crown of golden hair. She had no mask on, and even through the veil which seemed to hang before Gilles' eyes he could see that tantalizing little brown mole which gave such exquisite, roguish charm to her face and made of the angel vision a living, perfect piece of adorable womanhood.

Jacqueline de Broyart was not the sort of woman who would faint at sight of blood. Her country had suffered too much and too long for her to have remained ignorant and detached from all the horrors which perpetual warfare against tyranny and intolerance had sowed broadcast upon the land. She had ministered to the sick and tended, the wounded ever since her baby hands had been strong enough to apply a bandage. But at sight of this disordered room, of the ghastly faces of these men—ghastly above their blood-stained masks—of de Landas' weird, convulsive gesture, of Maarege's attitude of vacant imbecility, of all the litter of stained floor and soiled bits of finery, she recoiled with an involuntary cry of horror. The recoil, however, was only momentary; the next, she had come forward quickly, a cry of pity this time upon her lips. Her first thought was for de Landas—the friend, the playmate, the lover. She hurried to him, hardly looked on Gilles, who could not move or call, who tried not to stagger or to fall headlong at her feet.

Now Jacqueline had her arms round her lover, his head rested against her shoulder, soiling the white satin of her gown with ugly crimson stains. But that she did not heed. She could not conjecture what had happened! That stuttering, stammering creature, himself half dazed and bruised, had found his way to Monseigneur's living-room, had in incoherent language implored her to come. Monseigneur happened to be absent from the room at the moment, had gone to give orders to one of his servants. Jacqueline was alone, sitting by the hearth waiting for him when the creature came. She knew him for the henchman of the Prince de Froidmont, the man who had fought so valiantly to defend his master awhile ago in the banqueting hall. She could see that he was hurt and in grave distress and gathered from his confused stammer that something awful was happening somewhere in the Palace. She followed him without any hesitation, and now through that medley of hideous sights which confronted her in this room, the most vivid thing that struck her gaze was de Landas' convulsive gesture, pointing at Gilles.

Already, with a few quick words, she had despatched the torchbearer for assistance.

'Go, Anselm!' she said, 'and rouse Nicolle and two of my women. Tell them some gentlemen are hurt and that I order them to come hither at once and to bring all that is necessary for the dressing of wounds. And—stay!' she added in a tone of peremptory command. 'Not a word to Monseigneur or to his men—you understand?'

The man nodded in quick comprehension, fixed the torch into the wall-bracket and went. As soon as he had gone Jacqueline turned back to de Landas, pillowed his aching head upon her bosom and held his poor, trembling hand in her strong, warm grasp. Then only did she turn to look on Gilles.

He appeared unhurt, or nearly so. True, his doublet was stained— he might have received a scratch—and he bore about his person that unmistakable air of a fighting man who has been in the thick of a fight; but amongst these other fallen and fainting men he alone was standing—and standing firmly, on his feet. And he had a group of men around him, all of whom were quite obviously unhurt. They looked like his henchmen, for they crowded close behind him, looking up to him as to their master.

So, whatever had happened—and Jacqueline gave an involuntary shudder at the thoughts and conjectures which were crowding into her brain—whatever else had happened, the stranger had had plenty of minions and varlets with him to defend him, even if he had been set upon by de Landas and his friends.

It were easy to blame Jacqueline for the utterly false interpretation which she had put on what she saw; but de Landas was the friend, the playmate, and—yes!—the lover; whilst Gilles was only a stranger and an adventurer at best. Strangers were both feared and hated these days in this unfortunate, stricken country, that was tyrannized over and cowed by conquerors of alien blood; and though Jacqueline was shrewd enough to suspect de Landas and his companions of the treachery which they had indeed committed, yet in her mind she half-excused him on the plea that the Prince de Froidmont had been unchivalrous and timid enough to have his person guarded by a gang of paid varlets. Thus it was that the look which she threw on Gilles was both contemptuous and unpitying.

'I pray you, Messire,' she said coldly, 'to leave my guardian's house, ere I call to him to demand of you an explanation which I imagine you are not prepared to give.'

Her words, her look, were so different to what Gilles had expected that, for the moment, he remained absolutely speechless. He certainly had not his wits entirely about him, or he would not, after that one moment of silence, have burst into a harsh and prolonged laugh.

'Messire!' reiterated Jacqueline, more peremptorily, 'I have desired you to go, and to take your varlets along with you, ere they swoon with the excess of their terror.'

'Your varlets!' Gilles laughed more loudly than before—indeed, he felt that he could no longer stop himself from laughing now until he dropped down dead on the floor. Jacqueline was leaning over de Landas and saying something to him which he—Gilles—could not very well hear, but her whole attitude, the look wherewith she regarded the wounded man, sent such a pang of insensate jealousy through Gilles' heart that he could have groaned aloud with the misery of it.

'I entreat you, my beloved,' de Landas murmured more audibly after awhile, 'to go back to your apartments. This is no place for you, and my friends and I will struggle homewards anon.'

'I cannot leave you like this, José!' she broke in firmly. 'Not while—while that man and his varlets are here!'

Ye gods! the humour of the situation! No wonder that Gilles could not cease laughing, even though his side ached and his head felt like splitting with pain. But he obeyed her commands, peremptorily ordered the cowering group of knaves to go; and they, thankful to escape, rushed helter-skelter for the door. Probably they never understood what the noble lady had been saying, and they were too stupid with terror to say aught in protest. Whether M. le Marquis de Landas, who had employed them for this night's work, would pay them liberally on the morrow, as he had promised, or have them flogged for failing to murder the stranger, still remained to be seen. For the moment, they were only too thankful to escape with their skins whole. Jehan, who much against his will had been forced to remain at attention behind the door, relieved his feelings by giving each of them a vigorous kick ere they started to run madly down the corridor.

While the last of them was stumbling over the threshold Gilles managed to pull himself together sufficiently to stop that paroxysm of ungovernable laughter.

'Have no fear, Madame,' he contrived to say with moderate coherence and a full measure of contemptuous irony, 'I'll not harm M. le Marquis de Landas or his five gallant friends, on mine honour! All that remains for me to do now is to collect the half-dozen masks which I swore awhile ago to place as a trophy at your feet.'

'I forbid you, Messire,' she retorted coldly, 'to pursue this callous jest any further.'

'Jest? It was no jest, Madame! I swore to unmask these gentlemen, and— —'

'And took good care to protect yourself against their wrath by a crowd of ruffianly bullies! The victory—if, indeed, there be one— doth not redound to the credit of Messire le Prince de Froidmont.'

'Even so, I must redeem my pledge,' he riposted in a tone quite as cool now as hers. 'So, by your leave— —'

She watched him, fascinated—somewhat like a hare might watch the playful antics of a tiger—with blue eyes opened wide in wonder and horror, as he went lightly from one man to the other and with deft fingers removed their masks, then threaded them by the eye-slits along the length of his sword. De Borel never moved—he was quite unconscious, and La Broye only groaned and tried to turn away. But both Herlaer and du Prêt struggled in feeble self-defence, and Maarege, still clutching his broken rapier, made futile efforts to lunge at Gilles. But they too were faint from exhaustion and loss of blood, and Gilles, who had himself well in hand, had strength enough for his self-imposed task. Jacqueline never moved. Protests against this outrage were obviously of no avail, and physically she had not the strength to intervene. But when he finally turned to de Landas, she interposed with all her might, with the motherly instinct of a bird, striving to protect its mate.

'I forbid you, Messire!' she cried.

But even before the words were out of her mouth, de Landas with a hoarse cry of pent-up rage had struggled to his feet. With convulsed hands he fell heavily on Gilles, gripping him by the throat. Jacqueline could not suppress the cry of horror which rose to her lips: these two wounded men, one of them in the last stages of exhaustion, fighting and tearing, at grips with one another, like beasts convulsed in a desperate struggle for life.

But that same struggle could not help but be brief. De Landas was vanquished even before his last futile effort had fully matured. A minute or two later he was on his knees. Gilles held him down with one hand and with the other detached the mask from his face. He had thrown down his sword when de Landas attacked him with his hands. The row of masks had slid down the blade; they now lay in a mass upon the matting, right at Jacqueline's feet. De Landas' mask went to join the rest, and Gilles coolly picked up his sword. The light from the torch was full on him. Jacqueline still watched him, speechless and fascinated. It seemed as if she could not detach her eyes from him—his masked face, his broad shoulders, his hands; above all, his hands—the left one wherewith he tossed de Landas' mask at her feet; and the right, which clutched that exquisitely fashioned rapier with so much conscious power.

In a vague, dreamy kind of way, she noted how slender and nervy were those hands, despite their outward roughness and toil-worn look—the hands of a soldier, very obviously. The Prince de Froidmont must have been in many a bloody fray; had been wounded too on the left wrist—a severe cut. The scar gleamed white against the bronzed hue of the flesh. Jacqueline gazed on, strangely stirred. The scar was a very peculiar one, shaped like a cross, and at the time must almost have severed the wrist from the arm. She only remembered having once seen a similar wound, which must have left just such a peculiar scar. That was some three years ago, after that awful fight near Gembloux. Her brother Jan, since dead, was at the time lying sick at the monastery close by. She had wandered out for a breath of fresh air, feeling weary and desperately anxious. She was a mere child then, just past her sixteenth year. Outside the postern gate she and Nicolle had espied a soldier, lying wounded and unconscious on the ground. Nicolle had gone for help and two of the good monks had carried the poor man into the monastery. The leech who waited on Jan had tended him, and afterwards Jacqueline had ordered him to be transported back on the abandoned battle-field, where mayhap his comrades would presently find him; and she had seen that he was provided with food and with a pitcher of water, for she had been so sorry—so very sorry for him.

All that had happened three years ago, and Jacqueline had never thought on the matter again until now. Strange that the scar on Messire le Prince de Froidmont's wrist should so remind her of that little incident which had occurred in the monastery near Gembloux. Strange also that Messire should stand before her now and be searching her face with that intent glance of his, which she could feel right through the slits of his mask. He caught her looking at him so inquiringly and she straightway averted her gaze; but not before she had noted that with a quick gesture he had suddenly pulled the sleeve of his doublet well over his hand.

Gilles abruptly made for the door. But close to the threshold he turned and looked once more on Jacqueline. He could no longer see her face now, for she was stooping to de Landas, supporting him with her strong young arms. She had given one glance at the half-dozen masks which lay there on the floor where he had thrown them down. One or two were stained, others torn. She gave a shudder of horror and buried her face on de Landas' shoulder! Gilles could see that at sight of those things she had at last given way to tears and that convulsive sobs were shaking her lovely shoulders.

He felt a miserable brute—a callous ruffian who, for the sake of despicable vainglory, had done just the last thing that broke down this valiant woman's magnificent fortitude. A wave of self-contempt swept over him. He had meant to justify himself, to tell her that, far from being a common braggart who employed paid spadassins to save his own skin, he and his one faithful henchman had been set upon by her lover and his friends aided by half a dozen varlets to boot. He had meant to challenge de Landas to deny this truth, to force an avowal from his lips or from those of the young coxcombs who had played such a cowardly rôle in this night's work.

Yes, he had meant her to know the truth—the truth which would have shown her her lover and her friends in their true light. But when he saw those exquisite shoulders shaken with sobs, when he heard the pitiful little moans which at last found their way to her lips, he felt that he could not add yet another sorrow to the heavy burden which was weighing that golden head down. Now he was something of a knave in her sight; if she learned the truth from his lips he would become a cur in his own.

And, bidding Jehan to follow him, Gilles de Crohin hurried out of the room.

CHAPTER XII.
HOW TWO LETTERS CAME TO BE WRITTEN

I

'Madam la Reyne,' wrote Gilles the self-same night ere he laid down to rest, 'I entreat you to seek out Monseigneur le duc d'Anjou at once. Matters have occurred which might endanger the whole Success of this Enterprise. Madame Jacqueline is beautiful, exquisite, the most perfect Woman that ever graced a princely husband's house. So let Monseigneur come at once, Madame la Reyne, at once, I beg of you most humbly! and do entreat you to send me word by Maître Jehan when I may expect him.

'I am, your Majesty's
'Most Obedient and Most Faithful Servant,
'Gilles de Crohin.'

He felt more calm, more at peace with himself when he had written this letter, and allowed Jehan now to undress him and to attend to his wounds. They were not serious, certainly not so serious as many others which he had sustained in the past and recovered from without much trouble. But, somehow, this time he felt in a fever, the paltry scratches seemed unaccountably to throb, and his temples ached nigh to splitting.

Jehan, stolid and disapproving, pulled off his master's boots, took off doublet and hose with care and dexterity, but without making any attempt at conversation. What went on behind his low, square forehead could easily be conjectured: a towering rage against his own halting speech, which had prevented his proclaiming the truth before Madame Jacqueline, warred with a certain vague terror that Messire was angered with him for having brought Madame upon the scene.

But Messire apparently was too tired to scold. With unusual meekness he allowed Jehan to wash and dress that cut he had in the shoulder, and the one which had penetrated the fleshy part of his thigh. Maître Jehan was skilful in such matters. His father had been an apothecary at Grenoble and had taught the youngster something of the art of drugs and simples, until the latter's roving disposition had driven him to seeking fortune abroad. He still knew, however, how to minister to a wounded man, how to stem the flow of blood, and apply healing bandages. All this he did now in silence, and with the loving care engendered by his passionate affection for the master whom he served, the friend to whom he owed his life.

And all the while Gilles lay quite quiescent, so passive and patient that Jehan felt he must be very sick. Anger, self-contempt, self-reproach, had brought a heavy frown between his brows. Jacqueline's adorable image gave him a heart-ache more difficult to bear than any physical pain. For a long while he kept his eyes resolutely closed, in order to shut out the vision of a golden head and a demure, tantalizing face, which seemed to mock at him from out the dark angle of the room. It was only when Jehan had finished his ministrations and in his turn was ready to go to bed that he woke once more to the realities of life.

'Thou art a good soul, Jehan,' he murmured, with the first return to well-being brought about by the good fellow's restoratives.

'And you a mightily foolish one!' thought Jehan within himself, while he merely stuttered a moody: 'Aye—aye!'

'To-morrow morning,' continued Gilles; 'or rather, this morning—for 'tis past midnight now—thou'lt start for La Fère——'

'F-f-f-for La F-f-f——'

'For La Fère. Thou'lt take thy safe-conduct and this letter which I have just written for Madame la Reyne de Navarre.'

'B-b-b-but——'

'Hold thy tongue till I have finished. If Madame la Reyne hath perchance left La Fère, thou'lt follow her whithersoever she may have gone.'

'And if-f-f-f——'

'There is no "if" about the matter, my good Jehan,' quoth Gilles with a sigh and in a tone of unwonted firmness. 'Thou must find Madame la Reyne, and if she be not in La Fère then thou must follow her to Paris, or to Pau, or to the outermost ends of the earth; for Madame la Reyne must have my letter as soon as ever possible or the consequences for her, for me, for us all would be disastrous.'

Jehan made no further attempt at conversation. He only nodded his head in obedience and understanding.

'Madame la Reyne,' continued Gilles after a moment's pause, 'will, I doubt not, send me a letter in reply. I need not tell thee, Jehan, to guard both my letter and her reply with thy life.'

'N-n-no!' said Jehan with sudden glibness. 'You n-n-need not t-t-tell me that.'

'The letter would give us all away if it fell in alien hands. It must be destroyed, and thou too, honest Jehan, ere it leave thy hands.'

Jehan made a sign of comprehension, which Gilles evidently understood, for he continued more easily:

'Then get some rest now, Jehan, for thou must start as soon after daybreak as possible. And in God's name,' he added with a weary sigh, 'return with the answer within the week, or maybe thou'lt find my body rotting upon the gallows somewhere in the town.'

Jehan shrugged his wide shoulders. This meant that he thought his master must be slightly delirious, else he would never have spoken such rubbish. He took the letter which Gilles had folded into as small a compass as possible, and slipped it underneath his doublet and his shirt, against his skin. Then he tapped his breast and looked reassuringly on his master. Gesture and look conveyed all that he desired, and Gilles was satisfied.

He knew that he could trust Jehan as he would himself. With a final sigh which was almost one of content, he turned over on his side and went to sleep.

II

But faithful Jehan le Bègue did not go to sleep that night. Not until the late hours of the morning did he do that, and by then he was half a league away out of Cambray. As soon as he had seen his master lying in comparative comfort, he picked up the guttering candle and, walking cautiously on the tips of his toes, he went downstairs. Immediately under the stairs there was a narrow cupboard, and here upon the bare boards, rolled up In a blanket, Maître Julien was wont to sleep—of late with one eye open and one ear ready prepared to catch the slightest sound, since his liege-lady, the exquisite Queen of Navarre, had constituted him the guardian of Monseigneur le Prince de Froidmont.

Even now, at the first sound of those cautious footsteps, Julien was awake, and when, a minute or two later, Jehan peered into the narrow cupboard, he met the youth's eyes staring at him, glowing with that look of alertness and wariness which is peculiar to small animals at bay. He had raised himself on his elbow, but Jehan could see that underneath the ragged coverlet Julien's hand was grasping a pistol.

'F-f-f-friend,' he stuttered in a gruff whisper, 'g-g-get up. M-m-monseigneur's service,' he added significantly.

In a trice Julien was up.

'What is it?'

Jehan made several animated gestures, indicative of writing.

'Follow me,' rejoined Julien briefly.

He took the candle from Jehan and together the two men went into the room opposite, which served as taproom for the few guests who honoured 'Les Trois Rois' with their custom.

There was a long, narrow table at one end of the room. On this Julien placed the candle; then from a small cupboard in the wall he took paper, pen, sand and inkhorn, and placed these also upon the table.

There ensued then a long, whispered consultation between these two men. Julien with infinite patience gradually drew from Maître Jehan, bit by bit, almost word for word what he required. Ah! if Maître Jehan could only have put his wishes down on paper, matters would have been quite easy; but calligraphy was one of the arts which that worthy had never mastered in his youth, and which he certainly had not practised for the past twenty years. But what knowledge could not accomplish, that a boundless devotion on both sides contrived to do this night. Perspiration stood out in great beads upon Jehan's forehead, there was a deep frown of perplexity upon his brow as he stammered out laborious instructions to Julien. There was a strong vein of dogged obstinacy in his composition and a certain sound was still ringing in his ear, which spurred him to desperate efforts to make himself understood. It was the sound of Messire's weird laugh—harsh and uncontrolled—when Madame had taunted him with having a number of paid ruffians round him to help him in the fight against all those noble assassins. Paid ruffians, forsooth! Madame should know the truth, even if Maître Jehan's brain gave way under the terrible strain of making that cheesy-faced Julien understand what he wanted.

And Julien, intent, ghastly pale in his eagerness, listened with ear and mind and eyes and every sense strained to breaking point, to find sense and coherence in Jehan's stammering. For two hours these two men sat face to face with the guttering candle between them, glaring into one another's face, as if each would tear out the other's innermost brain and knead it to his will.

But at last Julien understood. By dint of broken monosyllables and emphatic gestures, Jehan had made it clear to him what had happened, and Julien, suddenly motioning the other to be silent, was at last able to put pen to paper.

'Most noble and gracious Seigneur,' he wrote, 'the writer is only a poor servant and you are a great and Puissant Lord; but I will tell you the Truth about what happened this night. Messire was set upon by six Noblemen, and the Writer was set upon by six Knaves. Messire was taken unawares and so was I. I feigned dead dog because I wanted to go and fetch help. Then the knaves were called away to help in the Murder of Messire, and I went to call Madame. Twelve against two, Monseigneur! Was that right? And Messire fought them all single-handed. This is the truth so help me God and I am Monseigneur's

'Most humble and obedient Servant,
'Jehan: servant to Monseigneur le Prince de Froidmont.'

When Julien had finished writing the letter he read it through aloud to Jehan three times; then, when the latter expressed himself completely satisfied with it, he folded it and Jehan slipped it inside his doublet, beside the one which Messire had given him.

After which, he took up the candle again and bade Maître Julien 'good-night.' He did not thank Julien, because he knew quite well that what the latter had done had given him infinite happiness to do. Every gesture, every look in the young man's face had proclaimed that happiness. In serving Monseigneur le Prince de Froidmont, he had indirectly served the goddess whom he worshipped from afar. His pale face still irradiated with joy, he went back to his poor, hard bed, to dream that She was smiling on him for his devotion to Her wishes.

And Jehan went straightway to his master's room.

III

The pale rays of a wintry moon came creeping in through the narrow casement-window. A lovely night had succeeded the drenching rain of awhile ago. Messire lay quite still upon his bed, but when Jehan crept close up to him he saw that his eyes were wide open.

'What's the matter, Jehan?' Gilles asked, when he saw his faithful henchman standing before him, booted and fully dressed.

'I can't sl-sl-sl-sleep,' replied Jehan unblushingly, 's-s-so I'll g-g-g-go now.'

'At once?'

Jehan nodded.

'Can you get your horse at this hour?'

Jehan nodded again.

'You have your safe-conduct? — the letter?'

More vigorous nods from Jehan.

'Take what money you want from there.' And Gilles with a jerk of the head indicated the valise which contained his effects.

Jehan knelt on the floor beside the valise and turned over his master's belongings. He took a small purse containing some gold, which he slipped into the pocket of his breeches; then he selected a fresh doublet, hose and mantle for Messire to wear and carefully folded and put away the tattered garments which had suffered so much damage during the fight. Oh! Maître Jehan was a tidy valet when he gave his mind to such trivial matters, and just now his mind was sorely exercised over Messire's future plight when he would be deprived of the services of so efficient a henchman.

Messire watched all his doings with much amusement.

"Tis not the first time that I shall be servantless, my good man,' he said lightly. 'And of a truth I have been too much pampered in that way of late. I still know how to dress myself and how to clean my boots—Aye!' he added, catching Jehan's look of reproach, 'and how to tend to these silly scratches which the very unskilful blades of M. de Landas and his friends did inflict upon my body.'

With a gesture of genuine affection he put out his hand, and good old Jehan took it in both his rough brown ones. When Gilles withdrew his hand again he noticed that there was a warm, wet spot upon it, whilst Jehan turned away very quickly, wiping his nose with the sleeve of his doublet.

But not another word was spoken by either of these two men—master and servant, friends and comrades—who understood one another to the last secret thought and the innermost heartbeat.

A moment or two later, Jehan had blown out the candle and was gone, and Gilles, lying on the narrow paillasse, wide awake, listened while he could hear his faithful servant's heavy footstep stumping along the corridor and down the stairs.

The wintry moon shed a weird, cold light into the narrow room, upon his valise, the elegant doublet which Jehan had so carefully laid out, the bottle of sedative, the fresh bandages, the pots of salve laid close to his hands. A heavy sigh rose involuntarily to his lips. Life appeared very difficult and very complicated just then. It had been so extraordinarily simple before: fighting for the most part, starving often, no cares, no worries, no thought for the morrow; then the axe finally laid to the root of life, somewhere on a battlefield, when Destiny had worked her will with the soldier of fortune.

But now——! And there was faithful Jehan, dragged too, and innocently, into this adventure, involved in an episode which might find the gallows for its conclusion. Gilles, listening, could hear his henchman's raucous stutter, rousing the echoes of the squalid little hostelry. Anon there was much scuffling and shuffling, doors opening and shutting, calls from Jehan and calls from Julien; then for awhile only distant and confused sounds of people stirring. Ten minutes or a quarter of an hour later the tramp of a horse's hoofs upon the cobblestones, more calls and some shouting, a good deal of clatter, the final banging of a heavy door—then nothing more.

And Gilles turned over, trying to get to sleep. In his hand he held, tightly clutched, a small, white, sweet-scented rag—a tiny ball of damp cambric; and ever and anon he raised that ball to his lips ... or to his eyes. But he could not get to sleep.

CHAPTER XIII.
HOW MADAME JACQUELINE
WAS GRAVELY PUZZLED

I

Old Nicolle and the women had known how to hold their tongues, so had Madame Jacqueline's torch-bearer. Indiscretion these days, where the affairs of noble gentlemen were concerned, was apt to bring terrible reprisals in its train. And above all, M. le Marquis de Landas was not a gentleman to be trifled with. If he desired secrecy, secrecy he would have, and woe betide the unfortunates who had not known how to hold their tongue.

Nicolle, aided by Maria and Bertine—two of Madame's most trustworthy serving-maids—had done their best to tend the wounds of the noble seigneurs, while the torch-bearer was despatched to their respective houses to summon immediate assistance. Messire de Borel was wealthy, owned horses and had an army of servants; the Comte du Prêt lived in a fine palace on the Place Verte, and the Seigneur de Maarege in the Rue St. George.

It was all done very quickly and very discreetly. Monseigneur the governor was never meant to know what had occurred in his Palace that night; servants came and went on tiptoe; the night watchmen had anyhow been bribed to secrecy. Martin et Martine at the Town Hall had only chimed the second hour of the morning and already the six young gallants had been conveyed back to their homes; the boudoir was locked up and the key given in charge of the night watchmen, who would see that order there was once more restored.

Jacqueline never deserted her self-appointed post until she was satisfied that the last vestige of that awful scuffle had been effectually obliterated. She helped Nicolle and her women to dress the wounds of the young seigneurs; she remained by de Landas' side until she saw him safely in the stalwart arms of his own henchmen. It was amazing how a girl, so young and so inexperienced, was able to give directions and to keep her head through this amazingly trying time. She had broken down once, when Gilles had thrown the masks at her feet; but directly he had gone she recovered herself, and from that moment everything was done at her command. Nicolle and the women, who were on the verge of losing their heads—of screaming and falling into a panic, were soon restored to order and efficiency by Madame's coolness and by her courage.

Jacqueline never flinched, nor did she ask any questions. She was affectionate with de Landas and gentle to all, but evidently her one care was to keep this miserable affair a secret from her guardian.

II

On the other hand, I, for one, am not going to say that Gilles de Crohin was not a sick man on the following morning, when he managed to crawl out of bed and to dress himself, inwardly cursing the absence of his faithful Jehan. He made light of 'scratches,' but he had no fewer than five about his body, and the flesh wound in his thigh was exceedingly unpleasant. He had sat moodily in his narrow room for some time, vaguely wondering what in the world he was to do with himself, or whether Madame Jacqueline would ever care to set eyes on him again.

He was smarting under the sense of injustice. What right had she to look on him as a braggart who would pay a set of knaves to help him in his quarrels? The feeling of insensate jealousy which was gnawing at his heart was still more unpleasant to bear. He almost understood de Landas' hatred of himself after the episode in the banqueting hall, for he—Gilles—was at this moment experiencing just that same torturing jealousy, which had caused de Landas to outrage every canon of chivalry and honour for the sake of getting even with an execrated rival.

In fact, neither his mental nor his physical condition was in an enviable state when a runner arrived that morning at 'Les Trois Rois' and asked for leave to speak with Messire Gilles de Crohin, equerry to Monseigneur le Prince de Froidmont.

Gilles, a little bewildered by this unexpected occurrence, met the runner in the taproom of the hostelry. Somewhat curtly, he told the man that Monseigneur le Prince was sick, and that he—Gilles—was in attendance on his master. But the messenger appeared in no way disconcerted at the rebuff; he seemed to have received instructions that would cover every eventuality.

'Monseigneur the governor,' he said, 'had heard a rumour that His Magnificence was sick. Therefore he begged that Messire de Crohin would forthwith come over to the Palace and reassure him as to the condition of his master, Monseigneur le Prince de Froidmont.'

The runner had long disappeared down the Rue aux Juifs and Gilles de Crohin was still standing in the middle of the taproom, clutching his chin with his hand in a state of most unenviable perturbation. A very severe test on his histrionic powers was about to be imposed upon him. Monseigneur's desire—nay! his command—could not be disregarded. He—Gilles—must present himself at the Palace just as he was—playing no rôle this time, save that of striving to obliterate all similarity between himself as he really was and would be to-day, and himself as he had been in Monseigneur's sight during the past five days.

No wonder that at the prospect he too—like Jehan last night—felt cold drops of sweat rising to the roots of his hair. I will not say that the thought of seeing Madame Jacqueline again, if he went to the Palace, did not in a measure give him courage; but even that courage was only fictitious, because in all probability she would scarce vouchsafe to look on the servant, seeing that her heart was filled with hatred and contempt for the master.

Nevertheless, he was at the Palace less than an hour later. Monseigneur was very gracious, and apparently not the least suspicious. He only expressed regret that it had not been his good fortune to meet Messire Gilles de Crohin ere this. On the other hand, his apologies for what had occurred the night before inside his own Palace were both profuse and humble—almost abject.

'I beg you, Messire,' he said earnestly, at the close of the interview, 'to assure Monseigneur le Duc d'Anjou that I would give ten years of my life—and I have not many left to give—to undo the mischief wrought by a few young nincompoops. I can but hope that

His Highness will exonerate me from any negligence or want of understanding in the matter.'

By this time Gilles was mentally quite at his ease. If his thigh was painful, he had nevertheless managed to walk into Monseigneur's presence without a limp, and to all appearances his host was at this hour very far from suspecting the slightest fraud.

'His Highness,' he said lightly, 'will recover from his scratches within the next day or two. The whole matter is unworthy of Monseigneur's anxiety.'

After which assurance, and mutual protestations of esteem and good-will, Gilles was allowed to take his leave.

III

Being a personage of no consequence, Messire Gilles de Crohin, equerry to Monseigneur le Prince de Froidmont, was not escorted to the gates by an army of ushers; rather was he allowed to find his way out as best he could. The interview with Monseigneur had taken place in a room on a floor above, and he was walking slowly along one of the wide corridors which, if memory served him, would lead him to the grand staircase. On his right the tall, deep-embrasured windows gave on the magnificent park which, with its stately trees still dressed in winter garb, lay bathed in the sunlight of this early spring day.

He paused just for a moment, looking over the park at the rich panorama of the city. The window nearest to him was slightly open, and the south-westerly breeze was apparently stirring the heavy curtains in front of it. From somewhere close by there came gently wafted the delicious penetrating fragrance of lilies. Was it a wonder that Gilles' thoughts should at once have flown to Jacqueline? and that an uncontrollable ache should suddenly grip his heart?

Throughout his long adventurous life he had seen so many women—had kissed a few, and loved none; and now Fate had placed in his path just the one woman in the whole wide world whom at first sight he had loved with unbounded passion, and who was as far removed from him as was the gold-crowned steeple of St. Géry far away, and infinitely more unattainable. For the first time in his life Gilles had looked into a woman's eyes, felt that they held in their depths a promise of paradise, only to realize that that promise could never be made to him.

The scent of the lilies brought with it a murmur of spring, of awakening nature, of twitter of birds, and the man who listened to that murmur, who thrilled at its insistent call, knew that he must for ever remain lonely, that the call of springtide for him must for ever remain unsatisfied.

Standing there alone, he was not ashamed of his emotion, not ashamed that hot tears welled up involuntarily to his eyes. But with a half-impatient gesture and a smile at his own folly, he brushed these with his hand resolutely away.

When the mist of tears was cleared from his eyes, he suddenly saw her—his dream—standing before him. She was in the window embrasure, with the flood of sunshine wrapping her like a mantle of gold. On the window sill beside her lay a bunch of white lilies. Her little hand—Gilles thought he had never seen such an exquisite little hand—held back the curtain, behind which she had apparently been sitting. A soft breeze blew in through the half-open window and stirred with its delicate breath the soft tendrils of her ardent hair. Her face against the light was in a tender, grey shadow, through which her eyes shone like a peep of azure sky, and on her cheek that tiny mole was provocatively asking for a kiss.

The apparition had come upon Gilles so suddenly, the transition from dark melancholy to joy was so abrupt, that he—poor man!— weak, sick, unnerved by weariness and constant strain, not only found nothing to say, but he clean forgot all the amenities of social life which the equerry of a prince of the House of Valois should have had at his finger-tips.

Jacqueline, too, strangely enough, felt embarrassed for the moment, angry with herself for being tongue-tied. What was there to be confused about? Messire Gilles de Crohin could not possibly guess that she had been sitting here in the window embrasure, waiting to see him pass, just because she desired to have news of his master. He could not guess that it had taken all her reserves of diplomacy to so explain to Monseigneur when he questioned her, what she knew of the events of the past night that, without being greatly angered against M. de Landas, he should feel sufficient compunction to send promptly for news of Messire le Prince de Froidmont. Certainly Messire's equerry could not guess that Madame Jacqueline's heart had been touched and her mind tickled when Monseigneur placed before her the naïve effusion of Maître Jehan, and that her own common sense and unerring feeling for justice had filled in the gaps which the worthy servant's missive had left in his exposé of what had actually occurred.

Therefore it was not the fear of what Messire de Crohin might think or guess that kept Jacqueline momentarily speechless and shy, rather was it a curious and undefinable sense of something strange—familiar yet mysterious—about the personality of this man who stood, equally silent, before her. It took her several seconds to free herself from this spell which appeared to have been cast over her, several seconds of fighting angrily with herself for the constraint which rendered her tongue-tied and shy. Fortunately he appeared quite unaware of her embarrassment, waited somewhat awkwardly, she thought, for her to speak.

'You are Messire de Crohin?' she contrived to say at last.

'At your service, Madame,' he replied.

'Equerry to Monseigneur le Prince de Froidmont?'

He bowed in affirmative response.

'And ... I have no doubt ... devoted to his person?'

He smiled.

'Why should Madame conclude that?' he asked.

She gave a little start. Somehow his tone—that bantering smile, had accentuated that feeling of familiarity which rendered his person so strangely mysterious.

'Monseigneur le Prince de Froidmont,' she rejoined coldly, 'is sure to command the devotion of those who serve him. He is brave and chivalrous— —'

'That was not Madame's opinion of him last night— —' he broke in dryly. Then, seeing that his tone had caused her to turn her eyes on him with unfeigned surprise he added somewhat lamely: 'At least ... that is ... that is what Monseigneur gave me to understand last night— —'

'It was all a misunderstanding,' she said gently. 'Will you say that to Monseigneur?'

'If Madame desires.'

'I do desire it. And since you know all about the incident, Messire, will you, I pray you, tell your master how deeply I regret the erroneous judgment which I formed of his conduct? Those abominable varlets all crowding round him— —'

'Appearances were against Monseigneur, no doubt.'

'And I behaved like a vixen, Messire,' she said with a smile.

'Then give me an army of vixens!' he retorted impulsively.

'Why, Messire, you were not there to see— —'

'No! But I imagine now that vixens must be adorable.'

'Do not jest, Messire,' she rejoined more earnestly. 'I was shrewish last night and ill-tempered and unjust. Will you tell your master that this morning— —'

'I will tell him, Madame, that this morning you are perfect, whatever you may have been last night.'

Poor Gilles by now would have given all that he possessed in the world to be allowed to go. He felt that this interview, which he had neither sought nor hoped for, was like a dangerous trap into which Fate and his own temperament might hurl him headlong. Every minute that he spent in this woman's company rendered her more desirable to him, rendered him more completely a slave to her charm. But for some strange and subtle reason she seemed disinclined to let him go just yet, and even now when, remembering his best manners, Gilles started on the preliminaries of a most elaborate farewell bow, she went on with a quick catching of her breath and a slight hesitation, which brought a soft glow to her cheeks:

'Messire Gilles— —'

'At your service, Madame.'

'Was Monseigneur de Froidmont very angered with me?'

'He was,' Gilles admitted, 'last night.'

"But ... but....'

'His anger hath since melted like snow in the spring.'

'Even before you came hither at the bidding of my guardian?'

'Even before that, Madame.'

'Did he tell you so?'

'I guessed it.'

'Do you know his innermost thoughts, then?'

'Most of them—yes, Madame.'

'You are very intimate with Monseigneur le Prince de Froidmont?' she asked, with a certain shy hesitancy which Gilles found adorable, because it caused a delicate flush of pink to suffuse her cheeks. This caused him, in his turn, to be confused and tongue-tied, staring at her with eyes that seemed as if they would devour her loveliness.

She had to repeat her question.

'Oh!—ah!—er!' he stammered vaguely. 'That is—yes! Yes, Madame! I am on ultimate terms with Monseigneur.'

'And—do tell me, Messire—is Monseigneur handsome?'

'No, by the Lord!' exclaimed Gilles with a loud laugh. Then he caught her look: it was not one of surprise, rather of amusement not unmixed with quaint, roguish mischief. He could not interpret that look rightly, and began to stammer, worse confused than before.

'Madame—I—that is——'

'You are no judge of your master's looks, shall we say?' she retorted with an enigmatic little smile. 'But you must remember that, though I found Monseigneur of noble bearing, I have no notion how he looks, for I have never seen him without a mask—that is——'

This time Gilles was quite sure that she was doing her best to suppress a laugh.

'Do you think,' she said, 'that you could persuade His Magnificence to pay his respects to me unmasked?'

'Monseigneur will, I feel sure,' he rejoined stiffly, 'be honoured by the command, but——'

'But what, Messire?'

'He is strangely ill-favoured, Madame.'

'Oh! a woman is the best judge of that. Some of the ugliest men have proved most attractive.'

'But—but Monseigneur is scarred—badly scarred. He——'

'What matter? There is naught so glorious as scars on a soldier's face. When I was a child I once saw the Duc de Guise—le Balafré! With that great cut across his cheek, he was still the most notable man in a room filled to overflowing with clever, brave and handsome men!'

'But—but, Madame, Monseigneur is also pock-marked. Yes, that's it! Pock-marked! An illness contracted in early childhood—Madame understands?'

'I do,' she replied with a little sigh of sympathy, and looked with those enchanting blue eyes of hers straight on poor Gilles. 'I do. It is very sad.'

'Very sad indeed, Madame.'

'Scarred and pock-marked. No wonder Monseigneur is shy to show his face. But no matter,' she continued gaily. 'He hath such a lovely voice, and oh! such beautiful hands! Slender and full of nerve and power! I always take note of hands, Messire,' she said with well-feigned ingenuousness. 'They indicate a man's character almost more than his face. Do you not think, so too?'

'I—Madame—that is——'

Gilles had, quite instinctively, drawn the lace of his sleeve over his left hand, even while Madame still looked at him with that tantalizing glance which had the effect of turning his brain to putty and his knees to pulp. Now she laughed—that merry, rippling laugh of hers—and I do verily assure you that the poor man was on the verge of making a complete fool of himself. Indeed, it were difficult to say whether or no the next second would have witnessed his complete surrender to Jacqueline's magic charm, his total loss of self-control and the complete downfall of Madame la Reyne de Navarre's cherished plan, for poor Gilles had lost consciousness of every other feeling and thought save that of a wild longing to fall on his knees and to kiss the tiny foot which peeped beneath the hem of that exquisite woman's gown, a wild longing, too, to hold out his arms and to fold her to his breast, to kiss her hair, her eyes, her lips, that tiny mole which had wrought the whole mischief with his soul. For the moment he forgot his past life, his present position, the Duc d'Anjou and Madame la Reyne: he had forgotten that he was a penniless adventurer, paid to play an unworthy trick upon this innocent girl, sworn to infamy on pain of greater infamy still! He had forgotten everything save that she was adorable and that an altogether new and ardent love had taken possession of his soul.

Of a truth it is impossible for a prosy chronicler to state definitely what might have happened then, if Monseigneur the governor had not chosen that very moment for coming out of his room and walking down the corridor, at one end of which Gilles was standing spell-bound before the living presentment of his dream of long ago. He heard Monseigneur's heavy footstep, pulled himself vigorously together, and with an impatient gesture which was habitual to him, he passed his left hand slowly across his forehead.

When he looked on Jacqueline again she was staring at him with an expression that appeared almost scared and wholly bewildered, and with a strange, puzzled frown upon her smooth forehead. For the space of a second or two it seemed as if she wanted to say something, then held back the words. After a slight hesitation, however, she finally went forward a step or two to meet her guardian, without looking again on Gilles.

'I was glad,' she said quietly to d'Inchy, 'to have had an opportunity of seeing Messire de Crohin and of begging him to offer to Monseigneur le Prince de Froidmont, his master, my sincere regrets for what occurred last night.'

'Messire has already assured me,' rejoined d'Inchy suavely, 'that Monseigneur harbours no resentment against any of us. Is that not so, Messire?'

'Indeed it is, Monseigneur,' replied Gilles stiffly. 'Whatever Monseigneur may have felt last night, I in his name do assure you that at this hour the incident of last night hath faded from his memory.'

He bowed now, ready to take his leave. But Jacqueline was apparently not yet ready to dismiss him. Something had gravely puzzled her, that was clear; and it was that something which seemingly made her loth to let him go.

'What, think you, Messire,' she said abruptly, 'caused Monseigneur to forget his resentment so quickly?'

'A journey, Madame,' he replied, looking her boldly between the eyes this time, 'which his thoughts took skywards, astride upon a sunbeam.'

She smiled.

'And did Monseigneur's thoughts wander far on that perilous journey?'

'As far as the unknown, Madame.'

'The unknown? Where is that?'

'There where we sow our dreams.'

'Where we sow our dreams? You speak in metaphors, Messire. If, as you say, we sow our dreams, what do we reap?'

'A perfect being such as you, Madame, can only reap joy and happiness.'

'But you, Messire?'

'Oh, I, Madame!' he replied with a shrug of his broad shoulders. 'What can a poor soldier of fortune garner from a crop of dreams save a bunch of memories?'

'Happy memories, I trust,' she said gently, as she finally extended her dainty hand for his kiss.

'Happiness is such an ephemeral flower, Madame: memory is its lasting perfume.'

For one brief moment her exquisite little hand, white, soft and tensely alive, like the petals of a fragrant lily, lay upon his own: for one brief moment of unalloyed happiness his lips rested upon her finger-tips, and he felt them quivering beneath his kiss, as if something of the passion which was searing his heart had been communicated to her through that kiss.

The moment went by like a flash: the next, Monsieur le Baron d'Inchy was already bidding him farewell with many an unctuous word, which Gilles never even heard. He had eyes and ears only for Jacqueline—Jacqueline, whom he had seen and loved at first sight, when she had been alternately proud and dignified, demure and arch, reproachful and contemptuous; but before whom he could now bend the knee in adoration when a softened mood filled her eyes with tears and caused her perfect lips to quiver with unexpressed sympathy.

'I entreat you, Messire,' she said finally, 'when you return to your master, to urge upon him the necessity of extreme prudence. Strangers are none too welcome in Cambray these days, and Monseigneur de Froidmont hath already made many enemies, some of whom are unscrupulous, others merely hot-headed; but all, alas! dangerous.

Guard him with your life, Messire,' she urged, with a quaint little catch in her throat. 'And, above all, I pray you to assure him that Jacqueline de Broyart would give much to undo the miserable work of the past night.'

She bowed her head in token that he was dismissed at last, and he—poor wretch!—could not at that moment have uttered a single word in response, for his throat was choked and his very sinews ached with the effort to appear calm and unconcerned before Monseigneur the governor.

So, I fear me, that Gilles de Crohin defied every social rule laid down by the aforesaid Maître Calviac, and that Monseigneur the governor was seriously shocked when he saw a mere equerry taking an unduly hasty leave from himself and from Madame Jacqueline de Broyart, who was Duchesse et Princesse de Ramèse, in rank far above any Sire de Crohin.

Monseigneur d'Inchy gave a quick sigh of impatience. The comedy invented by the Queen of Navarre was beginning to tax his powers of endurance heavily. Were it not for the great issues at stake, he would never have humbled himself before any man as he had done before a profligate Valois prince who was not worthy to lick the dust that stained Madame Jacqueline's velvet shoes. He looked down with conscious pride on his beautiful ward, more beautiful at this moment, he thought, than she had ever looked before. She was gazing straight down the length of the corridor; her lips were parted in an enigmatic smile which greatly puzzled her old guardian, a soft blush mantled over her cheeks and throat, and as she gazed—on nothing seemingly—her blue eyes shone with a strange, inward excitement.

And yet, all that there was to see down the corridor was the retreating figure of that somewhat ill-mannered equerry, Messire Gilles de Crohin.

CHAPTER XIV.
WHICH TREATS OF THE DISCOMFITURE
OF M. DE LANDAS

I

We may take it that M. le Baron d'Inchy, at whose invitation the Duc d'Anjou had come to Cambray, was not likely to let the matter of the midnight duel remain unpunished, the moment he learned the full facts about the affair. The epistle of Maître Jehan had put him on the scent, and it must be remembered that M. le Baron d'Inchy ruled over Cambray and the Cambrésis with the full autocratic power of a conqueror, and that he had therefore more than one means at his disposal for forcing the truth from unwilling witnesses if he had a mind.

That truth, as confessed by the night watchmen, was nothing short of appalling. Monseigneur the governor's first thought had been one of ample—not to say, obsequious—apologies to His Highness for the outrage against his person. But *Monsieur* being sick, and etiquette forbidding Monseigneur the governor's visit to so humble an hostelry as that of 'Les Trois Rois,' M. d'Inchy had bethought himself of Messire Gilles de Crohin, the equerry, had sent for him and begged him to transmit to His Highness all those excuses which he—the governor—would have wished to offer in person. Fortunately, the equerry had been able to assure Monseigneur that His Highness appeared inclined to look on the affair with leniency. Whereupon d'Inchy had seen him depart again, feeling still very wrathful but decidedly easier in his mind.

Then he sent for de Landas.

De Landas was sick of his wounds, feverish and in the leech's hands; but the order to present himself before the governor was so peremptory that he dared not refuse. He knew well that nothing but unbridled anger would cause Monseigneur to issue such an arbitrary order and that it would neither be wise nor even safe to run counter to his will.

So de Landas had his wounds re-dressed and bandaged; he took the cooling draught which the leech had prepared for him, and then he ordered four of his men to carry him on a stretcher to the Archiepiscopal Palace. But all this show of sickness did not have the effect of softening Monseigneur's mood. He ordered de Landas very curtly to dismiss his stretcher-bearers, then he motioned him to a seat, himself sat down behind his desk and fixed searching eyes upon his young kinsman.

'I have sent for you, José,' he began sternly, 'and for you alone, rather than for the whole of your gang, because you have constituted yourself their leader, and they invariably follow you like so many numskulls, in any mischief which you might devise.'

'Mon cousin— —' stammered de Landas, abashed, despite himself, by d'Inchy's dictatorial tone.

'One moment,' broke in the latter harshly. 'Let me tell you at once that explanations and prevarications are useless. I received a hint of what occurred last night primarily from an outside source, but you will understand that a clue once obtained can very easily be followed up. We questioned your varlets, put the night watchmen to the torture; they confessed everything, and you, M. le Marquis de Landas, my kinsman, and half a dozen of your precious friends, stand convicted of an attempt at assassination against the person of a stranger, who happens to be my guest.'

De Landas, feeling himself cornered, made no attempt to deny. It certainly would have been useless. Unfortunately he had allowed his jealousy to get the better of his prudence, and last night had made more than one mistake—such, for instance, as not killing the watchmen outright instead of merely overpowering them, and employing his own men rather than a few paid spadassins, who could not afterwards have been traced. So he sat on, sullen and silent, his arm resting on that of the chair, his chin buried in his hand.

'For that attempted crime,' resumed Monsieur le Baron d'Inchy, after a slight pause, and speaking in a trenchant and staccato tone, 'I have decided to expel you and your five friends out of the city.'

De Landas, forgetting his wounds and his sickness, jumped to his feet as if he had been cut with a lash.

'Expel me— —?' he stammered. He could scarcely frame the words. He was grey to the lips and had to steady himself against the table or he would have measured his length on the floor.

'You and your friends,' reiterated d'Inchy with uncompromising severity. 'Would you perchance prefer the block?'

But already de Landas had recovered some of his assurance.

'This is monstrous!' he exclaimed hotly. 'I, your kinsman! Herlaer, Maarege—some of your most devoted friends...!'

'No one is a friend,' retorted d'Inchy firmly, 'who is a law-breaker and a potential assassin!'

'Monseigneur!' protested de Landas.

'Well! What else were you all last night?'

'We had no intention of killing the rogue.'

'And attacked him, six to one!'

'His impudence deserved chastisement. We only desired to administer a lesson.'

'In what form, I pray you?' queried d'Inchy with a short ironical laugh.

'We had some sticks in reserve— —"

'Sticks!' thundered d'Inchy, who at the words had jumped to his feet and in his wrath brought down his clenched fist with a crash upon the table. 'Sticks!! You had thought ... you would dare ... to raise your hands against ... against ... Oh, my God!' he exclaimed in horror as he sank down once more into his chair and, resting his elbows on the table, he buried his face in his hands. Evidently he was quite unnerved.

De Landas had remained silent. Of a truth he had been struck dumb by this extraordinary show of what amounted almost to horror on the part of his usually dignified and self-contained kinsman. It seemed as if he—de Landas—had said something awful, something stupendous when he spoke of administering chastisement to a vagabond. A vagabond indeed! What else was this so-called Prince de Froidmont? Whence did he come? What was his purpose in coming to Cambray? And why should Monseigneur the governor be so completely unnerved at the bare possibility of any one laying hands on so obscure a personage?

But this was obviously not the moment for demanding an explanation. De Landas, ere he left his own fatherland in order to seek fortune in Flanders, had already been well schooled in those arts of diplomacy and procrastination for which Spanish statesmen were famous. He scented a mystery here, which he then and there vowed to himself that he would fathom; but this was not the time to betray his own suspicions. He knew well enough that these wooden-headed Flemings were for ever hatching plots for the overthrow of their Spanish conquerors, that His Majesty the King of Spain had hardly one faithful or loyal subject among these boors, who were for ever prating of their independence and of their civil and religious liberties. De Landas' quick, incisive mind had already jumped to the conclusion that, in this mystery which surrounded the personality of this enigmatic Prince de Froidmont, there was no doubt the beginnings of one of those subtle intrigues, which had already filched from the kingdom of Spain more than one of her fair Flemish provinces. But the young man had up to now been too indolent and too self-indulgent to trouble himself much about the dangers which threatened his country through the brewing of these intrigues. He was of a truth ready to find fortune in Flanders and to marry the richest heiress in the land if he could, and then to remain loyal to the country of his adoption if it continued to suit his purpose so to do; but if, as he began now vaguely to fear, his plans with regard to Jacqueline were thwarted for the sake of some unknown suitor, however highly placed, if the golden apple which he had hoped to gather in this mist-laden land turned to dead-sea fruit in his hand, then he would no longer consider himself bound by allegiance to this alien country; rather would his loyalty to King Philip of Spain demand that he should combat every machination which these abominable Flemings might set afoot, for the overthrow of Spanish power.

But all this was for the future. De Landas was astute enough not to betray a single one of his thoughts at the moment—not until he had surveyed the whole situation in cold blood and discussed it with his friends. For the nonce, conciliation was the only possible—the only prudent—course of action, and humility and resignation the only paths thereto.

So he waited a minute or two until d'Inchy had mastered his extraordinary emotion. Then he said meekly:

'Monseigneur, you see me utterly confounded by your anger. On my honour, I and my friends sinned entirely in ignorance. We thought the stranger presumptuous in the presence of Madame Jacqueline de Broyart, who in our sight is almost a divinity. We desired to teach a malapert a lesson for daring to approach the greatest lady in Flanders otherwise than on bended knees. We had no thought,' he added insidiously, 'that in so doing we might be attacking a personage whom Monseigneur desires to hold in especial honour.'

'Even if the stranger was a person of no consequence,' rejoined d'Inchy more calmly, 'your conduct was outrageous——'

'As it is, I am humbled in the dust at thought that it put a spoke in the wheel of some deep-laid political plans.'

'I did not say that——' broke in d'Inchy quickly.

'Oh, Monseigneur!' protested de Landas gently, 'you deign to belittle mine intelligence. I may be a young jackanapes, but I am not such a crass fool as not to realize that the person whom I only thought to chastise, as I might some insignificant groundling, must be a gentleman of more than ordinary consequence, else you would not punish me so severely for so venial an offence.'

'It is my duty——'

'To expel six noble gentlemen from their homes for laying hands on an unknown adventurer? Fie, Monseigneur! Your estimate of my reasoning powers must of a truth be a very low one.'

'You have gravely erred against the laws of hospitality.'

'I am prepared to lick the dust in my abasement.'

'You have offended a stranger who was my guest.'

'I will offer him my abject excuses, tell him that I mistook him for a caitiff.'

'He would not accept your excuses.'

'Is he such a high and mighty prince as all that?' retorted de Landas.

It was an arrow shot into the air, but it evidently hit the mark, for d'Inchy had winced at the taunt.

'M. le Prince de Froidmont has been too gravely affronted,' he said stiffly, 'for excuses to be of any avail.'

'Let me try them, at any rate,' riposted de Landas, almost servilely now.

'I don't know—I——'

'Ah! but Monseigneur, I entreat you, listen. I am your friend, your kinsman, have served this land faithfully, devotedly, for years! I have no wish to pry into your secrets, to learn anything of which you desire to keep me in ignorance. But think—think!! Others would not be so scrupulous as I. Gossip flies about very quickly in this city, and rumours would soon take wider flight, if it became known that you had punished with such unyielding rigour six of your best friends, one of them your own kinsman, for daring to quarrel with a masked stranger whom nobody knows, and who has entered this city in the strictest incognito. People will deduce unpleasant conclusions: some will call the stranger a Spanish spy, and you, Monseigneur, a paid agent of Spain. At best, rumour will be busy with speculations and conjectures which will jeopardize all your plans. In pleading for mercy, Monseigneur,' urged de Landas with well-feigned ingenuous enthusiasm, ''tis not so much mine own cause that I advocate, but rather that of your own peace of mind and the fulfilment of all your secret desires.'

D'Inchy made no immediate reply. No doubt the Spaniard's specious arguments had struck him as sound. He knew well enough how difficult it was, these days, to keep tongues from wagging, and until the affair with *Monsieur* Duc d'Anjou, was irrevocably concluded, gossip would prove a deadly danger, not only to the plans which he and de Lalain had laid so carefully, but also to themselves and to their adherents. This knowledge caused him to weaken in his attitude toward de Landas. He sat there, frowning, silent, obviously hesitating already.

We must always remember also that the Flemings—whether lords or churls—had never been able to hold their own against Spanish diplomacy and Spanish cunning. Their mind was too straightforward, too simple, yes! too childish, to understand the tortuous subtleties practised by these past masters of mental craftiness.

D'Inchy, de Lalain, de Montigny and their friends had plunged up to the neck in a sea of intrigue. They were already floundering, out of their depth. D'Inchy, ingenuous and inherently truthful, had never suspected de Landas of duplicity—had, of a truth, never had cause to suspect him—therefore now he took the young Spaniard's protestations, his meekness, his well-timed warning, entirely at their face value. De Landas was looking him straight in the face while he spoke, and d'Inchy was duly impressed by the air of straightforwardness, of youthful enthusiasm, wherewith the young man punctuated his impassioned tirade; and the latter, quick to note every change in the Fleming's stern features, pursued his advantage, pressed home his pleadings, half certain already of success.

'Let me go forthwith, Monseigneur,' he begged, 'to offer my humble apologies to—to—Monsieur—er—le Prince de Froidmont. Though you may think that we tried to murder him last night, we crossed swords with him like loyal gentlemen. I and my friends will meekly admit our errors. He is too chivalrous, believe me, not to forgive.'

Obviously d'Inchy was yielding. Perhaps he had never been very determined on punishing those young coxcombs, had been chiefly angered because he feared that in his wrath *Monsieur* Duc d'Anjou, might incontinently shake the dust of inhospitable Cambray from off his velvet shoes. Above all things, d'Inchy dreaded gossip about the affair, and de Landas had indeed proved himself a master in the art of self-defence when he prophesied the birth of countless rumours if wholesale expulsions and punishments followed the midnight brawl.

'Have I your permission to go, Monseigneur?' insisted de Landas. 'Sick as I am, I can yet crawl as far as the hostelry where lodges the enigmatic Prince de Froidmont.'

Again d'Inchy winced. He felt his secret escaping from the safe haven of his own keeping. He sat on in silence, meditating for awhile. After all, *Monsieur's* equerry had assured him that His Highness was disposed to look leniently on the episode, and who could be more royalist then the King? more Catholic than the Pope? Gradually the tensity of his attitude relaxed, the dark frown disappeared from between his brows; he still looked sternly on his young kinsman, but the latter saw that the look was no longer menacing.

A few minutes later Monseigneur d'Inchy had spoken the word which caused de Landas to give a deep sigh of relief.

'Very well!' he said. 'You may try. But understand,' he added inflexibly. 'If Monsieur—I mean, if M. le Prince de Froidmont does not accept your apology, if he demands your punishment, you leave Cambray to-night.'

'I understand, Monseigneur,' said de Landas simply.

'And if the Prince does accept your apology, and I do condone your offence this time, your punishment will be all the more severe if you transgress again. It would not be a sentence of expulsion then, but one of death. Now you may go!' he concluded curtly. 'My leniency in the future will depend upon your conduct.'

After which, he dismissed de Landas with a stiff inclination of the head, and the young Spaniard left the presence of the autocratic governor of Cambray with rage in his heart and a veritable whirlpool of conjectures, of surmises and of intrigues seething in his fertile brain.

II

But right through the wild medley of hypotheses which ran riot in de Landas' mind there raged also furious, unbridled wrath—wrath at his own humiliation, his own impotence—hatred against the man who had brought him to this pass, and mad, ungovernable jealousy whenever his thoughts turned to Jacqueline.

Somehow—it was only instinct, no doubt—he felt that all this pother about the masked stranger centred round the personality of Jacqueline. The first hint which Monseigneur had of last night's affray must of necessity have come from Jacqueline. She alone was there— varlets and wenches did not count—she alone could have a personal interest in putting Monseigneur on the scent.

A personal interest? De Landas' frown became dark and savage when first that possibility rose before his mind. He had ordered his servants, very curtly, to go and wait for him in the main entrance hall, for after his interview with the governor he felt the want of being alone for a few moments, to think over the situation as it so gravely affected him. He was in the same corridor where a couple of hours ago Jacqueline had waylaid and spoken with Messire Gilles de Crohin. On his right was the row of tall windows with their deep embrasures, which gave view upon the park. De Landas felt sick and fatigued, as much from choler and nerve-strain as from the effect of his wounds, and he sat down on one of the wide window-seats to think matters over.

A personal interest?

Yes! That was it. Jacqueline, capricious, hot-headed, impulsive, had been attracted by the mysterious personality of the stranger, and for the moment was forgetting the lover of her youth, the man who felt that he had an inalienable claim upon her allegiance. De Landas had heard rumours of a masked minstrel having serenaded Madame beneath her windows. Pierre, his own henchman, had received a broad hint to that effect from Nicolle, who was Madame's waiting-woman. Was it possible that the masked troubadour and the enigmatic Prince de Froidmont were one and the same person? and was it likely that Jacqueline's romantic fancy had been captured by his wiles?

A wild, unreasoning rage gripped at de Landas' heart at the thought: sheer physical pain caused him to groan aloud. He felt stifled and giddy, and with a rough, impatient gesture, he threw open the casement-window and leaned out, in order to inhale the pure, fresh air which rose from the park. As he did so, he caught sight of Jacqueline, who was wandering in and among the bosquets, attended only by one of her maids. She was dressed in a dark gown and had a hood over her head, but even thus garbed she looked adorable, and de Landas muttered an angry oath as he looked down on her, watching her sedate movements, the queenly walk, that quaint air of demureness and dignity which became her so well. He suddenly realized all that the past few days—nay! weeks—had meant in the shaping of his destiny. Monseigneur the governor's stern decree had already placed her out of his reach; she was slipping away from him, dragged from his side by her accession to wealth and power, by the political intrigues which centred around her—aye! and she was also slipping away from him through the gradual cooling of her attachment for him; that fact he could no longer disguise from himself. He had succeeded in winning her, when she was so young and so inexperienced that she fell readily enough—almost unconsciously—into his arms. He had ensnared her like the skilful fowler succeeds in trapping a fledgling unawares. Since then, so many things had changed. Jacqueline, from an obscure little country wench—almost the handmaid of an adulated brother—had become one of the most important personages in the land. She was fêted, courted, admired, on every side, surrounded by all that was most handsome, most chivalrous, in Europe. She had not actually turned from the lover of her girlhood—no! even de Landas was forced to admit that—but she had learned to appraise him in the same crucible as other men; and, with teeth set, and shame and anger gnawing in his heart, de Landas had to tell himself that she had apparently found him wanting. Time was when nothing on earth would have turned her admiration away from him, when, whatever the appearances might be, she would look up to him as the fount of all bravery and of all honour. But last night she had only been gentle and pitying, and a few hours later had led Monseigneur into investigating the whole affair.

De Landas' fist against the window ledge was clenched until the knuckles of his slender hand gleamed like ivory. Had the masked stranger himself aught to do with Jacqueline's disloyalty? Suddenly the Spaniard felt that at any cost he must know the truth about that, at any cost he must wring an avowal from Jacqueline's lips, whether in her innermost soul she had ever by one single thought been unfaithful to him.

As fast as his gathering weakness would allow, he hurried through the interminable corridors of the Palace, until he found himself down in the hall below, at the foot of the main staircase, not twenty paces away from the room where he had endured such bitter humiliation last night. Instinct drew him to that room, the window of which gave direct access on to a terraced walk and thence on to the park.

He pushed open the door behind which a few brief hours ago he and his friends had laid in wait so shamelessly for their unsuspecting enemy. Almost furtively he stepped over the threshold and peeped in. He scarce recognized the place, thought he had mistaken the door; and yet there were all the landmarks: the desk with its kidney-shaped top, which had proved such a useful rampart for the enemy; the chairs which the masked stranger had brandished like swivels above his head when the cowardly order was given to the varlets to help in the attack; the heavy curtain which had been the last, the most formidable weapon of defence.

All these things had been put back in their respective places; a fresh piece of matting covered the floor; the curtain had been hung once more in front of the window—not a stain, not a mark, not a break testified to the terrible orgy of bloodshed which had desecrated this noble apartment last night.

De Landas looked all about him in astonishment. He stepped further into the room, and even as he did so, a strong current of air caused the heavy door behind him to fall to with a bang. As de Landas looked across the room in order to see what had been the cause of this sudden gust he saw that the window opposite was open to the ground, and that Jacqueline had apparently just entered that way from the terraced walk beyond.

She did not see him just at first, but stood for awhile inert, as he had been, in noting the appearance of the room. The window framed her in like a perfect picture, with her dark gown and her golden hair and soft white skin. The hood of her cloak had fallen back over her shoulders and she held her heavy skirt gathered up in her hand.

'Jacqueline!' exclaimed the young man impulsively.

She looked up and saw him, and, quite serenely, stepped into the room, went forward to greet him with hand outstretched, her face expressing gentle solicitude.

'Why, José!' she said lightly, 'I had no thought of seeing you to-day.'

'Which,' he retorted glumly, 'doth not seem to have greatly troubled you.'

'I knew that you were sick. Surely the leech hath prescribed absolute rest.'

'I did not think of sickness or of rest,' he rejoined, with an undercurrent of grim reproach in his tone. 'I only thought of seeing you.'

'I would have come to you,' she said calmly, 'as soon as the leech advised.'

'And I could not wait,' he riposted with a sigh. 'That is all the difference there is, Jacqueline, between your love and mine.'

Then, as she made no reply, but led him gently, like a sick child, to a chair, he added sombrely:

'I came to bid you farewell, Jacqueline.'

'Farewell? I don't understand.'

'I am going away.'

'Whither?'

He shrugged his shoulders.

'*Chien sabe?*' he said. 'What does it matter?'

'You are enigmatical, dear cousin,' she retorted. 'Will you not explain?'

'The explanation is over simple, alas! Monseigneur the governor hath expelled me from this city.'

'Expelled you from this city?' she reiterated slowly.

'Yes! for daring to lay hands on His High and Mightiness, Monseigneur le Prince de Froidmont.'

'José, you are jesting!'

'I was never so serious in all my life.'

'And you are going?'

'To-night.'

'But whither?' she insisted.

'As I said before: *Chien sabe?*'

He spoke now in a harsh, husky voice. Obviously his nerves were on edge and he had some difficulty in controlling himself. He was sitting by the desk and his arm lay across the top of it, with fist clenched, while his dark eyes searched the face of the young girl through and through while he spoke. She was standing a few paces away from him, looking down on him with a vague, puzzled expression in her face.

'José,' she said after awhile, 'you are unnerved, angered, for the moment. You think, no doubt, that I am to blame for Monseigneur's knowledge of last night's affair. I swear to you that I am not, that on the other hand I did all that was humanly possible to keep the shameful affair a secret from every one.'

'Shameful, Jacqueline?' he protested.

'Yes, shameful!' she replied firmly. 'Monseigneur, it seems, received an inkling of the truth early this morning—how, I know not. But he sent for the watchmen and had them examined; then he told me what had occurred.'

'And you believed him?'

'I neither believed nor disbelieved. I was hideously, painfully puzzled. Now you tell me that my guardian hath expelled you from this city. He would not have done that, José, if he had not proof positive of your guilt.'

'Well!' he rejoined with sudden, brusque arrogance. 'I'll not deny it!'

'José!'

'I did waylay a malapert, an impudent rogue, with the view to administering a sound correction to his egregious vanity. I do not deny it. I am proud of it! And you, Jacqueline, should commend me for having done you service.'

'I cannot commend you for last night's work, José,' she said earnestly. 'It was cowardly and unchivalrous.'

'Pardieu!' he riposted roughly. 'I am going to be punished for it severely enough, methinks. Expelled from this town! Thrown to the tender mercies of the Duke of Parma and his armies, who will vent on me their resentment for my loyalty to the Flemish cause!'

'Nay, José! I swear to you that Monseigneur will relent.'

'Not he!'

'He only meant to frighten you, to cow you perhaps into submission. He was already angered with you after the banquet, for attacking Messire le Prince de Froidmont. He thought your action of the night not only a dishonourable one, but a direct defiance of his orders.'

'Not he!' quoth de Landas again. Then he added with a sudden burst of bitter resentment. 'He wants to get me out of the way—to separate me from you!'

'You must not be surprised, José,' she retorted quietly, 'that after what happened last night, my guardian's opposition has not undergone a change in your favour. But have I not sworn that he will relent? I will go to him now—I shall know what to say ... he so seldom refuses me anything I ask for.'

'I forbid you to go, Jacqueline!' he interposed quickly, for already she had turned to go.

'Forbid me? Why? I will not compromise your dignity; have no fear of that.'

'I forbid you to go!' he reiterated sullenly.

'You are foolish, José! I assure you that I understand Monseigneur's moods better than any one else in the world. I know that he is always just as ready to pardon as to punish. 'Tis not much pleading that I shall have to do.'

'You'll not plead for me, Jacqueline.'

'José!'

'You'll not plead. 'Tis not necessary.'

'What do you mean?'

'That I am already pardoned.'

'Already pardoned?'

'Yes. I am not expelled from the city.'

'But you told me——'

'It was all a ruse!'

'A ruse?'

'Yes!' he cried with a sudden outburst of rage, long enough held in check. 'Yes! A ruse to find out if you loved me still!'

Then, as instinctively, at sight of his face, which had become distorted with fury, she stepped back in order to avoid closer contact with him, he jumped up from his chair, and while she continued to retreat, he followed her step by step, and she watched him, fascinated and appalled by the look of deathly hatred which gleamed in his eyes.

'A year ago, Jacqueline,' he went on, speaking now through set teeth, so that his voice came to her like the hissing of an angry snake; 'a year—nay, a month, a week ago—if I had told you that I was going away from you, you would have thrown yourself in my arms in the agony of your grief; you would have wept torrents of tears and wrung your hands and yielded your sweet face, your full, red lips unasked to my caresses. But now——'

He paused. She could retreat no further, for her back was against the wall. Instinctively she put out her arms in order to keep him off. But he suddenly seized her with a fury so fierce that she could have screamed with the pain, which seemed literally to break her back in two. He held her close to him, his warm breath scorched her face, his lips sought her throat, her cheeks, her eyes, with a violence of passion so intense that for the moment she felt weak and helpless in his arms. Only for a moment, however. The next, she had recovered that dignified calm which was so characteristic of her quaint personality. She made no resistance, because of a truth she had not the power to shake herself free from his embrace; but her figure suddenly became absolutely rigid, and once or twice he met a look in her eyes which was so laden with contempt, that his exasperation gave itself vent in a long, impassioned tirade, wherein he poured forth the full venom of the pent-up rage, hatred, jealousy which was seething in his heart.

'You! Miserable Flemish cinder-wench!' he cried. 'So you thought that you could toy with the passion of a Spanish gentleman? You thought that you could use him and play with him for just as long as it suited your fancy, and that you could cast him aside like a torn shoe as soon as some one richer, greater, more important, appeared upon the scene. Well! let me tell you this, my fine Madame! That I'll not give you up! I'll not! No! Though I do not love you, any more than I do any slut who tosses me a passing kiss. But I'll not give you up—to that accursed stranger, or to any man; do you hear? You are mine, and I'll keep you—you and your fortune. I have reckoned on it and I want it—and I'll have it, if I have to drag you in the gutter first, or burn this confounded city about your ears!'

His voice had gradually grown more and more husky, until the last words came out of his parched throat like the screech of some wild animal gloating over its prey. But in his present state of health, the effort and the excitement proved too great for his endurance. He turned suddenly dizzy and sick, staggered and would have fallen headlong at her feet, if she herself had not supported him.

She had remained perfectly still while he poured forth that hideous torrent of insults and vituperation, which, in her sight, were akin to the writhings of some venomous reptile. She could not move or stop her ears from hearing, because he held her fast. Tall, stately and impassive, she had stood her ground like some unapproachable goddess whom the ravings of a raging cur could not in any way pollute.

Now that he became momentarily helpless, she gave him the support of her arm and led him quietly back to the chair. When he was once more seated and in a fair way of recovering from this semi-swoon, she—still quite calmly—turned to go.

'You are unnerved, José,' she said coldly, 'and had best remain here now till I fetch your servants. I could wish for your sake as well as for mine own that this had been an everlasting farewell.'

After which she walked quite slowly across the room, opened the door with a firm hand and went out. A moment or two later, de Landas could hear her giving instructions to his servants in a perfectly clear and firm voice. He leaned back in his chair and gave a harsh laugh of triumph.

'And now, Monseigneur le Prince de Froidmont,' he murmured under his breath, 'we shall see which of us will be the conqueror in the life and death struggle which is to come.'

CHAPTER XV.
HOW M. DE LANDAS PRACTISED THE GENTLE ART OF TREACHERY

I

The conduct of de Landas—of the one man whom in her childish way she had at one time loved—had been a bitter blow to Jacqueline's sensitive heart, also one to her pride. How she could have been so blind as not to see his baseness behind his unctuous speech, she could not imagine. How had she never suspected those languorous eyes of his of treachery, those full, sensual lips of falsehood? Now her cheeks still tingled with shame at the remembrance of those hateful kisses which he had forced on her when she was helpless, and her whole being quivered with the humiliation of his insults. He never, never could have loved her, not even in the past. He was just a fortune-hunter, goaded to desperation when he saw that her wealth and her influence were slipping from his grasp. 'Flemish cinder-wench,' he had called her, not just in a moment of wild exasperation, but because he had always hated her and her kin and the fair land of Flanders, which she worshipped and which all these Spanish grandees so cordially despised. Jacqueline, whose whole nature—unbeknown to herself—was just awakening from childhood's trance, felt that she, too, hated now that arrogant and outwardly pliant Spaniard, the man who with cajoleries and soft, servile words had wound his way into her heart and into the confidence of Monseigneur. She had realized in one moment, while he was pouring forth that torrent of abuse and vituperation into her face, that he was an enemy—a bitter enemy to her and to her country—an enemy all the more fierce and dangerous that he had kept his hatred and contempt so well concealed for all these years.

And now her whole mind was set on trying to find a means to undo the harm which her own weakness and her own overtrustfulness had helped to bring about. Monseigneur the governor had not of late shown great cordiality toward M. de Landas; at the same time, he did not appear to mistrust him, had not yet perceived the vicious claws underneath the velvet glove or the serpent's tongue behind the supple speech. To a sensitive girl, reared in the reserve and aloofness which characterized the upbringing of women of high rank in these days, the very thought of confiding to her guardian the story of de Landas' infamous conduct towards her was abhorrent in the extreme; but, in spite of that, she was already determined to put Monseigneur on his guard, and if mere hints did not produce the desired effect, she would tell him frankly what had happened, for Jacqueline's conscience was as sensitive as her heart and she had no thought of placing her private feelings in direct conflict with the welfare of her country.

But, strangely enough, when she broached the unpleasant subject with Monseigneur, she found him unresponsive. What to her had been a vital turning point in her life did not appear to him as more than a girlish and undue susceptibility in the face of an aggrieved lover. He made light of de Landas' fury, even of the insults which Jacqueline could hardly bring herself to repeat; and she—wounded to the quick by the indifference of one who should have been her protector and if need be her avenger—did not insist, withdrew into her own shell of aloofness and reserve, merely begging Monseigneur to spare her the sight of de Landas in the future.

This Monseigneur cordially promised that he would do. He meant to keep de Landas at arm's length for the future, even though he was quite genuine in his belief that Jacqueline had exaggerated the violence of the Spaniard's outburst of hatred. In his innermost heart, M. le Baron d'Inchy was congratulating himself that the young girl had been so completely, if somewhat rudely, awakened from her infatuation for de Landas. Matters were shaping themselves more and more easily with regard to the alliance which he and his party had so much at heart. *Monsieur* showed no sign of desiring to leave Cambray, which plainly proved that he had not abandoned the project. But for this, as for all delicate political situations, secrecy was essential above all things, and Monseigneur had received a severe shock when de

Landas had so boldly suggested that rumour would soon begin to stir around the mysterious personality of the masked stranger.

Because of this, too, d'Inchy did not desire to quarrel just then with de Landas—whose misdemeanour he had already condoned—and turned a deaf ear to Jacqueline's grave accusations against her former lover. The next few days would see the end of the present ticklish situation and in the meanwhile, fortunately for himself and his schemes, most of those young hotheads who had taken part in the midnight drama were more or less sick, and safely out of the way.

We may take it that M. le Baron d'Inchy heard no further complaints about the unfortunate affair from his exalted guest: certain it is that neither M. de Landas nor any of his friends suffered punishment for that night's dastardly outrage. Whether they actually offered abject apologies to Messire le Prince de Froidmont, we do not know; but it is on record that the latter made no further allusion to the affair, and that subsequently, whenever he chanced to meet any of his whilom enemies in the streets, he always greeted them with unvarying cordiality and courtesy.

II

De Landas had in effect burnt his boats. He knew that sooner or later Jacqueline's resentment would get the better of her reserve and that his position inside the city would become untenable, unless indeed he succeeded in winning by force what he had for ever forfeited as a right—the hand of Jacqueline de Broyart, and with it the wealth, the power and influence for which his ambitious soul had thirsted to the exclusion of every other feeling of chivalry or honour.

He had left her presence and the Archiepiscopal Palace that afternoon with hatred and rage seething in his heart and brain, his body in a fever, his mind torn with conflicting plans, all designed for the undoing of the man whom he believed to be both his rival and his deadly enemy. An hour later, Du Pret and Maarege, the only two of his friends who were able to rise from their bed of sickness in response to a hasty summons from their acknowledged chief, were closeted with him in his lodgings in the Rue des Chanoines. A man dressed in rough clothes, with shaggy hair and black, unkempt beard, stood before the three gallants, in the centre of the room, whilst Pierre, M. de Landas' confidential henchman, stood on guard beside the door.

'Well?' queried de Landas curtly of the man. 'What have you found out?'

'Very little, Magnificence,' replied the man. 'Messire le Prince de Froidmont is lying sick at the hostelry of "Les Trois Rois," and hath not been seen to-day. His equerry received a messenger in the course of the morning from Monseigneur the governor and went subsequently to the Archiepiscopal Palace, where he remained one hour; and the henchman started at dawn, on horseback, went out of the city, and hath not since returned.'

'Pardi! we knew all that,' broke in de Landas roughly, 'and do not pay you for such obvious information. If you have nothing more to say — —'

'Pardon, Magnificence; nothing else occurred of any importance. But I was entrusted with other matter besides following the movements of Messire le Prince de Froidmont and his servants.'

'Well! and what did you do?'

'Obeyed orders. The people of Cambray are in a surly mood to-day. For the first time this morning, food supplies failed completely to reach the town. Rumours are rife that the armies of the Duke of Parma are within ten kilometres of the gates of the city, and that already he proposes to starve Cambray into capitulation.'

'All that is good—very good!' assented de Landas, who nodded to his friends.

They too signified their approval of the news.

'It is most fortunate,' said young Maarege, 'that all this has occurred this morning. It helps our plans prodigiously.'

'Go on, Sancho,' broke in de Landas impatiently. 'What did you do in the matter?'

'I and my comrades mixed with the crowd. It was easy enough to throw in a word here and a word there ... the masked stranger in the city ... a banquet at once given in his honour, where the last food supplies intended for the people were consumed by those who would sell Cambray back to the Spaniards ... Spanish spies lurking in the city.... Oh! I know how to do that work, Magnificence!' the man went on with conscious pride. 'You may rely on me!'

'Parbleu, fellow!' retorted de Landas haughtily. 'I would not pay thee if I could not.'

'Well! what else?' queried one of the others eagerly.

'As luck would have it, Magnificence,' continued the man, 'one of the strangers—he who is said to be equerry to the Prince de Froidmont—chanced to be walking down the street when I was by. I had a small crowd round me at the time and was holding forth on the subject of Flanders and her wrongs and the wickedness and tyranny of our Spanish masters ... I had thrown out a judicious hint or two about strangers who might be Spanish spies ... Magnificence, you would have been satisfied with the results! The crowd espied the stranger, hooted him vigorously, though for the nonce they dared not actually lay hands on him. But 'tis only a matter of time. The seeds are sown; within the week, if food becomes more scarce and dear, you will have the crowd throwing stones at the stranger! ... I have earned my pay, Magnificence! Those Flemish dogs are yapping already ... to-morrow they'll snarl ... and after that...'

'After that, 'tis the Duke of Parma who will bring them back to heel,' concluded de Landas in a triumphant tone. 'And now, Sancho, I have other work for thee!'

'I am entirely at the commands of His Magnificence,' the man rejoined obsequiously.

'The seeds here are sown, as thou sayest! Let Sandro and Alfonzo and the others continue thy work amongst the loutish crowds of Cambray. Thou'lt start to-night for Cateau-Cambrésis.'

'Yes, Magnificence.'

'The Duke of Parma is there. Thou'lt take a message from me to him.'

'Yes, Magnificence.'

'A verbal message, Sancho; for letters may be stolen or lost.'

'Not when I carry them, Magnificence.'

'Perhaps not. But a verbal message cannot be lost or stolen. If it is not transmitted I'll have thee hanged, Sancho.'

'I know it, Magnificence.'

'Well then, thou'lt seek out His Highness the Duke of Parma. Tell him all that has occurred in this city—the arrival of the stranger; the manner in which he stalks about the town under cover of a mask; the extraordinary honour wherewith the governor regards him. Dost understand?'

'Perfectly, Magnificence.'

'Then tell the Duke—and this is the most important part of thy mission—that on any given day which he may select, I can provoke a riot in this city—a serious riot, wherein every civil and military authority will be forced to take a part—and that this will be the opportunity for which His Highness hath been waiting. While the rioters inside Cambray will be engaged in throwing stones at one another, the Duke of Parma need only to strike one blow and he can enter the city unopposed with his armies, in the name of our Most Catholic King Philip of Spain.'

He rose from his chair as he did so and crossed himself devoutly, his friends doing likewise. Though they were Flemish born—these two young men—they had for some unavowable reason espoused the cause of their tyrants, rather than that of their own people. A look of comprehension had darted from Sancho's eyes as he received these final instructions from his employer, a look of satisfaction, too, and of hatred; for Sancho was a pure bred Castilian and despised and loathed all these Flemings as cordially as did his betters. Whether he served his own country from a sense of patriotism or from one of greed, it were impossible to say. No one had ever found it worth while to probe the depths of Sancho's soul—a common man, a churl, a paid spadassin or suborned spy—he was worth employing, for he was sharp and unscrupulous; but as to what went on behind those shifty, deep-set eyes of his and that perpetually frowning brow, was of a truth no concern of his noble employers. All that mattered to them was that Sancho had—in common with most men of his type—an unavowable past, one which would land him on the cross, the gibbet or the stake, in the torture-chamber or under the lash, whenever his duties were ill-performed or his discretion came to be a matter of doubt.

'If you serve me well in this, Sancho,' resumed de Landas after a brief while, 'the reward will surpass your expectations.'

'In this as in all things,' said the man with obsequious servility, 'I trust in the generosity of your Magnificence.'

'Thou must travel without a safe-conduct, fellow.'

'I am accustomed to doing that, Magnificence.'

'No papers of any kind, no written word must be found about thy person, if perchance thou fall into Flemish hands ere thou canst reach His Highness the Duke of Parma's camp.'

'I quite understand that, Magnificence.'

'Nothing wilt thou carry save the verbal message. And if as much as a single word of that is spoken to any living soul save to the Duke of Parma himself, I pledge thee my word that twenty-four hours later thou shalt be minus thy tongue, thine ears, thine eyes and thy right hand, and in that state be dangling on the gibbet at the Pré d'Amour for the example of any of thy fellows who had thought or dreamt of treachery.'

While de Landas spoke, Sancho kept his eyes resolutely fixed upon the ground, and his shaggy black beard hid every line of his mouth. Nor were de Landas and his young friends very observant or deeply versed in the science of psychology, else, no doubt, they would have noticed that though Sancho's attitude had remained entirely servile, his rough, bony hand was clutching his cap with a nervy grip which betrayed a stupendous effort at self-control. The next moment, however, he raised his eyes once more and looked his employer squarely and quite respectfully in the face.

'Your Magnificence need have no fear,' he said. 'I understand perfectly.'

'Very well,' rejoined de Landas lightly. 'Then just repeat the message as thou wilt deliver it before His Highness the Duke of Parma, and then thou canst go.'

Obediently Sancho went through the business required of him. 'I am to tell His Highness,' he said, 'that on any day which he may select, Monseigneur le Marquis de Landas and his friends will provoke a riot within this city—a serious riot, wherein every civil and military authority will be forced to take a part—and that this will be the opportunity for which His Highness hath been waiting. I am to tell him also that while the rioters inside Cambray will be engaged in throwing stones at one another, the Duke of Parma need only to strike one blow and he can enter the city unopposed, with his armies, in the name of our Most Catholic King Philip of Spain.'

De Landas gave a short, dry laugh.

'Thou hast a good memory, fellow,' he said: 'or a wholesome fear of the lash—which is it?'

'A profound respect for Your Magnificence,' replied Sancho, literally cringing and fawning now before his noble master, like a dog who has been whipped; 'and the earnest desire to serve him well in all things.'

'Parbleu!' was de Landas' calm rejoinder.

Two minutes later, Sancho was dismissed. He walked backwards, his spine almost bent double in the excess of his abasement; nor did he straighten out his tall, bony figure till Pierre had finally closed the door after him and there was the width of an antechamber and a corridor between him and the possibility of being overheard. Then he gave a smothered cry, like that of a choking bull; he threw his cap down upon the floor and stamped upon it; kicked it with his foot, as if it were the person of an enemy whom he hated with all the bitterness of his soul. Finally he turned, and raising his arm, he clenched his fist and shook it with a gesture of weird and impotent menace in the direction from whence he had just come, whilst in his deep-set eyes there glowed a fire of rancour and of fury which of a truth would have caused those young gallants to think. Then he picked up his cap and almost ran out into the street.

III

But neither de Landas nor his friends troubled themselves any further about Sancho once the latter was out of their sight. They were too intent on their own affairs to give a thought to the susceptibilities of a down-at-heel outlaw whom they were paying to do dirty work for them.

'We could not have found a more useful fellow for our purpose than Sancho,' was de Landas' complacent comment.

'A reliable rascal, certainly,' assented Maarege. 'But it is not easy to get out of the city without a safe-conduct these days.'

'Bah! Sancho will manage it.'

'He might get a musket-shot for his pains.'

'That would not matter,' rejoined de Landas with a cynical laugh, 'so long as his tongue is silenced at the same time.'

'Yes, silenced,' urged one of the others; 'but in that event our message would not be delivered to the Duke of Parma.'

'We must risk something.'

'And yet must make sure of the message reaching the Duke. We want as little delay as possible.'

'If food gets short here our own position will be none too pleasant. These Flemings seem to think that the churls have just as much right to eat as their betters.'

'Preposterous, of course,' concluded de Landas. 'But, as you say, we'll make sure that our message does reach the Duke as soon as may be. Let Sancho take one chance. Pierre shall take the other.'

Pierre, motionless beside the door, pricked up his ears at sound of his own name.

'Here, Pierre!' commanded his master.

'Yes, Monseigneur.'

'Thou hast heard my instructions to Sancho.'

'Yes, Monseigneur.'

'And couldst repeat the message which I am sending to His Highness the Duke of Parma?'

'Word for word, Monseigneur.'

'Say it then!'

Pierre repeated the message, just as Sancho had done, fluently and without a mistake.

'Very well, then,' said de Landas; 'thine instructions are the same as those which I gave to Sancho. Understand?'

'Yes, Monseigneur.'

'Thou'lt leave the city to-night.'

'Yes, Monseigneur.'

'Without a safe-conduct.'

'I can slip through the gates. I have done it before.'

'Very good. Then thou'lt go to Cateau-Cambrésis and present thyself before His Highness. If Sancho has forestalled thee, thy mission ends there. If, however, there has been a hitch and Sancho has not put in an appearance, thou'lt deliver the message and bring me back His Highness' answer.'

'I quite understand, Monseigneur.'

Thus it was that M. le Marquis de Landas made sure that his treacherous and infamous message reached the Generalissimo of the Spanish armies. To himself and to his conscience he reconciled that infamy by many specious arguments, foremost among these being that Jacqueline had played him false. Well! he had still a few days before him wherein to study two parts, one or the other of which he would have to play on the day when Alexander Farnese, Duke of Parma, demanded the surrender of the city of Cambray in the name of His Majesty King Philip of Spain. The one rôle would consist in a magnificent show of loyalty to the country of his adoption, the rallying of the garrison troops under the Flemish flag and his own leadership; the deliverance of Cambray from the Spanish yoke and the overthrow of the Duke of Parma and his magnificent army. The other rôle, equally easy for this subtle traitor to play, meant handing over Cambray and its inhabitants to the tender mercies of the Spanish general, in the hope of earning a rich reward for services rendered to His Majesty the King of Spain. The first course of action would depend on whether Jacqueline would return to his arms, humbled and repentant: the second on whether the masked stranger was indeed the personage whom he—de Landas—more than suspected him of being, namely, *Monsieur* Duc d'Anjou et d'Alençon, own brother to the King of France, come to snatch the Sovereignty of the Netherlands, together with their richest heiress, from the arms of her former lover.

Well! whichever way matters went, de Landas stood to win a fair guerdon. He even found it in his heart to be grateful to that mysterious stranger who had so unexpectedly come across his path. But now he was tired and overwrought. His work for the day was done and there was much strenuous business ahead of him. So he took leave of his friends and, having ordered the leech to administer to him a soothing draught, he finally sought rest.

CHAPTER XVI.
WHAT NEWS MAÎTRE JEHAN
BROUGHT BACK WITH HIM

I

How Gilles spent the next two or three weeks he could never afterwards tell you. They were a long-drawn-out agony of body and of mind: of body, because the enforced inactivity was positive torture to such a man of action as he was; of mind, because the problem of life had become so complicated, its riddle so unanswerable, that day after day and night after night Gilles would pace up and down his narrow room in the Rue aux Juifs, his heart torn with misery and shame and remorse. The image of Jacqueline, so young, so womanly, so unsuspecting, haunted him with its sweet, insistent charm, until he would stretch out his arms toward that radiant vision in passionate longing and call to her aloud to go and leave him, alone with his misery.

He felt that, mayhap under simpler circumstances—she being a great lady, a rich heiress, and he an humble soldier of fortune—he could have torn her image from his heart, since obviously she could never become his, and he could have endured the desolation, the anguish, which after such a sacrifice would have left him finally, bruised and wearied, an old and broken man. But what lay before him now was, of a truth, beyond the power of human sufferance. A great, an overwhelming love had risen in his heart almost at first sight of an exquisite woman: and he was pledged by all that he held most sacred and most dear to play an unworthy part towards her, to deceive her, to lie to her, and finally to deliver her body and soul to that degenerate Valois Prince whom he knew to be a liar and a libertine, who would toy with her affections, sneer at her sensibilities and leave her, mayhap, one day, broken-hearted and broken-spirited, to end her days in desolation and misery.

And it was when the prospect of such a future confronted Gilles de Crohin in his loneliness that he felt ready to dash his head against the wall, to end all this misery, this incertitude, this struggle with the unsolvable problem which stood before him. He longed to flee out of this city, wherein she dwelt, out of the land which gave her birth, out of life, which had become so immeasurably difficult.

Maître Julien tended him with unwearying care and devotion, but he too watched with burning impatience for the return of Maître Jehan. There was little that the worthy soul did not guess just at this time. It had not been very difficult to put two and two together with the help of the threads which his Liege Lady had deigned to place in his hands. But Julien was too discreet to speak; he could only show his sympathy for a grief which he was well able to comprehend by showering kindness and attention on Messire, feeling all the while that he was thereby rendering service to his divinity.

II

Despite his horror of inaction, Gilles seldom went out during that time save at nightfall, and he had been content to let Monseigneur the governor know that he was still sick of his wounds. Indeed, those wounds inflicted upon him that night by a crowd of young jackanapes had been a blessing in disguise for him. They had proved a valid excuse for putting off the final day of decision which Monseigneur d'Inchy and his adherents had originally fixed a fortnight hence. That fortnight had long since gone by, and Gilles knew well enough that the Flemish lords were waxing impatient.

They were urging him earnestly for a decision. The pressure of the Duke of Parma's blockade upon the city was beginning to make itself felt. All access to the French frontier was now closed and it was only from the agricultural districts of the province itself that food supplies could be got into the town; and those districts themselves were overrun with Spanish soldiery, who pillaged and burned, stole and requisitioned, everything that they could lay hands on. The city of Cambray was in open revolt against her Sovereign Lord, the King of Spain, and the Duke of Parma had demanded an unconditional surrender, under such pains and penalties as would deliver the whole population to the tender mercies of a conqueror whose final word was always bloodshed and destruction.

A stout garrison, enthusiastic and determined, was in defence of the city, and there was no thought at present of capitulation in the valiant hearts of these Flemings, the comrades and equals of those who had perished in their hundreds in other cities and provinces of the Netherlands, whilst upholding their ancient rights and privileges against the greatest military organization of the epoch. There had been no thought of surrender, even though food was getting scarce and dear. Wheat and fresh meat had already become almost prohibitive for all save the rich; clothing and leather was unobtainable. The Duke of Parma was awaiting further troops yet, wherewith he proposed to invest the city from every side and to cut her population off from every possible source of supply.

This was the inexorable fact which M. le Baron d'Inchy placed before Gilles de Crohin when the latter presented himself one day at the Archiepiscopal Palace in his rôle as equerry to *Monsieur*.

'His Highness must see for himself,' d'Inchy said firmly, 'how impossible it is for us to wait indefinitely on his good pleasure. No one can regret more than I do the unfortunate circumstances which have brought His Highness down to a bed of sickness; and because of those circumstances—in which, alas! I, as Monseigneur's host, had an innocent share—I have been both considerate and long-suffering in not trying to brusque His Highness in his decision. But Parma is almost at our gates, and Orange is leading his own army from victory to victory. We gave in to Monseigneur's caprice when matters did not appear so urgent as they are now; time has come when further indecision becomes a rebuff.'

To these very just reproaches Gilles had no other answer save silence. Ill-versed as he was in the art of diplomacy, he did not know how to fence with words, how to parry this direct attack and to slip out of the impasse in which he was being cornered.

Jehan had been gone a fortnight, and still there was no answer from the Queen of Navarre!

'Monseigneur hath a delicate constitution,' he said somewhat lamely after awhile. 'He suffers grievously from his wounds and hath been delirious. It were unwarrantable cruelty to force a decision on him now.'

'So do our people suffer grievously,' retorted d'Inchy roughly. 'They suffer already from lack of food and the terror of Parma's armies. And,' he added with a touch of grim irony, 'as to His Highness' delicate constitution, meseems that if a man can hold six young gallants for half an hour at the sword's point, he hath little cause to quarrel with the constitution wherewith Nature hath endowed him.'

'Even the strongest man can be prostrated by fever.'

'Possibly. But there is no longer any time for procrastination, and unless I have His Highness' final answer at the end of the week, my messenger starts for Utrecht to meet the Prince of Orange.'

III

When Gilles had taken his leave of Monseigneur the Governor that afternoon, he felt indeed more perplexed than he had been before. Until Madame la Reyne's letter came, he felt that he could not pledge *Monsieur's* word irrevocably. When he thought over all the events which had finally landed him in face of so stupendous a problem his mind hung with dark foreboding on the Duc d'Anjou's cynical pronouncement: 'If any engagement is entered into in my name to which I have not willingly subscribed, I herewith do swear most solemnly that I would repudiate the wench at the eleventh hour—aye! at the very foot of the altar steps!' And Gilles, as he hurried along the interminable corridors of the Palace, was haunted by the image of Jacqueline—his flower o' the lily—tossed about from one ambitious scheme to another, subject to indifference, to aversion, to insults; unwanted and uncared for save for the sake of her fortune and the influence which she brought. It was monstrous! abominable! Gilles felt a wild desire to strangle some one for this deed of infamy, since he could not physically come to grips with Fate.

At the top of the stairs he saw Jacqueline coming towards him, and, whether it was the effect of his imagination or of his guilty conscience, certain it was that she seemed moody and pale. He stood aside while she walked past him; but though his whole being cried out for a word from her and his every sense yearned for the sound of her voice and a glance from her eyes, she did not stop to speak to him, only gave him a kind and gracious nod as she went by.

And after he had watched her dainty figure till it disappeared from his view, he took to his heels and ran out of the Palace and along the streets, like one who is haunted by torturing ghosts. It seemed to him that malevolent voices were hooting in his ear, that behind walls or sheltering doorways, there lurked hidden enemies or avenging ghosts, who pointed fingers of scorn at him as he ran past.

'There goes the man,' those accusing voices seemed to say, 'who would deliver an exquisite lily-flower to be crushed in the rough and thoughtless hands of an avowed profligate! There goes the man who, in order to attain that end, is even now living a double life, playing the part of a liar and a cheat!'

Self-accusation tortured him. He hurried home, conscious only of a desire to hide himself, to keep clear of *her* path, whom he was helping to wrong. He paid no heed to the real hooting that followed him, to the menacing fists that were levelled at him from more than one street-corner, wherever a few idlers had congregated or some poor, wretched churls, on the fringe of want, had put their heads together in order to discuss their troubles and their miseries. He did not notice that men spat in his trail, that women gathered their children to their skirts when he hurried past, and murmured under their breath: 'God punish the Spanish spy!'

IV

Twenty days went by ere Jehan returned—twenty days that were like a cycle of years to the unfortunate watcher within the city. Maître Jehan arrived during the small hours of the morning, drenched to the skin, having swum the river for a matter of a league or more to avoid the Spanish sentries, and finally, after having skirted the city walls, had climbed them at a convenient spot under cover of darkness, being in as great danger from the guard at the gates as he had been from the enemy outside. He had then lain for an hour or two, hidden in the Fosse-au-Pouilleul, the most notorious and most comprehensive abode of thieves and cut-throats known in any city of Flanders. But the letter which Madame la Reyne de Navarre had given him for Messire, with the recommendation not to part with it to any one else save with his life, was still safe in its leather sheath inside the pocket of his doublet.

By the time that the first grey streak of dawn had touched the tall spires of the ancient city with its wand of silver, the letter was in Gilles de Crohin's hands, and the two friends were sitting side by side in the narrow room of the dreary hostelry, whilst Gilles felt as if a load of care had been lifted from his shoulders.

'Your news, my good Jehan? Your news?' he reiterated eagerly; 'ere I read this letter.'

But Jehan, by dint of broken words and gestures, indicated that the letter must be read first.

So, while he partook of the solid breakfast which Maître Julien had placed before him, Gilles read the letter which the gracious Queen had sent to him. It ran thus:

'Highly Honoured Seigneur,

'My Faithful and Loyal Friend!

'The present is to tell You that all is well with our schemes. I have seen Monsieur, who already is wearied of Madame de Marquette, and like a School boy who has been whipped for disobedience, is at this moment fawning round my Skirts, ready to do anything that I may command. Was I not right? I prophesied that this would be so. Thus Your labours on My behalf have not been in fain. And now I pray you to carry through the matter to a triumphant conclusion. In less than three months Monsieur will be Sovereign Lord of the Netherlands, with the hand of the Flemish Heiress as a priceless additional guerdon. In the meanwhile, as no doubt You know already, the Armies of the Duke of Parma lie between Us and Cambray. Monsieur is busy collecting together the necessary Forces to do battle against the Spaniards. He is prepared to enter Cambray in triumph, to marry the Lady blindfolded, since *You* say that She is adorable; in fact He is in the best of moods and consents to everything which I desire. Meanwhile, Messire de Balagny, who is Chief of Monsieur's camp, is on his way with full details of our projects for the final defeat of the Spaniards. He has a small troop with him, whom he will leave at La Fère until after he hath spoken with You. I urge You, Messire, in the meanwhile to entreat M. le Baron d'Inchy not to surrender the City to the Duke of Parma. I pray You to assure Him—in Your name as Duc d'Anjou et d'Alençon—that the whole Might of France, of which Messire de Balagny's small troop is but the forerunner, is at Your beck and call; that You will use it in order to free the Netherlands from the Spanish yoke. Tell him that the next few months will see the final overthrow of King Philip's domination in the Netherlands and a prince of the house of France as their Sovereign Lord. Say anything, promise anything, Messire! I swear to You that Monsieur is prepared to redeem *any* pledge You may enter into in his Name. Then, when Messire de Balagny arrives in Cambray, You can make this Your excuse for quitting the City, nominally in order to place Yourself at the head of Your armies. Messire de Balagny, who is in My confidence, will then remain, not only to take command of the Garrison and help with his small troop to defend the City from within, but also as a guarantee for Monsieur's good faith. See how splendidly I have thought everything out, how perfectly events are shaping themselves for the success of Our schemes! Patience a brief while longer, Messire! Your time of trial is drawing to an end! Confess that it hath not been a very severe ordeal and that You have derived much enjoyment from mystifying some of those over obtuse Flemings. I count with pleasure and impatience upon Your arrival in La Fère very shortly, where the gratitude of a sorely tried Queen will be awaiting You. If You now help me to carry the affair through to a triumphant close, I vow that on the day that Monsieur makes his state entry into Cambray there will be naught that You can ask of Me and which if in My power to give that I would not bestow with a joyful heart upon you.

'Until then, I remain, Messire,
'Your earnest Well-Wisher,
'Marguerlte de Navarre.
'Given in Paris, under My hand and seal this 27th day
of March 1581.'

V

The letter fell from Messire Gilles' hand unheeded on to the floor.
He was staring straight out before him, a world of perplexity in his
eyes. Maître Jehan tried in vain to fathom what went on behind his
master's lowering brow. Surely the news which he had brought was
of the most cheering and of the best. The present humiliating position
could not now last very long. Messire de Balagny was on his way,
and within a few days—hours, perhaps—he and Messire could once
more resume those happy, adventurous times of the past. And yet it
seemed as if Messire was not altogether happy. There was something
in his attitude, in the droop of his listless hands, as if something bright
and hopeful had just slipped out of his grasp—which to Jehan's mind
was manifestly absurd.

So he shrugged his wide shoulders and solemnly picked up the
fallen letter and pressed it back into Messire's hand. The action roused
Gilles from his gloomy meditations.

'Well, my good Jehan!' he said with a grim laugh, which grated
very unpleasantly on faithful Jehan's ears. 'If the rest of your news is
as good as that contained in Madame la Reyne's letter, you and I will
presently find ourselves the two luckiest devils in Flanders.'

Jehan nodded. 'I have n-n-n-no f-f-f-further news,' he blurted out.
'Messire de B-b-b-b-balagny was at La F-f-f-fère when I was th-th-
there.'

'With a strong troop?'

Jehan nodded dubiously.

'A couple of hundred men?'

'Or s-s-s-s-so,' retorted Jehan.

'But he himself will be within sight of Cambray to-day?'

'A-a-a-at this hour.'

'And inside the city to-morrow?'

Jehan nodded again.

'And Monseigneur le Duc d'Anjou?'

'In P-p-p-p-aris: ready to st-st-st-start.'

'He does not mean to play a double game this time?'

'No-n-n-n-no-no!' came in rapid and vigorous protest from Maître Jehan.

'Then the sooner I secure his bride for him, the better it will be for Madame la Reyne's schemes,' concluded Gilles dryly. Then suddenly he jumped to his feet, gave a deep sigh, and stretching out his arms with a gesture of impatience and of longing, he said: 'If we could only vacate the field without further ado, honest Jehan! and let Fate do the rest of the dirty work for us!'

His hand as it fell back came in contact with his sword, which was lying across the table; not the exquisite Toledo rapier, the gift of a confiding Queen, but his own stout, useful one, which he had picked up some three years ago now, after his own had been broken in his hand on the field of Gembloux. There it lay, the length of its sheath in shadow; but the slanting rays of the early morning sun fell full upon the hilt, which was shaped like a cross. With it in his hand, with that cross-hilt before his eyes, Gilles de Crohin had sworn by all that he held most sacred and most dear that he would see this business through and would not give it up, until Marguerite of Navarre herself gave him the word. And these were days when the sworn word was a thing that was sacred above all things on this earth; and as Gilles himself had said it on that same memorable occasion, he was not a prince and he could not afford to toy with his word—it was the only thing he possessed. Therefore, though more than one historian, notably Enguerrand de Manuchet, has chosen to cast a slur upon Gilles de Crohin for his actions, I for one do not see how he could have acted otherwise and kept his honour intact. He was pledged to Marguerite de Navarre, had pledged himself to her with eyes open and full knowledge of the Duc d'Anjou's character. To have turned back on his promise, to have broken his word to the Queen, would have been the act of a perjurer and of a coward. He could at this precise moment have walked out of Cambray, that we know. The Duke of Parma's armies at the time that Balagny succeeded in reaching Cambray only occupied that portion of the Cambrésis which adjoined the French frontier. On the West the way lay open, and the whole world on that side was free to the soldier of fortune, even though he would have been forced, after such a course of action, to shake the dust of France for ever from his feet.

But he chose to remain. He chose to continue the deception which had been imposed upon him, even though it involved the happiness of the woman he loved, even though it meant not only to relinquish her to another man, but to a man who was wholly unworthy of her.

Far be it from the writer of this veracious chronicle to excuse Gilles de Crohin in what he did. I do not wish to palliate, only to explain. Far be it from me, I say, to run counter to Messire de Manuchet's learned opinion. But the history of individuals as well as that of nations has a trick of seeming more clear and more proportionate when it is viewed through the glasses of centuries, and it is just possible—I say it in all humility—that Messire de Manuchet, who in addition to being a very capable historian was also a firm adherent of the policy of a French alliance for the sorely stricken Netherlands, felt aggrieved that Madame Jacqueline de Broyart, the fairest heiress in Flanders, did not after all wed *Monsieur* Duc d'Alençon et d'Anjou, own brother to the King of France, and did not thereby consolidate that volatile Prince's hold upon the United Provinces, and that the learned historian hath vented his disappointment in consequence on the man who ultimately failed to bring that alliance about.

That, of course, is only a surmise. Messire de Manuchet's history of that stirring episode was writ three hundred years ago: he may have been personally acquainted with the chief actors in the palpitating drama—with d'Inchy and Jacqueline de Broyart, with Gilles de Crohin and the Marquis de Landas; even with the Queen of Navarre and *Monsieur* Duc d'Anjou. He may also have had his own peculiar code of honour, which was not the one laid down by Du Guesclin and Bayard, by Bussy d'Amboise and Gilles de Crohin, and all the protagonists of chivalry.

CHAPTER XVII.
HOW MESSIRE DE LANDAS'
TREACHERY BORE FRUIT

I

It is Messire Enguerrand de Manuchet who tells us that on the 3rd day of April of this same year of grace 1581, Messire de Balagny, Maître de Camp to *Monsieur* Duc d'Anjou succeeded under cover of darkness in entering the city by the Landrecy road on the West, which was still—an you remember—clear of the Spanish investing armies. He came alone, having left his troop at La Fère, a matter of three leagues or so. Toward nine o'clock of the morning he made his way to the hostelry of 'Les Trois Rois,' where we may take it that Gilles de Crohin was mightily glad to see him. Messire de Balagny's advent was for the unfortunate prisoner like a breath of pure air, something coming to him from that outside world from which he had been shut out all these weary weeks; something, too, of the atmosphere of camps and of clean fighting in the open, which for the moment seemed to dissipate the heavy fumes of political intrigues, with its attendant deceits and network of lies, that were so abhorrent to the born soldier.

'I do not envy you your position, my dear friend,' Balagny said dryly, after he had discussed the whole situation with Gilles.

'My God!' responded Gilles with almost ludicrous fervour. 'It has been a positive hell!'

'Although Madame la Reyne de Navarre is very grateful to you for what you have done; she was only saying to me, before I left, that there was nothing she would not do for you in return.'

'Oh!' said Gilles with a careless laugh. 'The gratitude of a Queen...!!'

'This one is above all a woman,' broke in the older man earnestly. 'She is a Queen only by the accident of birth.'

'I know, I know,' Gilles went on, somewhat impatiently. 'But for the nonce Her Majesty has conferred the greatest possible boon upon me by releasing me from my post; and I, being more than satisfied, will ask nothing better of her. But what about His Highness?' he added, after a slight pause.

Balagny shrugged his shoulders.

'He does not mean to play us false?' insisted Gilles.

'*Chien sabe?*' was the other's enigmatic reply. 'Does one ever know what François, Duc d'Anjou, may or may not do?'

'But Madame la Reyne declares— —'

'Madame la Reyne is blind where that favoured brother is concerned. But it is she who, even now, is moving heaven and earth to recruit the armies for the relief of Cambray—not he. As you know, brother Henri, King of France, will not stir a finger to help Monsieur conquer a possible kingdom, and *Monsieur* himself sits in his Palace in Paris, surrounded by women and young sycophants, idling away his time, wasting his substance, while his devoted sister wears herself out in his service.'

'Don't I know him!' concluded Gilles with a sigh. Then after awhile he added more lightly: 'Well, friend, shall we to the governor? He hath sent me a respectful but distinctly peremptory request this morning to present myself in person at the Archiepiscopal Palace.'

'The worthy Fleming is getting restive,' was de Balagny's dry comment.

'Naturally.'

'He wants to bring matters to a head.'

'To-day, apparently. He hath given me respite after respite. He will not wait any longer. Matters in this city are pretty desperate, my friend. And if *Monsieur* tarries with his coming much longer...'

De Balagny rose from his chair, and going up to Gilles, he placed a kindly hand on the younger man's shoulder.

'*Monsieur* will not tarry much longer,' he said earnestly. 'Madame la Reyne will see to that. Go to the governor, my good Gilles, and complete the work you have so ably begun. It was not pleasant work, I'll warrant, and there is little or no glory attached to it; but when you will have lived as many years as I have, you will realize that there is quite a deal of satisfaction to be derived out of inglorious work, if it be conscientiously done. And after to-day,' he added gaily, 'you will be free to garner a whole sheaf of laurels in the service of a grateful Queen and of a dissolute Prince.'

But Gilles was not in the humour to look on the bright side of his future career. He was fingering moodily the letter which Monseigneur the governor had sent him an hour or so ago. It was obviously intended to be the forerunner of the final decision which would throw Jacqueline—beautiful, exquisite Jacqueline of the merry blue eyes and the rippling laugh—into the arms of that same dissolute Prince of whom even de Balagny—his trusted Maître de Camp—spoke with so much bitterness.

> 'Were I a free agent,' d'Inchy said in his letter, 'I would not dream of asking Your Highness so signal a favour; but while Your Highness chooses to hide Your identity under a mask, and in an humble Abode altogether unworthy of Your rank, I have no option but to beg You most humbly to grace My own house with Your presence, in order that We may arrive at last to an irrevocable decision in the Matter which lies so closely to My heart.

Indeed the die was cast. Even Messire de Manuchet admits that Gilles could not do otherwise than present himself at the Palace in accordance with Monseigneur the governor's desire. De Balagny certainly did everything to cheer and encourage him.

'Will you not come with me?' Gilles asked of him, when he was ready to go. 'I could then present you at once to d'Inchy, and, please God! be myself out of Cambray ere the sun has begun to sink low in the West.'

But Balagny shook his head.

'You had best go alone, this once more,' he said firmly. 'Think of the coming interview as an affair of honour, my dear Gilles, and go to it as you would to a fight, with a bold front and unquaking heart. You will find it quite easy to confront the Fleming then.'

Gilles gripped the old man's hand with gratitude.

'You have put new life into me,' he said, with something of his habitual cheerfulness. 'Another few hours of this miserable business and I shall be free—free as air!' Then he added with a bitter sigh, which the other man did not quite know how to interpret: 'And I shall imagine myself as almost happy!'

After which, he sallied forth into the street with a firm and elastic step.

II

There are few things in the world quite so mysterious as the origin and birth of a rumour. It springs—who knows whence? and in a trice it grows, hurries from mouth to mouth, gathers crowds together, imposes its presence in every house, at every street corner, on every open space where men and women congregate.

Messire de Balagny had only been inside Cambray a few hours. He had entered the city under cover of darkness and in secrecy, and even before midday the rumour was already current in the town that the King of France was sending an army against the Spaniards, and that his ambassador had arrived in Cambray in order to apprise Monseigneur the governor of the happy event.

It was also openly rumoured that the arrival of this same ambassador of the King of France was not altogether unconnected with the activities of Spanish spies inside the city. The people, who were beginning to suffer grievously from shortage of food and lack of clothing, were murmuring audibly at the continued presence of strangers in their midst, who were more than suspected of aiding the Duke of Parma from within, by provoking riots or giving away the secrets of the garrison and of the stronghold.

Above all, there had been growing ill-will against the masked stranger, the mysterious Prince de Froidmont, whose persistent stay in this beleaguered city had given rise at first to mere gossip, but latterly to more pronounced suspicion, plentifully sprinkled with malevolence. The extraordinary deference which Monseigneur the governor had been observed to show him on more than one occasion fostered the growing suspicion that he was a stranger of great distinction, who for some unavowable reason desired to preserve an incognito, and chose to dwell in an obscure hostelry, in order that he might cany on some nefarious negotiations unchecked.

Crowds are always unreasonable when skilfully handled in the direction of suspicion and unrest by unscrupulous agitators, and we know that de Landas' paid hirelings had been busy for weeks past in fomenting hatred against the masked stranger, amongst a people rendered sullen and irritable both by hunger and by the threat of an invading and always brutal soldiery at their gates.

Certain it is that, the moment that Gilles set foot that day outside his lodgings in the Rue aux Juifs, he was followed not only by glances of ill-will, but also by open insults freely showered after him as he passed. He was wearing the rich clothes which would have been affected by *Monsieur* on such an occasion; his toil-worn hands were hidden beneath gloves of fine chamois leather and his face was concealed by a black velvet mask. Looking neither to right nor left, absorbed in his own thoughts, he hurried along the street, paying no heed to what went on around him. It was only when he reached the Place Notre Dame, in front of the cathedral, and tried in crossing toward the Archiepiscopal Palace to avoid a group of people who stood in his way, that he began to perceive something of the intense hostility which was dogging his every footstep.

'Look at the Spaniard!' a woman shouted shrilly out of the crowd. 'Wants the place to himself now!'

'Dressed in silks and satins, when worthy folk go half naked!' called out another, with bitter spite ringing in her husky voice.

'How much does the King of Spain pay you, my fine gallant, for delivering the girls of Cambray to his soldiery?' This from a short, square-shouldered man, only half-dressed in a ragged doublet and hose, shoeless and capless, who deliberately stood his ground in front of Gilles, with bare arms akimbo and bandy legs set wide apart, in an attitude of unmistakable insolence.

Gilles, with whom patience was at no time a besetting virtue, uttered an angry exclamation, seized the fellow incontinently by the shoulder and forced him to execute a wild pirouette ere he fell back gasping, after this unexpected attack, against his nearest companions.

This brief incident naturally exasperated the crowd: it acted as a signal for a fresh outburst of rage and a fresh volley of insults, which were hurled at the stranger from every side.

'Miserable Spaniard!' exclaimed one man. 'How dare you lay a hand on a free burgher of the city?'

'If a free burgher of the city chooses deliberately to insult me,' retorted Gilles, who, for obvious reasons, was trying to keep his temper, 'I do what every one of you would have done under like circumstances—knock the impudent fellow down.'

'Impudent fellow!' came from a harsh voice at the rear of the crowd. 'Hark at the noble Spanish Senor! Flemish burghers are like the dust beneath his feet.'

'I am no Spaniard!' said Gilles loudly. 'And whoever calls me one again is a liar. So, come out of there,' he added lightly, 'you who spoke from a safe and convenient distance; and Fleming, French or Spaniard, we'll soon see whose is the harder fist.'

'Fight with a masked spy like you?' was the defiant riposte. 'Not I! The devil, your accomplice, has taught you some tricks, I'll warrant, against which no simple Christian could stand.'

'Well said!' shouted one of the women. 'If you are no Spaniard and no spy, throw down that mask and show your face like an honest man!'

'Yes! Yes! Throw down the mask!' another in the crowd assented. 'We know you dress like a fine gallant; but we want to see how like your face is to the picture of Beelzebub which hangs in the Town Hall.'

A prolonged shout of ribald laughter, which had no merriment in it, was the unanimous response to this sally. The women were already raising their fists: the ever-recurring insult, 'Spanish spy!' had the effect of whipping up everybody's temper against the stranger. Gilles was defenceless save for his sword, which it would obviously have been highly impolitic to draw against that rabble. Whilst he parleyed with them, he had succeeded by a deliberate manoeuvre in drawing considerably nearer to the high wall of the Archiepiscopal Palace, where the latter abuts on the cathedral close, and he hoped with some good luck, or a sudden, well-thought-out ruse, to reach the gates ere the hostility of the crowd turned to open attack.

That both the men and the women—oh! especially the women!— meant mischief, there could be no doubt. There was that gruff murmur going the round, which means threats muttered between closed teeth; sleeves were being rolled above brawny or gaunt arms;

palms moistened ere they gripped stick or even knife a little closer. Gilles saw all these signs with the quick, practised eye of the soldier, and it was his turn to grind his teeth with rage at his own impotence to defend himself adequately if it came to blows. Just for the moment the crowd was still sullen rather than openly aggressive, and, much as the thought of beating a retreat went against the grain of Gilles' hot temperament, there was no doubt that it were by far the wisest course to pursue.

But there were one or two units in the midst of that gang who were determined that the flame of enmity against the stranger should not die for want of fuel. They were apparently on the fringe of the malcontents, in a safe position in the rear, and from there they threw out a word now and again, a sneer or an insult, whenever there appeared the slightest slackening in the hostile attitude of their friends.

'He wouldn't like to show us his face,' one of this gentry said now, with a mocking laugh; 'for fear we should see how bloated he is with good food and wine.'

'Spawn of the devil!' at once screeched a gaunt, hungry-looking wretch, and ostentatiously tightened his belt around his middle. 'They all gorge while we starve!'

'And wallow in riches, while honest citizens have to beg for their daily bread!'

A woman, still young, and who might have been comely but for the miserable appearance of her unwashed face and lank, matted hair, pushed her way through the throng right into the forefront of the men. She dragged a couple of half-naked children in her wake, who clung weeping to her ragged skirts.

'Look at these!' she screamed harshly, and thrust a fist as close to Gilles' face as she dared. 'Look at these children! You miserable spy! Starving, I tell you! Starving! While your satin doublet is bursting with Spanish gold!'

'Aye!' came with renewed vigour from the rear. 'The price of our sons' lives, of our daughters' honour, are sacrificed to the tyranny and the debauchery of such as you!'

'Shame! Shame!' came in a dull, ominous murmur from the rest of the throng.

There was no doubt that tempers were waxing more and more ugly. In more than one pair of bloodshot eyes which were glaring at him, Gilles saw the reflection of a lust which was not far removed from that of murder. It was no use looking on the matter with indifference; his life was being threatened, and there were men actually present among the crowd who were making it their business to goad this rabble into ever-increasing fury. The latter were in themselves too obtuse to realize that they were acting under guidance, that their choler would no longer be allowed to cool down nor they permitted to let the stranger go unmolested. Their tempers, their own stupidity, their miseries, poor wretches, had made them the slaves of de Landas' gang.

Gilles had been shrewd enough to suspect the plot almost from the first.

'I marvel,' he had already said to himself, 'if my gallant with the Spanish accent and the languorous eyes has had a finger in this delectable pie. Between employing paid spadassins to commit deliberate murder and egging on a set of hungry wretches into achieving manslaughter, there is little to choose, and Messire de Landas has no doubt adopted the less risky course.'

But for the nonce self-preservation became the dominant necessity, and Gilles, feeling himself so closely pressed that his free movements were becoming hampered, executed a swift manoeuvre of retreat which landed him a second or two later with his back against the high encircling walls of the Archiepiscopal Palace, and with the stately limes of the Palace gardens waving their emerald-laden branches above his head. Were his position not quite so precarious, he might have laughed aloud at its ludicrousness. He, Gilles de Crohin, masquerading as a Prince of Valois, and set upon for being a Spanish spy!! That fellow, de Landas, was a clever rogue! But it was a dirty trick to use these wretched people as his tools!

Aloud, he shouted, as forcibly and vigorously as he could: 'Now then, my friends! Have I not already told you that I am no Spaniard? I am a Frenchman, I tell you, and my Liege Lord the King of France is even at this hour busy trying to free you from your Spanish tyrants. He——'

'Hark at him!' came at once, to the accompaniment of deafening clamour, from the rear. 'Feeding us with lies. 'Tis the way of spies to assume any guise that may suit their fancy or their pocket. Friends! Citizens! Do not let the Spaniard trick you! Why is he here, I ask you? If he is a Frenchman, why doth he go about masked? What is he doing here? Bargaining with the Duke of Parma, I say, with your lives and your liberties.'

'Silence, you fool!' cried Gilles, in stentorian tones. 'You miserable cur! Who pays you, I would like to know, to incite these poor people to break the laws of peace and order?'

'Peace and order, forsooth!' retorted the voice from the rear, with a prolonged, harsh laugh. 'You want peace, no doubt, so that your master the Spanish King can work his way with Cambray, send his soldiers into our city to burn our houses, pillage our homes, outrage our wives and daughters! Citizens, remember Mechlin! Remember Mons! Beware lest this man sell your city to the Spaniards and you reap the same fate as your kinsmen there!'

A stupendous cry of rage and execration greeted this abominable tirade—as abominable, indeed, as it was ludicrous. One moment of sober reflection would have convinced these poor, deluded fools how utterly futile and false were the assertions made by those who were goading them to exasperation. But a crowd never does reflect once it is aroused, once a sufficient number of hotheads are there, ready to drive them from empty bluster to actual violence. The paid agents of M. de Landas had done their work well. They had sown seeds of disaffection, of mistrust and of hostility, for days past and weeks; now they were garnering just the amount of excitement necessary to bring about a dastardly crime.

Gilles, with his back against the wall, was beginning to think that he would have to make a fight for it after all. Already the crowd was closing in around him, pressing closer and closer, completing the semicircle which barred his only means of escape. He tried to make himself heard, but he was shouted down. The work of the agitators was indeed complete; the rabble needed no more egging on. Men and women were ready for any mischief—to seize the stranger, tear off the rich clothes from his back, ransack his pockets, knock him on the head and finally drag him through the streets and throw him either into the river or over the battlements into the moat.

It became a question now how dearly Gilles would be able to sell his life. He could no longer hope to reach the gates of the Palace, and the vast courtyard, gardens and precincts which surrounded the house itself rendered it highly improbable that any one would hear the tumult and come to his assistance. Over the heads of the crowd, he could see the great, open Place where a patrol of the town guard was wont to pass from time to time on its beat. For some unexplainable reason there appeared to be no patrol in sight to-day. Had they been bribed to keep out of the way? It was at least possible. Some one had evidently planned the whole of this agitation, and that some one—an unscrupulous devil, thought Messire, if ever there was one!—was not like to have left the town guard out of his reckoning.

Even while Gilles took this rapid, mental survey of his position, one of the men in the rear had suddenly stooped and picked up a loose stone out of the gutter. Gilles saw the act, saw the man lift the stone, brandish it for a moment above his head and then fling it with all his might. He saw it just in time to dodge the stone, which struck the wall just above his head.

'Not a bad fling, my man,' he said lightly. 'But 'twas the act of a coward!'

Then he drew his sword—was forced to do it, because the crowd were pressing him close, some with sticks, others with fists. The square-shouldered man of awhile ago—he with the bandy legs—had a butcher's knife in his hand.

'Murder!' shrieked the women, as soon as Gilles' sword darted out of its sheath like a tongue of living flame.

'Aye, murder!' he riposted. 'I can see it in your eyes! So stand back, all of you, or the foremost among you who dares to advance is a dead man.'

They did not advance. With a churl's natural terror of the sword, they retreated, realizing for the first time that it was a noble lord, an exalted personage whom, in their blindness, they had dared to attack. Spaniard or no, he was a gentleman; and suddenly the thought of floggings or worse for such an outrage dissipated the fumes of folly, which some unknown person's rhetoric had raised inside their brains.

De Landas' agents in the rear saw this perceptible retreat. Another moment or two, and their carefully laid schemes would certainly come to naught. Failure for them now was unthinkable. The eyes of their employer were undoubtedly upon them, even though they could not see him, and they knew from past bitter experience how relentless the young Spanish lord could be if his will was thwarted through the incompetence of his servants. One of them—I think his name was Jan—bolder than the others, called to his comrades and to those on the fringe of the crowd who had not been scared by the sight of that fine Toledo blade, gave them the lead, which they promptly followed, of picking up more stones out of the gutter and flinging them at the stranger one after another in rapid succession. Some of this stone-throwing was very wild, and Gilles was able to dodge most of the missiles, whilst others actually hit some of the crowd. A woman received one on the shoulder; the bandy-legged bully another on the head. Blood now was flowing freely, and the sight of blood acts on a turbulent crowd in the same way as it does on a goaded bull. No longer frightened of the sword, the riotous crew began to attack the stranger more savagely. One man struck at him with a stick, another tried to edge nearer in order to use a knife.

Stones were being flung now from every point, and soon it became impossible to dodge them all. The crowd had become a screeching mob, bent on outrage and on murder. The screams of women, the cries of little children, mingled with hoarse cries of rage and volleys of unspeakable insults. The sight of blood had of a truth turned a knot of malcontents into a pack of brute beasts, fuming with an insatiable desire to kill.

As fast as the stones fell around him, Gilles picked them up and flung them back. These seldom missed their mark, and already several of his assailants had been forced to retreat from the field. But now a piece of granite hit him on the sword-arm and he had barely the time to transfer his sword to his left hand in order to ward off a thrust aimed at him with a knife, just below the belt. His right arm hung limp by his side, aching furiously; a small piece of sharp stone had grazed his forehead, and with an unconsidered gesture, he tore the mask from his face, for the blood was streaming beneath it into his eyes. But that movement—wellnigh instantaneous as it was—placed him at a greater disadvantage still, for another stone, more accurately aimed than some others, hit his left arm so violently that, but for an instinctive, nervy clutch on the hilt, his sword would have fallen from his grasp.

After that, he remembered nothing more. A red veil appeared to interpose itself between his eyes and that mass of vehement, raging, perspiring humanity before him. Each individual before him seemed to the weary fighter to assume greater and ever greater proportions, until he felt himself confronted with a throng of giants with distorted faces and huge, ugly jaws, through which a hot fire came, searing his face and obscuring his vision. Instinctively he still dodged the missiles, still parried with his sword; but his movements were mechanical; he felt that they were becoming inefficient ... that he himself was exhausted ... vanquished. Vaguely he marvelled at Destiny's strange caprice, which had decreed that he should die, assassinated by a set of shrieking men and women, whom he had never wronged even by a thought.

Then suddenly the whole wall behind him appeared to give way, and he sank backwards into oblivion.

CHAPTER XVIII.
HOW A SECOND AWAKENING MAY BE MORE BITTER THAN THE FIRST

I

It all seemed like the recurrence of that lovely dream of long ago—the awakening to a sense of well-being and of security; the sweet-smelling couch; the clean linen; the fragrance of the air, and above all the tender, pitying blue eyes and the tiny brown mole which challenged a kiss.

When Gilles opened his eyes, he promptly closed them again, for fear of losing that delicious sensation of being in dreamland, which filled his whole body and soul with inexpressible beatitude. But even as he did so, a gentle voice, light and soothing as the murmur of a limpid stream, reached his ear.

'Will you not look up once more, Messire,' the angelic voice said softly, 'and assure me that you are not grievously hurt?' And oh! the little tone—half bantering, wholly sympathetic—which rippled through those words with a melodious sound that sent poor Gilles into a veritable heaven of ecstasy.

But he did look up, just as he was bidden to do—looked up, and encountered that tantalizing little mole at such close quarters that he promptly raised his head, so that his lips might touch it. Whereupon the mole, the blue eyes, the demure smile, the whole exquisite face, retreated with lightning rapidity into some obscure and remote distance, and Gilles, conscious that only gentle pity would bring them nearer to him again, groaned loudly and once more closed his eyes.

But this time these outward signs of suffering were greeted with a mocking little laugh.

'Too late, Messire! You have already betrayed yourself. You are not so sick as you would have me believe!'

'Sick? No!' he retorted; but made no attempt to move. 'Dead, more like! and catching my first glimpse of paradise.'

'Fie, Messire!' she exclaimed gaily. 'To make so sure of going speedily to Heaven!'

'How can I help being sure when angels are present to confirm my belief?'

'But you are not in Heaven,' she assured him, and smiled on him archly from out a frame of tender, leafless branches. 'You are in an arbour in the park, whither I and two of my servants brought you when you fell into our arms at the postern gate.'

He raised himself upon his elbow, found he could do it without much pain; then looked about him searchingly and wonderingly. He was lying on a couch and his head had apparently been resting on a couple of velvet cushions. All around him the still dormant tendrils of wild clematis wound in and out of skilfully constructed woodwork. Overhead, the woodwork was shaped to a dome, and straight in front of him there stretched out a vista over the park of a straight, grass walk, bordered with beds of brilliantly coloured tulips and hyacinths and backed by a row of young limes, on which the baby leaves gleamed like pale emeralds, whilst far away the graceful pinnacles of the cathedral stood out like perfect lace-work against the vivid blue of the sky.

'Well, Messire,' resumed Jacqueline lightly, after awhile, 'are you convinced now that you are still on earth, and that it was by human agency that you arrived here, not on angels' wings?'

'No, I am not convinced of that, Madame,' he replied. 'At the same time, I would dearly like to know how I did come here.'

'Simply enough, Messire. I was taking my usual walk in the park, when I heard an awful commotion on the other side of the wall. I and my two servants who were with me hurried to the postern gate, for of a truth the cries that we heard sounded threatening and ominous. One of my servants climbed over the shoulders of the other and hoisted himself to the top of the wall, from whence he saw that a whole crowd armed with knives and sticks was furiously attacking a single man, who was standing his ground with his back against the postern gate, whilst we could all hear quite distinctly the clash of missiles hurled against the wall. To pull open the gate was the work of a few seconds, and you, Messire, fell backwards into my—into my servants' arms.'

Then, as he made no sign, said not a word, only remained quite still—almost inert—resting on his elbow and gazing on her with eyes filled with passionate soul-hunger, she added gently:

'You are not in pain, Messire?'

'In sore pain, ma donna,' he replied with a sigh. 'In incurable pain, I fear me.'

The tone of his voice, the look in his eyes while he said this, made it impossible for her not to understand. She lowered her eyes for a moment, for his glance had brought a hot blush to her cheeks. There was a moment of tense silence in the little arbour—a silence broken only by the murmur of the breeze through the young twigs of the wild clematis and the call of a robin in the branches of the limes. Jacqueline was the first to rouse herself from this strange and sweet oppression. She gave a quick little sigh and, unable to speak, she was turning to go away, flying as if by instinct from some insidious danger which seemed to lurk for her in the wild, tremulous beating of her heart.

'Jacqueline!'

She had not thought that her name could sound so sweet as it did just then, when it came to her in a fervent, passionate appeal from the depths of the fragrant arbour, where awhile ago she and her servants had laid Messire down to rest. She did not turn her head to look on him now, but nevertheless paused on the threshold, for her heart was beating so fast that she felt almost choked, and her knees shook so that she was forced to cling with one hand to the curtain of young twigs which hung at the entrance of the arbour.

The next moment he was by her side. She felt that he was near her, even though she still kept her head resolutely turned away. He put one knee to the ground and, stooping, kissed the hem of her gown. And Jacqueline—a mere child where knowledge of the great passion is concerned—felt that something very great and very mysterious, as well as very beautiful, had suddenly been revealed to her by this simple act of homage performed by this one man. She realized all of a sudden why those few weeks ago, when the mysterious singer with the mellow voice had sung beneath her window, the whole world had seemed to her full of beauty and of joy, why during these past long and weary days while Messire lay sick and she could not see him, that self-same world became unspeakably drab and ugly. She knew now that, with his song, the singer had opened the portals of her heart, and that, unknown to herself, she had let Love creep in there and make himself a nest, from whence he had alternately tortured her or made her exquisitely happy. Tears which seared and soothed rose to her eyes; a stupendous longing for something which she could not quite grasp, filled her entire soul. And with it all, an infinite sadness made her heart ache till she could have called out with the pain of it—a sense of the unattainable, of something perfect and wonderful, which by a hideous caprice of Fate must for ever remain out of her reach.

'It can never be, Messire!' was all that she said. The words came like a cry, straight from her heart—a child's heart, that has not yet learned to dissemble. And that cry spoke more certainly and more tangibly than any avowal could have done. In a moment, Gilles was on his feet, his arms were round her shoulders and his face was buried in her fragrant hair. And she, unresisting, yielded herself to him, savoured the sweetness of his caresses, the touch of his lips on her eyes, her cheeks, her mouth. Her ardent nature, long held in fetters by convention, responded with all its richness to the insistent call of the man's passionate love.

'You love me, Jacqueline?' he asked, and looked down into the depths of those exquisite blue eyes which had captured his soul long ago and made him their slave until this hour, when they in their turn yielded entirely to him.

'Verily,' she replied quaintly, and looked shyly into his glowing face; 'I do believe, in truth, Messire, that I do.'

Let those who can, blame Gilles de Crohin for losing his head after that, and for promptly forgetting everything that he ought to have remembered, save the rapture of holding her to his breast. Of a truth, duty, honour, promises, the Duc d'Anjou and Madame la Reyne, were as far from his ken just now as is a crawling worm from the starry firmament above. He was going away to-day—out, out into a great world, into the unknown, where life could be made anew, where there would be neither sorrow nor tears, if he could carry this exquisite woman thither in his arms.

'I cannot let you go, ma donna,' he murmured as he held her closer and ever closer, and covered her lips, her neck, her throat with kisses. 'No power on earth can take you from me now that I have you, that I hold you, my beautiful, exquisite flower. You love me, Jacqueline?' he asked her for the tenth time, and for the tenth time she murmured in response: 'I love you!'

Time had ceased to be. The world no longer existed for these two happy beings who had found one another. There was only Love for them—Love, pure and holy, and Passion, that makes the world go round. There was spring in the air, and the scent of awakening life around them, the fragrance of budding blossom, the call of birds, the hum of bees—Nature, exquisite, wonderful in her perfect selfishness, and in her oblivion of all save her own immutable Self.

'You love me, Jacqueline?'

'I love you!'

'Then, in the name of God that made us to love one another,' he entreated with ever-growing fervour, 'let us forget everything, leave everything, dare all for the sake of our Love. It can never be, you say ... everything can be, mignonne; for Love makes everything possible. Rank, wealth, duty, country, King—what are they but shadows? Leave them, my flower! Leave them and come to me! Love is true, love is real! Come with me, Jacqueline, and by the living God who made you as perfect as you are, by your heavenly blue eyes and your maddening smile, I swear to you that I will give you such an infinity of worship that I will make of your life one long, unceasing rapture.'

She had closed her eyes, drinking in his ardour with her very soul. Hers was one of those super-natures which, when they give, do so in the fullest measure. Being a woman, and one nurtured in self-control and acute sensitiveness, she did not, even at this blissful moment, lose complete grasp of herself; unlike the man, her passion did not carry her entirely into the realm of forgetfulness. She yielded to his kisses, knowing that, as they were the first, so they would be the last that she would ever savour in the fullness of perfect ecstasy; that parting—dreary, inevitable, woeful parting—must follow this present transient happiness. Yet, knowing all that, she would not forgo the exquisite joy that she felt in yielding, the exquisite joy, too, that she was giving him. She deliberately plucked the rich fruit of delight, even though she knew that inexorable Fate would wrench it from her even before she had tasted its sweetness to the full.

It was only when Jacqueline, suddenly waking as from a dream and disengaging herself gently from his arms, said once again, more resolutely this time: 'It can never be, Messire!' that Gilles in his turn realized what he had done. He was brought back to earth with one of those sudden blows of reawakened consciousness which leave a man stunned and bruised, in a state of quasi-hebetude. For one supreme moment of his life the gates of an earthly paradise had been opened for him and he had been granted a peep into such radiant possibilities that, dazzled and giddy with joy, he had felt within himself that sublime arrogance which makes light of every obstacle and is ready to ride rough-shod over the entire world.

But the inexorable 'It can never be!' had struck at the portals of his consciousness, and even before he had become fully sentient he saw the grim hand of Fate closing those golden gates before his eyes, and pointing sternly to the path which led down to earth, left him once more alone with his dream.

'It can never be!'

He tried to wrestle with Fate, to wrest from cruel hands that happiness which already was slipping from his grasp.

'Why not?' he cried out defiantly. Then, in a final, agonized entreaty, he murmured once more, 'Why not?'

Ah! he knew well enough why not! Fool and criminal, to have forgotten it even for this one brief instant of perfect bliss! Why not? Ye gods, were there not a thousand reasons why a penniless soldier of fortune should not dare approach a noble and rich heiress? and a thousand others why he—Gilles de Crohin—should never have spoken one word of love to this one woman, who was destined for another man—and that man his own liege lord. There was a gateless barrier made up of honour and chivalry and of an oath sworn upon the cross between his love and Jacqueline de Broyart, which in honour he should never have attempted to cross.

Consciousness came back to him with a sudden rush, not only the consciousness of what he had done, but of what he had now to do. Not all the bitter tears of lifelong remorse would ever succeed in wiping out the past; but honour demanded that at least the future be kept unsullied.

A final struggle with temptation that was proving overwhelming, a final, wholly human, longing to keep and to hold this glorious gift of God; then the last renunciation as he allowed the loved one to glide out of his arms like a graceful bird, still a-quiver after this brief immersion in the torrential wave of his passion. Then, as she stood now a few paces away from him, with wide, sad eyes deliberately turned to gaze on the distant sky, he passed his hand across his forehead, as if with the firm will to clear his brain and chase away the last vestige of the sweet, insistent dream.

Once more there was silence in the fragrant arbour; but it was the silence of unspoken sorrow—a silence laden with the portent of an approaching farewell. Gilles was the first to break it.

'It can never be, ma donna,' he said quietly, his rugged voice still shaking with emotion, now resolutely held in bondage. 'I know that well enough. Knew it even at the moment when, in my folly, I first dared to kiss your gown.'

'I was as much to blame as you, Messire,' she said naïvely, her lips trembling with suppressed sobs. 'I don't know how it came about, but...'

'It came about, ma donna,' he rejoined fervently, 'because you are as perfect as the angels, and God when He fashioned you allowed no human weakness to mar His adorable work. The avowal which came from your sweet lips was just like the manna which He gave to the hungry crowd. I, the poor soldier of fortune, have been made thereby more enviable than a king.'

'And yet we must part, Messire?' she said firmly, and withal in her voice that touching note of childlike appeal which for the unfortunate dweller on the outskirts of paradise was more difficult to withstand than were a glass of water to one dying of thirst. 'I do not belong to myself, you know,' she continued, and looked him once more serenely in the face. 'Ever since my dear brother died I have been made to understand that my future, my person, belong to my country—my poor, sorrowing country, who, it seems, hath sore need of me. I have no right to love, no right to think of mine own happiness. God alone in His Omniscience knows how you came to fill my heart, Messire, to the exclusion of every other thought, of every other duty. It was wrong of me, I know—wrong and unmaidenly. But the secret of my love would for ever have remained locked in my heart if I had not learned that you loved me too.'

She made her profession of faith so firmly and earnestly and with such touching innocence that the hot passion which a while ago was raging in Gilles' heart was suddenly soothed and purified as if with the touch of a divine breath. A wonderful peace descended on his soul: he hardly knew himself, his own turbulent temper, his untamed and passionate nature, so calm and serene did he suddenly feel. 'Yes, we must part, ma donna,' he said, in a simple, monotonous voice which he himself scarcely recognized as his own. 'We must each go our way; you to fulfil the great destiny for which God has created you and to which your sorrowing country calls you; I to watch from afar the course of your fortunes, like the poor, starving astrologer doth watch the course of the stars.'

'From afar?' she said, and her delicate cheeks took on a dull, lifeless hue. 'Then you will go away?'

'To-day, please God!' he replied.

'But, I—'

'You, ma donna, my beautiful Flower o' the Lily, you will, I pray Heaven, forget me even as the young, living sapling forgets the stricken bough which the tempests have laid low.'

She shook her head.

'I will never forget you, Messire. If you go from me to-day I will never know another happy hour again.'

'May God bless you for saying this! But I have no fear that you will not be happy. Happiness comes as readily to your call as does a bird to its mate. You and happiness are one, ma donna. Where you are, all the joys of earth dwell and flourish.'

'Not when I am alone,' she said, the hot tears welling to her eyes, her voice shaken with sobs. 'And thoughts of you—lonely and desolate—will chase all joy from out my life.'

'But you must not think of me at all, ma donna,' he rejoined with infinite tenderness. 'And when you do, when a swift remembrance of the poor, rough soldier doth perchance disturb the serenity of your dreams, do not think of him as either lonely or desolate. I shall never again in life be lonely—never again be desolate. I am now rich beyond the dreams of men, rich with the boundless wealth of unforgettable memories.'

'You talk so readily of forgetting,' she said sadly. 'Will you find it so easy, Messire?'

'Look at me, ma donna, and read the answer to your question in mine eyes.'

She looked up at him, with that shy and demure glance which rendered her so adorable and so winning, and in his face she saw so much misery, such unspeakable sorrow that her heart was seized with a terrible ache. The sobs which were choking her could no longer be suppressed. She stuffed her tiny handkerchief into her mouth to stop herself from crying out aloud, and feeling giddy and faint, she sank on to a pile of cushions close by and buried her face in her hands, letting her tears flow freely at last, since she was not ashamed of the intensity of her grief.

Gilles could have dashed his head against the nearest tree-trunk, so enraged was he with himself, so humiliated at his own weakness. How deeply did he regret now that de Landas' sword had not ended his miserable life, before he had brought sorrow and tears to this woman whom he worshipped. What right had he to disturb her peace of mind? What right to stir to the very depths of her fine nature those strong passions which, but for his clumsy touch, might for ever have remained dormant?

And through it all was the sense of his own baseness, which had come upon him with a rush—his treachery to Madame la Reyne, his falseness to his sworn oath. Love for this beautiful woman had swept him off his feet, caught him at a weak and unguarded moment and left him now covered with humiliation and self-reproach, an object of hatred to himself, for ever in future to be haunted by the recurrent vision of the loved one's face bathed in tears and by the sound of those harrowing sobs which would until the end of time rend his soul with unutterable anguish.

'Would to God we had never met!' he murmured fervently.

And she had sufficient courage, sufficient strength, to smile up at him through her tears, murmuring with enchanting simplicity:

'Would to God we had not to part.'

What else could he do but fall on his knees in mute adoration, and with the final, heartbroken farewell dying upon his lips? He stooped low until his head nearly touched the ground. Her small foot in its velvet shoe peeped just beneath the hem of her gown, and with a last act of humble adoration, he pressed his lips upon its tip.

'Farewell, my adored one,' he said softly, as he straightened out his tall, massive figure once more. 'With my heart and my soul I worship you now and for all time. Even though I may never again look upon your loveliness, the memory of it will haunt me until the hour of death, when my spirit—free to roam the universe—will fly to you as surely as doth the swallow to its mate. And if in the future,' he added with solemn earnestness, 'aught should occur to render me odious in your sight, then I pray you on bended knees and in the name of this past unforgettable hour, to remember that, whatever else I may have done that was unworthy and base, my love for you has been as pure and sacred as is the love of the lark for the sun.'

And, before she could reply, he was gone. She watched his tall figure striding rapidly away along the grass walk, until he became a mere speck upon the shimmering distance beyond. Soon he disappeared from view altogether, and

CHAPTER XIX.
WHAT JACQUELINE WAS FORCED TO HEAR

I

Indeed, to Jacqueline, even more so than to her lover, this last half-hour appeared more unreal than a dream. For a long time after Gilles had gone she remained sitting on the pile of cushions at the entrance of the arbour, gazing, gazing far away into the translucent sky, struggling with that life-problem which to the ingenuous hath so oft remained unsolved: If God gave me that happiness, why did He take it away again so soon?

Life appeared before her now as one long vista of uninterrupted dreariness. With her heart dead within her, she would in truth become the pawn in political games which her guardian had always desired that she should be. Well! no doubt it was all for the best. Awhile ago, ere she had met Messire, ere he had taught her to read in the great Book of Love, she had been headstrong and rebellious. A loveless marriage of convention, a mere political alliance would have revolted her and mayhap caused grave complications in her troubled country's affairs. Now, nothing mattered. Nothing would ever matter again. Since happiness was for ever denied her, she was far more ready to sacrifice her personal feelings to her country's needs than she had been before.

Her joy in life would for the future be made up of sacrifice, and if she could do her beloved and sorely-stricken country a permanent benefit thereby, well! she would feel once more that she had not lived her life in vain.

At this stage she was not actively unhappy. Emotion had torn at her heartstrings and left her bruised and sore, but her happiness had been too brief to cause bitter regret. She was chiefly conscious of an immense feeling of pity for her lover, whose heartache must indeed be as great as her own. But, for herself, there was nothing that she regretted, nothing that she would have wished to be otherwise. All her memories of him were happy ones—except that moment of the midnight quarrel in the Palace, when for a brief while she had wilfully misjudged him. Even the final parting from him, though it broke her heart, had been wholly free from bitterness. She was so sure of his love that she could almost bear patiently to see him go away, knowing that she could always treasure his love in her heart as something pure and almost holy.

All through life that love would encompass her, would keep her from evil thoughts and evil intent, whilst nothing on earth could rob her of the sweets of memory. She loved him and he had wanted her, even long before she knew him; he had come to Cambray in disguise, under a mask, and had wooed her in his own romantic fashion, with song and laughter and joy of living, so different to the amorous sighs and languorous looks wherewith other swains had striven to win her regard. She loved the mystery wherewith he had surrounded his person, smiled at the thought how he had led Monseigneur her guardian by the nose, and had tried vainly to hoodwink even her— her, Jacqueline, who had loved him already that night when he had flung Pierre over the wall and run to her window, singing: 'Mignonne, venez voir si la rose— —'

And he had thought to hoodwink her after that! thought to throw dust in her eyes by playing a dual rôle, now masquerading as the Prince de Froidmont, now as the equerry—he, the chosen of her heart, the man whose every action, every word was fine and noble and dear.... How foolish of him to imagine that she could be deceived. Why, there was that scar upon his hand—a scar the sight of which had loosened a perfect floodgate of memories—a scar which she herself had helped to tend and bind three years ago, in the monastery of Gembloux. She could even remember the leech saying at the time: 'The rascal will be marked for life, I warrant. I've never seen such a strange wound before—the exact shape of a cross it is, like the mark on an ass's back.'

How well she remembered that night! Her own anxiety for the wounded man—a poor soldier, evidently, for he was miserably clad; his clothes were old and had been frequently darned and his pockets only contained a few sols. He had apparently fought with the French on that awful day, and had been discovered by herself, lying unconscious near the monastery wall, up on the hill, more than a league away from the field of battle. She remembered insisting that the leech should tend him, and afterwards that he should be taken back to the spot where the fighting had taken place, in case some friend or comrade be searching for him. After that, the death of her dear brother and the change in her fortunes had chased all other memories away, until that awful night in the Palace, when de Landas had behaved like a coward and she like a vixen, and the Prince de Froidmont had threaded the masks of his vanquished enemies upon his sword and thrown them at her feet. She had seen the scar then upon his hand, and the sight had troubled her, because of the mystery which it evoked. Then came the next day, when she sat in the window embrasure in wait for the Prince's equerry. At once his face had seemed so strangely familiar to her—and then there was the scar!

Jacqueline remembered how deeply she pondered over the puzzle then. The Prince de Froidmont and his equerry were one and the same person; that was evident, of course. And both these personalities were also merged in that of the poor soldier whom she had helped to tend in the monastery of Gembloux. But, unlike most women, she had never tried to pry into his secrets. Somehow the mystery—if mystery there was—seemed to harmonize with his whole personality. She loved him as he was—rough at times, at others infinitely gentle; and oh! the strength of his love and its ardour when he held her in his arms! She would be quite satisfied if the mystery remained for ever unsolved. It was a part of him, not by any means the least amongst his many attractions in her sight.

Now he had gone, never to return, leaving her alone with only memory for company—memory and a huge longing to rest once more in the safe fold of his protecting arms.

'Come back to me, Messire!' she called out to him in her heart. 'Take no heed of what I said when in my blind folly I vowed that it could never be. It shall and must be if you'll only come back to me— just once—only once—and I should be content. God never meant that you and I should part before we had each drained the cup of Love to the end. The world is ours, our Love shall conquer it. Not the world of riches and of pomp; not even the world of glory. Just a little kingdom of our own, wherein no one shall dwell but you and I—a little kingdom bound for me by the span of your arms, my throne your heart, my crown your kiss.'

II

Dreaming, sighing, longing, Jacqueline sat on in the arbour, unmindful of time. It was only when the cathedral bell boomed the midday hour that she awoke—vaguely, still—to the actualities of life. Of a truth, it seemed difficult to conceive that life in the future must go on just the same: the daily rounds, the conventionalities, the social flummeries must all go on, and she—Jacqueline—would have to smile, to speak, to live on—just the same.

And yet nothing, nothing on earth could ever be quite the same again. It is impossible to delve deeply into the Book of Passion, to have mastered the lesson which God Himself forbade His children to learn, and then to look on Life with the same vacant, ignorant eyes as before. The daily rounds would certainly go on; but life itself would henceforth be different. The girl—a mere child—had in one brief half-hour become a woman. Love had transfigured the world for her.

But she tried to think of life as he—her knight—would have wished her to do, to fulfil her destiny so that from afar he might be proud of her. Above all, she would show a serene face to her world. Her fellow-citizens here in Cambray had quite enough sorrow to behold, without having the sight of Madame Jacqueline de Broyart's tear-stained face constantly before them. There would be much to do in the near future—much grief to console, many troubles to alleviate. What was one solitary heartache beside the sufferings of an entire nation?

She rose to her feet, feeling more valiant and strong. One last look she gave round the little arbour which had sheltered her short-lived happiness. The pale sun peeped in shyly through the interstices of the woodwork, and threw a shaft of honey-coloured light upon the couch where he had lain unconscious, after she and her servants had saved him from the mob. With an impulsive movement which she did not try to check, she ran up to the couch, and, kneeling down beside it, she buried her face in the pillows whereon his head had rested. A few more tears, one long convulsive sob, a heart-broken sigh; then nothing more. That was the end! the last word in the final chapter of her romance, the lifelong farewell to her girlish dream.

Then she dried her eyes resolutely, rose to her feet, and prepared to return to the Palace.

III

But at the entrance of the arbour she was met by de Landas. He was standing there, looking at her, with a hideously evil sneer upon his face.

She had not spoken with him since that day when she had for ever cast him out of her heart, had always succeeded in avoiding him when the exigencies of their mutual social position forced her to be in the same room with him. To-day she felt as if his very presence was an outrage. How long he had been there she could not say; how much of her soul agony he had witnessed caused her a sense of intolerable humiliation. For the moment he had trapped her, obviously had lain in wait for her, and was not like to let her go without forcing his company upon her. There was no other exit to the little arbour, and she, unable to avoid him, yet loathing the very sight of him, could only take refuge in an attitude of haughty indifference and of lofty scorn.

'I will not pollute you with my touch,' he said coolly, seeing that at sight of him she had retreated a step or two, as she would have done had she encountered a noisome reptile. He remained standing in the doorway, leaning against the woodwork, with arms folded and legs crossed and an insolent leer in his dark eyes.

'Then I pray you to let me pass,' was her calm rejoinder.

'Not,' he riposted, ''till you have allowed me to say something to you, which hath weighed on my heart these past three weeks.'

'There is nothing that you can wish to say to me, M. le Marquis, that I would care to hear.'

'You are severe, Jacqueline,' he said. Then, as she made no reply save an indifferent shrug of the shoulders, he added with well-feigned humility: 'Not more so than I deserve, I know. But I was delirious on that day. I did not know what I was saying. Jealousy had completely obscured my brain. You would not make a madman responsible for his ravings!'

'Let us leave it at that, M. le Marquis,' she rejoined calmly. 'But you will understand that I do not care to listen to that same madman's ravings again.'

'How cold you are!' he murmured, sighed dolefully like one in utter grief. His whole attitude suddenly betokened contrition and overwhelming sentiment; his fine dark eyes even contrived to fill themselves with tears. 'Have you forgotten so soon, Jacqueline?' he asked, 'all that you and I have meant to one another in the past; how oft your golden head hath rested against my heart!'

But she was not like to be taken in by this mood, the falseness of which was transparent enough.

'An' you do not cease to insult me with your ramblings,' she said, with all the scorn which his contemptible ruse deserved, 'I will call to my servants to rid me of your presence.'

'Your servants are too far away to hear you,' he retorted with a cynical laugh. 'And if you do not listen to me to-day, Jacqueline, you will put it out of my power to save you from humiliation and your lover from death.'

'How dare you!' she exclaimed aloud, roused at last out of her indifference by his wanton insolence. Whereupon he, seeing that she was not to be won by honeyed words, threw down the mask in an instant, appeared in his true colours—false, vengeful and full of venom, his face distorted by jealous rage, breathing greed and spite as he spoke.

'Oh!' he said with a sneer. 'A man who has been flouted and scorned and who sees a hated rival assuming a position which once was his, is not like to mince his words. I have nothing to lose at your hands—remember that, my fine Madame. The full measure of your hate and of your scorn are my portion now, it seems; while Messire le Prince de Froidmont is the recipient of your smiles.'

Outraged to her innermost being by hearing that name, which to her was almost sacred, profaned by that vile creature's lips, Jacqueline would readily now have forgotten her dignity, and fled from his presence if she could, as she would from that of a spirit of evil. But he divined her wish to flee, feared that she might succeed in slipping past him; so he seized her by the wrist just as she meditated a dash past him, and held her so fast and with such a brutish grip, that but for her courage and sense of dignity, she could have screamed with pain.

'Listen to me, Jacqueline,' he said menacingly. 'You must listen! Think you I will stand by any longer and see the man whom I hate worse than any man I have ever hated in all my life before, in the full enjoyment of what I have lost—of your fortune, my winsome Flemish scrub, the only thing about you which is worth a Spanish gentleman's while to covet? Oh! but I know more about your love intrigue, my proud lady, than you think! I knew something of it before to-day, when, half an hour ago I saw the noble Prince de Froidmont stealing unmasked out of the postern gate. Unmasked, my tricksy lady,' he continued with a harsh laugh, 'in more senses than one; for though he was dressed in the rich clothes affected by the master, the man who stole out of the postern gate had the features of the equerry. A pretty story, indeed, this would make for Monseigneur the governor! Madame Jacqueline de Broyart meeting clandestinely, like a flirtatious kitchen wench, some nameless adventurer who hath captured her fancy!'

'M. de Landas,' she said quite calmly, as soon as he gave her a chance of making herself heard, 'an you have a spark of manhood left in you, you will cease these insults and let me go.'

'What else was it but a clandestine meeting?' he riposted savagely. 'Your flaming cheeks and tear-filled eyes proclaim it loudly enough. I saw him, I tell you; then I searched for you, but I did not know of this arbour. Such private trysting-places were never granted me!'

'M. de Landas,' she reiterated for the third time, 'I desire you to be silent and to let me go.'

'So you shall, my dear,' he riposted with his insolent leer. 'So you shall! You shall be free in a moment or two—free to go quietly back to your own room and there to ponder over one or two questions which I am going to put to you, and which mayhap have never occurred to you before. Who is this Prince de Froidmont? Where did he spring from? Why does he masquerade, now as the master, anon as his own equerry? What unavowable secret doth he hide beneath that eternal mask of his? Can you answer that, my specious lady, who are still fresh from that enigmatic person's arms? Was it the Prince who kissed you in this arbour, or was it his servant?'

Then, as she drew herself up to her full height, looking a veritable statue of lofty disdain, a world of withering contumely in her fine eyes, he went on more insidiously:

'Let me tell you one thing, Jacqueline, of which you obviously are ignorant. There is no Prince de Froidmont inscribed in France's book of Heraldry. There is an out-at-elbows Seigneur de Froidmont, whose fortunes are at so low an ebb that he sells his sword to the highest bidder. He was last seen in the company of the Duc d'Anjou, the most dissolute scion of an abandoned race. And those who knew him then, say that he is tall and broad-shouldered, hath a martial mien and the air of a soldier. They also say that he has a curiously shaped scar on the back of his hand. Now, I warn you, Jacqueline, that when next I meet Monseigneur le Prince de Froidmont, I shall ask him to give me his hand in friendship, and if he refuses, which he certainly will do, I shall challenge him to take off his glove ere I smite him in his lying face with mine.'

'When you have finished with those vile calumnies, Messire...' began Jacqueline coldly.

'Calumnies!' he exclaimed. 'Calumnies, you call them? Then Heaven help you, for your infatuation has indeed made you blind! But take care, Jacqueline, take care! The eyes of hate are keener than those of love.'

'The eyes of some miserable informant, you mean!' she retorted.

'Informant? I had no need of an informant to tell me that if a man shuns the gaze of his fellow-creatures it is because he hath something unavowable to hide. Beware the man who conceals his face behind a mask, his identity behind an assumed name! He has that to conceal which is dishonourable and base. Think on it all, Jacqueline. 'Tis a friendly warning I am giving you. The path which you have chosen can only lead to humiliation. Already the people of Cambray are enraged against the mysterious stranger. Take care lest Madame Jacqueline de Broyart, duchesse et princesse de Ramèse, be found bestowing her favours upon a common spy!'

He released her wrist, having had his say, felt triumphant and elated too because she had been forced, in spite of herself, to listen to him. Hers was an intensely mobile face, with sensitive brow and lips that readily betrayed her thoughts and emotions; and, as he had said very pertinently, the eyes of hate are sharper than those of love. He had studied her face while he was pouring the pernicious poison into her ear. He saw that poison filtrating slowly but surely into her brain. For the moment she looked scornful, aloof, dignified; *but she had listened*; she had not called to her servants; she had not even made a second attempt to escape. Eve once listened to the smooth persuasion of the serpent; Elsa heard to the end what Ortrude had to say, and Jacqueline de Broyart, her soul still vibrating in response to Gilles de Crohin's passionate love, had not closed her ears to de Landas' perfidy.

The serpent, having shed his venom, was content. He was subtle enough not to spoil the effect of his rhetoric by any further words. Obviously Jacqueline no longer heard him. Her thoughts were already far away, wandering mayhap in those labyrinthine regions to which a miscreant's blind hatred had led them. He turned on his heel and left her standing there, still dignified and scornful. But there was that in her pose, in the glitter of her eyes and the set of her lips, which suggested that something of her former serenity had gone. She still looked calm and indifferent, but her quietude now was obviously forced; there was a tell-tale quiver round her lips, the sight of which gave de Landas infinite satisfaction. In her whole person there was still determination, valour and perfect faith; but it was militant faith, the courage and trust of a woman fighting in defence of her love—not the sweet tenderness of childlike belief.

And with an inward sigh of content, the serpent wriggled quietly away.

CHAPTER XX.
HOW MORE THAN ONE PLOT WAS HATCHED

I

And now the die was cast.

Gilles de Crohin stood before Monseigneur the governor of Cambray and Monsieur le Comte de Lalain in the library of the Archiepiscopal Palace, and in the name of Monsieur Duc d'Anjou et d'Alençon, asked for the hand of Madame Jacqueline de Broyart in marriage.

It was a solemn hour wherein the fate of nations rested in the hand of men, whilst God withheld His final decree. Gilles had kept his word to the end. Madame la Reyne could be satisfied. He had put resolutely behind him all thoughts of his dream and of his own happiness. His exquisite Jacqueline had ceased to be aught but a vision of loveliness, intangible, and for him—the poor soldier of fortune—for ever unattainable. For once in his life he was thankful for the beneficence of the mask. At least he was spared the effort of concealing the ravages which misery had wrought upon his face. What the final struggle had cost him, no one would ever know; even Maître Jehan had been shut out from the narrow room, wherein a man's imprisoned soul fought out the grim fight 'twixt love and duty.

When, an hour later, Messire called to his faithful henchman to help him don his richest attire, the battle had been won. The man himself was left heart-broken and bruised, a mere wreck of his former light-hearted self; but honour and the sworn word had gained the day. Love lay fettered, passion vanquished. God's will alone should now be done.

A great sigh of relief came from d'Inchy when *Monsieur* had pronounced the final word which bound him irrevocably to the destinies of Flanders. He and de Lalain bowed their heads almost to the ground. Gilles extended his hand to them both and they each kissed it almost reverently.

Then they both rose, and d'Inchy said solemnly:

'No Prince could wear a more glorious crown than that of the Sovereignty of the Netherlands.'

And de Lalain added with equal earnestness:

'And no King could wed a worthier mate.'

A worthier mate! Ye gods! Gilles could have laughed aloud at the abjectness of this tragic farce. A worthier mate? Who knew that better than the unfortunate man who had held her for one brief, blissful moment in his arms, just long enough to feel how perfect, how exquisite she was—just long enough to realize all that he had lost. Truly hell's worst torture could not be more harrowing than this.

Wearied to the very top of his bent, Messire did his best to bring the interview to an end.

'And now, Messeigneurs,' he said at last, 'I will, by your leave, bid you farewell. My Maître de Camp, Messire de Balagny, has, as you know, arrived in Cambray. He will represent me here the while I go to rejoin my armies.'

'Your Highness would leave us?' exclaimed d'Inchy with a frown. 'So soon?'

'Only to return in triumph, Messire,' replied Gilles, 'at the head of my armies, after I have brought the Spaniard to his knees.'

'But Madame Jacqueline,' protested de Lalain. 'The betrothal—'

'While Cambray is starving, Messire, and the Duke of Parma is at her gates, there is no time for public festivities. You will convey to Madame Jacqueline de Broyart my earnest desire that she should confer the supreme honour upon me by consenting to be my wife.' Then, as the two men appeared wrapt in moody silence, he added quickly, with I know not what faint ray of hope within his heart: 'You are doubtful of her consent?'

'Doubtful? Oh, no, Monseigneur,' replied d'Inchy. 'Jacqueline de Broyart is, above all, a daughter of Flanders. She is ready to give her fortune, herself, all that is asked of her, to the man who will free her country from its oppressors.'

'Then the sooner I go ... and return to claim my bride,' rejoined Gilles dryly, 'the better it will be for us all.'

'Yes, Monseigneur—but——'

'But what?'

'The people of Cambray will wish to see Your Highness with Madame Jacqueline by your side—her hand in yours—in token of an irrevocable pledge.'

'Starving people care little for such flummery, Messire. They will prefer to see the sentimental ceremony when mine armies have driven the foe from their city's gates.'

'But——'

'Ah, ça, Messeigneurs!' suddenly queried Gilles with growing impatience. 'Do you, perchance, mistrust me?'

The protest which came from the two Flemish lords in response to this suggestion was not perhaps as whole-hearted as it might have been. Gilles frowned beneath his mask. Here was a complication which he had not foreseen. He could part from Jacqueline—yes!—he could tear her sweet image from out his heart, since she could never become his. He could play his part in the odious comedy to the end—but only on the condition that he should not see her again or attempt to carry through the deception which, in her presence, would anyhow be foredoomed to failure.

A public betrothal! A solemn presentation to the people, with Jacqueline's hand in his own, her dear eyes having found him out in the very first minute that they met again, despite every mask, every disguise and every trickery! Heavens above! but there was a limit to human endurance! and Gilles had already reached it, when he envisaged his beloved as the wife of another man—and that man wholly unworthy of her. Now he had come to the end of his submission. Honour and loyalty could go no further.

Of a truth, it seemed as if some impish Fate would upset, at this eleventh hour, Madame la Reyne's perfectly laid schemes. The Flemish lords looked obstinate. It seemed to Gilles that while he himself had stood silent for the space of a quick heart-beat, cogitating as to his next course of action, a secret understanding had quickly passed between the two men.

This in its turn had the effect of stiffening Gilles' temper. He felt like a gambler now, whose final stake was in jeopardy.

'For my part, Messeigneurs,' he said with a clever assumption of haughty insolence, 'I could not lend myself to a public pageant at this hour. His Majesty my brother would not wish it. When I enter Cambray as its conqueror I will claim my promised bride—and not before.'

This final 'either—or' was a bold stroke, no doubt: the losing gambler's last throw. If the Flemings demurred, all was lost. Gilles, by an almost superhuman effort, contrived to remain outwardly calm, keeping up that air of supercilious carelessness which had all along kept the Flemish lords on tenterhooks. Obviously the tone had aroused their ire, just as it had done many a time before, and Gilles could see well enough that a final repudiation of the whole bargain hovered on M. d'Inchy's lips. But once again the counsels of prudence prevailed; the implied 'take it or leave it,' so insolently spoken by *Monsieur*, had the effect of softening the two men's obstinacy. Perhaps they both felt that matters had anyhow gone too far, even for a man of Monsieur's vacillating temperament to withdraw from the bargain with a shred of honour. Be that as it may, when Gilles rejoined a moment or two later with marked impatience: 'Which is it to be, Messire? Is a Prince of the House of Valois not to be trusted to keep his word?' d'Inchy replied quite glibly:

'Oh, absolutely, Monseigneur!'

'Well, then?' queried Gilles blandly.

'There is nothing more to be said,' concluded de Lalain. 'And if your Highness really desires to leave us——'

'I do desire to rejoin my armies as soon as may be.'

'Then it shall be in accordance with Monseigneur's wishes. I will see that everything is made ready for the safety and secrecy of your journey.'

'You are more than gracious, Messire,' said Gilles, who had some difficulty in disguising the intense relief which he felt. 'As you know, my Maître de Camp, Messire de Balagny, is in Cambray now. He will be my representative during my brief absence.'

After that, little more was said. Formal leave-taking took up the last few minutes of this momentous interview. Gilles had some difficulty in concealing his eagerness to get away: a dozen times within those same few minutes he was on the point of betraying himself, for indeed it seemed ludicrous that the Duc d'Anjou should be quite so eager to go. However, the two Flemings were in a distinctly conciliatory mood now. They appeared to desire nothing save the keeping of His Highness' good graces.

'Monseigneur will remember that Cambray is on the edge of starvation!' said d'Inchy earnestly at the last.

'Give me three months, Messire,' rejoined Gilles lightly, 'and her joy-bells will be ringing for her deliverance.'

'For the entry of *Monsieur* Duc d'Anjou, within her walls?'

'And the betrothal of Madame Jacqueline de Broyart to a Prince of the House of France.'

'A happy hour for the Netherlands, Monseigneur.'

'And a proud one for me, Messire,' concluded Gilles solemnly. 'For the Prince of the House of France will not lead his bride to the altar empty-handed. The freedom of the Netherlands will be her marriage-portion.'

'Amen to that,' said the Flemish lords fervently.

II

They kissed the gracious hand which was extended to them; they bent the knee and took leave of their exalted guest with all the ceremonial due to his rank.

But the moment that Gilles had finally succeeded in effecting his escape, and even before his firm footstep had ceased to echo along the corridors of the Palace, a complete change took place in the demeanour of these two noble lords.

Monseigneur the governor drew inkhorn, pen and paper close to him, with almost feverish haste; then he began to write, letter after letter, while his friend watched him in silence. For over half an hour no sound was heard in tie room save the ceaseless scratching of d'Inchy's pen upon the paper. Only when half a dozen letters were written and each had been duly signed and sealed did de Lalain make a remark.

'You are sending out orders for a holiday to-morrow?' he asked.

'Yes,' replied d'Inchy.

'And orders to de Landas not to allow any one to leave the city?'

'Yes.'

'I thought so. You do not trust our wily Prince?'

'No,' retorted the other curtly. 'Do you?'

Then, as de Lalain made no reply, since indeed that reply was obvious, d'Inchy went on, in a quick, sharp tone of command:

'Will you see the Chief Magistrate yourself, my good de Lalain? Explain to him just what we have in contemplation. A reception in the Town Hall, the presence of the Provosts of the city and of the Mayors of the several guilds; the announcement of the betrothal to be read to the people from the balcony. The Provosts must see to it that there is a large concourse of people upon the Grand' Place and that the whole city is beflagged by ten o'clock in the morning, and wears an air of general festivity.'

'It shall be done at once,' said de Lalain simply.

D'Inchy then rang the bell and summoned one of his special messengers to his presence. As soon as the man appeared, he gave him one of the letters which he had just written.

'This to Messire de Landas,' he commanded. 'And see that he has it without delay.'

The man retired, and when d'Inchy was once more alone with his friend, he added complacently:

'This will close the trap, methinks, on our wily fox.'

'So long as he doth tumble into it,' remarked de Lalain dryly.

'He will! He will! You may be sure of that! Imagine him a few hours hence, ready for his journey and finding every gate closed against him and the town garrison afoot. I have warned de Landas of what was in the wind, and given him an outline of my plans for to-morrow. I can safely trust him to see that no one leaves the city within the next four and twenty hours, for I have made him personally accountable to me if any suspected person should effect an escape. So our fine *Monsieur* will fume and rage, and demand to see Monseigneur the governor. The latter, weary and sick, will have long ago retired to bed. In the morning he will still be sick and unable to attend to business, until past ten o'clock, when quite unexpectedly he will have given his exalted guest the slip and already be engaged on important matters at the Town Hall. Thither *Monsieur* will repair at once—you may take your oath on that—fretting to receive his safe-conduct and be out of the city ere another twenty-four hours go by. In the meanwhile——'

'You will have spoken with Madame Jacqueline,' broke in de Lalain eagerly. 'The Magistrate and the Provosts will have issued their proclamations, the city will be beflagged and the people assembled on the Grand' Place, eager to see Madame and her royal betrothed. What a programme, my good d'Inchy!' he concluded with unstinted enthusiasm. 'And how wisely conceived! Of a truth, you have enchained our fox. He cannot now slip out of our sight.'

When the two old cronies finally took leave of one another, they had prepared everything for their next day's box of surprise. A surprise it would be for everybody, and Monseigneur d'Inchy could indeed congratulate himself on the happy cannon-shot which he would fire off on the morrow, and which would wake this sad and dormant city from its weary somnolence. The alliance with the Royal House of France would prove a splendid stimulus for the waning courage of the people, whilst a fickle Valois Prince would at the same time learn that it is not easy to play fast and loose with a nation that was ruled by such diplomatic and determined men as were M. le Comte de Lalain and Monseigneur d'Inchy, governor of Cambray.

III

As for de Landas, he probably spent that evening some of the happiest hours which he had experienced for some time. It seemed indeed as if Fate, having buffeted him about so unmercifully these past few weeks, was determined to compensate him for everything that he had suffered.

When he received Monseigneur's letter, he was still fresh from his stormy interview with Jacqueline, still fresh from the discovery which he had made of at any rate a part of his rival's secret. As to what use he would make of this discovery, he had not yet made up his mind: his dark, vengeful soul was for the nonce consumed with rage at thought of seeing Jacqueline happy in the love of the man whom he so cordially hated. In the ordinary course of events, he would have been perfectly content to see her married—for political reasons, lovelessly or even unhappily—to any man who was influential enough to win her at the hands of her ambitious guardian. But to think of her bestowing her love and her kisses on another was wont to drive de Landas to the verge of mania. He did not love Jacqueline de Broyart. He had told her so, and he knew that her fortune would never be his. But he had always desired her, and did so still; and such are the tortuous ways of a depraved heart, that he would have been content to lose her only if he knew that she would be unhappy.

Now, suddenly, Fate had changed everything. Instead of impotent rage and futile scheming, Monseigneur's orders had placed in his hands the very weapon which he needed to consummate that revenge of which he dreamed.

'See to it, My dear de Landas,' Monseigneur had written, 'that for the next four and twenty Hours a full Company of the Town garrison is afoot, and that no one leave this City on any pretext whatsoever. I have prepared a special pageant for the People—a day of Festivity, wherein I will make a joyful Announcement to them from the Balcony of the Town Hall. This announcement has a direct bearing not only on the Future of our sorely-stricken Province, but also on that of her fairest Daughter. Both these great Issues are inextricably bound together, and to-morrow will see them ratified before our assembled people. So, see to it, My dear de Landas, that the Garrison under your Command do keep Order in the Town, so that there should be no disturbance likely to mar the solemnity of the occasion. There are always Malcontents in every Community and dissentients to every measure of public good. But I know that You at least have always been at one with Me in earnest desire to see our beloved country placed under the protection of our mighty neighbour, and that You will therefore rejoice with Me that that desire will at last be fulfilled. Because of Your unswerving loyalty to me and to Our cause, You shall be the first to know that the mysterious stranger whom We have so long harboured within Our gates and who chose to be known to Us all as the Prince de Froidmont, is none other than Monsieur duc d'Anjou et d'Alençon, Brother of His Majesty the King of France, who came to Cambray for the express purpose of wooing Madame Jacqueline de Broyart, Our Ward, to be his Wife. That he has succeeded in winning her promise is the announcement which I desire to make to our People to-morrow. I also will give them the assurance that, in consequence of this alliance with the royal House of Valois, We may reckon on the full might and support of France to deliver Us from Our enemies.'

De Landas crushed the welcome letter in his hand in the excess of his joy. He could have screamed aloud with unholy rapture.

'There is a fraud here, of course. Monseigneur has been hoodwinked. The Prince de Froidmont is not Duc d'Anjou!' he cried exultantly. 'This much I know. And now, friend Beelzebub and all your myrmidons, grant me aid, so that I may unmask that miscreant in a truly dramatic manner! Something must and shall be done, to turn that fateful hour to-morrow into one of triumph for me, and of humiliation for the woman who has dared to scorn my love. As for the man who has filched her from me, this same hour will be one which shall cover him with such boundless infamy, that for Jacqueline the very memory of his kisses will for ever remain an agony of shame.'

He sent a hasty summons to his intimates—to Maarege, de Borel, du Prêt and the whole of the gang of hot-headed malcontents, and just like in the Archiepiscopal Palace, so in the lodgings occupied by Messire de Landas, a Council of War was held which lasted late into the night.

IV

It was a dark and stormy evening after a brilliant day; and some time after the cathedral bell had struck the hour of ten, Messire de Landas, commanding the town garrison, was making the round of the city gates.

He had his man, Pierre, with him—a fellow well known to the guard. At the gate of Cantimpré, Messire desired that the bridge be lowered, for he wished to assure himself that everything was as it should be, over on the right bank of the river. Far away to the right and left, the lights of the Duke of Parma's encampment could be distinctly seen. The archers at the gate begged Messire not to venture too far out into the darkness, for the Spanish patrols were very wide-awake, and they were like cats for sighting a man in the dark. But Messire thought it his duty to cross the bridge, and to see if all was well on the other side. He refused to take a bodyguard with him in case the Spanish patrols were on the alert. Messire de Landas was known to be very brave; he preferred to take such risks alone.

Only his man Pierre accompanied him.

The archers kept a sharp look-out. But the night was very dark, a veritable gale was blowing from the south-west, and the driven rain was blinding. Messire crossed the bridge with Pierre, after which the darkness swallowed them both up.

Ten minutes later, the guard at the gate, the archers and gunners, heard the sharp report of two musket shots, following closely upon one another, and coming from over the right bank of the river. Trembling with anxiety, they marvelled if Messire were safe. The sheriff, who had no special orders from the commandant to meet the present eventuality, did not know what to do. He was ready to tear out his hair in an agony of apprehension. Had it not been quite so dark he would have sent out a search-party, for Messire still tarried. But, as it was, his men might fall straight into a *guet-apens* and be massacred in the gloom, without doing any good to any one. Skilled and able-bodied men were becoming precious assets in Cambray: their lives could not be carelessly jeopardized.

A quarter of an hour of heartrending suspense went by, after which Messire's footstep was suddenly heard upon the bridge. He returned alone. The archers and gunners crowded round him, with the anxious query upon their lips: 'Pierre?'

No one really cared about Pierre. Messire de Landas and his gang were not popular in Cambray. But the incident had been rendered weird and awesome by the darkness and the bad weather, and Messire's obstinacy in venturing out so far.

M. de Landas appeared moody and silent. No doubt he felt responsible for his servant's fate. But he answered the men's questions quite straightforwardly, more fully too and with less brusqueness than was his wont when speaking with subordinates.

'I had my suspicions aroused to-day,' he said, 'by something which our spies reported to me, that the Spaniards contemplated one of their famous surprise attacks under cover of this murky darkness. So I was determined to venture on the Bapaume Road and see if I could discover anything. Pierre insisted on coming with me. We kept our eyes and ears open and crawled along in the ditch on hands and knees. Suddenly we were fired on without any warning. I lay low under cover of the ditch, not moving, hardly breathing, and thought that Pierre was doing likewise. I heard the Spanish patrols move noiselessly away. Then I crept out of my hiding-place, almost surprised at finding myself alive. I called softly to Pierre, but received no answer; then I groped about for him. Presently I found him. He had been shot twice—through the back—and must have died on the instant.'

The story was plausible enough, nor did any one doubt it. The men cared so little about Pierre, who was overbearing and surly. But what had actually happened was vastly different.

It was this—Messire le Marquis de Landas, accompanied by Pierre, had in truth crossed the bridge, and as soon as the darkness had swallowed them up, the two men had walked rapidly along the Bapaume Road, until they were challenged by a Spanish patrol on duty. Messire gave the password, and the patrol not only halted but also stood at attention, for the password which had been given was one used only by Spanish gentlemen of high rank in the King's armies.

'You will conduct my servant at once before His Highness the Duke of Parma,' Messire de Landas said to the man in command of the patrol.

And to Pierre he added in a whisper: 'All that you have to do when you see His Highness is to give him this letter from me and tell him that we are quite prepared for to-morrow.'

He gave Pierre a letter, then ordered the patrol to fire a couple of musket-shots. After which, he waited for a few minutes, and finally returned alone to the city gate.

CHAPTER XXI.
HOW SOME OF THESE SUCCEEDED

I

Jacqueline was sitting in the self-same deep window-embrasure from whence she had listened — oh, so long ago! — to that song, which would for ever remain for her the sweetest song on earth:

'Mignonne, allons voir si la rose——'

Only a few hours had gone by since she had reached the sublimal height of ecstatic happiness — only a few hours since she had tasted the bitter fruit of renunciation. Since then she had had a good cry, and felt better for it; but since then also she had encountered a venomous reptile on her way, and had been polluted by its touch.

Even to suggest that Jacqueline's pure faith in the man she loved had been troubled by de Landas' insidious suggestions, would be to wrong her fine and steadfast character. She did not mistrust her knight; for her he still stood far above the base calumnies hurled at him by a spiteful rival; but, somehow, de Landas' venom had succeeded in making her sorrow more acute, less endurable. Oh! if only she could have shared with her beloved all his secrets and his difficulties, if only he had thought her worthy of his entire trust!

Words which he had spoken ere he finally went away rang portentously in her ear — ominous words, which she had not heeded at the moment, for her heart was then over-full with the misery of that farewell, but which now took on, despite herself, a menacing and awesome significance.

With frowning brows and hands tightly clasped together, Jacqueline sat there, motionless, the while memory called back those words which in very truth did fill her heart with dread.

'If within the future,' Messire had said, 'aught should occur to render me odious in your sight, will you at least remember that, whatever else I may have done that was unworthy and base, my love for you has been as pure and sacred as is the love of the lark for the sun.'

He had gone after that—gone before she could ask him for an explanation of these ununderstandable words, before she could affirm her perfect faith and trust in him. Then the memory of them had faded from her ken, merged as it was in her great, all-embracing sorrow, until the wand of a devilish magician had brought them forth from out the ashes of forgetfulness, and she was left more forlorn than she had been before.

II

Monseigneur the governor found her in the late afternoon, still sitting in the window embrasure, the large, lofty room in darkness, save for the fitful glow of the fire which was burning low in the monumental hearth. The patter of the rain against the window panes made a weird, melancholy sound, which alone broke the silence that hung upon the place with an eerie sense of desolation. Monseigneur shuddered as he entered.

'B-r-r!' he exclaimed. 'My dear Jacqueline! I had no thought that you were moping here all alone—and in the dark, too!—or I would have been here sooner to cheer your spirits with my good news.'

'You and your good news are right welcome, Monseigneur,' responded Jacqueline with a pathetic effort at gaiety. 'I was out in the garden most of the day,' she continued composedly, 'and was resting for awhile in the gathering dusk, as this awful weather hath made it impossible to go out again.'

'Gathering dusk, forsooth!' he retorted. 'Send for your women, Madame, and order them to bring in the candles. Light! We want more light, laughter and joy at this hour! I would I could light a bonfire, to turn the night into day!'

He was obviously nervy and excited, paced up and down the room in a state of nerve-tension, very unlike his usual dignified self. Jacqueline, a little puzzled, obeyed him promptly. She rang the bell and ordered Nicolle to send in the candles, and while the women busied themselves about the room, disposing candelabra upon the tables and consols, she watched her guardian keenly. He certainly appeared strangely excited, and now and then he darted quick, inquiring glances upon her, and when she met those glances, he smiled as if in triumph.

'Let us sit by the fire, my dear,' he said genially, after he had dismissed Nicolle and the women with an impatient gesture. 'I came to see you alone and without ceremony, because I wished for the selfish pleasure of imparting my good news to you myself.'

She sat down in the tall chair beside the fire, and Monseigneur sat opposite to her. She had on a dress of dark-coloured satin, upon the shiny surface of which the flickering firelight drew quaint and glowing arabesques. She rested her elbow on the arm of her chair and leaned her head against her hand, thus keeping her delicate face in shadow, lest Monseigneur should note the pallor of her cheeks and the tear-stains around her eyes. But otherwise she was quite composed, was able to smile too at his eagerness and obvious embarrassment.

It was his turn to study her keenly now, and he did so with evident pleasure. Not so very many years ago he, too, had been a young gallant, favoured by fortune and not flint-hearted either where women were concerned. He had buried two wives, and felt none the worse for that, and still ready to turn a compliment to a pretty woman, and to give her the full measure of his admiration. He would have been less than a man now, if he had withstood the charm of the pretty picture which his ward presented, in the harmonious setting of her high-backed chair, and with the crimson glow of the fire-light turning her fair hair to living gold.   —

'Put down your hand, Jacqueline,' he said, 'so that I may see your pretty face.'

'My head aches sadly, Monseigneur,' she rejoined with a pathetic little sigh, 'and mine eyes are heavy. 'Tis but vanity that causes me to hold my hand before my face.'

'Neither headaches nor heavy eyes could mar the beauty of the fairest lily of Flanders,' he went on with elaborate gallantry. 'So I pray you humour me, and let me see you eye to eye.'

She did as he asked, and dropped her hand. Monseigneur made no remark on her pallor, was obviously too deeply absorbed in his joyful news to notice her swollen eyes. She tried to smile, and said lightly:

'And why should Monseigneur desire to see a face, every line of which he knows by heart?'

He leaned forward in his chair and said slowly, keeping his eyes fixed upon her:

'Because I wish to behold the future Duchesse d'Anjou and d'Alençon, the future sister of the King of France!'

She made no reply, but sat quite still, her face turned toward the fire, presenting the outline of her dainty profile to the admiring gaze of her guardian. Monseigneur was silent for a moment or two, was leaning back in his chair once more, and regarding her with an air of complacency, which he took no pains to disguise.

'It means the salvation of the Netherlands!' he said with a deep sigh of satisfaction. 'We can now count on the whole might of France to rid us of our enemies, and after that to a long era of prosperity and of religious liberty, when Madame Jacqueline de Broyart shares with her lord the Sovereignty of the Netherlands.'

Jacqueline remained silent, her aching eyes fixed in the hot embers of the fire. So the blow had fallen sooner than she thought. When, in the arbour, she had made her profession of faith before her knight, and told him that she belonged not to herself but to her country, she did not think that her country would claim her quite so soon. Vaguely she knew that some day her guardian would dispose of her hand and fortune, and that she would have to ratify a bargain made for her person, for the sake of that fair land of Flanders which was so dear to her. But awhile ago, all that had seemed so remote; limitless time seemed to stretch out before her, wherein she could pursue her dreams of the might-have-been.

Monseigneur's announcement—for it was that—came as a hammer-blow upon her hopes of peace. She had only just wakened from her dream, and already the bitter-sweet boon of memory would be denied to her. Stunned under the blow, she made no attempt at defiance. With her heart dead within her, what cared she in the future what became of her body? Since love was denied her, there was always the altruistic sentiment of patriotism to comfort her in her loneliness; and the thought of self-sacrifice on the altar of her stricken country would, perhaps, compensate her for that life-long sorrow which was destined to mar her life.

'No wonder you are silent, Jacqueline,' Monseigneur was saying, and she heard him speaking as if through a thick veil which smothered the sound of his voice; 'for to you this happy news comes as a surprise. Confess that you never thought your old guardian was capable of negotiating so brilliant an alliance for you!'

'I knew,' she rejoined quietly, 'that my guardian would do everything in his power to further the good of our country.'

'And incidentally to promote your happiness, my dear.'

'Oh!' she said, with an indifferent shrug of the shoulders, 'my happiness is not in question, is it? Else you would not propose that I should wed a Prince of the House of Valois.'

'I am not so sure,' he replied, with a humorous twinkle in his old eyes. '*Monsieur* Duc d'Anjou, is not—or I am much mistaken—quite the rogue that mischievous rumour hath painted.'

'Let us hope, for my sake,' she retorted dryly, 'that rumour hath wronged him in all particulars.'

'In one, at any rate, I'll vouch for that. *Monsieur* is more than commonly well-favoured—a handsome figure of a man, with the air and the voice of a soldier.'

'You know him well?'

'I have seen much of him,' said Monseigneur with an enigmatic smile, 'these past four weeks.'

'These past four weeks?' she exclaimed. 'But you have not been out of Cambray.'

'Nor has he,' put in Monseigneur quietly.

She frowned, deeply puzzled.

'*Monsieur* Duc d'Anjou hath been in Cambray?' she asked, 'these past four weeks?'

He nodded.

'And I have never seen him?'

'Indeed you have, my dear Jacqueline; on more than one occasion.'

'Not to my knowledge, then.'

'No. Not to your knowledge.'

'I don't understand,' she murmured. 'Why should so exalted a prince as the Duc d'Anjou be in Cambray all this while?'

'Because he desired to woo Madame Jacqueline de Broyart, duchesse et princesse de Ramèse.'

'Without my knowledge?'

'Without your knowledge—outwardly.'

'What do you mean?'

'Oh! nothing very obscure, my dear; nothing very remarkable. *Monsieur* Duc d'Anjou is young—he hath a romantic turn of mind. He admired you and desired you in marriage, but chose to woo you—have I not said that he is romantic?—chose to woo you under a mask.'

She gave a gasp, and quickly put her hand to her mouth to smother a cry. She sat bolt upright now, her two hands clutching the arms of her chair, her eyes—wide open, glowing, scared—fixed upon her guardian. He, obtuse and matter-of-fact, mistook the gasp and the tense expression of her face.

'No wonder you are aghast, my dear,' he said cheerily. 'Not unpleasantly, I hope. More than once it seemed to your old guardian that *Monsieur's* martial presence was not altogether distasteful to you. He hath sharper eyes, hath the old man, than you gave him credit for—what? Ah, well! I was young too, once, and I still like to bask in the sunshine of romance. 'Twas a pretty conceit on *Monsieur's* part, methinks, to pay his court to you under a disguise—to win your love by the charm of his personality, ere you realized the great honour that a Prince of the Royal House of France was doing to our poor country, by wooing her fairest maid.'

Monseigneur continued to ramble on in the same strain. Jacqueline hardly heard what he said. She was striving with all her might to appear composed, to understand what the old man was saying, and to reply to him with some semblance of coherence. Above all, she was striving to get the mastery over her voice, for presently she would have to speak, to say something which would shake her guardian's complacency, open his eyes to the truth, the whole hideous, abominable truth; without ... without ... Heavens above, this must be a hideous dream!

'It was all arranged with de Montigny, you remember?' Monseigneur continued, still engrossed in his own rhetoric, too blind to see that Jacqueline was on the verge of a collapse. '*Monsieur* was so fanciful, and we had to give in to him. We all desired the alliance with our whole hearts, and Madame la Reyne de Navarre did approve of our schemes. I must say that de Lalain and I were against the masquerade at first, but *Monsieur's* soldierlike personality soon won our approval. And imagine our joy when we realized that our dear Jacqueline was not wholly indifferent to him either. He came to us this afternoon and made formal demand for your hand in marriage.... So de Lalain and I have taken measures that our poor people do have a holiday to-morrow, when Madame Jacqueline de Broyart, duchesse et princesse de Ramèse, will solemnly plight her troth to *Monsieur* Duc d'Anjou. So, my dear Jacqueline, I entreat you to wear your loveliest gown. Flanders is proud of her fairest flower. Monsieur desired to rejoin his armies to-day and leave the ceremony of betrothal waiting for happier times; but de Lalain and I would not hear of it. Everything is prepared for a festive holiday. Of a truth, to-morrow's forenoon will see the happiest hour which our sadly-afflicted province hath seen these many years.'

He paused; I think, for want of breath: he certainly had been talking uninterruptedly for the past ten minutes, going over the whole ground of de Montigny's mission, *Monsieur's* romantic desire and the final demand in marriage, till Jacqueline could have screamed to him to cease torturing her. The hideousness of the mystery appalled her: some dark treachery lurked here somewhere and she was caught in a net of odious intrigues, out of which for the moment she could see no issue. A feeling of indescribable horror came over her—a nameless, unspeakable terror, as in the face of a yawning, bottomless abyss, on the brink of which she stood and into which an unseen and mighty hand would presently hurl her.

Something of that appalling state of mind must have been reflected in her face, despite the almost superhuman effort which she made not to allow Monseigneur to guess at what was going on in her mind; for presently he looked at her more keenly, and then said gently:

'Jacqueline, my dear, you look so strange. What is it? Hath my news so gravely startled you?'

She shook her head, and when he reiterated his question, and leaned forward in order to take her hand, she contrived to say, moderately calmly, even though every word came with an effort from her parched throat:

'The man with the mask? ... The Prince de Froidmont? ... You are sure?'

'Sure of what, my dear?' he riposted.

'That he is the Duc d'Anjou?'

Monseigneur laughed loudly and long, apparently much relieved.

'Oh! is that what troubles you, my child?' he said gaily. 'Well then, let me assure you that I am as sure of that as that I am alive. Why!' he added, evidently much surprised, 'how could you ask such a funny thing?'

'I did not know,' she murmured vaguely. 'Sometimes an exalted prince will woo a maid by proxy ... so I thought...'

But evidently the idea of Jacqueline's doubts greatly tickled Monseigneur's fancy.

'What a strange conceit, my child!' he said with condescending indulgence. 'By proxy, forsooth! His Highness came himself, not more than three days after Messire de Montigny completed negotiations with him at La Fère. He desired to remain incognito and chose to lodge in a poor hostelry; but Madame la Reyne de Navarre begged us in a letter writ by her own august hand, to make *Monsieur* Duc d'Anjou, her dear brother, right welcome in Cambray. By proxy!' and Monseigneur laughed again, highly amused. 'Why, His Highness was in my study but two hours ago, and made formal proposal for your hand in marriage!'

Then, as the door behind him was thrown open and old Nicolle, shuffling in, announced M. le Comte de Lalain, d'Inchy turned to his old friend and said, highly delighted with what he regarded as a good joke:

'Ah, my good de Lalain! You could not have come at a more opportune moment. Here is our ward, so bewildered at the news that she asks me whether I am sure that it is truly *Monsieur* Duc d'Anjou who has been masquerading as the Prince de Froidmont. Do reassure the child's mind, I pray you; for in truth she seems quite scared.'

De Lalain, always a great stickler for etiquette, had in the meanwhile advanced into the room, and was even now greeting Jacqueline with all the ceremonial prescribed by Maître Calviac. Then only did he reply soberly:

'Sure, Madame? Of course we are sure! Why, 'tis not two hours since he was standing before us and asking for the hand of Madame Jacqueline de Broyart in marriage. We knelt before him and kissed his hand, and to-morrow we'll present him to the people as the future Sovereign Lord of the Netherlands.'

'And so, my dear Jacqueline——' concluded d'Inchy. But he got no further, gave a loud call to Nicolle and the women; for Madame had uttered a pitiful moan, slid out of her chair, and was now lying on the floor in a swoon.

CHAPTER XXII.
WHILE OTHERS FAILED

I

Of a truth, Monseigneur the governor was not gravely perturbed by his ward's sudden attack of faintness. He knew that women were subject to megrims and sundry other fancies, and he was willing to admit that in his excitement he had, perhaps, been too abrupt with her and too brusque. She had been scared, bewildered, no doubt, and lost consciousness in her agitation. But old Nicolle had quickly come to the rescue with restoratives; and with the prerogative of an old and trusted servant, she had bundled Monseigneur and Monsieur de Lalain incontinently out of the room. Madame would soon be well, she said, only needed rest. She was overwrought and over fatigued with so many banquets and public functions—such late hours, too; and Madame not twenty! Young people needed plenty of sleep, and Madame, after a good and peaceful night, would be quite well on the morrow.

So Monseigneur, fully reassured, went back to his apartments and to his own business. There was still a great deal to be done, a great deal to see to—many people to interview and many more orders to give, to ensure that to-morrow's ceremony should be conducted not only with perfect smoothness, but also that the preparations for it be concluded with perfect secrecy.

M. de Lalain, d'Inchy's old friend, was an invaluable helpmate, and de Landas too had for the occasion thrown off that supercilious manner which he had adopted of late, and had entered fully into the spirit of the affair. There was no fear that the wily Valois fox would slip from out the trap which was being so skilfully laid for him.

Already messengers, dressed in Monseigneur the governor's livery, were flying all over the town, carrying letters and sign-manuals.

Directly these were delivered, extraordinary bustle and activity came at once into being in the official and municipal centres of the city. The Provosts could be seen, wearing their chain of office and hurrying to the Town Hall, where they were received by the Chief Magistrate. Orders and counter-orders flew from one end of the town to the other, from the Citadel to the Palace and from Cantimpré to the Château, while, by special command of M. le Marquis de Landas, the entire garrison, which manned the forts, was under arms during the whole of that night.

The humbler folk, scared by this unwonted turmoil, shut themselves up with their families inside their houses, until a persistent rumour reassured them that no fresh assault on the part of the besieging army was expected, but rather that a happy, joyful and hopeful proclamation would be made by Monseigneur the governor on the morrow, from the balcony of the Town Hall. Whereupon fear and trouble were for the moment put resolutely away. The people were beginning to suffer so acutely, that they were abjectly thankful for any ray of hope, which gleamed through the darkness of their ever-present misery. With the Duke of Parma's armies at their gates, they were still clinging to the thought that some mighty Power would take compassion on them, and come to their rescue with a force strong enough to inflict a severe defeat upon the Spaniard. They had not yet reached the final stages of despair. They were still ready to seize every opportunity for forgetfulness, for enjoyment even, whenever it was offered or allowed them. Rumour had been persistent about the help which was to come from France. Messire de Balagny's presence in the city had confirmed the hopes which had rested upon those rumours. Now, with the knowledge that Monseigneur had a joyful announcement to make, mercurial temperaments rose for awhile — especially among the young. The older people had been too often deluded with flowery promises to believe in any good fortune for their unfortunate city. They had seen the fate of others — of Mons and of Mechlin and of Gand. The might of the Spanish armies always conquered in the end, and the rebellious cities had been made to suffer untold brutalities, as a punishment for their heroic resistance.

Fortunately for the morale of Cambray, these older people, these wiseacres, were still in the minority, and hope is of all human attributes the strongest and the most persistent. So, despite the prognostications and fear of pessimists, people rose early on the following morning, in order betimes to decorate their houses. Soon after dawn, activities began; flags were dragged out of old, disused coffers and hung out of windows and balconies; the women sought, in their worm-eaten dower chests, for any scraps of finery that may have survived from the happy olden days, before their Spanish tyrants had made of this prosperous land a forlorn wilderness.

By eight o'clock the beleaguered city looked almost gay. The shops were closed; soldiers paraded the streets; the city guilds, their masters and their 'prentices, came out with banners flying, to stand in groups upon the Grand' Place. If a stranger could have dropped into Cambray from the skies on that fine April morning, he would of a truth have doubted if any Spanish army was encamped around these walls.

II

Even Gilles de Crohin, absorbed as he was in his own affairs, could not fail to notice the generally festive air which hung about the place. In the quarter where he lodged, it is true that very little of that holiday mood had found its way down the narrow streets and into the interior of squalid houses, where the pinch of cold and hunger had already made itself insistently felt. But as soon as he was past the Place aux Bois, he began to wonder what was in the wind. The populace had been at obvious pains to put aside for the moment every outward sign of the misery which it endured. The women had donned their best clothes, the men no longer hung about at street corners, looking hungry and gaunt. They did not even scowl in the wake of the masked stranger, so lately the object of their ire, as the latter hurried along on his way to the Palace.

And then there were the flags, and the open windows, the draped balconies and pots of bright-coloured early tulips—all so different to the dreary, drab appearance which Cambray had worn of late.

But, nevertheless, Gilles himself would have told you afterwards that no suspicion of Monseigneur d'Inchy's intentions crossed his mind. Vaguely he thought that Messire de Balagny's arrival had been announced to the townfolk, and that the promise of help from France had been made the occasion of a public holiday. And he himself was in too much of a fume to pay serious heed to anything but his own affairs—to anything, in fact, but his own departure, which had been so provokingly delayed until this morning.

And this veracious chronicle has all along put it on record that Messire Gilles de Crohin was not a man of patience. Imagine his choler, his fretting rage when, fully prepared for his journey, mounted upon the same horse which had brought him into Cambray a month ago, and duly accompanied by Maître Jehan, who had a pack-horse on the lead, he had presented himself on the previous afternoon at the Porte Notre Dame with his original safe-conduct, and was incontinently refused exit from the city, owing to strict orders issued by the commandant of the garrison that no one should be allowed to pass out of the gates under any pretext whatsoever.

Gilles had argued, persuaded, demanded; but he himself was too thorough a soldier not to have realized from the first that every argument would be futile. The captain of the guard assured him that he could do nothing in the face of the strict and uncompromising orders which he had received. Gilles was of course quite certain that some one had blundered—a mere matter of formality, which Monseigneur the governor could put right with a stroke of the pen—but it was obviously not for a subordinate officer to question his orders, or to take any revision thereto upon himself; and Gilles, after receiving the captain's courteous regrets, had no option but to ride away.

It was then six o'clock of the afternoon, and the brilliance of the early spring day was quickly fading into dusk. A boisterous wind had sprung up, which brought heavy banks of cloud along, threatening rain. But, rain or shine, Gilles had no thought as yet of giving up his purpose. There were other gates within the city walls, and wrapping his mantle closely round his shoulders, he gave spur to his horse and started on a new quest, closely followed by Maître Jehan. It is on record that he went the round of every gate, armed with his safe-conduct and with as much patience as he could muster. Alternately he tried bribery, persuasion, stealth; but nothing availed. The town garrison was everywhere under arms; orders had been given, and no one, be he the highest in the land, was allowed to leave.

Had the matter been vital or the adventure worth the trial, I doubt not but what Messire would have endeavoured to get through at all costs—have scaled the city walls, swam the river, challenged the

Spanish lines and run the gauntlet of archers and gunners, in order to accomplish what he wanted, if he had wanted it badly. But a few hours' delay in his journey could make no matter, and truth to tell he was in no mood for senseless adventure.

In the meanwhile, however, several hours had been wasted on fruitless errands. It was late evening. The heavy gale had brought along its due complement of rain. It were certainly not seemly to disturb Monseigneur the governor in the Palace at this hour, so Gilles and Jehan returned, sorely disappointed, to their lodgings, there to spend a sleepless night, waiting for the first reasonable hour in the morning wherein Monseigneur the governor might be expected to transact business. And I can confidently affirm that no suspicion of what was in contemplation for the confusion of the fickle Prince, crossed Gilles' mind, as he lay half the night, staring into the darkness, with the image of Jacqueline haunting his tortured brain.

III

At eight o'clock the next morning, he was once more at the Archiepiscopal Palace, demanding to see Monseigneur. Not wishing to challenge any comparison at this eleventh hour between his two entities, he had elected to present himself under his disguise and his mask, and to send in a greeting to Monseigneur with the message that Messire le Prince de Froidmont desired to speak with him immediately.

But it seems that Monseigneur had been very ill all night and had not yet risen. A leech was in attendance, who, ignorant of the true rank of this early visitor, strictly forbade that the sick man should be disturbed. No doubt if Messire le Prince de Froidmont would present himself a couple of hours later—the leech added suavely—Monseigneur would be prepared to see him.

It was in very truth a trial of patience, and I marvel how Gilles' temper stood the strain. The fact that he was a stranger in the city, without a friend, surrounded too by a goodly number of enemies, may be accountable for his exemplary patience. Certain it is that he did once again return to his lodgings, anathematizing in his heart all these stodgy and procrastinating Flemings, but otherwise calm and, I repeat, wholly unsuspecting.

At ten o'clock, a runner came to him with a message that Monseigneur had been unexpectedly summoned to the Town Hall, but, not wishing to disappoint M. le Prince de Froidmont, he begged the latter to go forthwith to see him there. So Gilles left horses and baggage in Maître Julien's charge and, accompanied by Jehan, he proceeded on foot to the Town Hall. He had much difficulty in forcing his way through the crowd, which had become very dense, especially in and about the Grand' Place.

Gilles, indeed, could not help but notice the festive appearance of the town, the flags, the flowers, the banners of the guilds. Above all, the good-humour of the crowd was in such strange contrast to their habitual surliness. Instead of uttering insults against the masked stranger, as he jostled them with his elbows and a rapid 'By your leave!' they chaffed and teased him, laughed and joked among themselves in perfect good-humour.

In and about the Town Hall there was a large concourse of people, city fathers and high dignitaries in official attire. The perron steps were decorated with huge pots of Dutch earthenware, placed at intervals all the way up as far as the entrance doors and filled with sheaves of white Madonna lilies, produced at great cost at this season of the year in the hothouses of the Archiepiscopal Palace. Pots containing the same priceless flowers could also be seen up on the huge balcony above the entrance, and showing through the interstices of the stonework of the splendid balustrade. There was also a guard of honour—halbardiers in their gorgeous attire—who lined the hall and the grand staircase as far as the upper floor.

When Gilles appeared outside the huge entrance gates, an usher in sober black came forward from some hidden corner of the hall, and approached him with marked deference. Monseigneur the governor had given orders that directly M. le Prince de Froidmont presented himself at the Town Hall he was to be shown up to the Council Room.

Gilles, having ordered Jehan to wait for him below, followed the usher up the grand staircase, noting with the first gleam of suspicious surprise that the guard presented arms as he went by.

But even then he did not guess.

IV

The Council Room was crowded when Gilles entered. At first
he felt quite dazed. The whole scene was so ununderstandable,
so different to what he had expected. He had thought of finding
Monseigneur the governor alone in a small apartment; and here he
was ushered into a magnificent hall, harmoniously ornamented with
priceless Flemish tapestry above the rich carving of the wainscoting.
The hall was crowded with men, some of whom he had vaguely seen
on the night of the banquet at the Archiepiscopal Palace. There was
the Chief Magistrate, a venerable old man, gorgeously decorated with
a massive gold chain and other insignia of authority; there were the
Mayors of the City guilds, each recognizable by their robes of state
and the emblems of their trades; there were the Provosts and the
Captains of the guard and the Chiefs of the Guild of Archers, with
their crimson sashes, and there was also Monseigneur the governor,
looking more pompous and solemn than he had ever done before.

Gilles was once more deeply thankful for the mask which covered
his face, together with its expression of boundless astonishment,
amounting to consternation, which must inevitably have betrayed
him. Already he would have retreated if he could; but even as the
swift thought crossed his mind, the ushers closed the doors behind
him, the guard fell in, and he was—there was no mistaking it—a
virtual prisoner.

Dressed for the journey, booted and spurred, with leather jerkin
and heavy belt, he stood for a moment, isolated, at the end of the
room, a magnificent and picturesque figure, mysterious and defiant—
yes, defiant! For he knew in one instant that he had been trapped and
that he, the gambler, had been set to play a losing game.

His quick, keen glance swept over the dignified assembly.
Monseigneur, in the centre, was advancing to greet him, bowing
almost to the ground in the excess of his deference. Every head
was bared, the captains of the guard had drawn their swords and
held them up to the salute. Through the wide-open, monumental
windows, the pale April sun came peeping in, throwing a glint of
gold upon the rich robes of the Provosts and the Mayors. A murmur
of respectful greeting went round the room, followed immediately
by loud and prolonged cheering; and Gilles—suddenly alive to the

whole situation—took his plumed hat from off his head and, with a splendidly insolent gesture, made a sweeping bow to the assembled dignitaries. His life, his honour, his safety, were hanging by a thread. He stood like a trapped beast before a number of men who anon would be clamouring perhaps for his blood; but the whole situation suddenly struck him as so boundlessly humorous, the solemnity of all these worthy Flemings would presently be so completely ruffled, that Gilles forgot the danger he was in, the precariousness of the position in which he stood, only to remember its entirely ludicrous aspect.

'Long live His Highness le Duc d'Anjou et d'Alençon!' came in rousing cheers, which woke the echoes of the old Town Hall.

And outside, on the Grand' Place, the people heard the cheering. They did not know yet what it was about, but they had come out on this fine April morning to enjoy themselves, to forget their troubles, their danger, their miseries; and when they heard the cheering, they responded with full throat and heart, and acclaimed not what they knew but what they hoped.

'You have beaten me, Messire,' Gilles said in a good-humoured whisper to Monseigneur the governor, as the latter bent one knee to the ground and kissed the gracious hand of the Valois Prince. 'Never was game so skilfully trapped! All my compliments, Messire. You are a born——' 'liar' he would have said, but checked himself just in time and used the smoother word—'diplomatist.'

'Your Highness will not grudge us our little ruse,' d'Inchy riposted under his breath with a suave smile. 'It is all for your glorification and the exaltation of our promised union with France.'

'Take care, Messire!' retorted Gilles, 'that your want of trust in me doth not receive the punishment it deserves.'

He had still the thought that he might run away. The only time in the whole course of his life that Gilles de Crohin had the desire to show a clean pair of heels to the enemy! If he could only have seen the slightest chance of getting away, he would have taken it—through door or window, up the chimney or the side of a house—any way, in fact, out of this abominable trap which these astute Flemings had so skilfully laid for him. And this, despite the fact that he had spied his arch-enemy, de Landas, at the far end of the room—de Landas, who was gazing on him, not only in mockery but also in triumph.

Nevertheless, Gilles was ready to turn his back even on de Landas—anything, anything, in fact, to get away; for the situation, besides being ludicrous, was tragic too, and desperate. One false move on his part, one unconsidered word, and the whole fabric of Madame la Reyne's schemes would totter to the ground. He seemed to see her now, with her gracious hand extended towards him and the tears streaming down her cheeks, while she said with solemn earnestness: 'When a prince of the house of Valois breaks his word, the shame of it bears upon us all!' He seemed to see himself with his hand upon the crosshilt of his sword, swearing by all that he held most sacred and most dear that he would see this business through to the end. Indeed, the end was in sight, and he felt like a soldier who has been left all alone to defend a citadel and ordered to hold it at all costs.

That citadel was the honour of France.

And the soldier-nature in him not only refused to give in, but at this supreme hour rejoiced in the task. He *would* hold on at all costs for the honour of *Monsieur*, his master; but, above all, for the honour of France. If contumely, disgrace or shame was to fall, in consequence of this gigantic hoax, then it must fall entirely on him—Gilles de Crohin, the penniless adventurer—not upon a Prince of the Royal House of France. Either he would be able to extricate himself from this desperate position with the mask still upon his face and *Monsieur's* secret still inviolate before these assembled Flemings, or the whole burden of knavery and imposture must fall upon him alone—the shameless rogue who had impersonated his master for some unavowable purpose, and perpetrated this impudent fraud for the sake of some paltry gain.

It only took him a few seconds thus to pass the whole situation, present and future, in a brief review before his mind. Having done it, he felt stronger and keener for the fight and ready for any eventuality. The honour of France!—and he left here to guard it! ... Ye gods! but he felt prouder than any king! Contumely, disgrace, exposure, an ignominious flight—mayhap a shameful death. Bah! what mattered anything so long as the honour of France and of her Royal House remained untarnished before the world?

Fortunately Jacqueline was not here! Perhaps she would not come! Perhaps these wily fools, when they had set their trap, had left her out of their reckoning. In which case, all might be well; the chances of exposure remained remote. A little more impudence, a brief half-hour still of this abominable rôle, and the curtain must fall at last upon the farcical tragedy and he, Gilles, would be free to become an honest man once more.

A little luck!! And, remember that he was a gambler, and staking his all upon the last throw!

And as, one by one, the city dignitaries came up to be presented by the governor to His Highness, and as the minutes sped away, hope once more knocked at the gateway of the adventurer's heart. One by one they came, these solemn Flemings. They bent the knee and kissed the hand of the Prince who was to be their Sovereign Lord. And some of them were old and others very rheumatic; most of them appeared to Gilles highly ridiculous in this homage rendered to an impostor. The desire to laugh aloud became positive torture after awhile, and yet nothing but self-possession *could* carry the day, now that every second rendered Gilles' position more hopeful.

For still Jacqueline did not come! Jacqueline! the only person inside this city who could betray him, and she the one being in the entire world before whom he would have wished to remain deserving and unimpeached. She of a truth would know him amongst a thousand; her loving, searching eyes would laugh at masks and disguises! Her finger alone could, at sight of him, point at him with scorn; her voice, like that of an avenging angel, could be raised against him, saying:

'That man is a liar and a cheat! He is not the Duc d'Anjou!'

V

Monseigneur the governor acted throughout as the Master of Ceremonies. Obsequious and suave, he seemed to have no wish save to please His Highness in all things, and to make him forget the want of trust that the present ceremony implied. He hovered round Gilles, executing a manoeuvre which the latter was certainly too guileless to notice. It was a case of: 'On this side, I entreat Your Highness!' and 'Here is Messire de Haynin, who craves the honour...' or 'If Your Highness would deign to speak with Messire d'Anthoin.' All very subtle and unnoticeable, but it meant that every time a city father came to kiss hands, Gilles, in order to greet him, had to take a step or two forward, and that each step brought him a trifle nearer to the open window. That window gave directly on La Bretèque, the vast terrace-like balcony which overlooked the Grand' Place and which had so often been the scene of historic proclamations. Suddenly Gilles found himself there, in the open, with a huge concourse of people down below at his feet.

He had Monseigneur the governor on his left, and the company of city fathers and dignitaries had followed him out on La Bretèque. They were standing in a compact group around him; and all down the length of the balcony, at the foot of the balustrade, there were huge pots filled with those Madonna lilies, which seemed like the very emblem of Jacqueline.

Time had gone on; the crowd had cheered at sight of him, and Gilles had gradually been lulled into a semblance of security. Then suddenly, from the far end of the balcony, some fifty paces away, there came the sound of an usher's voice calling in stentorian tones:

'Make room for Madame Jacqueline de Broyart, Duchesse et Princesse de Ramèse, d'Espienne et de Wargny! Make room!'

And down the vista of the long terrace, he caught sight of Jacqueline advancing towards him between the avenue of lilies. She was dressed in a white satin gown, and she had pearls round her neck and in her hair. The April sun fell full upon her, and the soft breeze blew the tendrils of her hair, like strands of gold, about her face. With a sinking of the heart, Gilles saw that she walked with a weary and listless step; but she held herself very erect, with head slightly thrown back, looking straight out before her as she came. A mask of black satin hid her face, but even though he could not see those heavenly blue eyes of hers, Gilles had realized in a moment that his beloved knew everything.

An access of wellnigh savage rage sent the hot blood up to his head. For the space of one second everything around him took on a blood-red hue, and he turned on d'Inchy with convulsed fingers, prepared to grip him by the throat. Already the cry 'You miserable scoundrel!' hovered on his lips.... Then he checked himself. What was the good? D'Inchy had acted rightly, in accordance with his own lights. He wished to make sure that the Valois Prince, who had broken so many promises in his life, should at least on this one occasion be irrevocably fettered. The assembled dignitaries, the crowd down below, the whole city of Cambray should witness the solemn plighting of his troth. And Jacqueline—the unfortunate, innocent pawn in all these intrigues—should be the one whose weak, small hands would hold him indissolubly to his bond.

There was a moment of tense silence. Gilles could hear his own heart beating in his breast. He had of a truth ceased to feel and to think. The situation was so hopeless now, so stupendous, that it was beyond human power to grapple with. He hardly felt that he was alive; a kind of greyish veil had interposed itself between his eyes and that group of solemn Flemish worthies around him. And through that veil he could see their podgy faces, red and round, and grinning at him with great cavern-like mouths, and eyes that darted fierce flames upon him. Of a truth, he thought that he was going mad, had a wild desire to throw back his head and to laugh—laugh loudly and long; laugh for ever at the discomfiture of some fool who was standing there in his—Gilles de Crohin's—shoes; at that fool who had thought to carry through a long farce unchecked, and who presently would be unmasked by the very woman whom he loved, and driven forth under opprobrium and ignominy into an outer world, where he could never look an honest man in the face again.

Perhaps he would have laughed—for the muscles round his mouth were itching till they ached—only that, just then, in the very midst of the crowd below, he caught sight of de Landas' mocking glance—de Landas, who had been in the Council Room awhile ago, and who apparently had since mixed with the crowd for the sole purpose of witnessing his successful rival's discomfiture. This seemed to stiffen him suddenly, to drag him back from out that whirlpool of wild sensations wherein he was floundering, and which was bowling him along, straight to dementia.

'No, my friend Gilles!' he said to himself. 'Since you are to die dishonoured, at least die like a man. Not before all these people; not before that man who hates you, not before that woman who loves you, shall you flinch in the face of Destiny. You have played many ignoble parts these days; do not now play that of a coward!'

And he stood quietly there, still picturesque and magnificent, still defying Fate which had played him this last, desperate trick, while Monseigneur advanced to Jacqueline, took her hand and said aloud in measured tones of ceremony, so that every one there might hear:

'My dear Jacqueline, it is with inexpressible joy that mine old eyes behold this happy hour. *Monsieur* Duc d'Anjou et d'Alençon, Prince of the House of France, hath asked your hand in marriage. We, your guardians, do but await your consent to this union which we had planned for the great good of our beloved country. Say the word, my dear Jacqueline, and I myself will proclaim to our poor, sorrowing people the joyful news that a Liberator hath come to them at last, and that the United Provinces of the Netherlands may look to him as their Sovereign Lord and King.'

Jacqueline had listened to Monseigneur's peroration with perfect composure. She stood then not ten paces away from Gilles—the only woman in the midst of all these men who were gambling with her destiny. Through her mask she was looking on Gilles, and on him only, feeling that the whole abyss of loathing, which filled her soul for him, would be conveyed to him through her look.

She had believed in him so completely, trusted him so implicitly, that now that she knew him to be both a liar and a cheat, she felt that the very well-spring of her love had turned to bitter hate. And hate in a strong and sensitive nature is at least as potent as love. What the mystery was wherewith he chose to surround himself, she did not know. What the object of the hideous comedy which he had played could be, she hardly cared. All that she knew was that he had cheated her and played her false, stolen her love from her to suit some political intrigue of which he held the threads—helped in any case in a hideous and clumsy deception which would leave her for ever shamed.

But now she knew just what she had to do. She might have unmasked the deception last night, told Monseigneur the truth and opened his eyes to the stupid fraud that was perpetrated upon him. What stopped her from doing that she did not know. Perhaps she still hoped that something would occur that would give a simple explanation of the difficult puzzle. Perhaps she thought that when she would be brought face to face with the man who was impersonating the Duc d'Anjou, that man would prove to be some low impostor, but not her knight—not the man who had held her in his arms and sworn that his love for her was as pure as that of the lark for the sun. And if, indeed, she had been so hideously deceived, if her idol prove to have not only feet of clay but heart of stone and soul of darkness, then she would unmask him, publicly, daringly, before the entire people of

Cambray, humiliate him so utterly that his very name would become a by-word for all that was ignominious and base, and find some solace for her misery in the satisfaction of seeing him brought to shame.

Therefore Jacqueline had said nothing last night to Monseigneur—nothing this morning. When requested by her guardian to prepare for this day's ceremony, she had obeyed without a word. Now she listened to his speech until the end. After which, she said calmly:

'Like yourself, Monseigneur, I am covered with confusion at thought of the great honour which a Prince of the House of France will do to our poor country. I would wish, with your permission, to express my deep respect for him ere I place my hand in his.'

Whereupon Monseigneur stood a little to one side, so that Jacqueline and Gilles remained directly facing one another. Every one was watching the young pair, and kindly murmurs of approval at the beauty of the girl, and the martial bearing of the man, flew from mouth to mouth.

Jacqueline, stately and dignified as was her wont, advanced a step or two. Then she said slowly:

'And is it of a truth *Monsieur* Duc d'Anjou et d'Alençon who stands before me now?'

She looked straight at him, and he in imagination saw beneath the mask which hid the expression of her face—saw those blue eyes which had looked on him yesterday with such ineffable tenderness; saw those exquisite lips which had murmured words of infinite love. An utter loathing overcame him of the part which he had to play, of the fraud which was to deliver his beloved into the keeping of a worthless reprobate. He was conscious only of a wild desire to throw himself at her feet in an agony of remorse and repentance, to kiss her gown, the tips of her velvet shoes; and then to proclaim the truth, to put it for ever out of that profligate Prince's power to claim this exquisite woman as his bride—to proclaim the truth, and then to run away like a second Cain, from the scene of an unforgivable crime; to flee like the treacherous soldier who hath deserted the citadel; to flee, leaving behind him the tattered rag of France's honour lying for ever soiled in the dust, beneath the feet of a duped and credulous nation.

Just then she put out her hand—that perfect hand, which he had held in his and which to his touch had seemed like the petal of a flower, and she said, with the same solemn deliberation:

'Is it in truth to the Duc d'Anjou himself that I herewith plight my troth?'

The avowal was on Gilles' lips.

'Madame——' he began, and looked unflinchingly, straightforwardly at her.

But before he could speak another word, a cry suddenly rang out—shrill and terrifying—out of the crowd.

'Do not touch him, Madame! Do not touch him! He is not the Duc d'Anjou! He is an impostor and a liar! A Spanish spy! Beware!!'

Monseigneur, the city fathers, the Mayor—every one on La Bretèque, in fact—gasped with horror. How dared these abominable agitators mar the beauty of this affecting ceremony? Monseigneur went forward, leaned over the balustrade in order to try and ascertain who it was who was trying to create a disturbance. He saw de Landas down below in the midst of the throng, vaguely wondered what the young commandant was doing there, when his place was up on La Bretèque amongst those of his own rank. Anyway, he spoke to de Landas, shouted himself hoarse to make the young man hear, for an unpleasant turmoil had followed that first cry of 'Spanish spy'— people were shouting and gesticulating and the call 'Down with him!' came repeatedly from several points in the rear of the crowd.

De Landas looked up, but he pretended not to hear, laughed and shrugged his shoulders, as if the matter did not concern him. And yet there was no mistaking the persistence with which that ominous cry 'Spanish spy!' was taken up again and again, nor the disturbing effect which it had upon the crowd.

Monseigneur then tried to harangue the mob, to point out to them the evil of their ways. Had they forgotten that they were out to enjoy themselves, to forget their troubles, to forget the very fact that the words 'Spaniard' and 'Spanish' existed in their lexicon. But Messire de Landas' paid agents would not let him speak. They had been paid to create a disturbance, not to let the people stand about placidly, listening to windy harangues.

So, the moment Monseigneur opened his mouth, the whole gang of them took up the provocative cry: 'A Spanish spy! Take care, Madame Jacqueline!' until it was repeated over and over again by numberless voices, hoarse with excitement and with spite. The crowd oscillated as if driven by a sudden blast; ominous murmurs came from those points where women and men stood in compact and sullen groups.

'Spanish spy! Beware!' rang out again and again.

Monseigneur the governor was in a wild state of agitation. He could not understand what it was that had set some rowdy malcontents to disturb the peaceful serenity of this eventful morning. Unable to make himself heard, he turned in helpless bewilderment to Gilles.

'Monseigneur,' he began, in a voice quivering with consternation. 'I do entreat you...'

But he got no further. Above this peroration, above the shuffling and the mutterings of his friends on the balcony, above the cries and murmurs down below, there had suddenly resounded the dull boom of distant cannon. The crowd gave one terrific, full-throated roar of terror:

'The Spaniards! They are on us!'

And in the seething mass of humanity on the Grand' Place could be seen just that awful, ominous swaying which precedes a stampede. Already the women screamed and some men shouted: 'Sauve qui peut!'

'The Spanish spy!' cried a voice. 'What did I tell you, citizens? He hath taken advantage of this holiday to bring the Spaniards about your ears!'

Now the swaying of the crowd became like a tidal wave upon the bosom of the ocean. Hundreds of men and women and little children started to move, not in one direction but in several, like frightened sheep who know not whither to go. Yells and screams, some of rage, others of terror, rose in a wild tumult from below. And through it all a few persistent voices—recognizable by the well-known guttural tone peculiar to those of Spanish blood—shouted themselves hoarse with the persistent cry: 'The Spaniards are on us! We are betrayed!'

VI

Monseigneur the governor, unable to make himself heard, helpless and gravely perturbed, hurried into the Council Room, and after him trooped the city fathers like a flock of scared hens. Confusion at once reigned inside the Town Hall as much as out on the Place—a confusion that could be felt rather than heard, a dull murmur of voices, a scurrying and pattering of feet.

Once more the cannon roared, and the weird sound was followed by a prolonged volley of musket shot.

'They are on us! Sauve qui peut!'

Then, suddenly, far away in the direction of Cantimpré, a huge column of smoke rose to the sky. It was immediately followed by a stupendous report which literally shook the ground beneath the feet of this terror-stricken mass of humanity. A shower of broken glass fell at several points with a loud clatter on to the pavements below, and in absolutely wild and unreasoning terror, the crowd began to push and to jostle, to drive, and shove, and batter anything or any one that came in the way. Men and women in their terror had become like a herd of stampeding beasts, tearing at every obstacle, hurling maledictions and missiles, fighting, pushing, to get back to their homes, hammering at doors that had already been hastily barred and bolted, by those who happened to have found shelter inside the houses close by.

'They are on us! Sauve qui peut!'

This time it was a company of the city guard, who came running helter-skelter from the direction of the Citadel, halbertmen and pikemen, most of them unarmed, others with their steel bonnets set awry upon their heads, not a few leaving a trail of blood behind them as they ran.

'Sauve qui peut!' The deathly call of the runaway soldier, the most awesome sound the ear of man can hear. And over from St. Géry came others running too, the archers from Notre Dame, and on the right there were the gunners from Seille. They were running; like hunted deer, swiftly, panting, their jerkins torn, the slashings of their doublets hanging on them in strips.

They added the final horrible note of hopelessness to the terror and the confusion. From every corner of the city there rose cries of distress, shrill screams from women and children, loud curses from the men. The very air was filled with these dismal sounds, whilst the Unseen which was happening somewhere upon the ramparts of the city, appeared vastly more terrifying than the Seen.

And, far away, the cannon still roared and columns of fire and smoke rose with lurid significance to the sky.

VII

And yet it had all occurred within a very few minutes. Gilles and Jacqueline were left alone now on La Bretèque, and neither of them had thought of fleeing. For each of them the awesome moment was just a pause wherein their minds faced the only important problem — how to help and what to do, singly, against that terrible tide.

It was just a moment—the space, perhaps, of a dozen heart-beats. All around them the turbulent passions of men—fear, enmity, greed—were raging in all their unbridled frenzy. The cannons roared, the walls of the ancient city tottered; but they stood in a world apart, he—the man who unknowingly had played so ignominious a part— and she, the woman whom he had so heinously wronged. He tried to read her innermost thoughts behind that forbidding mask, and a mad appeal to her for forgiveness rose, even at this supreme instant, to his lips.

But the appeal was never made. The man's feelings, his grief, his shame were all swept aside by the stirring of the soldier's soul. It was the moment when first the cannon roared and the runaway guard came running through the streets, Gilles saw them long before they had reached the Grand' Place. He realized what it all meant, saw the unutterable confusion and panic which would inevitably render the city an easy prey to the invader. He gave a cry of horror and dismay.

'My God! but 'tis black treachery that has been at work this day!' he exclaimed involuntarily.

She had not yet seen the runaway guard, did not perhaps for the moment realize the utter imminence of the peril. Her mind was still busy with the difficult problem—how to help, what to do. But his involuntary cry suddenly roused her ire and her bitter disillusionment.

'You should know Messire,' she retorted. 'You are well versed in the art.'

'God forgive me, I am!' he ejaculated ruefully. 'But this!' he added with a smothered oath, and pointed down to the panic-stricken soldiers. 'This! ... Oh, my God! Your safety, your precious life at stake! You'll not believe, Jacqueline,' he pleaded, 'that I had a hand in selling your city to your enemies?'

'In selling the city!' The words appeared to have whipped up her spirit as with a lash. She looked at him, wrathfully, boldly, with a still unspoken challenge lurking in her eyes. 'You do not believe that— —'

'That traitors have engineered her perdition?' he broke in rapidly. 'I do!'

'But— —'

'The disturbance in the crowd ... the panic ... the deserters ... those abominable agitators! In a few hours the Spaniards will be inside the city—and Cambray lost!'

'Cambray lost! Impossible!'

'With no discipline, no leaders.... She cannot resist— —'

'Then you must lead her,' she said firmly.

'I?'

'Yes! You!'

She had taken the mask from off her face and confronted him now with a glowing challenge in her eyes.

'You!' she reiterated, speaking very rapidly. 'Whoever you are, save Cambray ... defend her ... save her! I know that you can.'

In the look which she gave him he read something which filled his very soul with rapture. He gave her back glance for glance, worship for this trust.

'I can at any rate die for her,' he said quietly. 'If you, ma donna, will forgive.'

'Save Cambray,' she reiterated with superb confidence, 'and I'll forgive everything!'

'Then may God have you in His keeping,' he called to her. And, before she could realize what was in his purpose, he had climbed to the top of the tall balustrade, stood for one moment there high above her, silhouetted against the clear blue of the sky, like a living statue of youth and enthusiasm and springtide, animated by that faith which moveth mountains and sets out to conquer the world in order to lay it at the loved one's feet.

'Jehan!' he called. 'À moi!'

Then, swinging himself with the easy grace of perfect strength, he jumped down on to the perron below.

CHAPTER XXIII.
WHILE TRAITORS ARE AT WORK

I

And now, I pray you think of Jacqueline running to the balustrade and, with glowing eyes looking over the stonework upon the perron beneath her. Jehan has caught his master as the latter touches the ground, and for the space of two or three seconds the two men stand at the top of the steps, locked in each other's arms, steadying one another. During those few seconds Messire whispers hurriedly in his faithful henchman's ears:

'De Balagny's troops from La Fère ... at all costs.... Understand?'

Jehan nods.

'Tell them to attack from the Bapaume Road, with as much clatter and shouting as may be. We'll hold on till they come. Go!'

He waits another few seconds until he sees Jehan's burly form disappear through the throng, then with a loud call, 'À moi! all you citizens of Cambray who are not cowards and traitors!' he draws his sword and faces the crowd.

He has a clear and resonant voice, which rises above the tumult. The panic-stricken throng of men and women pause mechanically in their unconsidered flight, to look on that strange apparition on the perron steps—strange, in truth; for towering up there, he looks preternaturally tall, and the black mask on his face gives him an air of mystery.

'Citizens of Cambray,' he continues lustily. 'The Spaniard is at your gate! Are you going to let the traitors have their day?'

The crowd sways towards him. Frightened as every one is, there is a momentary lull in the wild stampede, while scared, wide-eyed, pallid faces are turned towards the stranger. The runaway soldiers, too, pause, in their headlong rush. A company of pikemen stand in a compact group on the edge of the crowd, some fifty paces away from Gilles. Their captain, bonnetless, with tattered jerkin and face streaming with sweat, is in their midst. Messire sees him, and shouts to him with all his might.

'Captain of the guard, Cambray is in peril! What are you doing here?'

The man evidently wavers; he looks shamed and overcome, tries to hide himself behind his subordinates. But some one close at his elbow—Jacqueline cannot see who it is—appears to egg him on, and after an instant's hesitation he says sullenly:

'The Spaniards are on us, and——'

'Then why are you not on the Spaniards?' retorts Gilles.

'They have made a breach at Cantimpré.'

'Then where are your counter-mines?'

'Under the bastion.'

'Did you fire them?'

'No. The whole fort is crumbling already. It would tumble about our ears.'

'Then why are you not at the breach to make a rampart of your body?'

Again the man wavers. He is a soldier and a tried one, appears bewildered at his own act of treachery. It seemed at the time as if some one—some devil—had put cowardice into his heart at the very moment when courage and presence of mind were most urgently needed. The men, too, had faltered, broken most unexpectedly at the first assault, throwing down their arms. Even the gunners.... But it wouldn't bear thinking of. In truth, some devil had been at work, is at work now; for when the men and the captain, already stirred by Gilles' enthusiasm, looking ashamed and crestfallen, are on the point of cheering, a peremptory voice, laden with spite, rises from somewhere in the rear.

'Captain of the guard! I forbid you to listen to this man! He is a cheat and an impostor!'

It is de Landas, who, hidden at the back of the crowd, has seen Gilles jump down from the balcony, and scenting danger to his infamous scheme, has been at pains to force his way to the forefront of the mob. It has taken him some time and vigorous play of the elbows, for the crowd has become interested in the masked stranger—in the man whom they had nearly murdered twenty-four hours ago, but whose appearance and words to-day are distinctly inspiriting and reassuring.

De Landas has one of his favourite familiars with him— the Fleming, Maarege—and together the two men stand now, commanding and arrogant, in front of the soldiers and their captain. And they, recognizing the chief commandant of the garrison, are once more panic-stricken and dumb. Vague ideas of discipline and punishment, to which the young Spaniard had accustomed them, check their enthusiasm for the stranger.

Now de Landas has taken a step or two nearer to the captain of the guard. His eyes are aflame with fury, and his whole attitude is one of authority and of menace.

'If you dare parley with this man,' he says savagely, 'you will answer for it with your life. The Spanish armies are at your gates; in a few hours they will be in this city. Your only hope of pardon for yourself, for your wife, your children and your kindred, lies in complete and immediate surrender to the will of His Majesty the King of Spain, my master and yours!'

'To hell with the King of Spain, your master!' Gilles' stentorian voice breaks in from above. 'Soldiers of Cambray!' he continues lustily, 'You have nothing to fear from the King of Spain, or from any of his minions! 'Tis you who will punish them for all their past insolence! You who will dictate to them the terms of victory!'

'You miserable varlet!' exclaims de Landas, and turns on Gilles with unbridled savagery. 'How dare you raise your voice when the King of Spain speaks through my lips? How dare you speak to all these besotted fools of victory, when in submission lies their only chance of safety? Fools!' he goes on, and turns once more to the crowd. 'Self-deluded dupes! Do you not feel the might of Spain closing in upon you? Surrender, I say! Submit! You are wretched and starved and weak. You cannot defend yourselves, and no one will come to your aid.'

'Then do I proclaim you a liar, M. de Landas!' is Gilles' firm retort. 'The armies of France are on their way for the relief of Cambray, even at this hour.'

'It is false!'

'True as I live. True as that you are a miserable traitor! True as there is a Heaven above us and as there are angels who visit this earth. Citizens of Cambray, I swear to you that the army of the King of France will be outside your city before the April sun that smiles upon your valour has sunk down to rest. So give a cheer for France, citizens of Cambray! France, your deliverer and friend!'

His sally is greeted with a gigantic outburst of cheering.

'France! France!'

The crowd has listened spellbound while the masked stranger bandied words with that bastard Spaniard, whom they had all learned to loathe long ago. His cheery voice, his confident bearing, his exultation, have already warmed their hearts. Something of their terror has vanished; they are no longer like a herd of awestruck beasts, driven aimlessly along by senseless terror. There is nothing in the world so infectious as fear, except courage and enthusiasm: and Gilles' martial figure, the proud carriage of his head, his vibrant voice and flashing sword, are there to infuse valour even in the most abject.

The captain of the guard and his men had winced before de Landas' threats. Old habits of discipline could not all in a moment be shaken off. But now they feel that the crowd is at one with them in their enthusiasm for the stranger, and also that they will be given a chance of retrieving their shameful act of cowardice of awhile ago. So, when the crowd cheers, the soldiers, despite de Landas' black looks and his brutal menaces, following their captain's lead, cheer too. They cheer until the very walls of the ancient city reverberate with the sound.

'France! France!'

Then suddenly Gilles, at the top of the perron steps, quick as lightning, runs to the nearest earthenware pot which is filled with the Madonna lilies. He plucks out a sheaf of the flowers, and with a loud cry: 'Soldiers of Cambray, rally to the standard of France! To the unconquered Flower o' the Lily!' he throws the flowers one by one to the soldiers and their captain. The men seize them as they fly through the air and fasten them to their bonnets or their belts. The crowd acclaims the spirited deed:

'Long live the flower o' the lily!' they shout.

Now Gilles is running from pot to pot. He snatches sheaf after sheaf of lilies and throws them to the crowd. The flowers are caught up with ever growing ardour, whilst every corner of the Place rings with the triumphant call: 'France! France!'

Far away the cannon is roaring, the air is rent with the sharp report of muskets and the crumbling of masonry. The translucent April sky hath taken on a lurid hue. Around the city walls the brutal enemy is already swarming; he is battering at the gates, has climbed the fortifications, run triumphantly to the assault. Awhile ago the crowd had cowered at the sound, fled terrified at his approach. Now every heart is thrilled with fervour, every soul responds to the appeal of an enthusiast, and is glowing with the hope of victory.

And de Landas, blind with fury, sees the fruits of his abominable treachery crumbling to dust before his eyes. He glowers on every one around him like a stricken bull, with rage and frenzy enkindled in his eyes. And suddenly, before any one there can guess his purpose, he has laid savage hands on the Captain of the guard, and drawing a pistol from his belt he points it at the unfortunate man's breast.

'If one of you dares to utter another sound, or to stir from this spot,' he shrieks out in a shrill and husky voice, 'I'll shoot this dog where he stands.'

At once the cheers immediately near him are stilled, a groan of horror and of execration rises from an hundred throats, and for the space of a few seconds the soldiers stand quite still, holding their breath; for in truth it is murder which gleams out of the young Spaniard's eyes.

'Down on your knees, you miscreant!' shouts de Landas fiercely. 'Maarege, à moi! Help me to make a clean sweep of this herd of rebels. Down on your knees, every one of you! You Flemish swine!'

'Down on your knees, M. le Marquis!' Gilles' sonorous voice rings out like a bronze bell beneath the clapper. With that rapidity which characterizes his every action, he runs down the perron steps, catches de Landas' right arm from behind and gives it such a brutal wrench that the pistol falls from the miscreant's hand and the Spaniard himself, sick with the pain, comes down on one knee.

'Out of the way, you hell-hound!' Gilles goes on mercilessly. 'There is no room for traitors in Cambray.'

He kicks the pistol on one side and throws de Landas, semi-inert, from him, as if he were a bale of noisome goods. Then he turns and, with an instantaneous gesture, has gripped de Landas' familiar by the throat.

'I'll kill every one of your gang with mine own hands,' he says in a fierce and rapid whisper, 'unless you all slink away at once like the curs that you are!'

The words are hardly out of his mouth, and Maarege, faint and sick, is bending under that powerful grip, when from somewhere overhead there comes a sudden, heart-rending cry of warning.

'Take care!'

But the warning has come just a second too late. De Landas, recovering from semi-consciousness, has succeeded in crawling on hands and knees and retaking possession of his pistol. He points it straight at his hated rival. There is a sharp report, followed by screams from the women. For a second or two Gilles remains standing just where he was, with his sinewy fingers round Maarege's throat. Then his grip relaxes; Maarege totters back, panting and half dead, whilst Gilles instinctively puts his hand to his shoulder. His jerkin is already deeply stained with blood.

De Landas gives an almost demoniacal shout of glee, which, however, is but short-lived. The soldiers, who had been cowed by his brutality a moment ago, are roused to a passion of fury now at the dastardly assault on one who has already become their idol. They fall on the recreant, regardless of his rank and power. They drag him up from the ground, wrench the pistol out of his hand and hold him there, a panting, struggling, impotent beast, breathing hatred and malediction.

'Give the word, Monseigneur,' the Captain says coolly, 'and we'll kill the vermin.' He holds the pistol to de Landas' breast, whilst his eyes are fixed on Gilles, waiting for the order to fire.

'Let the serpent be, captain,' Gilles replies quietly.

'But you are hurt, Monseigneur,' the captain urges.

'Nothing but a scratch—'tis healed already.'

Far away the cannon thunders once more. Once more a terrific explosion rends the air. Gilles, still upright, still cheery, still brimful of enthusiasm, holds his sword up high over his head, so that the April sun draws sparks of fire from its shining blade.

'To the breach, friends!' he cries. 'If breach there be! À moi, soldiers of Cambray! Form into line and to the ramparts! I'll be there before you! And you, proud citizens of a valiant city, à moi! Pick up your staves and your sticks, your chisels and your rakes! À moi! All of you, with your fists and your knees and your hearts and your minds! Remember Mons, and Mechlin and Gand! Remember your hearths! your wives! your daughters! and let the body of each one of you here be a living rampart against the foe for the defence of your homes. À moi!'

The captain gives the order, the men fall in, in straight, orderly line. On their bonnets or in their belts the white lily gleams like shining metal beneath the kiss of the April sun. From the Town Hall the bodyguard comes trooping down the perron steps. They are joined by the halberdiers who had lined the Grand' Place, by the archers from St. Géry and the musketeers from the citadel. The banners of the city guilds flutter in the breeze; fair hands and white kerchiefs are waved from windows and balconies above, and a terrific cheer for France rends the air with its triumphant echo, as the crowd begins to move slowly in the wake of the soldiers.

'Long live France!'

'Long live the Defender of Cambray!'

II

For a moment Gilles stands quite still, almost isolated where he is, a little dizzy with excitement and with loss of blood. An uncomfortable veil is fast gathering in front of his eyes. 'I shall have to see to this stupid scratch,' he murmurs to himself.

It had all occurred so quickly—within a brief quarter of an hour. And yet the destinies of nations had been recast during that time. Now the city fathers, the provosts, Monseigneur himself, are crowding round the one man who they feel might still save them from dishonour.

'Your Highness, we look to you,' Monseigneur is saying.

'Tell us what you wish done,' adds the Chief Magistrate.

'The Provosts await your Highness' orders,' rejoins a pompous dignitary, whilst yet another continues in the same strain: 'We are body and soul at your Highness' commands.'

Their voices come to Gilles as if from somewhere far away. They are drowned by the tumult of the beleaguered city preparing for a last stand. But the instinct of the soldier keeps him steadfast on his feet. He makes a violent effort to keep his head clear and his voice firm. He gives orders to the Chief Magistrate, the Provosts, the Mayors of the Guilds. The forts must be visited at once, the men encouraged, the officers admonished. Every hour, every minute almost is now of priceless value. The troop brought over by Messire de Balagany, encamped at La Fère cannot be here before sundown. Until then the men must stand. Oh! they must stand, Messires! Despite crumbling walls and hecatombs of dead! Let the men know that the existence of their country is hanging to-day by a thread!

The Guild of Armourers must open up its stores: pikes, lances, halberts, muskets, must be distributed to a contingent of citizens, who, though untrained, will help to strengthen the living wall. The Guild of Apothecaries must be ready with ambulances and dressings, and stretcher-bearers must work wonders so that the fighters are not encumbered by the dead.

The Chief Engineer of the city must see to barricading the streets with double rows of hurdles, or boxes, or furniture, or lumber of any sorts, with sacks filled with earth, empty carts, wagons, clothing, anything and everything that may be handy. The reservoirs of the city must be patrolled, and if it be deemed necessary, they must be opened and the water allowed to flood the low-lying streets by the river, if the enemy succeed in obtaining a foothold there. Countermines must be laid; every one must to his task, and he who does not fight must think and work and endure.

Every one obeys. One by one, the dignitaries file away to execute the orders which have been given them. They all accept the leadership of this man, whom they still believe to be the Duc d'Anjou, their future Sovereign Lord.

'Ah, Monseigneur!' exclaims d'Inchy warmly. 'I thank God on my knees that you are with us to-day, and that it is you who will defend our city—the most precious pearl in your future inheritance.'

'Your Highness must save yourself as much as possible,' comes in cordial echo from M. de Lalain. 'We could ill spare you now.'

'What would we do if Monseigneur fell?' adds another.

And then an angelic voice breaks in suddenly, saying with sweet compassion:

'Fie, Monsieur my guardian, to weary Monseigneur so! Cannot you see that he is fainting?'

But Gilles hardly hears. Tired nature is asserting her rights over him at last. He sinks wearied upon the nearest step. It seems to him as if soft arms are thrown around him, whilst others—more powerful and insistent—busy themselves dexterously with his jerkin.

It is all very vague and infinitely sweet. Soft linen is laid upon his wounded shoulder, something pungent and sweet-smelling is held to his nostrils, whilst from very far away, in the regions of dreams and of paradise, a soft voice murmurs with angelic solicitude:

'Think you it will heal?'

'Very quickly, gracious lady,' a gruff voice replies. ''Tis only a flesh wound. Excitement hath brought on a brief swoon. It is nothing.'

After which Gilles remembers nothing more.

—

CHAPTER XXIV.
THE DEFENCE OF CAMBRAY

I

Of that terrible day in Cambray, that fourth of April, 1581, nothing has survived but a memory—a glowing memory of fervour and enthusiasm, of reckless disregard of danger and magnificent deeds of valour; a heartrending memory of sorrow and misery and death.

Five times in as many hours did the armies of the Duke of Parma rush to the assault of the city. Five times did a living rampart of intrepid bodies interpose itself between the mighty hordes and the crumbling walls of Cambray—those intrepid bodies more steadfast than the walls. At one hour after noon the redoubt of Cantimpré is a black mass of charred débris, the Château de Seille is in flames. On the right bank of the Scheldt the walls have a breach through which twenty men can pass, the moats and the river are filled with dead.

But the living rampart still stands. The walls of Cambray are crumbling, but her citizens are steadfast. Halbertmen and pikemen, archers and gunners, they all have a moment's weakness to retrieve, and do it with deeds of indomitable valour. And as they fall, and their numbers become thinned, as that breathing, palpitating wall sustains shock after shock of the most powerful engines of warfare the world has ever known, its gaps are made good by other breasts and other hearts, and with all the spirit which will not rest until it has conquered.

Outside and in, at this hour, all is confusion. A medley of sights and sounds which the senses cannot wholly grasp, dull roar of cannon, sharp retort of musketry, clash of pike and lance and halbert, the terrified shrieks of women and the groans of the wounded and the dying. Round about the walls, in the narrow streets and up on the battlements, a litter of broken steel and staves, of scrap-iron and fragments of masonry and glass, torn jerkins cast aside; for the April sun is hot and the smell of powder goes to the head like wine.

II

And from the tall steeples of Cambray's many churches the tocsin sends its ominous call above the din.

Cambray is fighting for her liberty, for her existence. Her sons and daughters are giving their lives for her. And not only for her, but for the Netherlands—the brave and stricken country which has fought against such terrible odds while the very centuries have rolled by.

A last stand, this; for no mercy is to be expected from the Spaniard if he enters the city in his numbers. Cambray hath withstood the might of Philip II, hath rebelled against his authority, hath dared to think that men are free to think, to work and to worship, that children are not slaves or women chattels. Cambray hath unfurled the flag of liberty. If she fall, she becomes a prey to rapine and brutality, to incendiaries and libertines.

So Cambray to-day must conquer or die.

Traitors have plotted against her, laid her open, unsuspecting, to a surprise attack by an army which is past-master in the art. Caught unawares in a holiday mood, she has flinched. Worked upon by treachery, her sons have wavered at first, panic seized hold of them— they all but fell, shamed and destined to never-ending disgrace and remorse.

But the cowardice had been momentary, fostered by past months of privations and misery, fomented by the insidious voice of traitors. One man's voice hath rallied the sinking spirits, one man's valour revived the dormant courage. All they wanted was a leader—a man to tell them to hope, a man to cheer and comfort them, to kindle in their hearts the dying flame of indomitable will. So, in the wake of that man they have followed in their hundreds and their thousands; the soldiers have regained discipline; the men, courage; the women, resignation. The masked stranger whom they had been taught to hate, they have already learned to worship.

Heroic, splendid, indomitable, he is the bulwark which strengthens every faltering heart, the prop which supports every wavering spirit. From end to end of the ramparts his sonorous voice vibrates and echoes, commanding, helping, cheering. If courage fails, he is there to stiffen; if an arm tires, his is there to take its place. Sword or lance, or pike or halbert, culverine or musket or bow; every weapon is familiar to his hand. At the breach with a pistol, on the ramparts with falconet, on the bastion with the heavy cannon; he is here, there and everywhere where danger is most threatening, where Spanish arrows darken the sky like a storm-cloud that is wind-driven, and deal death when they find their goal. His jerkin is torn, the sleeve of his doublet hangs tattered from his shoulder, his arm is bare, his face black with powder and grime. Around him the Provosts and Sheriffs and Captains of the Guard vainly beg him not to expose himself to unnecessary peril.

'The soldiers look to your Highness alone,' they cry in desperation. 'If you fall, what should we do?'

They still believe him to be the Duc d'Anjou, brother of the King of France, and marvel that so degenerate a race could breed such a magnificent soldier. He has said nothing to disillusion them. The mire of battle masks him better than a scrap of satin or velvet, and whilst fighting to save Cambray, he is also redeeming the honour of France.

'If you fall, what should we do?' implores d'Inchy on one occasion, during a lull in the attack.

Gilles laughs, loudly and long. 'Do?' he exclaims gaily. 'Hold Cambray to the last man and turn the Spaniard from her walls!'

Unflinching and resolute, a pack of Flemish bourgeois hold their ground against the might and main of the Duke of Parma's magnificent army—clerks, some of them, others shopkeepers or labourers, against the most powerful military organization of the epoch! But it is not only Cambray that is threatened now; it is the freedom of their province and the honour of their women. And so they make a wall of their bodies whilst the flower of the Duke of Parma's hordes is hurled time after time against them.

Musketeers and crossbowmen, lancers and halberdiers—up they come to the charge like an irresistible tidal wave against a mighty cliff. Like a torrent they rush over the moat and on to the breach, or the bastions, or the ramparts; attacking from every side, using every engine of warfare which the mightiest kingdom of the age has devised for the subjugation of rebellious cities. The sound of metal-headed arrows against the masonry is like a shower of hailstones upon glass; the battlements gleam with flashing steel, with sparks from brandished swords and flame-spitting falconets.

Of a truth, the mind cannot grasp it all, eyes cannot see nor ears perceive all the horrors, the misery and the devotion. Men fighting and women working to soothe, to comfort or to heal. Burghers' wives, humble maids, great ladies, are all fighting with the men, fighting with their hearts and their skilled hands, with clean bandages and soothing potions, with words of comfort for the dying and prayers for the dead.

In the streets behind the ramparts, rough ambulances have been set up, mattresses dragged under sheds or outhouses, fresh straw laid, on which the wounded might find momentary solace. The women, too, are doing their part. Jacqueline de Broyart, one of the many, the most untiring where all give of their best, the most selfless where all are ready for sacrifice. From time to time during the lull between terrific assaults, she sees Gilles hurrying past—her knight, the defender of her beloved city. She bade him go and save Cambray and sees him now, begrimed, in rags, unheedful even of her, but cheerful and undaunted, certain of victory.

'You will be proud, my dear,' says d'Inchy to her, during one of those nerve-racking lulls, 'to place your hand in that so valiant a soldier, to plight your troth to Monsieur Duc d'Anjou.'

'I shall be proud,' she retorts simply, 'if, indeed, I might plight my troth to the defender of Cambray.'

'The defender of Cambray, my dear,' rejoins d'Inchy lustily. 'The saviour of Cambray, you mean! 'Tis on our knees we shall have to thank him and offer him all that we have of the best!'

A strange, elusive smile flits for a moment round Jacqueline's mouth, and a look of infinite longing softens the light of her blue eyes.

'If only it could be!' she sighs, and returns to her task.

III

Later in the afternoon, the picture becomes more clear. We see the crumbling walls, the girdle around Cambray falling away bit by bit; we see the breach at Cantimpré wider by many feet now and a handful of men making a last stand there, with muskets, crossbows, sticks—anything that is ready to hand. We see the bastions a mass of smouldering ruins and the ramparts around on the point of giving way.

And all about the city a mighty hecatomb—Spaniards and Flemings, soldiers, burghers or churls, lie scattered on the low-lying ground, in the moat, the ramparts or the streets. Might and glory have claimed their victims as well as valour and worship of liberty.

Cambray's walls are falling. The breach becomes wider and wider every hour, like a huge gaping wound through which the life-blood of the stricken city is oozing out drop by drop.

But, guarding that breach, not yet yielding one foot of the city which shelters his Jacqueline, Gilles de Crohin, with that handful of men, still holds the ground. His anxious eyes scan the low horizon far away where the April sun is slowly sinking to rest. That way lies La Fère and de Balagny's few picked men, whom Jehan has gone to fetch, and who could even in this desperate hour turn Spanish discomfiture into a rout.

'My God! why does Jehan tarry?' he calls out with smouldering impatience.

Up on the battlements the guard stand firm; but the Spaniards have succeeded in throwing several bridges of pikes across the moat and one mine after another is laid against the walls. Captains and officers run to Gilles for instructions or orders.

'There are no orders,' he says, 'save to hold out until France comes to your aid.'

And out in the open country, outside those city walls which hold together so much heroism and such indomitable courage, the Duke of Parma, angered, fierce, terrible, has rallied the cream of his armies around him. The sixth assault has just been repulsed, the breach cleared by a terrific fusillade from that handful of men, whilst a murderous shower from above, of granite and scrap-iron and heavy stones, has scattered the attacking party. A fragment of stone has hit the Duke on the forehead; blood is streaming down his face. He sets spurs to his horse and gallops to where a company of archers is scrambling helter-skelter out of the moat.

'Cowards!' he cries savagely. 'Will you flee before such rabble?'

He strikes at the soldiers with his sword, sets spurs to his horse until the poor beast snorts with pain, rears and paws the air with its hoofs, only to bring them down the next moment, trampling and kicking half a dozen soldiers to death in its mad and terrified struggle.

'You know the guard has fled,' Alexander Farnese cries to his officers. ''Tis only an undisciplined mob who is in there now.'

His nephew, Don Miguel de Salvado, a brave and experienced captain, shrugs his shoulders and retorts:

'A mob led by a man who has the whole art of warfare at his finger-tips. Look at him now!'

All eyes are turned in the direction to which Don Miguel is pointing. There, in the midst of smouldering ruins of charred débris and crumbling masonry, stands the defender of Cambray; behind him the graceful steeples of St. Géry and of St. Waast, the towers of Notre Dame and of the Town Hall, are lit up by the honey-coloured rays of the sinking sun. Superb in his tattered clothes, with chest and arms bare, and ragged hose, he stands immovable, scanning the western sky.

De Landas laughs aloud.

'He is still on the look-out for that promised help from France,' he says, with a shrug of his shoulder.

The traitor has made good his escape out of the city which he has betrayed. What assistance he could render to the Duke in the way of information, he has done. The measure of his infamy is full to the brim, and yet his hatred for the enemy who has shamed him is in no way assuaged.

He, too, looks up and sees Gilles de Crohin, the man whose invincible courage has caused the Spanish armies so many valuable lives this day and such unforgettable humiliation.

'A hundred doubloons,' he cries aloud, 'to the first man who lays that scoundrel low!'

The word is passed from mouth to mouth. The archers and musketeers set up a cheer. Parma adds, with an oath: 'And a captain's rank to boot!'

An hundred doubloons and a captain's rank! 'Tis a fortune for any man. It means retirement, a cottage in sunny Spain, a home, a wife. The men take heart and look to their arrows and their muskets! Every archer feels that he has that fortune in his quiver now and every musketeer has it in his powder horn. And with a loud cry of 'Long live King Philip of Spain!' the infantry once more rush for the breach.

IV

Don Miguel de Salvado leads the attack this time. The breach now looks like a gate which leads straight into the heart of the city, where pillage and looting are to be the reward of the conquerors; and the booty will be rich with the precious belongings of a pack of overfed bourgeois.

That open gate for the moment seems undefended. It is encumbered with fallen masonry, and beyond this appear piles of rubbish, overturned wagons, furniture, débris of all sorts, evidently abandoned by the wretched inhabitants when they fled from their homes. Of Gilles de Crohin and his burghers there is for the moment no sign.

Don Miguel has with him half a company of musketeers, the finest known in Europe, and a company of lancers who have been known to clear an entire city of rebels by their irresistible onrush.

'No falling back, remember!' he commands. 'The first who gives ground is a dead man!'

Up the lancers run on the slippery ground, clinging to the wet earth with naked feet, to the coarse grass and loose stones with their knees. The musketeers remain on the hither side of the moat, three deep in a long battle array; the front lying flat upon the ground, the second kneeling, the third standing, with their muskets levelled against the first enemy who dares to show his face. The pikemen have reached the breach. There is silence on the other side. The officer laughs lustily.

'I told you 'twas but a rabble playing with firearms!'

The words are hardly out of his mouth when a terrific volley of musketry shakes the fast crumbling wall to its foundation. It comes from somewhere behind all those débris—and not only from there, but from some other unknown point, with death-like precision and cold deliberation. The Spanish officer is hit in the face; twelve pikemen throw up their arms and come rolling down on the wet ground.

'What is this hell let loose?' cries the officer savagely, ere he too, blinded with the flow of blood down his face, beats a hasty retreat.

Quick! a messenger to His Highness the Duke of Parma! The breach is so wide now that twenty men could walk easily through it. The enemy is not in sight—and yet, from somewhere unseen, death-dealing musketry frustrates every assault.

'Return to the charge!' is the Duke of Parma's curt command, and sends one of his ablest officers to lead a fresh charge. He himself organizes a diversion, crosses the small rivulet, which flows into the Schelde at the foot of Cantimpré, and trains his artillery upon a vulnerable piece of wall, between the bastion and the river bank. He has the finest culverines known in Europe at this time, made on a new pattern lately invented in England; his cannon balls are the most powerful ever used in warfare, and some of his musketeers know how to discharge ten shots in a quarter of an hour—an accomplishment never excelled even by the French.

So, while one of his ablest officers is in charge of the attacking party on the breach, His Highness himself directs a new set of operations. Once more the roar of artillery and of musketry rend the air with their portentous sound. The Duke of Parma's picked men attack the last bastion of Cantimpré, whilst from the roads of Arras, of Sailly and Bapaume, the whole of the Spanish infantry rush like a mighty wave to the charge.

Pikemen and halberdiers, archers and lancers, once more to the assault! Are ye indeed cowards, that a pack of Flemish rabble can hold you at bay till you sink back exhausted and beaten? Up, Bracamonte and Ribeiras! Messar, with your musketeers! Salvado, with your bow-men! Up, ye mighty Spanish armies, who have seen the world at your feet! With Farnese himself to lead you, the hero of an hundred sieges, the queller of an hundred rebellions; are ye dolts and fools that you cannot crush a handful of undisciplined rabble?

And in close masses, shoulder to shoulder, they come!—exhausted, but still obstinate, and with the hope of all the rich booty to lure them on. Down the declivity of the moat—no longer deep, now that it is filled with dead! And up again to below the walls! The setting sun is behind them and gleams on their breastplates and their bonnets, and gilds the edges of the battlements with lines of flame.

And, up on the crumbling battlements, the defenders of Cambray—the clerks and shopkeepers and churls—hear the tramp of many feet, feel the earth quivering beneath this thunder of a last mighty assault. Sturdy, undaunted hands grip lance and pike tighter still, and intrepid hearts wait for this final charge, as they have waited for others to-day, and will go on waiting till the last of them has stilled its beating.

And Gilles de Crohin in their midst, invincible and cool, scours the battlements and the breach, the bastions and the ramparts— always there where he is needed most, where spirits want reviving or courage needs the impetus of praise. He knows as well as they do that gunpowder is running short, that arrows are few and thousands of weapons broken with usage: he knows, better than they do, that if de Balagny's troop tarries much longer all this heroic resistance will have been in vain.

So he keeps his own indomitable little army on the leash, husbanding precious lives and no less precious ammunition; keeping them back, well away from the parapets, lest the sight of the enemy down below lead them on to squander both. Thus, of all that goes on beneath the walls, of the nature of the attack or the chances of a surprise, the stout defenders can see nothing. Only Gilles, whilst scouring the lines, can see; for he has crawled on his hands and knees to the outermost edge of the crumbling parapet and has gazed down upon the Duke of Parma's hordes.

V

Now the Spanish halbertmen have reached the hither side of the moat. The breach is before them, tantalizingly open. The lancers are following over the improvised bridges, and behind them the musketeers are sending a volley of shot over their heads into the breach. It is all done with much noise and clash of steel and thundering artillery and cries of 'Long live King Philip!'—all to cover the disposing of scaling ladders against the walls.

The pikemen are executing this surprise attack, one in which they are adepts. The noisy onslaught, the roar of artillery, the throwing of dust in the eyes of wearied defenders; then the silent scaling of the walls, the rush upon the battlements, wholesale panic and slaughter.

Alexander Farnese hath oft employed these devices and hath never known them to fail. So the men throw down their pikes, carry pistols in their right hand and a short dagger-like sword between their teeth. They fix their ladders—five of them—and begin quite noiselessly to mount. Ten on each ladder, which makes fifty all told, and they the flower of the Duke of Parma's troops. Up they swarm like human ants striving to reach a hillock. Now the gunners have to cease firing, lest they hit those ladders with their human freight.

And while at the breach the men of Cambray make their last desperate stand, the first of the Spanish pikemen has reached the topmost rung of his ladder. The human ants have come to the top of their hillock. Already the foremost amongst them has begun to hoist himself up, with his hands clinging to the uneven masonry. The next second or two would have seen him with his leg over the parapet, and already a cry of triumph has risen to his lips, when suddenly, before his horror-stricken gaze, a man surges up, as if out of the ground, stands there before him for one second, which is as tense as it is terrifying. Then, with a mighty blow from some heavy weapon which he holds, he fells the pikeman down. The man loses his footing, gives a loud cry of horror and falls headlong some forty feet. In his fall he drags two or three of his comrades with him. But the ladder still stands, and on it the human ants, reinforced at once by others, resume their climb. Only for a minute—no more! The next, a pair of hands with titanic strength and a grip of iron seizes the ladder by the shafts, holds it for one brief, agonizing moment, and then hurls it down with the whole of its human freight into the depth below.

An awful cry rends the air, but is quickly drowned by the roar of cannon and musketry. It has been a mere incident. The Duke has not done more than mutter an oath in his beard. He is watching the four other ladders on which his human ants are climbing. But the oath dies on his lips—even he becomes silent in face of the appalling catastrophe which he sees. That man up there whom already he has learned to fear, that man in the tattered doublet and the ragged hose—he it is who has turned the tables on Farnese's best *ruse de guerre*. With lightning rapidity and wellnigh superhuman strength, he repeats his feat once more. Once more a scaling ladder bearing its precious human freight is hurled down into the depth. The man now appears like a Titan. Ye gods! or ye devils! which of you gave him that strength? Now he has reached the third ladder. Just perhaps one second too late, for the leading pikeman has already gained a foothold upon the battlements, stands there on guard to shield the ladder; for he has scented the danger which threatens him and his comrades. His pistol is raised even as Gilles approaches. The Duke of Parma feels as if his heart had stilled its beating. Another second, and that daring rebel would be laid low.

But Gilles too has seen the danger—the danger to himself and to the city which he is defending. No longer has he the time to seize the ladder as he has done before, no longer the chance of exerting that titanic strength which God hath lent him so that he might save Cambray. One second—it is the most precious one this threatened city hath yet known, for in it Fate is holding the balance, and the life of her defender is at stake. One second!

The Spanish pikemen are swarming up dangerously near now to the battlements. The next instant Gilles has picked up a huge piece of masonry from the ground, holds it for one moment with both hands above his head, then hurls it with all his might against the ladder. The foremost man is the first to fall. His pistol goes off in his hand with a loud report. Immediately below him the weight of the falling stone has made matchwood of the ladder and the men are hurled to their death, almost without uttering a groan. The Flemish halbertmen in the meanwhile have rushed up to the battlements; seeing Gilles' manoeuvre, they are eager to emulate it. There are two more ladders propped against the falling walls and their leader's strength must in truth be spent. And there are still more Spaniards to come, more of those numberless hordes, before whom a handful of untrained burghers are making their last and desperate stand.

Just then Gilles has paused in order to gaze once more into the far-away west. Already the gold of the sun has turned to rose and crimson, already the low-lying horizon appears aflame with the setting glow. But now upon the distant horizon line something appears to move, something more swift and sudden and vivid than the swaying willows by the river bank or the tall poplars nodding to the evening breeze. Flames of fire dart and flash, a myriad specks of dust gleam like lurid smoke and the earth shakes with the tramp of many horses' hoofs. Far away on the Bapaume road the forerunners of de Balagny's troops are seen silhouetted against the glowing sky.

Gilles has seen them. Aid has come at last. One more stupendous effort, one more superhuman exertion of will, and the day is won. He calls aloud to the depleted garrison, to that handful of men who, brave and undaunted, stand around him still.

'At them, burghers of Cambray! France comes to your aid! See her mighty army thundering down the road! Down with the Spaniard! This is the hour of your victory!'

As many times before, his resonant voice puts heart into them once again. Once again they grip halberds and lances with the determination born of hope. They rush to the battlements and with mighty hands hurl the Spanish scaling ladders from their walls, pick up bits of stone, fragments of granite and of iron, use these as missiles upon the heads of the attacking party below. The archers on one knee shoot with deadly precision. They have been given half a dozen arrows each—the last—and every one of them finds its mark.

Surprised and confounded by this recrudescence of energy, the Spaniards pause. An hundred of them lie dead or dying at the foot of the wall. Their ranks are broken; don Miguel tries to rally them. But he is hit by an arrow in the throat, ere he succeeds. De Landas is close by, runs to the rescue, tries to re-form the ranks, and sees Gilles de Crohin standing firm upon the battlements and hears his triumphant, encouraging cry:

'Citizens of Cambray, France has come to your aid!'

Confusion begins to wave her death-dealing wand. The halbertmen at the breach stand for full five minutes almost motionless under a hail of arrows and missiles, waiting for the word of command.

And on the Bapaume road, de Balagny and his troops are quickly drawing nigh. Already the white banner with the gold Fleur-de-Lys stands out clearly against the sky.

Parma has seen it, and cursed with savage fury. He is a great and mighty warrior and knows that the end has come. The day has brought failure and disgrace; duty now lies in saving a shred of honour and the remnants of a scattered army. He cannot understand how it has all happened, whence this French troop has come and by whose orders. He is superstitious and mystical and fears to see in this the vengeful finger of God. So he crosses himself and mutters a quick prayer, even as a volley of musketry fired insolently into the air, reverberates down the Bapaume road.

France is here with her great armies, her unconquered generals: Condé, Turenne, have come to the rescue. Parma's wearied troops cannot possibly stand the strain of fighting in the rear whilst still pushing home the attack in front. How numerous is the French advancing troop it is impossible to guess. They come with mighty clatter and many useless volleys of musketry, with jingling of harness and breastplates and clatter of hoofs upon the road. They come with a mighty shout of 'Valois! and Fleur-de-Lys!' They wave their banners and strike their lances and pikes together. They come! They come!

And the half-exhausted Spanish army hears and sees them too. The halbertmen pause and listen, the archers halt halfway across the moat, whilst all around the whisper goes from mouth to mouth:

"The French are on us! Sauve qui peut!"

Panic seizes the men. They turn and scurry back over the declivity of the moat. The stampede has commenced: first the cavalry, then the infantrymen, for the French are in the rear and legions of unseen spirits have come to the aid of Cambray.

The Duke of Parma now looks like a broken wreck of his former arrogant self. His fine accoutrements are torn, the trappings of his charger are in tatters, his beard has been singed with gunpowder, he has no hat, no cloak. Raging fury is in his husky voice as he shouts orders and counter-orders to men who no longer hear. He calls to his officers, alternately adjures and insults them. But the French troops draw nearer and nearer, and nothing but Death will stop those running Spanish soldiers now.

To right and left of the Bapaume road they run, leaving that road free for the passage of de Balagny's small troop. Out in the western sky, the sun is setting in a mantle of vivid crimson, which is like the colour of human blood. The last glow illumines the final disgrace of Parma's hitherto unconquered hordes. The cavalry is galloping back to the distant camp, with broken reins and stirrups hanging loose, steel bonnets awry, swords, lances, broken or wilfully thrown aside.

Behind them, the infantry, the archers, the pikemen, the halberdiers—all running and dragging their officers away with them in their flight.

Parma's unconquered army has ceased to be.

VI

Then it is that Gilles de Crohin stands once again on the very edge of the broken parapet and fronts the valiant men of Cambray, who have known how to conquer and how to die. The setting sun draws lines of glowing crimson round his massive figure. His clothes are now mere tattered rags; he is bleeding from several wounds; his face is almost unrecognizable, coal-black with grime and powder; but his eyes still sparkle with pride of victory.

'Citizens of Cambray, you are free!' he cries. 'Long live France! Long live the Flower o' the Lily!'

And down in the plain below, where the remnants of a disintegrated army are being slowly swallowed up by the gathering dusk, the Duke of Parma has paused for one moment before starting on his own headlong flight. He sees the man who has beaten his mighty armies, the man whose valour and indomitable will has inflicted untarnishable humiliation upon the glory of Spain. With a loud curse, he cries:

'Will no one rid me of that insolent rebel?'

De Landas is near him just then. He too had paused to look once again on the city which had been his home and which he had so basely betrayed, and once again on the man whom he hated with an intensity of passion which this day of glory and infamy had for ever rendered futile.

'If I do,' he retorts exultantly, 'what will your Highness give me?'

'Cambray and all it contains,' replies the Duke fiercely.

De Landas gives a cry of prescient triumph. A lancer is galloping by. The young man, with a swift, powerful gesture, seizes the horse by the bridle, forces it back on its haunches till it rears and throws its rider down into the mud. De Landas swings himself into the saddle, rides back to within a hundred paces of the city walls. Here confusion is still holding sway; belated runaways are darting aimlessly hither and thither like helpless sheep; the wounded and the maimed are making pitiable efforts to find a corner wherein to hide. The ground is littered with the dead and the dying, with abandoned cannon and spent arrows, with pikes and halberts and broken swords and lances.

De Landas halts, jumps down from his horse, looks about him for a crossbow and a quiver, and finds what he wants. Then he selects his position carefully, well under cover and just near enough to get a straight hit at the man whom he hates more than anything else in the world. Opportunity seems to favour him. Gilles is standing well forward on the broken parapet, his throat and chest are bare, his broad figure stands out clear-cut against the distant sky. He is gazing out towards the west, straight in the direction where de Landas is cowering—a small, unperceived unit in the inextricable confusion which reigns around.

He has found the place which best suits his purpose, has placed his stock in position and adjusted his arrow. Being a Spanish gentleman, he is well versed in the use of every weapon necessary for war. He takes careful aim, for he is in no hurry and is determined not to miss.

'Cambray and all it contains!' the Duke of Parma has promised him if he succeeds in his purpose.

One second, and the deed is done. The arrow has whizzed through the air. The next instant, Gilles de Crohin has thrown up his arms.

'Citizens of Cambray, wait for France!' he cries, and before any of his friends can get to him, he has given one turn and then fallen backwards into the depth below.

De Landas has already thrown down his crossbow, recaptured his horse and galloped back at break-neck speed in the wake of the flying army.   –

And even then the joy-bells of Cambray begin to ring their merry peal. Balagny's troops have entered the city through the open breach in her walls, whilst down there in the moat, on a pile of dying and dead, her defender and saviour lies with a murderous arrow in his breast.

VII

De Landas rides like one possessed away from the scene of his dastardly deed; nor does he draw rein till he has come up once more with the Duke of Parma.

'At any rate, we are rid of him,' he says curtly. 'And next time we attack, it will only be with an undisciplined mob that we shall have to deal.'

All around him the mighty army of Parma is melting like snow under the first kiss of a warm sun. Every man who hath limbs left wherewith to run, flies panic-stricken down the roads, across fields and rivulets and morasses, throwing down arms, overturning everything that comes in his way, not heeding the cries of the helpless and trampling on the dead.

Less than an hour has gone by since France's battle-cry first resounded on the Bapaume road, and now there is not one Spanish soldier left around the walls of Cambray, save the wounded and the slain. These lie about scattered everywhere, like pawns upon an abandoned chess-board. The moat below the breach is full of them. Maître Jehan le Bègue has not far to seek for the master and comrade whom he loves so dearly. He has seen him fall from the parapet, struck by the cowardly hand of an assassin in the very hour of victory. So, whilst de Balagny's chief captains enter Cambray in triumph, Jehan seeks in the moat for the friend whom he has lost.

He finds him lying there with de Landas' arrow still sticking in the wound in his breast. Maître Jehan lifts him as tenderly as a mother would lift her sick child, hoists him across his broad shoulders, and then slowly wends his way along the road back to La Fère.

CHAPTER XXV.
HOW CAMBRAY STARVED AND ENDURED

I

As for the rest, 'tis in the domain of history. Not only Maître Manuchet, but Le Carpentier in his splendid *History of Cambray*, has told us how the Duke of Parma's armies, demoralized by that day of disasters, took as many weeks to recuperate and to rally as did the valiant city to recover from her wounds.

Too late did Parma discover that he had been hoaxed, that the massed French troops, who had terrified his armies, consisted of a handful of men, who had been made to shout and to make much noise, so as to scare those whom they could not have hoped to conquer in open fight. It was too late now for the great general to retrieve his blunder; but not too late to prepare a fresh line of action, wait for reinforcements, reorganize the forces at his command and then to resume the siege of Cambray, with the added hope of inflicting material punishment upon the rebel city for the humiliation which she had caused him to endure.

The French armies were still very far away. Parma's numerous spies soon brought him news that Monsieur Duc d'Anjou, was only now busy in collecting and training a force which eventually might hope to vie in strength and equipment with the invincible Spanish troops, whilst the King of France would apparently have nothing to do with the affair and openly disapproved of his brother's intervention in the business of the Netherlands.

The moment therefore was all in favour of the Spanish commander; but even so he did not again try to take Cambray by storm. Many historians have averred that a nameless superstition was holding him back, that he had seen in the almost supernatural resistance of the city, the warning finger of God. Be that as it may, he became, after the day of disaster, content to invest the approaches to the French frontier, and after awhile, when his reinforcements had arrived, he formed with his armies a girdle around Cambray with a view to reducing her by starvation.

A less glorious victory mayhap, but a more assured one!

II

So Cambray starved and endured.

For four months her citizens waited, confident that the promised help from France would come in the end. They had hoped and trusted on that never-to-be-forgotten day four months ago when they covered themselves with glory, and their trust had not been misplaced. The masked stranger whom they had followed unto death and victory, the man who had rallied them and cheered them, who had shown them the example of intrepid valour and heroic self-sacrifice, had promised them help from France on that day, and that help had come just as he had promised. Now that he was gone from them, the burghers and the soldiers, the poor and the rich alike—aye! even the women and the children—would have felt themselves eternally disgraced if they had surrendered their city which he had so magnificently defended.

So they tightened their belts and starved, and waited with stoicism and patience for the hour of their deliverance.

And every evening when the setting sun threw a shaft of crimson light through the stately windows of Notre Dame, and the gathering dusk drew long shadows around the walls, the people of Cambray would meet on the Place d'Armes inside the citadel, and pray for the return of the hero who had fought for their liberty. Men and women with pale, gaunt faces, on which hunger and privations had already drawn indelible lines; men and women, some of whom had perhaps never before turned their thoughts to anything but material cares and material pleasures, flocked now to pray beneath the blue vault of heaven and to think of the man who had saved them from ruin and disgrace.

Nobody believed that he was dead; though many had seen him fall, they felt that he would return. God Himself had given Cambray her defender in the hour of her greatest peril: God had not merely given in order to take away again. Vague rumours were afloat that the mysterious hero was none other than the Duc d'Anjou, own brother of the King of France, who one day would be Sovereign Lord over all the United Provinces; but as to that, no one cared. He who was gone was the Defender of Cambray: as such, he was enshrined in thousands of hearts, as such he would return one day to receive the gratitude and the love of the people who worshipped him.

III

Le Carpentier draws a kindly veil over the sufferings of the unfortunate city. With pathetic exactitude, he tells us that a cow during the siege fetched as much as three hundred francs—an enormous sum these days—a sheep fifty francs, an egg forty sols and an ounce of salt eight sols; but he altogether omits to tell us what happened to the poor people, who had neither fifty francs nor yet forty sols to spend.

Maître Manuchet, on the other hand, assures us that at one time bread was entirely unobtainable and that rats and mice formed a part of the daily menu of the rich. He is more crude in his statements than Le Carpentier, and even lifts for our discreet gaze just one corner of that veil, wherewith history has chosen to conceal for ever the anguish of a suffering city. He shows us three distinct pictures, only sketched in in mere outline, but with boldness and an obvious regard for truth.

One of these pictures is of Jacqueline de Broyart, the wealthy heiress who shared with the departed hero the worship of the citizens of Cambray. Manuchet speaks of her as of an angel of charity, healing and soothing with words and hands and heart, as of a vision of paradise in the midst of a torturing hell—her courage and endurance a prop for drooping spirits; her voice a sweet, insistent sound above the cries of pain, the curses and the groans. Wide-eyed and pale, but with a cheering smile upon her lips, she flits through the deserted streets of Cambray, bringing the solace of her presence, the help that can be given, the food that can be shared, to many a suffering home.

Of the man who hath possession of her heart, she never speaks with those in authority; but when in a humble home there is talk of the hero who has gone and of his probable return, she listens in silence, and when conjectures fly around her as to his identity, she even tries to smile. But in her heart she knows that her knight—the man whom the people worship—will never come back. France will send troops and aid and protection anon; a puissant Prince will enter Cambray mayhap at the head of his troops and be acclaimed as the saviour of Cambray. She would no doubt in the fullness of time plight her troth to that man, and the people would be told that this was indeed the Duc d'Anjou et d'Alençon, who had once before stood upon the ramparts of Cambray and shouted his defiant cry: 'À moi, citizens; and let the body of each one of you here be a living rampart for the defence of your homes!'

But she would know that the man who spoke those inspiring words had gone from her for ever. Who he was, where he came from, what had brought him to Cambray under a disguise and an assumed name, she would perhaps never know. Nor did she care. He was the man she loved: the man whose passionate ardour had thrilled her to the soul, whose touch had been as magic, whose voice had been perfect music set in perfect time. He was the man she loved — her knight. Throughout that day upon the ramparts she had seen him undaunted, intrepid, unconquered — rallying those who quaked, cheering those who needed help, regardless of danger, devoted even unto death. So what cared she what was his name? Whoever he was, he was worthy of her love.

IV

The second picture which the historian shows us is more dispiriting and more grim. It is a picture of Cambray in the last days of July. The Spanish armies have invested the city completely for over eight weeks, and Cambray has been thrown entirely on her own resources and the activities of a few bold spirits for the barest necessities of life. Starvation — grim and unrelenting — is taking her toll of the exhausted population; disease begins to haunt the abodes of squalor and of misery.

France has promised aid and France still tarries.

Mayhap France has forgotten long ago.

In Cambray now a vast silence reigns — the silence of impending doom. The streets are deserted during the day, the church bells are silent. Only at evening, in the gloom, weird and melancholy sounds fill the air, groans and husky voices, and at times the wild shriek of some demented brain.

Cambray has fought for her liberty; now she is enduring for it—and enduring it with a fortitude and determination, which is one Of the most glorious entries in the book of the recording angel. Every morning at dawn the heralds of the Spanish commander mount the redoubt on the Bapaume road, and with a loud flourish of brass trumpets they demand in the name of His Majesty the King of Spain the surrender of the rebel city. And every day the summons is answered by a grim and defiant silence. After which, Cambray settles down to another day of suffering.

The city fathers have worked wonders in organization. From the first, the distribution of accumulated provisions has been systematic and rigidly fair. But those distributions, from being scanty have become wholly insufficient, and lives that before flickered feebly, have gone out altogether, while others continue a mere struggle for existence, which would be degrading were its object not so sublime.

Cambray will not surrender! She would sooner starve and rot and be consumed by fire, but with her integrity whole, her courage undoubted, the honour of her women unsullied. Disease may haunt her streets, famine knock at every door; but at least while her citizens have one spark of life left in their bodies, while their emaciated hands have a vestige of power wherewith to grasp a musket, no Spanish soldier shall defile her pavements, no Spanish commander work his tyrannical will with her.

Cambray will not surrender! She believes in her defender and her saviour!—in his words that France will presently come with invincible might and powerful armies, when all her sufferings will be turned to relief and to joy. And every evening when lights are put out and darkness settles down upon the stricken city, wrapping under her beneficent mantle all the misery, the terrors and the heroism, men and women lay themselves down to their broken rest with a last murmur of hope, a last invocation to God for the return of the hero in whom lies their trust.

V

And in the Town Hall the city fathers sit in Council, with Messire de Balagny there, and Monseigneur d'Inchy presiding. They, too, appear grimly resolved to endure and to hold out; the fire of patriotism and of enthusiasm burns in their hearts, as it does in the heart of every burgher, noble or churl in the city. But, side by side with enthusiasm, stalks the grim shadow of prescience—knowledge of the resources which go, diminishing bit by bit, until the inevitable hour when hands and mouths will still be stretched out for food and there will be nothing left to give.

Even now, it is less than bare subsistence which can be doled out day by day; and in more than one face assembled this day around the Council Board, there is limned the grim line of nascent despair.

It is only d'Inchy who has not lost one particle of his faith, one particle of self-confidence and of belief in ultimate triumph.

'If ye begin to doubt,' he exclaims with tragic directness, 'how will ye infuse trust in the hearts of your people?'

The Chief Magistrate shakes his head; the Provosts are silent. More than one man wipes a surreptitious tear.

'We must give the people something to hearten them,' has been the persistent call from those in authority.

De Balagny interposes:

'Our spies have succeeded in evading the Spanish lines more than once. One of them returned yesterday from La Fère. He says the Duc d'Anjou is wellnigh ready. The next month should see the end of our miseries.'

'A month!' sighs the Chief Magistrate. 'The people cannot hold out another month. They are on the verge of despair.'

'They begin to murmur,' adds one of the Provosts glumly.

'And some demand that we surrender the city,' concludes de Lalain.

'Surrender the city!' exclaimed d'Inchy vehemently. 'Never!'

'Then can Monseigneur suggest something?' riposts the Chief Magistrate dryly, 'that will restore confidence to a starving population?'

'The help from France almost within sight,' urges Monseigneur.

The Provosts shrug their shoulders.

'So long delayed,' one of them says. 'The people have ceased to believe in it.'

'Many declare the Duke is dead,' urges another.

'But ye know better than that, Messires,' retorts d'Inchy sternly.

Again one or two of the older men shrug their shoulders.

'I saw him fall from the ramparts,' asserts one.

'He was struck full in the breast by an arrow,' says another, 'shot by an unseen hand—some abominable assassin. His Highness gave one turn and fell into the moat below.'

'And was immediately found and picked up by some of my men,' retorts de Balagny hotly. 'Mine oath on it! Our spies have seen him—spoken with him. The Duc d'Anjou is alive and on his way to Cambray. I'd stake on it the salvation of my soul!'

The others sigh, some of them dubiously, others with renewed hope. From their talk we gather that not one of them has any doubt in his mind as to the identity of the brave defender of Cambray. Nothing had in truth happened to shake their faith in him, and de Balagny had said nothing to shake that faith. On that fateful day in April they had been convened to witness the betrothal of Madame Jacqueline de Broyart to *Monsieur* Duc d'Anjou, had been presented to His Highness and kissed his hands. Then suddenly all had been confusion—the panic, the surprise attack, the runaway soldiers, and finally the one man who rallied every quaking spirit and defended the city with heart and mind, with counsel and strength of arm, until he fell by an unseen assassin's hand: he, the Duc d'Anjou, of the princely House of France—the future Sovereign Lord of a United Netherlands.

For awhile there is absolute stillness in the Council room. No one speaks; hardly does any one stir. Only the massive clock over the monumental hearth ticks out every succeeding second with relentless monotony. Monseigneur is buried in thought. The others wait, respectfully silent. Then suddenly d'Inchy looks up and gazes determinedly on the faces round him.

'Madame Jacqueline must help us,' he says firmly.

'Madame Jacqueline?' the Chief Magistrate exclaims. 'How?'

'On the Place d'Armes—one evening—during the intercession,' Monseigneur goes on, speaking rapidly and with unhesitating resolve. 'She will make a solemn declaration before the assembled people—plight her troth to the Duc d'Anjou, who, though still absent, has sent her a token of his immediate arrival.'

'Sent her a token?' most of them murmur, astonished. And even de Balagny frowns in puzzlement.

'Yes,' rejoins d'Inchy impatiently. 'Cannot you see? You say the people no longer believe in the coming of His Highness. Our spies and the news they bring no longer carry weight. But if we say that the Duke hath sent a token....'

'I understand,' murmurs the Chief Magistrate, and the others nod in comprehension.

'Madame Jacqueline will not demur,' d'Inchy continues insistently. 'She will accept the assurance from me that one of our spies has come in contact with *Monsieur* and brought back a fresh token of his promise to her ... a ring, for instance. We have many valuable ones in our city treasury. One of them will serve our purpose.' Then, as the city dignitaries are still silent, somewhat perturbed at all that sophistry — ''Tis for the sake of our city, Messires,' d'Inchy urges with a note of pleading in his usually commanding voice. 'A little deception, when so much good may come of it! what is it? Surely you can reconcile it with your consciences!'

To him the matter seems trivial. One deception more or less — hitherto the path had been so easy. He frowns, seeing that this tiresome pack of old men hesitate, when to acquiesce might even now save their city. Anyhow, he is the governor. His word is law. For the nonce he chooses to argue and to persuade, but anon he commands.

The city dignitaries—the old men for the most part, and with impaired health after weeks of privation—have but little real resistance in them. D'Inchy was always a man of arbitrary will and persuasive eloquence. De Balagny is soon won over. He ranges himself on the side of the governor, and helps in the work of demolishing the bulwark of the Magistrate's opposition. The latter yields—reluctantly, perhaps— but still he yields. After all, there is no harm whatever in the deception. No one could possibly suffer in consequence. Madame Jacqueline has always expressed herself ready to marry the Duc d'Anjou—a hero and a doughty knight, if ever there was one!—and in any case it were an inestimable boon to put fresh heart into the starving population.

So gradually the others yield, and Monseigneur is satisfied. He elaborates his plan, his mind full of details to make the result more sure. A public ceremony: Jacqueline once more publicly betrothed to the Duc d'Anjou—dedicated, in fact, like a worshipper to some patron saint. Then the people made to realize that the Duc d'Anjou is already known to them as their hero, their defender and their saviour; that he is not dead, but coming back to them very soon at the head of his armies this time, to save them once for all from the Spaniards, whilst he remains with them to the end of his days as their chosen Sovereign Lord and King.

Monseigneur has worked himself up to a high pitch of enthusiasm, carries the others with him now, until they cast aside all foreboding and gloom and hope springs afresh in their hearts.

VI

Thus we see the third and last picture which Enguerrand de Manuchet shows us of Cambray in her agony. It is a picture that is even more vivid than the others, more alive in the intensity of its pathos. We see inside the citadel on the last day of July, 1581. And of all the episodes connected with the memorable siege of Cambray and with its heroic defence, not one perhaps is more moving than that of this huge concourse of people—men, women and tiny children—assembled here and for such a purpose, under the blue dome of the sky.

The grim walls of the ancient castle around them are hung with worn and tattered flags; they are like the interior of a church, decked out with all the solemnity of a marriage ceremony and all the pathos of a De Profundis.

Jacqueline, indifferent to everything save to the welfare of the city, has accepted without resistance or doubt Monseigneur's story of the spy, the Duc d'Anjou and the token. The ring, borrowed for the occasion from the city treasury, she has taken without any misgiving, as coming straight from the man whom she is destined to marry. She had promised long ago to wed *Monsieur* Duc d'Anjou, because the weal of her country was, it seems, wrapped up in that union. All those who worked for the glorious future of Flanders had assured her that much of it depended in her acquiescence to this alliance with France.

With her heart for ever buried beneath the ramparts of Cambray, side by side with the gallant knight who had given his life for the beloved city, she cared little, if at all, what became of her. The Duc d'Anjou or another—what did it matter?—but preferably the Duc d'Anjou if her country's welfare demands that he should be the man.

No wonder that this last picture stirs even the heart of the dry-as-dust old historian to enthusiasm. Noble and churl, burghers and dignitaries and soldiers, toilers and ragamuffins, all are there—those who can walk or stand or crawl. Those who are hale drag or support those that are sick, bring tattered mattresses along or a litter of straw for them to lie on. But they all come to see a woman make a solemn profession of faith in the man who is to bring deliverance to the agonizing city.

They come in their thousands; but thousands more are unable to find room upon the Place or within the Citadel. Even so, they line the streets all the way to the Archiepiscopal Palace, whilst all those who are so privileged watch Madame Jacqueline's progress through the streets from their windows or their balconies. Fortunately the day has been brilliantly fine ever since morning, and the sun shines radiant upon this one day which is almost a happy one.

For many hours before that fixed for the ceremony, the streets seethe with the crowd—a pathetic crowd, in truth: gaunt, feeble, weary, in tattered clothes, some scarce able to drag themselves along, others sick and emaciated, clinging to the posts at the corners of the streets, just to get one peep at what has come to be regarded as a tangible ray of hope. A silent, moveless crowd, whose husky voice has scarce a cheer in it; as Jacqueline passes by, walking between Monseigneur the governor and the Chief Magistrate, bare arms are waved here and there, in a feeble attempt at jubilation. But there is no music, no beating of drums or waving of banners; there is no alms-giving, no largesse! All that the rich and the prosperous possessed in the past has been shared and distributed long ago.

In spite of the brilliant weather, the scene is dark and dreary. The weary, begrimed faces do not respond to the joyous kiss of the sun; the smile of hope has not the power to dry every tear.

VII

And now Jacqueline stands, like a white Madonna lily, in the centre of the Place d'Armes. Monseigneur the governor is beside her and around her are grouped the high dignitaries of the city, standing or sitting upon low velvet-covered stools. The Chief Magistrate and Messire de Balagny are in the forefront, and behind them are the members of the States General and of the Town, the Provosts and Captains of the City Guard. The picture is sombre still, despite the banners of the guilds and the flags of various provinces which hang along the walls of the Citadel. The russets and browns, the blacks and dull reds, absorb the evening light without throwing back any golden reflections. The shadows are long and dense.

The white satin of Jacqueline's gown is the one bright note of colour against the dull and drab background; its stiff folds gleam with honey-coloured lights in the slowly sinking sun. She has allowed old Nicolle to deck her out in all her finery, the gown which she wore on that night—oh! so very long ago—at the banquet, the one with the pale green underdress which Messire declared made her look so like a lily; the pearls in her hair; the velvet shoes on her feet.

'I will plight my troth publicly to the Defender of Cambray!' she had said to her guardian, when Monseigneur had first spoken of the proposed ceremony.

'To Monsieur Duc d'Anjou et d'Alençon, my child,' Monseigneur had insisted, and frowned slightly at what he called his ward's romantic fancies.

''Tis to the Defender of Cambray that I will dedicate my faith,' she had continued obstinately.

'Let the child be!' de Lalain had interposed, seeing that d'Inchy was about to lose his temper. 'After all, what does it matter, seeing that the Defender of Cambray and Monsieur Duc d'Anjou are one and the same?'

D'Inchy gave in. It did not really matter. If Jacqueline still harboured a doubt as to the identity of the masked stranger, it would soon be dispelled when Monsieur entered Cambray and came to claim her openly. Women were apt to have strange fancies; and this one, on Jacqueline's part, was harmless enough.

In any case, she appeared satisfied, and henceforth was quite submissive. In the midst of her sorrow, she felt a sweet, sad consolation in the thought that she would publicly plight her troth to the man whom she loved, proclaim before the whole world—her world that is, the only one that mattered—that she was for ever affianced to the brave man who had given his life, that Cambray might be saved.

In an inward vision she could see him still, as she saw him on that day upon the ramparts, with the April sun gilding his close-cropped head, with the light of enthusiasm dancing in his eyes, his arms bare, his clothes torn, his vibrant voice resounding from wall to wall and from bastion to bastion, till something of his own fire was communicated to all those who fought under his command.

To Jacqueline he was still so marvellously, so powerfully alive, even though his body lay stark and still at the foot of those walls which he had so bravely defended. He seemed to be smiling down on her from the clear blue of the sky, to nod at her with those banners which he had helped to keep unsullied before the foe. She heard his voice through the lengthy perorations of Monseigneur, the murmured approbation of the Provosts, through the cheers of the people. She felt his presence now as she had felt it through the past four weary months, while Cambray suffered and starved, and bore starvation and misery with that fortitude which he had infused into her.

And while Monseigneur the governor spoke his preliminary harangue, to which the people listened in silence, she stood firm and ready to speak the words which, in accordance with the quaint and ancient Flemish custom, would betroth her irrevocably to the man chosen for her by her guardians, even though he happened to be absent at the moment. For her, those words, the solemn act, would only register the vow which she had made long ago, the vow which bound her soul for ever to the hero who had gone.

'It is my purpose,' Monseigneur said solemnly, 'to plight this my lawful ward, Jacqueline, Dame de Broyart et de Morchipont, Duchesse et Princesse de Ramèse, d'Espienne et de Wargny, unto His Royal Highness, Hercule François de Valois, Duc d'Alençon et d'Anjou, and I hereby desire to ask the members of my Council to give their consent to this decree.'

And the Chief Magistrate, speaking in the name of the States General and of the City and Provincial Council, then gave answer:

'Before acceding to your request, Monseigneur, we demand to know whether Hercule François of Valois, Duc d'Alençon et d'Anjou, is an honourable man, and possessed of sufficient goods to ensure that Madame Jacqueline de Broyart et de Morchipont, Duchesse et Princesse de Ramèse, d'Espienne et de Wargny, continue to live as she hath done hitherto and in a manner befitting her rank.'

Whereupon Messire de Balagny made reply:

'His Royal Highness is a prince of the House of France; he defended our city in the hour of her gravest peril and saved her from destruction and from the fury of our Spanish foe. He is in every way worthy to have our ward for wife.'

'Wherefore, most honourable seigneurs,' continued the governor solemnly, 'I do desire by your favour to grant the hand of Madame Jacqueline to him in marriage.'

'This request we would grant you, Monseigneur,' rejoined the Chief Magistrate, 'but would ask you first how it comes that the bridegroom himself is not here to claim his bride.'

'The bridegroom,' replied d'Inchy, slowly and loudly, so that his voice could be heard, clear and distinct, in every corner of the great courtyard. 'The bridegroom is even at this hour within sight of our beleaguered city. He is at the head of his armies and only waits a favourable opportunity for demanding from the Spanish commander that the latter do give him battle. The bridegroom, I say, hath sent us a token of his goodwill and an assurance that he will not tarry. He hath asked that Madame Jacqueline do plight her troth to him before the assembled people of Cambray, so that they may know that he is true and faithful unto them and take heart of courage against his speedy coming for their deliverance.'

A murmur—it could not be called a cheer, for voices were hoarse and spent—went the round of the crowd. There were nods of approval; and a gleam of hope, almost of joy, lit up many a wan face and many a sunken eye. After so many deceptions, so much weary waiting and hope deferred, this was at least something tangible, something to cling to, whilst battling against the demons of hunger and disease which so insidiously called for surrender.

The Chief Magistrate, who together with Monseigneur had been chiefly instrumental in engineering the present situation, waited for a moment or two, giving time for the governor's cheering words to soak well into the minds of the people. He was a tall, venerable-looking old burgher, with a white beard clipped close to his long, thin face, and a black velvet bonnet, now faded to a greenish hue by exposure to all weathers, set upon his scanty hair. He drew up his bent shoulders and threw back his head with a gesture expressive both of confidence and of determination, and he allowed his deep-set eyes beneath their bushy brows to wander over the populace, as if to say: 'See how right I was to bid you hope! Here you have an actual proof that the end of your sufferings is in sight, that the deliverance for which you pray is already at your gate!' After which, he turned once again to d'Inchy and said loftily:

'Monseigneur the governor! the people of Cambray here assembled have heard with profound respect the declaration which you have deigned to make, as to the intentions of His Royal Highness the Duc d'Anjou et d'Alençon. On their behalf and on the behalf of the States of this Town and Province whom I represent, I hereby affirm most solemnly that we have the weal of our city at heart; that we will resist the armies of the Duke of Parma with the whole might of our arms and our will, awaiting tranquilly and with fortitude the hour of our deliverance. We trust and believe that he who defended us so valiantly four months ago will soon return to us, and rid us once and for ever from the menace of our foe.'

Once more a murmur of approval went round the Place. Wearied, aching heads nodded approval; firm lips, thin and pale, were set with a recrudescence of energy. All the stoicism of this heroic race was expressed in their simple acceptance of this fresh term of endurance imposed upon them, in their willingness to hope on again, to wait and to submit, and in their mute adhesion to the profession of faith loudly proclaimed by their Chief dignitary: 'awaiting tranquilly and with fortitude the hour of our deliverance.'

'And now, Monseigneur,' concluded the Magistrate impressively, 'in the name of your Council, I herewith make acceptance of His Royal Highness, Hercule François of Valois, Duc d'Alençon et d'Anjou, prince of the House of France, defender and saviour of Cambray, to be the future husband and guardian of Madame Jacqueline de Broyart, our ward.'

Monseigneur the governor now drew his sword, held it upright and placed on it a hat and round his arm a mantle; then he took the ring, which had been borrowed from the city treasury for the occasion, and hung it on a projecting ornament of his sword-hilt. After which he said, with great solemnity:

'With these emblems I hereby entrust to His Royal Highness Hercule François de Valois, Duc d'Anjou et d'Alençon, prince of the House of France, the defender and saviour of Cambray in the hour of her gravest peril, the custody of my ward Jacqueline, Dame de Broyart et de Morchipont, Duchesse et Princesse de Ramèse, d'Espienne et de Wargny; and as I have been her faithful custodian in the past, so do I desire him to become her guardian and protector henceforth, taking charge of her worldly possessions and duly administering them faithfully and loyally.'

After which he lowered his sword, put down the hat and the mantle and presented the ring to Jacqueline, together with seven gloves, saying the while:

'Jacqueline, take these in exchange for the emblems of marital authority which I herewith hold for and on behalf of your future lord, and in the presence of all the people of Cambray here assembled, I demand that you do plight your troth to him and that you swear to be true and faithful unto him, to love and cherish him with your heart and your body, to obey and serve him loyally as his wife and helpmate, until death.'

Jacqueline, by all the canons of this quaint custom, should have held the ring and the gloves in her left hand and taken the solemn oath with her right raised above her head. Instead of which, Manuchet assures us that she laid down the ring and the gloves upon the chair nearest to her, and clasped her two hands together as if in prayer. She raised her small head and looked out upon the sky — there where the setting sun hid its glory behind a filmy veil of rose-tinted clouds.

'In the name of the living God who made me,' she said, with solemn and earnest fervour, 'I do hereby plight my troth to my lord, the noble and puissant hero who defended Cambray in the hour of her gravest peril, who saved her from destruction and taught her citizens how to conquer and to endure, and I swear upon my life and upon my every hope of salvation that I will be true and faithful unto him, that I will love and cherish him with my heart and with my body and will serve him loyally and unswervingly now and alway until our souls meet in the presence of God.'

A great hush had fallen on the vast courtyard while Jacqueline de Broyart made her profession of faith; nor did a sound mar the perfect stillness which lay over the heavy-laden city. This was a time of great silences—silence of sorrow, of anxiety and pain. The women frankly gave way to tears; but they were tears that fell soundlessly from hollow eyes. The men did not weep—they just set their teeth, and culled in that one woman's fervour fresh power for their own endurance.

The city dignitaries crowded round Jacqueline, kissing and pressing her hands. Monseigneur the governor was looking greatly relieved. From the tower of Notre Dame, the bells set forth a joyous peal—the first that had been heard for many months. And that peal was presently taken up, first by one church tower and then another, from St. Waast to St. Martin, Ste. Croix to St. Géry. The happy sound echoed and reverberated along the city walls, broke with its insidious melody the gloomy silence which had lain over the streets like a pall.

Far away in the west the sun was slowly sinking in a haze of translucent crimson, and tipped every church spire, every bastion and redoubt with rose and orange and gold. For the space of a few more minutes the citadel with its breathless and fervid crowd, with its waving banners and grey walls, was suffused as with a flush of life and hope. Then the shadows lengthened—longer and longer they grew, deeper and more dense, like great, drab arms that enfold and conceal and smother. Slowly the crimson glow faded out of the sky.

Now the group in the centre appeared only like a sombre mass of dull and lifeless colours; Jacqueline's white satin gown took on a leaden hue; the brilliance of the sky had become like a presage of storm. The women shivered beneath their ragged kerchiefs; some of the children started to cry.

Then, one by one, the crowd began to disperse. Walking, halting, crawling, they wended their way back to their dreary homes,—there to wait again, to suffer and to endure; there to conceal all the heroism of this patient resignation, all the stoicism of a race which no power could conquer, no tyranny force into submission.

And once more silence descended on the hapless city, and the mantle of night lay mercifully upon her grievous wounds.

VIII

And far away in the Spanish camps, the soldiers and their captains marvelled how joy-bells could be ringing in a city which was in the throes of her death agony. But the Duke of Parma knew what it meant, as did the members of his staff—del Fuente, his second in command, de Salvado, Bracamonte, de Landas and the others. More than one of their wily spies had succeeded before now in swimming across the Schelde and in scaling the tumble-down walls of the heroic city, and had brought back the news of what was doing in there, in the midst of a starving and obstinate population.

'The public betrothal to a fickle Prince who will never come,' said the Duke grimly, between his teeth. 'At any rate, not before we have worked our will with those mulish rebels.'

'We could take their pestilent town by storm to-morrow,' remarked de Landas, with a note of fierce hatred in his voice, 'if your Highness would but give the order.'

'Bah!' retorted the Duke. 'Let them rot! Why should we waste valuable lives and precious powder, when the next few days must see the final surrender of that peccant rat-hole?'

He gave a coarse laugh and shrugged his shoulders.

'I believe,' he said to de Landas, 'that I once promised you Cambray and all that it contains—what?'

'For ridding your Highness of the abominable rebel who organized the defence last April,' assented de Landas. 'Yes! Cambray and all that it contains was to be my reward.'

'You killed the miscreant, I believe?'

'I shot him through the heart. He lies rotting now beneath the walls.'

'Well!' riposted the Duke. 'You earned your reward easily enough. There will be plenty left in Cambray, even after I have had my first pick of its treasures.'

De Landas made no protest. It would have been not only useless, but also impolitic to remind His Highness that, at the moment when he offered Cambray and all its contents to the man who would rid him of a valiant foe, he had made no proviso that he himself should fill his pockets first. There was no honour among these thieves and no probity in these savage tyrants—brute beasts, most of them, who destroyed and outraged whatever resisted their might. So de Landas held his tongue; for even so, he was not dissatisfied. The Duke, being rid of the rebel whom he feared, might easily have repudiated the ignoble bargain in its entirety, and de Landas would have had no redress.

As it was, there was always Jacqueline. The Spanish commanders were wont to make short shrift of Flemish heiresses who happened to be in a city which they entered as conquerors. By decree of His Highness, Jacqueline de Broyart would certainly be allocated to him—de Landas—if he chose to claim her. Of a truth, she was still well worth having—more so than ever, perhaps; for her spirit now would be chastened by bodily privations, broken by humiliation at the hands of the faithless Valois and by the death of her mysterious lover.

'So long as the heiress is there for me,' he said carelessly to the Duke, 'I am satisfied to let every other treasure go.'

'Oh! you shall have the heiress,' riposted His Highness hilariously. 'Rumour hath described her as passing fair. You lucky devil! Methinks you were even betrothed to her once.'

'Oh! long ago, your Highness. Since then the oily promises of the Duc d'Anjou have helped to erase my image from the tablets of Madame Jacqueline's heart.'

'Then she'll be all the more ready to fall back into your arms, now that she has discovered the value of a Valois prince's faith.'

After which pronouncement, the Duke of Parma dismissed the matter from his mind and turned his attention to the table, richly spread with every kind of delicacy, which had been laid for him in his tent. He invited the gentlemen of his staff to sit, and as he dug his fork into the nearest succulent dish, he said complacently:

'Those pestiferous rebels out there cannot have as much as a mouse between the lot of them, to fill their Flemish paunches. Messeigneurs, here is to Cambray!' he added, as he lifted his silver goblet filled to the brim with Rhenish wine. 'To Cambray, when we march through her streets, ransack her houses and share her gold! To Cambray, and the pretty Flemish wenches, if so be they have an ounce of flesh left upon their bones! To de Landas' buxom heiress and his forthcoming marriage with her! To you all, and the spoils which these many months of weary waiting will help you to enjoy! To Cambray, all ye gallant seigneurs!'

His lusty toast was greeted with loud laughter. Metal goblets clicked one against the other, every one drank to the downfall of the rebellious city. De Landas accepted the jocose congratulations of his boon-companions. He, too, raised his goblet aloft, and having shouted: 'To Jacqueline!' drained it to its last drop.

But when he set the goblet down, his hand was shaking perceptibly. Cain-like, he had seen a vision of the man whom he had so foully murdered. Accidentally he knocked over a bottle of red Burgundy, which stood on the table close by, and the linen cloth all around him was spread over with a dark crimson stain, which to the assassin appeared like the colour of blood.

CHAPTER XXVI.
WHAT VALUE A VALOIS PRINCE
SET UPON HIS WORD

I

To Gilles de Crohin, when he woke to consciousness one morning in his former lodging in La Fère, the whole of the past few weeks appeared indeed like a long dream.

Cambray—Jacqueline—his mask—his deceit—that last day upon the ramparts—were they not all the creations of his fevered brain? Surely a whole lifetime could not be crowded into so short a space of time. No man could have lived through so much, loved so passionately, have lost and fought and conquered so strenuously, all within a few weeks.

And when, after many days' enforced rest and a good deal of attention from a skilful leech backed by Maître Jehan's unwavering care, he was once more on his feet and was able to relate to Madame la Reyne de Navarre the many vicissitudes of his perilous adventure, it seemed to him as if he were recounting to a child, fairy tales and dream stories which had never been.

It was only at evening, when he wandered round the little Dutch garden at the back of the house where he lodged, that Jacqueline came to him, aglow with life—a living, breathing, exquisite reality. For the Madonna lilies were all abloom in that garden just then: tall, stately white lilies, which bordered one of the narrow paths. They had slender, pale green stems, their fragrance filled the evening air and the soft breeze stirred their delicate crowns. Then it would seem to Gilles as if his Jacqueline were walking down the path beside him, that the breeze blew the tendrils of her fair hair against his nostrils and that her voice filled his ear with its sweet, melodious sound. A big heartache would make the rough soldier sigh with longing then. Unseen by any one, alone with his thoughts of her, he would stretch out his arms to that tantalizing vision which seemed so real and was yet so far, so very far away.

Madame la Reyne would at times chaff him about his moodiness, and he himself was ready to laugh aloud at his own folly. What right had he—the uncouth soldier of fortune, the homeless adventurer—to think of the great and noble lady, who was as far removed from him as were the stars? What right indeed? Even though Marguerite de Navarre, lavish in her gratitude, had already showered honours and wealth upon the man who had served her so faithfully.

'Monseigneur le Prince de Froidmont,' she had said to him with solemn earnestness, on the day when first she had realized how completely he had worked out her own schemes; 'the lands of Froide Monte, which are some of the richest in Acquitaine, were a part of my dowry when I married. They are yours now, as they once were the property of your forebears. They are yours, with their forests, their streams and their castles. Take them as a poor token of my lifelong gratitude.' And when Gilles demurred, half-indifferent even to so princely a gift, she added with her habitual impatience: 'Pardieu, Messire, why should you be too proud to accept a gift from me, seeing that I was not too proud to ask so signal a service of you?'

Even so, that gift—so graciously offered, so welcome to the man's pride of ancestry—had but little value in his sight, since he could not do with it the one thing that mattered, which was to lay it at Jacqueline's feet.

'Do not look so morose, Messire,' Marguerite de Navarre said teasingly. 'I vow that you have left your heart captive in Cambray.' Then as Gilles, after this straight hit, remained silent and absorbed, she added gaily: 'Have no fear, Messire! When *Monsieur* is Lord of the Netherlands, he will force the lady of your choice into granting you her favours. Remember!' she said more seriously, 'that the Prince de Froidmont can now aspire to the hand of the richest and most exalted lady in the land.'

'Monseigneur is still far from being Lord of the Netherlands,' Gilles said dryly, chiefly with a view to inducing a fresh train of thought in the royal lady's mind.

Marguerite shrugged her pretty shoulders.

'He still procrastinates,' she admitted. 'He should be at La Fère by now, with five thousand troops. Everything was ready when I left Paris.'

'He has found something else to distract him,' rejoined Gilles, with unconscious bitterness. 'Perhaps Mme. de Marquette has resumed her sway over him, the while Cambray waits and starves.'

'Chien sabe?' allowed Madame la Reyne with an impatient sigh.

II

The while Cambray waits and starves! That was indeed the deathly sting which poisoned Gilles de Crohin's very life during those four dreary months, while *Monsieur* Duc d'Anjou was ostensibly making preparations for his expedition for the relief of the beleaguered city. Ostensibly in truth, for very soon his fond sister had to realize that, now as always, that fickle brother of hers was playing his favourite game of procrastination and faithlessness. With him, in fact, faithlessness had become an obsession. It seemed as if he could not act or think straight, as if he could not keep his word. Now, while he was supposed to recruit his troops, to consult with his officers, to provide for engines and munitions of war, he actually deputed his long-suffering and still faithful friend, Gilles de Crohin, to do the work for him. His own thoughts had once more turned to a possible marriage—not with Jacqueline de Broyart, to whom he was bound by every conceivable tie of honour and of loyalty—but with Elizabeth of England, whom he coveted because of her wealth, and the power which so brilliant an alliance would place in his hands.

But of these thoughts he did not dare to speak even to the adoring sister, who most certainly would have turned her back on him for ever had she known that he harboured such dishonourable projects. He did not dare to speak of them even to Gilles, for he felt that this would strain his friend's loyalty to breaking point. He entered outwardly into the spirit of the proposed expedition with all the zest which he could muster, but the moment he was no longer under Marguerite de Navarre's own eyes he did not lift another finger in its organization.

'Turenne and la Voute are quite capable of going to the relief of Cambray without me,' he said to Gilles with a yawn and a lazy stretch of his long, loose limbs. 'I have never been counted a good commander, and Parma is always a difficult problem to tackle. Let Turenne go, I say. My brother Henri lauds him as the greatest general of the day, and the rogue hath fought on the Spanish side before now, so he hath all their tricks at his fingers' ends.'

Monsieur was in Paris then, and Marguerite de Navarre, wellnigh distraught, had entreated Gilles to stir him into immediate activity.

'Cambray will fall before that indolent brother of mine gets there, Messire,' she had pleaded, with tears of impotent anger in her eyes.

Gilles had gone. He needed no goad even for so distasteful a task. 'Cambray might fall!' The thought drove him into a fever, from which he could find no solace save in breathless activity. He found *Monsieur* in his Palace in Paris, surrounded by the usual crowd of effeminate youngsters and idle women, decked out in new-fangled, impossible clothes, the creations of his own fancy, indolent, vicious, incorrigible. Just now, when Gilles had come to speak to him of matters that meant life or death, honour or shame, the future welfare or downfall of a nation, he was lounging in a huge armchair, his feet resting on a pile of cushions. He was wearing one of his favourite satin suits, with slashed doublet all covered with tags and ribbons; he had gold earrings in his ears and was nursing a litter of tiny hairless puppies, whom he was teasing with the elaborate insignia of the Order of the Holy Ghost, wrought in gold and set with diamonds, which he wore on a blue ribband round his neck.

Gilles looked down on him with a contempt that was no longer good-humoured. Cambray was waiting and starving whilst this miserable coxcomb idled away the hours! Two months had gone by and practically nothing had been done. There were no troops, no munitions, no arms; and Cambray was waiting and starving! God alone knew what miseries were being endured by those valiant burghers over there, whom Gilles' own voice had so easily rallied once to a stubborn and heroic defence! God alone knew what his exquisite Jacqueline was being made to suffer! At the thought, his very soul writhed in torment. He could have raised his hands in measureless anger against that effeminate nincompoop, and crushed the last spark of a profligate and useless life out of him. As it was, he had to entreat, to argue, almost to kneel, pleading the cause of Cambray and of his proud Jacqueline—his perfect and unapproachable lily, whom this miserable rag of manhood was casting aside and spurning with a careless wave of the hand.

Ye gods! That he, of all men, should have been assigned such a rôle! That Fate should have destined him to plead for the very honour and safety of the woman whom he worshipped, with a man whom he despised! And yet he argued and he entreated because Madame la Reyne herself vowed that no one could keep her brother in the path of integrity now, except his friend Gilles de Crohin. She had begged him not to leave Monsieur, not for a day, not if possible for an hour!

'He will give us the slip again,' she begged most earnestly; 'and be off to England after his wild-goose chase. Elizabeth will never marry him—never! And we shall remain before the world, uselessly discredited and shamed.'

Alas! much precious time had in the meanwhile been lost. News had come through that the Duke of Parma had given up the thought of taking Cambray by storm and had left del Fuente in temporary command with orders to reduce her by starvation.

But this was two months ago.

Marguerite de Navarre, wearied to death, harassed by *Monsieur's* inactivity, obstructed by the King of France, was on the verge of despair. Cambray, according to the most haphazard calculations, must be on the point of surrender.

III

Early in July, *Monsieur*, stung into a semblance of activity by perpetual nagging from his sister and constant goading from Gilles, did send M. de Turenne with an insufficient force, ill-equipped and ill-found, to effect a surprise attack against the Spanish army.

We know how signally that failed. The blame naturally was lavishly distributed. M. de Turenne, ignorant of his ground, had, it was averred, employed guides who led him astray. Spies and traitors amongst his troops were also supposed to have got wind of his plans and to have betrayed them to the Spanish commander. Certain it is that Turenne's small force was surprised, cut up, Turenne himself taken prisoner and that la Voute, his second, only escaped a like fate by disguising himself as a woman and running with the best of them back to La Fère.

The blow had fallen, sudden, swift and terrible. When the news was brought to Marguerite of Navarre she was seized with so awful an attack of choler, that she fell into unconsciousness and had to take to her bed.

She sent for Gilles, who was eating out his heart in Paris, playing the watch-dog over a dissolute Prince. At her command he proceeded at once to La Fère.

'All is not lost, Messire,' she said to him, as soon as his calm, trust-inspiring presence had infused some semblance of hope into her heart. 'But we must not allow *Monsieur* to exert himself any more in the matter. His incapacity alone matches his indolence.'

She felt so ashamed and so humiliated, that Gilles wellnigh forgot the grudge, which he really owed her for that pitiable adventure into which she had thrust him, and which was even now ending in disaster.

'My spirit is wellnigh broken,' she continued, with pathetic self-depreciation. 'If only, out of all this misery, we could save one shred of our honour!'

'Will your Majesty let me try?' Gilles said simply.

'What do you mean?' she riposted.

'Let me gather an army together. Let me do battle against the Duke of Parma. Monseigneur hath proved himself unwilling. We court disaster by allowing him thus to fritter away both time and men. It was Turenne yesterday; it will be Condé to-morrow, or Montmorency or Bussy—anybody, any unfortunate or incompetent who is willing to serve him! In God's name, Madame la Reyne,' urged Gilles, with a tone of bitter reproach, 'do not let us procrastinate any longer! Cambray is in her death-agony. Let *me* go to her aid!'

She made a final, half-hearted protest.

'No! No!' she said. 'You cannot, must not leave your post. If you do not keep watch over *Monsieur*, we shall lose him altogether.'

'Better that,' he retorted grimly, 'than that we should lose Cambray.'

'There you are right, Messire. Cambray now is bound up with our honour.'

She had become like a child—so different to her former self-assured, almost arrogant self. Gilles, whose firm purpose gave him the strength, had little ado to mould her to his will. She had become malleable, yielding, humble in her helplessness. Marguerite de Navarre was actually ready to listen to advice, to let another think for her and scheme. She accepted counsel with a blindness and submissiveness which were truly pathetic. And Gilles—with the vision before him of Jacqueline enduring all the horrors of a protracted siege—was experiencing a semblance of happiness at thought that at last he would have the power of working for her. So he set to with a will, to make the harassed Queen see eye to eye with him, to make her enter into his ideas and his plans.

'Your Majesty,' he said, 'has offered me the richest lands in Aquitaine. I entreat you to take them back and to give me their worth in money, and I'll gather together an army that will know how to fight. Then, when we are sure of victory, *Monsieur* can come and himself take command. But in the meanwhile, we will beat the Duke of Parma and relieve Cambray. This I swear to you by the living God!'

Marguerite was soon swept off her feet by his determination and his enthusiasm. With naïve surrender, she laid down her burden and left Gilles to shoulder it. Now at last he could work for his Jacqueline! He could fight for her, die for her when the time came! He could drive the foe from her gates and bequeath to her, ere he fell, the freedom of the country she loved so well.

Night and day he toiled, not only with heart and will but with the frenzy of despair; while Marguerite, ever hopeful, ever deluded where that contemptible brother of hers was concerned, flew to Paris to keep a watch over him, then back to La Fère to concert with Gilles—hoping against hope that all would still be well, ready to forgive Monsieur even for the seventy times seventh time, confident that she would still see him entering Cambray and marching thence from city to city, the chosen Lord of the Netherlands, more puissant than any King.

IV

On the last day of July, Gilles de Crohin had his forces ready, equipped, armed, provisioned, at La Fère, where Marguerite de Navarre came herself in order to wish him and the expedition God speed.

But *Monsieur*—who had promised, nay sworn, he would come too, in order to take command in person at the last, when victory was assured—*Monsieur* had not arrived.

For two sennights the devoted sister and the faithful friend waited for him; but he did not come. Marguerite sent courier upon courier after him to Paris, but he evaded them all, and at one time nobody knew where he had hidden himself. To his other vices and failings, this descendant of a once noble race had added the supreme act of a coward. What that final weary waiting meant for Gilles, not even a veracious chronicler can describe. With Cambray almost in sight, with the Spanish armies not two leagues away, with his Jacqueline enduring every horror and every misery which the aching heart of an absent lover can conjure up before his tortured mind, he was forced to remain in idleness, eating out his heart in regret, remorse and longing, doubtful as to what the future might bring, tortured even with the fear that, mayhap, in Cambray only a flower-covered mound of earth would mark the spot where his Jacqueline slept the last sleep of eternal rest.

Then at last, upon the fourteenth day of August, a letter came by runner from *Monsieur*, for the Queen of Navarre. It had been written in Paris more than a week ago, and obviously had been purposely delayed. It began with many protestations of good-will, of love for his sister and of confidence in his friend. Then the letter went on in a kind of peevish strain:

> 'I am quite convinced, My dear sister, that I am
> altogether unfit for the kind of attack which the present
> Situation demands. Now Gilles has a great deal more
> Energy than I have, and a great deal more Knowledge.
> As you know, I never had any longing for military Glory,
> and feel absolutely no desire to make a State Entry into
> Cambray with a swarm of starved or diseased Flemings
> hanging to my stirrup-leathers. Let Gilles to all that. He
> seems to have had a liking for that unsavoury Crowd.
> Then, by and by, if the Spaniards, in the meanwhile,
> do not frustrate his Designs by giving him a beating,
> I shall be ready to take up once more the negotiations
> for my proposed Sovereignty of the Netherlands. But
> understand, My dear Sister, that this happy Event must

come to pass without the co-operation of a Flemish bride. Frankly, I have no liking for the Race, and would be jeopardising My whole Future, by selling Myself to the first Dutch wench that an untoward Fate would throw in My way. Entre nous, Elizabeth of England has not been so haughty with Me of late. Get Me that Kingdom of the Netherlands by all means, My dear. I verily believe that this accrued Dignity would ensure the favourable Acceptance of My suit by the English Queen.'

Marguerite had never made any secret before Gilles of her brother's perfidy. Even this infamous letter she placed loyally before him now. When he had finished reading it and she saw the look of measureless contempt which flashed through his eyes, she could have cried with shame and misery.

'What to do, Messire?' she exclaimed piteously. 'Oh, my God! what to do?'

'Relieve Cambray first and foremost, Madame,' he replied firmly. 'After that, we shall see.'

'But the Flemish lords!' she rejoined. 'Their anger! Their contempt! I could not bear it, Messire! The shame of it all will kill me!'

'It has got to be borne, Madame! Cambray has suffered enough. It is our turn now.'

Nor would he discuss the matter any further, even with her. The expedition had been entrusted to his hands, and nothing would delay him now. Cambray was waiting and starving, every hour might mean her final surrender. The Spanish commander — apprised of *Monsieur* le Duc d'Anjou's arrival with a strong force — had already offered battle. Gilles was only too eager to accept the issue.

On the fifteenth day of August, 1581, that battle was fought on the plains outside Cambray. The issue was never in doubt for one moment. Le Carpentier asserts that the Duke of Parma, after six hours' stubborn fighting, surrendered his position and all his forts and retired in great haste in the direction of Valenciennes.

CHAPTER XXVII.
AND THIS IS THE END OF MY STORY

I

And into the silent desolation of Cambray's deserted streets, there penetrated once again the sounds of that life which was teeming outside her walls. From the north and the south, from the east and the west, rumour, like a wily sprite, flew over the crumbling walls and murmured into ears that scarcely heard, that the promise given long ago was being redeemed at last. Anxiety, sorrow and suffering were coming to an end, so the elf averred. The hero who fought and conquered once, had returned to conquer again.

Whereupon, those who had enough strength left in them to drag themselves along, found their way to the ramparts, from whence they could watch the approach of the man who would bring them liberty if he succeeded, or bequeath them an heroic death if he failed. There was no other issue possible. The sands of Cambray's endurance had run down; she had no more resistance left in her, scarcely the power to suffer any longer. If the relieving army failed to-day, the setting sun would see the Spanish soldiery, drunk with victory, swarming over the lonely streets, destroying all that famine and disease had left whole, all that a dying population had no longer the strength to defend.

Little could be seen of what went on in the distant plain, and hollow eyes, wearied with weeping and anxiety, scanned in vain the horizon far away. But those who had come to watch remained to pray, while their minds, rendered super-sensitive by bodily want, conjured up visions of that grim fight which was going on beyond their range of vision.

The history of this heroic people has no more poignant page than that which tells of this long watch by a crowd of miserable, half-starved people, the while, out there upon the plain, brave men fought and died for their sake.

Not only for their sake, but for the honour of France.

II

Once more the roar of artillery and of musketry fills the air with its awe-inspiring sound. It is early morning, and the sky heavily overcast. To the anxious watchers, that grim struggle out there is only a dimly-perceived confusion, a medley of sights and sounds, a clash of arms, the dull thunder of culverines and sharp report of musketry. And, as the grey light of day begins to pick out with crude precision the more distant objects, a kaleidoscope of colour vies in brilliancy with the flash of steel, and tears asunder the drab mist which lies upon the bosom of the plain.

The yellow and red of the Spaniards becomes easily distinguishable, then the white and blue and gold of the French, the green of the arquebusiers, the black of the archers, and even that tiny moving speck, more brilliant even than the gleam of metal, the white banner of France, sown with her Fleur de Lys.

But the watchers up on the ramparts vainly strain their hollow eyes to see the man who has come to save Cambray. They can only guess that he is there, where the fight is fiercest, where death stands most grim and most relentless. They have a knowledge of his presence keener than sight can give, and though voices at this hour are spent and hoarse with pain, yet to every roar of cannon, to every volley of musketry, there comes, like an answering murmur, the triumphant call, which now sounds like a prayer and which their hero taught them four months ago: 'Fleur de Lys and Liberty!'

The French lancers and halberdiers rush the Spanish forts. The arquebusiers are fighting foot by foot; the musketeers and archers stand firm—a living wall, which deals death and remains unmoved, despite furious onslaughts from a foe who appears to be desperate. The plain around is already strewn with dead.

The French have fought valiantly for close on six hours, have repelled nine assaults against their positions, and now, at one hour after noon, they still stand or crouch or kneel on one knee, crossbow in hand or musket, they fire, fall out, reform and fire again. Shaken, battered, decimated, they still shoot with coolness and precision, under the eye of one who never tires. Their ranks are still unbroken, but the Spaniards are giving ground at last.

'This time we are undone!' Parma cries in the excess of his rage.

He himself has been twice wounded; four of his young officers have been killed. The French musketeers, the finest the world has ever seen, work relentlessly upon his finest positions. And he feels—this great captain, who hitherto hath not known defeat—he feels that now at last he has met his match. Not a great leader like himself, perhaps, not the victorious general in an hundred fights; but a man whose stubbornness and daring, whose blind disregard of danger and sublime defiance of evil fortune, gives strength to the weakest and valour to the least bold.

'I thought you had rid me once of that pestilential rebel!' he exclaims to de Landas, pointing to where Gilles de Crohin's tall figure towers above the pressing mass of Spanish halberdiers.

De Landas murmurs an imprecation, crosses himself in an access of superstitious fear.

'My God!' he says under his breath. 'He hath risen from the dead!'

In truth, Gilles appears endowed at this hour with superhuman strength. His doublet and jerkin are torn, his breastplate riddled with arrow-shot, he bleeds profusely from the hand, his face is unrecognizable under a coating of smoke and grime. Enthusiasm and obstinacy have given him the power of giants; his hatred of the foe is supreme; his contempt of death sublime. De Landas sees in him the incarnation of his own retributive destiny. 'Oh, that God's thunder would smite him where he stands!' he mutters fervently.

''Tis too late now,' retorts Parma, with ferocious spite. 'Too late to call to God to help you. You should have bargained with the devil four months ago, when you missed your aim. Risen from the dead, forsooth!' he adds, purple with fury. 'Very much alive now, meseems, and with the strength of Satan in his arm.'

He strikes at de Landas with his sword, would have killed him with his own hand, so enraged is he with the man for his failure to murder an enemy whom he loathes and fears.

'Unless those cowards rally,' he calls savagely, and points to where, in the heart of the *mêlée*, confusion and disorder wield their grisly sceptres, 'we shall have to retreat.'

But de Landas does not stop to hear. The fear of the supernatural which had for the moment paralysed his thinking faculties, is soon merged in that boundless hatred which he feels for the rival whom he had thought dead long ago. In the heart of that confusion he has spied Gilles, fighting, pursuing; slashing, hitting—intrepid and superb, the centre and the life of the victorious army. De Landas sets spurs to his horse and, calling to his own troop of swordsmen to follow, dashes into the *mêlée*.

The battle now is at its fiercest. A proud army, superior in numbers, in arms, in knowledge, feels itself weakening before an enemy whose greatest power is his valour. The retreat has not yet sounded, but the Spanish captains all know that the humiliating end is in sight. Already their pikemen have thrown down their cumbersome weapons. Pursued by the French lancers, they turn and fight with hands and fists, some of them; whilst others scatter in every direction. The ranks of their archers are broken, and the fire of their musketeers has become intermittent and weak. Even the horsemen, the flower of Parma's army, gentlemen all, are breaking in the centre. With reins loose, stirrup-leathers flapping, swords cast away and mantles flying loose, they are making a stand which is obviously the last, and which within the next few minutes will with equal certainty turn into rout.

Here it is that Gilles is holding his own with a small troop of French horsemen. His steel bonnet has been knocked off, his wounded arm roughly bandaged, the sleeves of his jerkin fly behind him like a pair of wings, his invincible sword strikes and flashes and gleams in the grey afternoon light.

For a few seconds, while the distance between himself and his enemy grows rapidly less, de Landas sees and hears nothing. The blood is beating in his temples, with a weird thumping which drowns the din of battle. His eyes are blinded by a crimson veil; his hand, stiff and convulsed, can scarcely grasp the pistol. The next instant he is in the very thick of the turmoil.

'For Spain and Our Lady!' he cries, and empties his pistol into the seething mass of Spanish horsemen who bar the way twixt him and his enemy. The horsemen are scattered. Already on the verge of a stampede, they are scared by this unexpected onslaught from the rear. They fear to be taken between cross-fires, are seized with panic, turn and flee to right and left. Two of them fall, hit by that madman's pistol. All is now tumult and a whirling ferment. The air is thick with smoke and powder, horses, maddened with terror, snort and struggle and beat the air with their hoofs. De Landas' own troop join in the *mêlée*; the French horsemen dash in pursuit; there is a scrimmage, a stampede; men fight and tear and hit and slash, for dear life and for safety.

But de Landas does not care, is past caring now. Another disaster more or less, another scare, final humiliation, what matters? The day is lost anyhow, and all his own hopes finally dashed to the ground by the relief of Cambray and the irrevocable loss to him of Jacqueline and her fortune. Already he has thrown aside his smoking pistol, seized another from the hand of his nearest follower, and points it straight at Gilles.

'For Spain and Our Lady!'

'Fleur de Lys and Liberty!'

The two cries rang out simultaneously—then the report of de Landas' pistol, and Gilles' horse hit in the neck, suddenly swerves, rears and paws the air, and would have thrown its rider had not the latter jumped clean out of the saddle.

To de Landas' maddened gaze the smoke around appears to be the colour of blood. Blindly he gropes for another pistol. His henchman is near him, thrusts a weapon into the young Spaniard's trembling hand. For the fraction of a second, destiny, waiting, stays her hand. Gilles is free of his struggling horse, he has his sword in his hand; but de Landas once more points a pistol straight at him.

'Satan! guide thou my hand this time!' he calls out, in a passion of fury.

Then suddenly a raucous cry rises above the din; there is a double, sharp report, a loud curse, a final groan of despair and of rage, and de Landas, struck in the breast by an almost savage blow from a lance, throws up his arms, falls, first on his knees, then backwards on the soft earth, would have been buried then and there under a seething mass of struggling men and beasts, had not Gilles rushed to him with one bound, caught him by the shoulders and dragged his now lifeless body to comparative shelter a few paces away. Now Gilles picks up a fallen cloak from the ground and lays it reverently over his fallen foe.

'Because Jacqueline loved you once,' he murmurs under his breath.

Then he turns to his faithful Jehan. 'You were just in time,' he says simply.

Jehan has been glancing down with mingled rage and contempt on the man whom in his loyal heart he hated in life with a wellnigh ferocious intensity. Now he looks at his master—his friend whom he loves—sees him on one knee by the side of that abominable murderer, trying to struggle back to his feet, but evidently weak and dizzy.

With a cry like an enraged tiger, Jehan casts his still streaming lance away, is already kneeling beside Gilles, supporting him in his arms as gently as a mother would shelter her child.

'H-h-h-hurt?' he stammers laconically. 'That d-d-d-devil hit you?'

'Only in the thigh,' replies Gilles. 'You diverted his aim right enough, my dear Jehan! And once more I owe my life to you. Just help me to get up,' he adds with his wonted impatience. 'Do not let me miss another second of the glorious spectacle of our victory!'

III

Out in the western sky, a vivid band of blue and gold breaks the bosom of the clouds. The afternoon sun illumines with its glowing rays the final rout of the Spanish army. Le Carpentier's laconic words tell us more than any lengthy chronicle could do.

'The Duke of Parma,' he says curtly, 'abandoned his forts and retired in haste to Valenciennes.'

So much that was mighty and great and invincible has succumbed before the power which comes from a sense of justice, from valour and enthusiasm and the decrees of God. God has decided that Cambray has suffered enough; He has broken the might of Parma and set an end to the miseries of an heroic people. And when, like a tidal wave of steel, the Spanish troops begin to oscillate toward the north, where lies Valenciennes and safety, up on the ramparts of Cambray hundreds of men and women and children fall on their knees, and thank God with fervour for their freedom and for victory.

They are too weak to shout, too weak even to raise their arms. The pikemen lean upon their arms, the musketeers upon their muskets, the gunners lie half-exhausted upon their culverines. Of the twenty-five thousand citizens of Cambray, scarce fifteen thousand have remained to bid the returning hero welcome.

Up in the fort of Cantimpré, the city guard—what is left of it—wait for the entry of the victorious army. The bridge is lowered, the men stand as if on parade. The city fathers are there too, and amongst them stands Monseigneur the governor.

Gaunt and careworn they all look. Their ranks too have been rudely thinned. Monseigneur's hair is now snow-white; the hand with which he leans upon a stick is emaciated almost to the bone. His other arm rests on that of Jacqueline de Broyart, whose pale, wan face hath a curious air of mystery and of detachment.

'Here they come!' Monseigneur says at last, as on the horizon far away a glowing speck begins to move, to gather shape as it draws nearer, catching, reflecting and throwing back the roseate flashes of the setting sun.

The whole city now is watching; her very soul is in the eyes of her expectant children. A curious, nervous thrill has taken the place of bodily exhaustion. Only Jacqueline stands quite silent and impassive. Boundless gratitude fills her heart for the deliverance of the city; but the overwhelming joy which she feels is drowned in the immensity of her sorrow. For her, in truth, life is gone, happiness lies buried beneath the city walls. She can rejoice at the coming of the man whom the people believe to be their hero, but for her he is the stranger. The real defender of Cambray—her brave and spotless knight—gave his precious life for her city all these weary months ago.

People crowd more insistently round her. The speck on the horizon has become a moving multitude. Steel and gold flash in the evening light, banners wave in the gentle, summer breeze. The French army, glorious after victory, wends its way to the city which it has saved.

In the forefront march the halberdiers, with their blue hose and huge, unwieldy trunks, small bonnets on their heads and a cloak about their shoulders. Then the pikemen, in striped doublets, their enormous hats slung behind their backs, and the musketeers with tall boots which reach half-way up their thighs. Immediately behind them comes a long train of carts and waggons—the provisions collected together for the starving city. The Master of the Camp is in charge of these. He is mounted on a black charger, surrounded by his staff. The ends of his blue silk scarf are smothered in dust, as are his boots and his plumed hat. Some way behind the waggons, the archers come, marching three abreast, and then the foot-soldiers, with huge steel gauntlets covering their hands, their heavy lances borne upon their shoulders.

Nearer and nearer the procession comes, and as it approaches, a strange exultation born of weakness and of fever, rises in the hearts of the watchers. It seems as if an unendurable weight were lifted from their shoulders, as if they themselves had in a mysterious manner been dead for weeks and months, and now had risen again in order to gaze into the setting sun, from whence their liberator had come to them again.

The streets are no longer deserted now. Furtive forms, gaunt and haggard, stand under doorways or congregate upon the open places. Women in ragged kirtles with children clinging to their skirts, sick and maimed and halt from disease and want, crawl out of the squalid houses to watch the entry of the French troops. Many, at sight of those brave men all covered with smoke and powder and dust, fall down on their knees and a long-forgotten prayer rises to their lips.

Anon down the Bapaume road it is quite easy to perceive the white banner sown with the gold Fleur de Lys. It is borne by a herald who sits upon a cream charger, and immediately behind him a man rides alone. He is hatless; but he holds his head erect and looks straight out towards the city. He has the reins of his horse in one hand, the other is hidden under his cloak. Some little way behind him ride a number of cavaliers in brilliant multi-coloured doublets and hose, with drawn swords in their hands, which flash and gleam in the setting sun. They are still close on half a league away, but adown the long, flat road Monseigneur's keen eyes have already perceived them.

'It is His Highness the Duc d'Anjou!' he exclaims.

But, with a strange instinct which has for ever remained inexplicable, Messire de Balagny retorts:

'It is the saviour of Cambray!'

And while he goes at once to transmit the governor's orders that all the church bells in the city shall at once begin to ring, Jacqueline de Broyart's gaze is fixed upon the road which lies like a winding ribbon down below, stretching as far as the glowing horizon far away. The sky is suffused with a joy-blush of crimson and orange and gold, the sinking sun illumines with a roseate hue that distant group of cavaliers, in the forefront of whom rides the defender of Cambray.

After the turmoil of battle, an immense silence reigns over the bosom of the plain. Even the tramp of thousands of men, the clatter of horses' hoofs and of arms, seem like an integral part of that great and solemn silence, which has its birth in the stricken city. The victorious army has entered Cambray, not with music and with cheering, not with shouts of joy. Joy is in every heart, but an abundance of sorrow has stilled its outward expression. The plain itself is strewn with dead and wounded; hundreds of valiant lives have been freely given for the deliverance of Cambray. Those that remain—some five thousand of them—cross the bridge at the foot of Cantimpré, marching three abreast. It takes an hour for the first portion of the victorious army to enter the city. The service men bring provision waggons in plenty, together with news that more will follow as quickly as may be. By nightfall there would not be one hungry mouth left in Cambray.

Relief, content, the shadow of happiness, are too poignant to find expression in words—perhaps they have come just a little too late. But gratitude is immense. Soon the streets of Cambray are encumbered with train and equipment, with carts and waggons and barrows, horses loosely tethered, litters of straw for the wounded and the ailing. The distribution of the food is the most pressing need. Everywhere men in faded, ragged clothing, with gaunt faces and hollow eyes, hurry to the Grand' Place and to the Marche aux Bois, where the food waggons are set up under the eye of the Master of the Camp.

A pathetic procession of eager, half-starved shadows—women and children too—with the humble, deprecating air of the desperately indigent, crowd around the waggons. Fifteen thousand mouths gaping for food. There is only a very little for everybody at first. More will come to-night. More again to-morrow. France, who has saved, will also provide. Of order there is none. People push and scamper as the hungry are wont to do, but all are too feeble to do one another much harm. The soldiers, flushed with victory, are patient and good-natured. My God! the very aspect of the streets is enough to make any staunch heart quake with horror! Some of the men have wife and family in far-off Artois or Provence. They can hardly restrain their tears as wee, grimy hands, thin to the bone, are stretched out to them in pitiable eagerness. They are as lavish as they can be, giving up their own supper to feed these unfortunates: generous now as they were brave out there, when they fought under the eye of the staunchest man they had ever seen in battle.

"Tis a fine candle you folk of Cambray owe to Monseigneur de Froidmont!' the Master of the Camp says to a group of burghers who, self-restrained and stoical, are giving help in the distribution, waiting till all the poor and the ignorant are fed before they themselves receive their share.

'Monseigneur de Froidmont?' one of them exclaims. 'Why, who is he?'

'Who is he?' retorts the Master of the Camp. 'Nay, by the Mass! He is above all the most doughty knight who hath ever wielded a sword. He it is who has saved your city for you, my friends. If the Spanish soldiery is not inside your walls this night, 'tis to him that ye owe it, remember!'

Most of the burghers look gravely puzzled. Their spokesman ventures on the remark:

'To His Highness the Duc d'Anjou, surely!'

The Master of the Camp shrugs his shoulders.

'That is as it may be,' he says dryly. 'But you might all have rotted inside your walls but for the valour of Monseigneur de Froidmont.'

'But the Duc d'Anjou...' hazards some one timidly.

'A murrain on the Duc d'Anjou!' breaks in the Master of the Camp good-humouredly. "Tis of the defender of your city you should think at this hour. Ah!' he exclaims, with a sigh of satisfaction, "tis good to hear that your city fathers at the least are giving him a rousing welcome!'

He himself sets up a cheer, which is taken up by his soldiers; for just then the bells of Notre Dame have begun their joyous peal. Soon Ste. Croix follows suit and St. Géry from the heights toward the north.

Peal after peal resounds, till the whole air vibrates with that most inspiriting sound, chasing away with its melody the very shadow of silence and desolation.

The last rays of the sun have now sunk in the west. Twilight is slowly fading into dusk. Out beyond Cantimpré, the herald upon his charger has halted at the foot of the bridge, the white banner of France, gay with its golden Fleur de Lys, is gently stirred by the evening breeze. The group of cavaliers has halted too, while the defender of Cambray rides slowly into the city.

IV

Monseigneur the governor awaited the victor in the courtyard of the citadel. He stood in the midst of his Sheriffs and his Provosts and the other dignitaries of the city, all of them still dignified and imposing, despite the faded appearance of their clothes and the gaunt, hungry look in their wan faces. All around the courtyard was lined with troops, the mere remnants of the garrison who had fought so valorously on that never-to-be-forgotten day in April, a little over four months ago, and of the small body of French troops who had come to their assistance then.

Gilles dismounted at the bridge-head, disdaining, despite his wounds, the aid of his faithful henchman's arm. Only limping very slightly, the bandage on his hand hidden in the folds of his cloak, he passed in on foot and alone under the gateway. For the space of one heart-beat he paused just inside the courtyard, when he saw before him this large concourse of people who, at his appearance, had slowly dropped on their knees. They were for the most part faces which had been familiar to him all those months ago—faces which even now wore an expression of deference and of awed respect.

A bitter sigh rose to Gilles' lips. For him, despite the grandeur of his victory, this was a bitter hour. Within the next few moments these proud and brave people would have to be told that a prince of the House of France had proved himself to be both fickle and base. Messire de Balagny was not there; and at first he did not see Jacqueline. She had retired into the guard-room at the desire of her guardians. 'It were seemly,' they had said, 'that we, your protectors, should first receive His Highness and pay him our respects. Then he will ask for his future bride, and ours shall be the honour of bringing you to him!'

So she was not there for the moment, and Gilles felt freer in her absence—even caught himself hoping that he would not be put to the torture of seeing her again. It were best for him and best for her that she should not hear that awful confession from his lips, that a Valois prince had broken his word to her, and in his wanton infamy had repudiated the perfect gift of God which had been offered to him.

'Do not tarry one moment, Messire,' Marguerite de Navarre had entreated of him at the last. 'Take advantage of the moment of boundless relief and gratitude when your victorious troops enter Cambray to release *Monsieur* of his promise to wed the Flemish heiress. Do not enter the city till you have made it clear to the Flemish lords that the Duc d'Anjou will accept the Sovereignty of the Netherlands, and in exchange will give the support of France, of her wealth and of her armies; but that he will not enter into personal alliance with one of his future subjects.'

So now, when at Gilles' approach the governor and the city fathers all bent the knee before him, he said at once, directly and simply:

'I entreat you, Messeigneurs, not to kneel to me. That honour belongs by right only to the puissant Prince whom I represent.'

'Your Highness——' began d'Inchy humbly.

'I am no Highness, Monseigneur,' he rejoined firmly. 'Only the servant of the Duc d'Anjou, who will be here as soon as may be, to claim from you that gratitude which you owe to him and not to me.'

D'Inchy and the others did not move. Their limbs were paralysed, their lips dumb. Their ears refused to convey to their over-tired brains that which they had just heard. It all seemed like a dream; the gathering dusk made everything appear unreal—the ringing of the joy-bells, the far-away crowd of soldiers and cavaliers, who filled the very air with clatter and jingle of spurs and accoutrements, with creaking of waggons, snorting of horses and snatches of songs and laughter. And in the centre of the courtyard, this tall figure of a man, with the tattered doublet and the bleeding hand, and the voice which seemed as if it rose straight out of a glorious grave.

'Do not look so puzzled, Messeigneurs,' Gilles went on with a smile, half-sad, wholly good-humoured. 'The Duc d'Anjou will not tarry, my word on it. He bids me say that he accepts the Sovereignty of the Netherlands, and will place at the disposal of her people the might and the armies of France, his own power, wealth and influence.'

Still as in a dream, d'Inchy and the Sheriffs and the Provosts staggered to their feet. The mystery, in truth, was greater than their enfeebled minds could grasp. They were for the most part chiefly conscious of a great feeling of disappointment.

Here stood before them, tall and magnificent even beneath rags and grime, the man whom they revered above all others, the hero whose personality was enshrined in the very hearts of the people of Cambray. What the mystery was which clung round him they did not know, nor did they care: he was the man of their choice, the saviour of Cambray now, as he had been their defender in the hour of their gravest peril. The victor of this glorious day was the hero of the ramparts on that memorable April day, the man who four months ago had defended them with heart and will and undaunted courage then, and to whom they owed their freedom, the honour of their wives and daughters and the future of their race.

To think of him as other than the Duc d'Anjou, their chosen Sovereign Lord, the husband of Jacqueline de Broyart, was positive pain. Most of them even now refused to believe, stared at Gilles as if he were a wraith set to mock them in their weakness and their dependence.

'Not the Duc d'Anjou?' the Chief Magistrate murmured. 'Impossible!'

Gilles could not help but smile at the farcical aspect of his own tragedy.

'It is not only possible, Messeigneurs,' he said, 'but is e'en a positive fact. Messire de Balagny would soon tell you so: and His Highness the Duc d'Anjou himself will be here on the morrow to prove to you that I am but an humble substitute, a representative of His Graciousness.'

'But,' stammered d'Inchy, still in a state of complete bewilderment, 'that day in April ... your—you, Monseigneur ... in the Town Hall ... Madame Jacqueline...'

With a quick gesture, Gilles put up his hand.

'I entreat you, Monseigneur,' he said earnestly, 'to wait awhile ere you probe further into His Highness' secrets. For the moment, will you not be content to rejoice with me at your deliverance? His Highness accepts from you the Sovereignty of the Netherlands. To-morrow he will be here, ready to receive the acclamations and the welcome of his people. He hath proved himself not only ready, but able, to defend you against all your enemies. He hath this day gained a signal victory over the powerful armies of the King of Spain. Henceforth the whole might of France will stand between you and the relentless foe who threatens your lives and your liberties. Join me, Messeigneurs,' he concluded earnestly, 'in acclaiming His Highness the Duc d'Anjou et d'Alençon, prince of the House of France, as your Sovereign Lord!'

His inspiring words were received in silence. Not one voice was raised in response to his loyal call. Gilles frowned, feeling that the supreme hour had come. A moment or two longer, and the inevitable question would be put 'And what of Madame Jacqueline, Monseigneur? What of the lady whom His Highness has sworn to wed?'

Already he had steeled himself to give answer, though the answer could only proclaim dishonour, both for himself and for the Valois prince whom he was trying so faithfully to serve unto the end. He saw the frown of puzzlement which gathered on d'Inchy's brow. The governor, in truth, was the first to recover his presence of mind. Leaning upon his stick, with back bent, but his whole attitude one of supreme dignity, he came nearer to Gilles and fixed a stern gaze upon his face.

'If you are not the Duc d'Anjou, Monseigneur,' he said slowly, 'will you tell us who it was who defended Cambray with such indomitable valour four months ago? Will you tell us who it is that saved Cambray to-day? For, of a truth, my friends and I are bewildered, and the mystery before us is one which we cannot fathom. Therefore I dare ask you once again in all respect—I may say in all affection: if you are not the Duc d'Anjou, who is it that stands before me now?'

'The saviour of Cambray!' came in a clear, ringing voice from the further end of the courtyard. 'My promised Lord and King!'

The sound of Jacqueline's voice sent a spark of living flame through those minds, atrophied by all this mystery. All eyes were at once turned to where she stood, dimly outlined in the gathering gloom. She was clad in a sombre gown and wore a dark veil over her fair hair. Her young, girlish figure, free from the hideous trammels of hoops or farthingale, appeared ethereal against the background of grim, frowning walls. Only the last lingering grey light in the west brought into bold relief her pale face and graceful shoulders, smooth like ivory. Just for a minute or two she stood quite still, like an exquisitely graven image, rigidly still yet pulsating with life. Then she advanced slowly towards Gilles. Her eyes held his and he scarcely dared to breathe, for fear that perfect vision should vanish into the skies, whence, of a truth, it must have descended. He could not have uttered a word then, if his very existence had depended on it. It seemed to him as if his very heart had stopped in its beating, as if life and time and the whole universe was stilled while Jacqueline's blue eyes sought his own, and she came, with hands extended as if in entreaty, to him.

Was it a minute or a cycle of years! He himself could not tell you. He saw nothing of what went on around; the city walls had fallen away, the men in their sombre clothes become mere shadows, the very sky overhead had receded into the realm of nothingness.

And through that state of semi-consciousness, her exquisite voice came to him as from another world.

'Nay! my dear Lord,' she said, with her enchanting smile, 'you'll not refuse me the joy of paying something of my country's eternal debt of gratitude to you.'

He still stood half-dazed and silent. Then suddenly he took her hands and slowly bent the knee, and buried his battle-stained face in her sweet-scented palms.

It had all occurred within half a dozen seconds. The governor, the Chief Magistrate, the city fathers, gazed on uncomprehending, silent and puzzled at what they saw. After awhile, d'Inchy murmured vaguely:

'Madame Jacqueline ... we ... that is...'

But quickly now she turned and faced them all, while Gilles still knelt and rested his hot forehead against her cool white hand. Through the gloom they could just discern her face, white and serene and withal defiant and firm, and irradiated with an enormous happiness.

'Messeigneurs,' she said with solemn earnestness, 'you heard, two sennights ago, the profession of faith which I made publicly before the assembled people of Cambray. There I swore by the living God Who made me that I would cherish and serve, loyally and faithfully, even until death, the noble and valorous hero who defended our city in the hour of her gravest peril. That dauntless hero is before you now. Once again he has saved our city from destruction, our sisters from dishonour, our men from shame. To him did I plight my troth, to him alone will I be true!'

Then, as all the men around her remained silent, moved to the depth of their hearts by the sublime note of passion which rang through her avowal, she continued, and this time with a note of unswerving defiance and magnificent challenge in her voice:

'Ask the people of Cambray, Messeigneurs! Let them be the arbiters of my fate and their own. Ask them to whom they would have me turn now — to the mighty Prince who would only use me and them and our valiant race as stepping stones to his own ambition, or to the hero who has offered his life for us all.'

A low murmur went round the assembly. Grave heads were shaken, toil-worn hands were raised to wipe a furtive tear. The evening gloom descended upon this strange scene, upon the reverend seigneurs and the stolid soldiers, upon the man who was kneeling and the woman — a mere girl — who stood there, commanding and defiant, secure in her love, proud of her surrender, ready to fight for her happiness.

'Ask the people of Cambray, Messeigneurs,' she reiterated boldly, 'if you have a doubt!'

She let her eyes wander slowly over the crowd. One by one, she looked these grave seigneurs in the face,—these men who arrogated the right to rule over her destiny. They were her friends, had been her daily companions in the past four months of horror and of misery. They had trembled with her over Cambray's danger, had wept with her over Cambray's woes. With her they had acclaimed the hero who had defended them, had wept when they saw him fall; and to-day, again to-day, had been ready to deify him as their hero and her knight.

'Messeigneurs,' she pleaded, 'ask the people of Cambray.'

She knew what would be the people's answer. Now that the hour of their liberty had struck, now that the Spaniard no longer thundered at their gates, they were ready to carry their Liberator shoulder-high and give him the universe in their gratitude, if they had it to give. What cared they if their Liberator was a Duc d'Anjou or a nameless knight? He was the man whom they worshipped, the man who had made them free.

And now, when she still saw doubt, hesitation, embarrassment, upon the face of all these grave dignitaries, she frowned with wounded pride and with impatience.

'Messeigneurs,' she said boldly, 'Heaven forgive me, but ye seem to hesitate! The man to whom you owe your life, your future, the honour of your name, asks nothing more of your gratitude. But I, who am privileged to read in his heart, know that it is in my power to repay him in full for all that he hath done. And yet you hesitate! I am content to make appeal to the people of Cambray. But I know too what goes on in your minds. Ye think that ye are pledged to *Monsieur* Duc d'Anjou! that Jacqueline de Broyart, if she refuse to wed him, would sully your honour and, what were infinitely worse, would besmirch the fair fame of Flanders. Isn't that so, Messeigneurs?'

Their silence had become eloquent.

'The honour of Flanders— —' Monseigneur began, then paused. A premonition of something which he could not put into words caused him to remain silent too, and to let the girl plead her cause without any interruption from him.

'The honour of Flanders, as you say, Monseigneur,' Jacqueline went on firmly, 'demands above all things that you and I and the guardians of our city do keep our word. Therefore, even before we make appeal to the people of Cambray, we will ask Monseigneur de Froidmont, who is here on behalf of His Highness, the Duc d'Anjou, to renew in His Highness' name the demand of my hand in marriage. On his answer should depend our future conduct. Is that not so, Messeigneurs?' she asked once again, and let her calm gaze wander from one solemn face to the other, search serenely every troubled eye.

D'Inchy this time realized that he must be the spokesman for all these representatives, his city and of his province. Vaguely troubled still by the mystery which surrounded the man to whom Cambray owed her deliverance, he thought once for all, by a straight question, to put an end to the many doubts and fears which assailed him and his friends. Jacqueline already had turned once more to Gilles; with a slight pressure of her hand she asked him to rise. This he did, feeling strangely elated, just as if Destiny, tired of buffeting him, was smiling encouragingly to him from afar. In the midst of the many confused impressions which had struck his wearied mind during the past quarter of an hour, one thought stood out with heavenly clearness: Jacqueline loved him! Her love had neither faltered nor tired through these weary months. She was as steadfast and true to him at this hour as she had been when in the clematis-covered arbour she had lain against his breast. Now her woman's quick wit had divined the truth and come to the aid of her love. Even when she challenged those grave seigneurs to ask him the straight and momentous question, she knew what his answer would be.

The task which lay before him no longer seemed irksome and humiliating. He still blushed for the shame which rested on the fickle Prince whom he served, but already in his heart he had registered the vow that, God helping as He had done hitherto, the honour of France should shine forth before these heroic people, in all its brightness and glory, through the glorious deeds of her sons.

'Monseigneur,' began d'Inchy tentatively, 'you have heard what Madame Jacqueline de Broyart hath said. We have all passed through much sorrow, have witnessed the miseries and the patience of our people. The hour of victory has come, but found us weak in body and tortured in mind. We place our faith with complete confidence in the honour and integrity of France. We are prepared to receive His Highness, the Duc d'Anjou with open hearts and to acclaim him as our Sovereign Lord. Will he in exchange keep faith with us, and wed our ward, Madame Jacqueline de Broyart, to whom he hath akeady plighted his troth?'

Even while the governor spoke, the city dignitaries all tried to read the expression on Gilles' face through the fast-gathering gloom, and anxious eyes scanned those war-worn features which they had learned to love. Even through the darkness they could see him, standing there in his rags and his battered breastplate, hatless and begrimed, splendid in his valour and his pride, and with Jacqueline's hand held tightly in his own—splendid still, now that he stood silent and shamed before them all.

To Monseigneur's peremptory question he had given no reply, remained almost motionless, while Jacqueline, proud in the face of the crying insult which a faithless Prince had put upon her, threw back her head and gave a deep sigh of content.

Monseigneur the governor had received his answer in Gilles de Crohin's obstinate silence. A bitter cry of unbridled anger rose to his lips, his emaciated hand trembled visibly upon the stick which he held.

Then, just as suddenly, his wrath gave way. It almost seemed as if an angel of reconciliation and of love had whispered into his ear, and had, with cool and gentle fingers, smoothed away the angry frown upon his brow. All that was fine and noble in the heroic race from which he sprang clamoured for the only possible solution of the present difficulty, a solution which would ensure the happiness of a brave and proud woman, and the dignity of the country which he represented.

One last second of hesitation, one final regretful sigh for the ambitious personal schemes which he saw crumbling into ashes at his feet, then Monseigneur d'Inchy, governor of Cambray, sank slowly down on his knees.

'Monseigneur,' he said slowly and impressively, 'Madame Jacqueline de Broyart has spoken and shown us the path of our duty. To-morrow we will acclaim His Highness the Duc d'Anjou et d'Alençon as our Sovereign Lord; but to-day we welcome you as the saviour of our city. Whatever your wishes are, they are a law unto us. You have heard what Madame Jacqueline has said. Will you in your turn plight your troth to her? Will you love and cherish her and serve her faithfully and loyally as her liege lord, until death?'

'And beyond!' Gilles murmured softly.

The last streak of grey light was still lingering in the sky. Everything in the enclosure of the tall, grim walls became mysterious and shadowy; darkness drew her kindly mantle over the scene. She hid from prying eyes what went on under the immediate shadow of the great gate, where for one brief moment Jacqueline lay against her loved one's heart.

From the towers of the city's churches the bells were still sending their happy carillon through the evening air. A group of pikemen brought torches into the courtyard. A wild shout of delight—the first which Cambray had heard, for many months—sent its joyous sound through the evening air.

And in the homes which all these months of misery had devastated, the sick and the weary roused themselves for a moment, marvelling what these shouts of joy might mean. And those who had suffered for so long and who were now comforted, those who had been hungry and were now fed, ran into the houses of sickness and of sorrow, in order to bring the gladsome, the great, the wonderful news.

'The Duc d'Anjou, brother of the King of France, is to be Sovereign Lord of the Netherlands. He will enter Cambray to-morrow, with his great army. He will be proclaimed Protector of the Liberties of Cambray and Sovereign of the Cambrésis!'

'And he will wed Madame Jacqueline de Broyart, the great heiress?—our Jacqueline?'

'Oh, no! The Duc d'Anjou will be our Sovereign Lord. But Madame Jacqueline will wed the saviour of Cambray.'